THE SNOW SPIDER TRILOGY

A magical story and winner of the Smarties Grand Prix,
Jenny Nimmo's superb tale of good against evil – set
against the shimmering backdrop of a magical domed city
– will capture the imagination of young and old alike.

Also by Jenny Nimmo

Griffin's Castle
Ultramarine

For younger readers

Delilah Alone
Delilah and the Dishwasher Dogs
Delilah and the Dogspell
Hot Dog, Cool Cat
Seth and the Strangers

THE SNOW SPIDER TRILOGY

Jenny Nimmo

Winner of the Smarties Grand Prix

Illustrated by Joanna Carey

EGMONT

The Snow Spider was first published in Great Britain 1986
by Methuen Children's Books Ltd

Emlyn's Moon was first published in Great Britain 1987
by Methuen Children's Books Ltd

The Chestnut Soldier was first published in Great Britain 1989
by Methuen Children's Books Ltd

Published in one volume as *The Snow Spider* trilogy 2003
by Egmont Books Limited
239 Kensington High Street, London W8 6SA

Text copyright © 1986, 1987, 1989 Jenny Nimmo
Illustrations copyright © 1986, 1987, Joanna Carey
Cover illustration copyright © 2003 Jessica Meserve

The moral rights of the author and illustrators have been asserted

ISBN 1 4052 1051 6

1 3 5 7 9 10 8 6 4 2

A CIP catalogue record for this title is available from the British Library

Printed and bound in Great Britain by the CPI Group

Contents

The Snow Spider

For David

Contents

1.
The
Five
Gifts

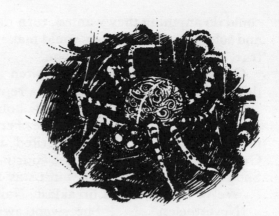

Gwyn's grandmother gave him five gifts for his birthday, his ninth birthday. They were very unusual gifts and if Gwyn had not been the sort of boy he was, he might have been disappointed.

'Happy Birthday!' said his grandmother, turning her basket upside down.

Gwyn stared at the objects on the kitchen floor, none of them wrapped in bright birthday paper: a piece of seaweed, a yellow scarf, a tin whistle, a twisted metal brooch, and a small, broken horse.

'Thank you, Nain!' said Gwyn, calling his grandmother the name she liked best.

'Time to find out if you are a magician, Gwydion Gwyn!' said Nain.

'A magician?' Gwyn inquired.

'Time to remember your ancestors: Math, Lord of Gwynedd, Gwydion and Gilfaethwy!'

'Who?'

'The magicians, boy! They lived here, in these mountains, maybe a thousand years ago, and they

7

could do anything they wanted, turn men into eagles and soldiers into dust; they could make dreams come true, and so, perhaps could you!'

On special occasions Nain often said peculiar things. Gwyn could not think of a reply.

'There has been an ache in this house since your sister – went,' said Nain, 'the ache of emptiness. You need help. If you have inherited the power of Gwydion you can use it to get your heart's desire.' She turned on her heel. 'I won't stay for tea!'

'We've only just had breakfast, Nain!'

'Nevertheless . . . ' She swept away, down the passage and through the open front door, her black hair sparkling in the golden mist that hung over the garden, her dress as gaudy as the autumn flowers crowding by the gate. Then she looked back and sang out, 'Give them to the wind, Gwydion Gwyn, one by one, and you'll see!'

Gwyn took the gifts up to his bedroom and laid them on the windowsill. They looked the most improbable effects for a magician.

'What's she on about now?' He scratched at his uncombed hair. From his tiny attic window he could see Nain's dark head bobbing down the mountain track. 'She travels too fast for a grandmother,' Gwyn muttered. 'If my ancestors were magicians, does that make her a witch?'

His father's voice roared up the stairs, 'Have you done the chickens then, Gwyn? It's Saturday. What about the gate? The sheep will be in the garden again. Was that your grandmother? Why didn't she stay?'

Gwyn answered none of these questions. He

gathered Nain's gifts together, put them in a drawer and went downstairs. His father was outside, shouting at the cows now, as he drove them down the track to pasture.

Gwyn sighed and pulled on his boots. His grandmother had delayed him, but she had remembered his birthday. His father did not wish to remember. There was no rest on Saturday for Gwyn. No time for football matches, no bicycle to ride down to the town. He was the only help his father had on the farm, and weekends were days for catching up with all the work he had missed during the week.

He tried not to think of Bethan, his sister, as he scattered corn to the hens, and searched for eggs in the barn. But when he went to examine the gate, he could not forget.

Beyond the vivid autumn daisies there was a cluster of white flowers nestling beneath the stone wall. Bethan had brought them up from the wood and planted them there, safe against the winds that tore across the mountain. Perhaps, even then, she had known that one day she would be gone, and wanted to leave something for them to remember her by.

'Gwyn, I've something for you.' His mother was leaning out of the kitchen window.

'I've to do the gate, Dad says!'

'Do it later; it's your birthday, Gwyn. Come and see what I've got for you!'

Gwyn dropped his tool box and ran inside.

'I've only just wrapped it,' his mother apologized. 'Did Nain bring you anything?'

'Yes. I thought everyone else had forgotten.'

9

'Of course not. I was so busy last night, I couldn't find the paper. Here you are!' His mother held out something very small, wrapped in shiny green paper.

Gwyn took the present, noticing that the paper had gold stars on it.

'I chose the paper specially.' Mrs Griffiths smiled anxiously.

'Wow!' Gwyn had torn off the paper and revealed a black watch in a transparent plastic box. Replacing the numbers, tiny silver moons encircled the dark face of the watch and, as Gwyn moved it, the hands sparkled like shooting stars.

'Oh, thanks, Mam!' Gwyn clasped the box to his chest and flung his free arm round his mother's neck.

'It's from us both, Gwyn. Your dad and me!'

'Yes, Mam,' Gwyn said, though he knew his mother had not spoken the truth. His father did not give him gifts.

'I knew you'd like it; always looking at the stars, you are, you funny boy. Take care of it now!'

''Course I will. It's more the sort of present for a magician. Nain gave me such strange things.'

His mother drew away from him. 'What things? What do you mean, a magician? Has Nain been spouting nonsense again?'

'Come and see!' Gwyn led his mother up to the attic and opened his top drawer. 'There!' he pointed to Nain's gifts.

Mrs Griffiths frowned at the five objects laid in a row on Gwyn's white school shirt. 'Whatever is she on about now? I wish she wouldn't.' She picked up the broken horse and turned it over in her hands.

10

'It has no ears, Mam,' Gwyn remarked, 'and no tail. Why did she give me a broken horse?'

'Goodness knows!' His mother held the horse closer and peered at a tiny label tied round its neck. 'It's in Welsh,' she said, 'but it's not your grandmother's writing. It's so faint. "Dim hon" I think that's what it says. "Not this!"'

'What does it mean, Mam, "Not this"? Why did she give it to me if I'm not to use it?'

His mother shook her head. 'I never know why Nain does things.'

'She said it was time to see if I was a magician, like my ancestors.'

'Don't pay too much attention to your grandmother,' Mrs Griffiths said wearily. 'She's getting old and she dreams.'

'Her hair is black,' Gwyn reminded her.

'Her hair is black, but her eyes don't see things the way they used to!' Mam picked up the yellow scarf. 'This too? Did Nain bring this?'

'Yes. It's Bethan's isn't it?'

His mother frowned. 'It disappeared with her. She must have been wearing it the night she went, but the police found nothing next morning, nothing at all. How strange! If Nain found it why didn't she say?' She held the scarf close to her face.

'You can smell the flowers,' said Gwyn. 'D'you remember? She used to dry the roses and put them in her clothes.'

His mother laid the scarf back in the drawer. 'Don't talk of Bethan now, Gwyn,' she said.

'Why not, Mam? We should talk of her. It was on

11

my birthday she left. She might come back . . . if we think of her.'

'She won't come back! Don't you understand Gwyn? We searched for days. The police searched, not only here, but everywhere. It was four years ago!' His mother turned away, then said more kindly, 'I've asked Alun Lloyd to come up for tea. We'll have a proper tea today, not like your other birthdays. You'd better get on with your work now.'

When Mrs Griffiths had left the room Gwyn lifted the scarf out of the drawer and pressed it to his face. The scent of roses was still strong. Bethan seemed very near. How good she had looked in her yellow scarf, with her dark hair and her red mac, all bright and shining. He remembered now; she had been wearing the scarf that night; the night she had climbed the mountain and never come back. Why had Nain kept it secret all this time, and given it to him now, on his birthday?

'If Bethan left her scarf,' Gwyn exclaimed aloud, 'perhaps she meant to come back.'

He laid the scarf over the broken horse, the seaweed, the whistle and the brooch, and gently closed the drawer. He was humming cheerfully to himself when he went out into the garden again.

Mam kept her word. Alun Lloyd arrived at four o'clock. But he had brought his twin brothers with him, which was not part of the arrangement.

There were nine Lloyds all crammed into a farmhouse only one room larger than the Griffiths', and sometimes Mrs Lloyd, ever eager to acquire a

little more space, took it upon herself to send three or four children, where only one had been invited. She was, however, prepared to pay for these few precious hours of peace. Alun, Gareth and Siôn had all brought a gift and Mrs Griffiths, guessing the outcome of her invitation, had provided tea for seven.

Kneeling on the kitchen floor, Gwyn tore the coloured paper off his presents. A red kite, a pen and a pair of black plastic spectacles with a large pink nose, black eyebrows and a black moustache attached.

'Looks like your dad, doesn't it?' giggled Siôn, and he snatched up the spectacles, put them on and began to prance up and down the room, chest out and fingers tucked behind imaginary braces.

Suddenly it was like other people's birthdays. The way a birthday should be, but Gwyn's never was.

Nain arrived with a box under her arm. 'For your birthday,' she said. 'Records, I don't want them any more.'

'But you've given your presents, Nain,' said Gwyn.

'Don't look a gift-horse in the mouth,' Nain retorted. 'Who are these nice little boys?'

'You know who they are. The Lloyds, Alun and Gareth and Siôn, from Ty Llŷr. Don't you ever see your neighbours?' chided Gwyn.

'Not the one with the specs; I don't know that one. Looks like your father,' chuckled Nain. 'Put on some music, Glenys!'

'Well, I don't know . . . ' Mrs Griffiths looked worried. 'Ivor put the record-player away; we

14

haven't used it since . . . '

'Time to get it out then,' said Nain.

Somewhat reluctantly, Mrs Griffiths knelt in a corner of the kitchen and, from a small neglected cupboard, withdrew the record-player. She placed it on the kitchen table while the boys gathered round.

'I can't remember where to plug it in,' said Mrs Griffiths.

'The light, Mam,' Gwyn explained. 'Look, the plug is for the light.'

'But . . . it's beginning to get dark.' His mother sounded almost afraid.

'Candles! We can have candles!' Gwyn began to feel ridiculously elated. He fetched a box of candles from the larder and began to set them up on saucers and bottles all round the room.

Then they put on one of Nain's records. It was very gay and very loud: a fiddle, a flute, a harp and a singer. The sort of music to send you wild, and the Lloyds went wild. They drummed on the table, jumped on the chairs, stamped on the floor, waved the dishcloths and juggled with the cat. The cat objected and Siôn retired, temporarily, from the merry-making, bloody-eared but unbowed.

Nain began to dance, in her purple dress and black lace stockings, her dark curls bouncing and her coloured beads flying. She wore silver bracelets, too, that jangled when she raised her arms, and a black shawl that swung out and made the candles flicker.

'Mae gen i dipyn o dŷ bach twt
A'r gwynt i'r drws bob bore.

15

Hei di ho, di hei di hei di ho,
'A'r gwynt i'r drws bob bore . . . '

sang the singers, and so sang Nain, in her high quivering voice.

The Lloyds thought it the funniest thing they had ever seen and, clutching their sides, they rolled on the floor, gasping and giggling.

Gwyn smiled, but he did not laugh. There was something strange, almost magical, about the tall figure spinning in the candlelight.

Down in the field, Gwyn's father heard the music. For a few moments he paused and listened while his cows, eager to be milked, ambled on up to the farmyard. Mr Griffiths regarded the mountain, rising dark and bare beside the house, and remembered his daughter.

When the boys had breath left neither for dancing nor laughter, Mrs Griffiths tucked the record-player away in its corner, stood up and removed her apron. Then she patted her hair, smoothed her dress and said, rather quiet and coy, 'Tea will be in here today, boys!' and she walked across the passage and opened the door into the front room.

Gwyn was perplexed. Teas, even fairly smart teas with relations, were always in the kitchen these days. He moved uncertainly towards the open door and looked in.

A white cloth had been laid on the long oak table, so white it almost hurt his eyes. And upon the cloth,

16

the best blue china, red napkins, plates piled with brightly wrapped biscuits, with sugar mice and chocolate pigs. There were crisps and popcorn, and cakes with coloured icing on a silver stand. There were crackers too, decorated with gold and silver paper, and in the centre of the table a magnificent green jelly, rising above a sea of ice-cream.

The Lloyds crowded into the doorway beside Gwyn and gazed at the splendid spread. Gwyn felt so proud. 'Oh, Mam,' he breathed, 'Oh, Mam!' Then Gareth and Siôn rushed past him and drew out their chairs exclaiming, 'Gwyn! Gwyn, come on, let's start, we're starving!'

'It's the grandest birthday table I've ever seen,' said Alun. 'Our Mam has never done anything like that.'

'Nor has his, until today,' said Nain. 'It was about time.'

Gwyn took his place at the head of the table and they began. There was so much chatter, so much laughter, no one heard Mr Griffiths come in from milking and go upstairs. And Mrs Griffiths, happy and gratified, did not notice her husband's boots beside the back door, nor his coat upon the hook, when she went into the kitchen to fetch the birthday cake.

The cake was huge and white, with chocolate windows and silver banners and, on each of the nine towers, a flaming candle.

'Turn out the lights!' cried Gareth, and he sprang to the switch, plunging the party into cosy candlelight again.

'Blow out the candles, Gwyn, and wish!'
commanded Siôn.

Gwyn drew a deep breath and then paused. 'Let's
cut the cake and leave the candles,' he said, 'they look
so good. Let's leave them till they die.'

They were still alight when Mr Griffiths came
downstairs again. Crackers were banging, and no
one heard feet upon the tiled kitchen floor, tapping in
unfamiliar shoes. When the door opened the tiny
flames glowed fiercely for a moment, and then died.

Except for a white shirt Mr Griffiths was dressed
entirely in black. He stared at the table in cold
disbelief.

The shock of the electric light jolted the party out of
its homely cheerfulness. The birthday table looked
spoiled and untidy; someone had spilt orange juice on
the white cloth.

'What's this? Celebrating are we?' Mr Griffiths'
mouth was tight, his face white with displeasure.

Siôn was still wearing the spectacle mask and his
brothers began to giggle. He did resemble Mr
Griffiths.

'It's Gwyn's birthday, Ivor,' Mrs Griffiths
explained nervously. 'You're just in time for . . . '

'I know what day it is.' Her husband spoke the
words slowly, through clenched teeth, as though the
taste was bitter. 'There are candles wasting in the
kitchen, chairs on the floor, and look at this – litter!'
He flung out his hand, indicating the table.

'Sit down, Ivor Griffiths, you miserable man,' said
Nain, 'and celebrate your son's birthday!'

'Miserable is it?' Mr Griffiths big red hands were

18

clasped tight across his chest, one hand painfully rubbing and pressing at the other. 'Miserable is it, to be remembering my own daughter who is gone? My daughter who went on this day, four years ago?'

Suddenly Mrs Griffiths stood up. 'Enough! We've had enough, Ivor!' she protested. 'We remember Bethan too. We've mourned her going every year on this day, for four years. But it's Gwyn's birthday, and we've had enough of mourning! Enough! Enough!' She was almost crying.

Gwyn turned his head away. He did not want to look at the bright colours on the table; did not want to see his friends' faces. He knew that his birthday was over. His mother was talking, but he could not listen to the words. She was taking his friends away, he heard them shuffling into the kitchen, murmuring 'good-bye', but he could not move. His father was still standing by the table, sad and silent in his black suit.

'How could you do that, Ivor?' Nain reproached her son as the front door slammed.

'How could I? I have done nothing. It was that one!' and he looked at Gwyn. 'She is gone because of him, my Bethan is.'

It was said.

Gwyn felt almost relieved. He got up slowly and pushed his chair neatly back to the table then, without looking at his father, he walked out to the kitchen.

His mother was standing by the sink, waving to the Lloyds through a narrow window. She swung round quickly when she heard her son. 'I'm sorry, Gwyn,' she said quietly. 'So sorry.' She came towards him and hugged him close. Her face was flushed and she had put her apron on again.

'It was a great party, Mam! Thanks!' said Gwyn. 'The other boys liked it too, I know they did.'

'But I wanted your father to . . .'

'It doesn't matter, Mam,' Gwyn interrupted quickly. 'It was grand. I'll always remember it!'

He drew away from his mother and ran up to his room, where he sat on the edge of his bed, smiling at the memory of his party and the way it had been before his father had arrived. Gwyn knew his father could not help the bitterness that burst out of him every now and again, and he had acquired a habit of distancing himself from the ugly words. He thought hard about the good times, until the bad ceased to exist.

A tiny sound caused him to go to the window. There was a light in the garden, a lantern swaying in the evening breeze.

Gwyn opened the window. 'Who's there?' he called.

He was answered by a high, girlish laugh, and then his grandmother's voice, 'Remember your gifts, Gwydion Gwyn. Remember Math, Lord of Gwynedd, remember Gwydion and Gilfaethwy!'

'Are you being funny, Nain?'

There was a long pause and then the reply, 'It's not a game I'm playing, Gwydion Gwyn. Once in every seven generations the power returns, so they say. Your father never had it, nor did mine. Let's find out who you are!'

The gate clicked shut and the lantern went

swinging down the lane, while the words of an old song rose and fell on the freshening wind, and then receded, until the light and the voice faded altogether.

Before he shut the window, Gwyn looked up at the mountain and remembered his fifth birthday. It had been a fine day, like today, but in the middle of the night a storm had broken. The rain had come pouring down the mountainside in torrents, boulders and branches rumbling and groaning in its path. The Griffiths family had awakened, pulled the blankets closer to their heads and fallen asleep again, except for Gwyn. His black sheep was still up on the mountain. He had nursed it as a motherless lamb, himself, tucking it in Mam's old jumper, cosy by the fire. Feeding it with a bottle, five times a day, until it had grown into a fine ewe.

'Please, get her! Please, save her!' Gwyn had shaken his sister awake again.

Bethan had grumbled but because she was older, and because she was kind, she had complied.

The last time Gwyn saw her she had been standing by the back door in her red mac, testing the big outdoor torch. It was the night after Halloween and the pumpkin was still on the windowsill, grimacing with its dark gaping mouth and sorrowful eyes. Bethan had become curiously excited, as though she was going to meet someone very special, not just a lonely black ewe. 'Shut the door tight, when I am gone,' she had whispered, 'or the wind will howl through the house and wake Mam and Dad!' Then, swinging the yellow scarf round her dark hair, she

21

had walked out into the storm. She had never been afraid of anything.

Through the kitchen window, Gwyn had watched the light of the big torch flashing on the mountainside until it disappeared. Then he had fallen asleep on the rug beside the stove.

They never saw Bethan again, though they searched every inch of the mountain. They never found a trace of her perilous climb on that wild night, nor did they find the black ewe. The girl and the animal seemed to have vanished!

2.
Arianwen

Unlike most Novembers, calm days seemed endless that autumn. Gwyn had to wait three weeks for a wind. It was the end of the month and the first snow had fallen on the mountain.

During those three weeks he found he could not broach the subject of his ancestors, though he dwelt constantly on Nain's words. Since his birthday the atmosphere in the house had hardly been conducive to confidences. His father remote and silent. His mother in such a state of anxiety that, whenever they were alone, he found he could only discuss the trivia of their days; the farm, the weather and his school activities.

But every morning and every evening Gwyn would open his drawer and take out the yellow scarf. He would stand by his window and run his hands lightly over the soft wool, all the time regarding the bare, snow-capped mountain, and he would think of Bethan.

Then, one Sunday, the wind came; so quietly at

23

first that you hardly noticed it. By the time the midday roast had been consumed, however, twigs were flying, the barn door banging, and the howling in the chimney loud enough to drive the dog away from the stove.

Gwyn knew it was time.

'Who were my ancestors?' he asked his mother.

They were standing by the sink, he dutifully drying the dishes, his mother with her hands deep in the soapy water. 'Ancestors,' she said. 'Well, no one special that I know of . . . '

'No one?' he probed.

'Not on my side, love. Your grandfather's a baker, you know that, and before that, well . . . I don't know. Nothing special.'

'What about Nain?'

Gwyn's father, slouched in a chair by the stove, rustled his newspaper, but did not look up.

Gwyn screwed up his courage. 'What about your ancestors, Dad?'

Mr Griffiths peered, unsmiling, over his paper. 'What about them?'

'Anyone special? Nain said there were magicians in the family . . . I think.'

His father shook the newspaper violently. 'Nain has some crazy ideas,' he said. 'I had enough of them when I was a boy.'

'Made you try and bring a dead bird back to life, you said,' his wife reminded him.

'How?' asked Gwyn.

'Chanting!' grunted Mr Griffiths. It was obvious that, just as Nain had said, his father had not

24

inherited whatever strange power it was that those long ago magicians had possessed. Or if he had, he did not like the notion.

'They're in the old legends,' mused Mrs Griffiths, 'the magicians. One of them made a ship out of seaweed, Gwydion I think it . . . '

'Seaweed?' Gwyn broke in.

'I think it was and . . . '

'Gwydion?' Gwyn absentmindedly pushed his wet tea-cloth into an open drawer. 'That's my name?'

'Mind what you're doing, Gwyn,' his mother complained. 'You haven't finished.'

'Math, Lord of Gwynedd, Gwydion and Gilfaethwy. And it was Gwydion made the ship? Me . . . my name!'

'It's what you were christened, Nain wanted it, but,' Mrs Griffiths glanced in her husband's direction, 'your father never liked it, not when he remembered where it came from, so we called you Gwyn. Dad was pretty fed up with all Nain's stories.'

Mr Griffiths dropped his newspaper. 'Get on with your work, Gwyn,' he ordered, 'and stop flustering your mother.'

'I'm not flustered, love.'

'Don't argue and don't defend the boy!'

They finished the dishes in silence. Then, with the wind and his ancestors filling his thoughts, Gwyn rushed upstairs and opened the drawer. But he did not remove the seaweed. The first thing he noticed was the brooch, lying on top of the scarf. He could not remember having replaced it in that way. Surely the scarf was the last thing he had returned to the drawer?

25

The sunlight, slanting through his narrow window, fell directly on to the brooch and the contorted shapes slowly assumed the form of a star, then a snowflake, next a group of petals changed into a creature with glittering eyes before becoming a twisted piece of metal again. Something or somebody wanted him to use the brooch!

Gwyn picked it up and thrust it into his pocket. Grabbing his anorak from a chair he rushed downstairs and out of the back door. He heard a voice, as he raced across the yard, calling him to a chore. 'But the wind was too loud, wasn't it?' he shouted joyfully to the sky. 'I never heard nothing!'

He banged the yard gate to emphasise his words and began to run through the field; after a hundred yards the land began to rise; he kept to the sheeptrack for a while, then climbed a wall and jumped down into another field, this one steep and bare. He was among the sheep now, scattering them as he bounded over mounds and boulders. Stopping at the next wall, he took a deep breath. The mountain had begun in earnest. Now it had to be walking or climbing, running was impossible.

A sense of urgency gripped him; an overwhelming feeling that today, perhaps within that very hour, something momentous would occur.

He stumbled on, now upon a sheeptrack, now heaving himself over boulders. He had climbed the mountain often, sometimes with Alun, sometimes alone, but the first time had been with Bethan, one summer long ago. It had seemed an impossible task then, when he was not five years old, but she had willed him to the top, comforting and cajoling him with her gentle voice. 'It's so beautiful when you get there, Gwyn. You can see the whole world, well the whole of Wales anyway, and the sea, and clouds below you. You won't fall, I won't let you!' She had been wearing the yellow scarf that day. Gwyn remembered how it had streamed out across his head, like a banner, when they reached the top.

It was not a high mountain, nor a dangerous one, some might even call it a hill. It was wide and grassy, a series of gentle slopes that rose, one after another, patterned with drystone walls and windblown bushes. The plateau at the top was a lonely place, however. From here only the empty fields and surrounding mountains could be seen and, far out to the west, the distant grey line of the sea. Gwyn took shelter beside the tallest rock, for the wind sweeping across the plateau threatened to roll him back whence he had come.

He must surely have found the place to offer his brooch. 'Give it to the wind,' Nain had said. Bracing himself against the rock, Gwyn extended his up-turned hand into the wind and uncurled his fingers.

The brooch was snatched away so fast that he never saw what became of it. He withdrew his hand and waited for the wind to answer, not knowing what the answer would be, but wanting it to bring him something that would change the way things were, to fill the emptiness in the house below.

But the wind did not reply. It howled about Gwyn's head and tore at his clothes, then slowly it died away taking, somewhere within its swirling streams and currents, the precious brooch, and leaving nothing in return.

Then, from the west, came a silver-white cloud of snow, obscuring within minutes the sea, the surrounding mountains and the fields below. And, as the snow began to encircle and embrace him, Gwyn found himself chanting, 'Math, Lord of Gwynedd, Gwydion and Gilfaethwy!' This he repeated, over and over again, not knowing whether he was calling to the living or the dead. And all the while, huge snowflakes drifted silently about him, melting as they touched him, so that he did not turn into the snowman that he might otherwise have become.

Gwyn stood motionless for what seemed like hours, enveloped in a soft, serene whiteness, waiting for an answer. Yet, had Nain promised him an answer? In the stillness he thought he heard a sound, very high and light, like icicles on glass.

His legs began to ache, his face grew numb with cold and, when night clouds darkened the sky, he began his descent, resentful and forlorn.

The lower slopes of the mountain were still green, the snow had not touched them and it was difficult for

28

Gwyn to believe he had been standing deep in snow only minutes earlier. Only from the last field could the summit be seen, but by the time Gwyn reached the field the mountain was obscured by mist, and he could not tell if snow still lay above.

It was dark when he got home. Before opening the back door he stamped his boots. His absence from the farm all day would not be appreciated, he realized, and he did not wish to aggravate the situation with muddy boots. He raised his hand to brush his shoulders free of the dust he usually managed to collect, and his fingers encountered something icy cold.

Believing it to be a snowflake or even an icicle, Gwyn plucked it off his shoulder and moved closer to the kitchen window to examine what he had found. His mother had not yet drawn the curtains and light streamed into the yard.

It was a snowflake; the most beautiful he had ever seen, for it was magnified into an exquisite and intricate pattern: a star glistening like crystal in the soft light. And then the most extraordinary thing happened. The star began to move and Gwyn stared amazed as it gradually assumed the shape of a tiny silver spider. Had the wind heard him after all? Was he a magician then?

'Gwyn, is that you out there? You'll have no tea if you hang about any longer.' His mother had spied him from the window.

Gwyn closed his fingers over the spider and tried to open the back door with his left hand. The door was jerked back violently and his father pulled him into

29

the kitchen.

'What the hell are you doing out there? You're late! Can't you open a door now?' Mr Griffiths had flecks of mud on his spectacles; Gwyn tried not to look at them.

'My hands are cold,' he said.

'Tea'll be cold too,' grumbled Mr Griffiths. 'Get your boots off and sit down. Where were you this afternoon? You were needed. That mad cockerel's out again. We won't have a Christmas dinner if he doesn't stay put.'

With some difficulty Gwyn managed to remove his boots with his left hand. 'I'm just going upstairs,' he said airily.

'Gwyn, whatever are you up to?' asked his mother. 'Wash your hands and sit down.'

'I've got to go upstairs,' Gwyn insisted.

'But Gwyn . . .'

'Please, Mam!'

Mrs Griffiths shrugged and turned back to the stove. Her husband had begun to chew bacon and was not interested in Gwyn's hasty flight through the kitchen.

Tumbling into his bedroom Gwyn scanned the place for something in which to hide his spider. He could think of nothing but the drawer. Placing the spider gently on to the yellow scarf, he pushed the drawer back, leaving a few centimetres for air, then fled downstairs.

He got an interrogation in the kitchen.

Mrs Griffiths began it. 'Whatever made you run off like that this afternoon,' she complained. 'Didn't

30

you hear me call?'

'No, it was windy,' Gwyn replied cheerfully.

'Well, what was it you were doing all that time? I rang Mrs Lloyd, you weren't there.'

'No,' said Gwyn, 'I wasn't!'

'Not giving much away, are you?' Mr Griffiths muttered from behind a mug of tea. 'It's no use trying to get that cockerel now it's dark,' he went on irritably. 'We'll have to be up sharp in the morning.'

'Won't have any trouble waking if he's out,' Gwyn sniggered.

'It would take more than a cockerel to wake you some mornings,' laughed his mother. At least she had recovered her good humour.

After tea Mr Griffiths vanished into his workshop. His work-load of farm repairs seemed to increase rather than diminish, and Gwyn often wondered if it was his father's way of avoiding conversation.

He thought, impatiently, of the drawer in his room, while his mother chattered about Christmas and the cockerel. Then, excusing himself with a quick hug, Gwyn left his mother to talk to the cat and, trying not to show an unnatural enthusiasm for bed, crossed the passage and climbed the stairs slowly, but two at a time.

His bedroom door was open and there appeared to be a soft glow within. On entering the room Gwyn froze. There were shadows on the wall: seven helmeted figures, motionless beside his bed. He turned, fearfully, to locate the source of light. It came from behind a row of toy spacemen standing on the chest of drawers. Gwyn breathed a sigh of relief and

31

approached the spacemen.

The silver spider had climbed out of the drawer. It was glowing in the dark!

Gwyn brushed his toys aside and hesitantly held out his hand to the spider. It crawled into his open palm and, gently, he raised it closer to his face. The spider's touch was icy cold, and yet the glow that it shed on his face had a certain strange warmth that seemed to penetrate every part of his body.

He held the spider for several minutes, admiring the exquisite pattern on its back and wondering whether there was more to the tiny creature than a superficial beauty. It had come in exchange for the brooch, of that he was certain. But was it really he who had transformed the brooch. Or had the extraordinary spider come from a place beyond his world. He resolved to keep it a secret until he could consult his grandmother the following evening.

Replacing the spider in the drawer, Gwyn went downstairs to fetch a book. When he returned the 'glow' came from the bedpost and, deciding that he had no need of an electric light, he sat on the bed and read his book beside the spider. It was an exceptional sensation, reading by spiderlight.

Nain was gardening by lamplight when Gwyn found her. She was wearing her sunhat and a bright purple cardigan. The sky was dark and frost had begun to sparkle on the ground.

'It's a bit late for that, isn't it?' said Gwyn, approaching his grandmother down the cinder path.

'I like to poke a few things about,' she replied, 'just

to let them know I've got my eye on them.'

'There's not much growing, Nain,' Gwyn remarked. 'Not that you can see anything in this light.'

'There's tatws!' she said defiantly, and heaved a plant out of the ground, scattering earth all over Gwyn's white trainers. Not satisfied with this, she shook the plant violently and Gwyn sprang back, too late, to save the bottoms of his new school trousers.

'Oh heck, Nain!' he cried. 'What did you do that for. I'll get a row?'

'Why didn't you put your boots on, silly boy?' she replied. 'There's mud all down the lane.'

'I came for a chat, didn't I? How was I to know I'd be attacked by a madwoman.'

'Ha! Ha! Who's mad, Gwydion Gwyn?' Nain loved being teased. 'Have you brought good news. Are you a magician, then?'

'Can't we go inside, Nain?' Gwyn fingered the matchbox in his pocket. He did not want to confide under the stars, someone could be listening, out there in the dark.

'Come on, then! We'll leave the plants to doze for a bit and have a cup of tea.' Nain dropped her potatoes, shook out her purple cardigan and stamped across to open the back door.

The inside of her house was like a bright bowl. All the corners had been rounded off with cupboards and book-cases, and upon every item of furniture there was heaped a jumble of books, bright clothes and exotic plants. The fronds of shawls, trailing leaves and garlands of beads festooned the furniture to such

33

a degree that its identity could not easily be ascertained. The only source of light came from an oil-lamp, and as this was partially obscured by a tall fern, the whole place had a wild and mystical air about it.

Somewhere, through the jumble, a kettle lurked, and soon this was whistling merrily, while Nain sang from behind a screen embroidered with butterflies, and a canary chattered in its cage.

Gwyn looked round for a vacant seat. There was none. 'What shall I do with the eggs, Nain?' he called.

'How many?'

Gwyn counted the eggs, nestling in a red woolly hat on the only armchair. 'Seven,' he replied.

'Well! Well! They've all been in here today, then, and I never noticed.' Nain chuckled to herself.

'Why d'you let the hens in, Nain?' Gwyn asked. 'They're such mucky things. Mam would have a fit.'

'Huh! Your mam would have a fit if she looked under my bed, I expect,' Nain giggled, 'but there's no need to go upsetting people for nothing. Bring the eggs out here.'

Gwyn held out the bottom of his jumper and gathered the eggs into it. He looked for his grandmother behind the screen but she had vanished, and so had the kitchen. There was only a narrow space between rows of plants and metres of crimson velvet. He found the kettle on the windowsill and put the eggs in a green hat beside it. Nain did not seem to be short of hats, so he felt the eggs would be safe enough for the moment. However, she had been

34

known to wear two at a time and so he called out, 'Don't put your green hat on yet, Nain!'

His grandmother's head popped out from a gap in the velvet. 'Isn't it grand?' she purred. 'I'm going to dance in it.'

'The hat?' Gwyn inquired.

'This, silly boy.' His grandmother stroked the crimson material.

'Where?' he asked.

'Who knows?'

'Nain, would you find yourself a cup of tea and then sit down and – concentrate. I've got something to show you!' Gwyn fingered his matchbox again.

'Was it the wind?' Nain asked. 'It was windy yesterday. I thought of you. Quick, a cup of tea.' She withdrew her head and reappeared a moment later, carrying two blue enamel mugs. 'One for you?'

'No thanks, Nain!' His grandmother did not use conventional tea-leaves. Her tea was made from nettles or dried roots. Sometimes it was palatable, most often it was not. Today Gwyn preferred not to risk it.

He waited until his grandmother had settled herself in the armchair and sipped her tea before he knelt beside her and took out the matchbox. He wanted her undivided attention for his revelation. Even so he was unprepared for the ecstatic gasp that accompanied Nain's first glimpse of the spider, when he gently withdrew the lid. The tiny creature crawled on to his hand, glowing in the dark room, and Nain's eyes sparkled like a child's. 'How did it come?' Her whisper was harsh with excitement.

35

'In the snow,' Gwyn replied. 'I thought it was a snowflake. It was the brooch, I think. I gave it to the wind, like you said, and this . . . came back!'

'So,' Nain murmured triumphantly, 'you are a magician then, Gwydion Gwyn, as I thought. See what you have made!'

'But did I make it, Nain? I believe it has come from somewhere else. Some far, far place . . . I don't know, beyond the world, I think.'

'Then you called it, you brought it here, Gwydion Gwyn. Did you call?'

'I did but . . . ' Gwyn hesitated, 'I called into the snow, the names you said: Math, Lord of Gwynedd, Gwydion and Gilfaethwy. Those were the only words.'

'They were the right words, boy. You called to your ancestors. The magicians heard your voice and took the brooch to where it had to go, and now you have the spider!' Nain took the spider from Gwyn and placed it on her arm. Then she got up and began to dance through the shadowy wilderness of her room. The tiny glowing creature moved slowly up her purple sleeve, until it came to her shoulder, and there it rested, shining like a star beneath her wild black curls.

Gwyn watched and felt that it was Nain who was the magician and he the enchanted one.

Suddenly his grandmother swooped back and, taking the spider from her hair, put it gently into his hands. 'Arianwen,' she said. 'White silver! Call her Arianwen; she must have a name!'

'And what now?' asked Gwyn. 'What becomes of

Arianwen? Should I tell about her? Take her to a museum?'

'Never! Never! Never!' said Nain fiercely. 'They wouldn't understand. She has come from another world to bring you closer to the thing you want.'

'I want to see my sister,' said Gwyn. 'I want things the way they were before she went.'

Nain looked at Gwyn through half-closed eyes. 'It's just the beginning, Gwydion Gwyn, you'll see. You'll be alone, mind. You cannot tell. A magician can have his heart's desire if he truly wishes it, but he will always be alone.' She propelled her grandson gently but firmly towards the door. 'Go home now or they'll come looking, and never tell a soul!'

3.
The
Girl
in the
Web

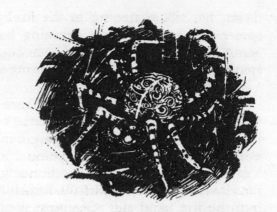

The farmhouse was empty when Gwyn reached home. Mr Griffiths could be heard drilling in his workshop. Mrs Griffiths had popped out to see a neighbour, leaving a note for her son on the kitchen table,

'SOUP ON THE STOVE.
STOKE IT UP IF IT'S COLD'

'The soup or the stove?' Gwyn muttered to himself. He opened the stove door, but the red embers looked so warm and comforting he was reluctant to cover them with fresh coal. He turned off the light and knelt beside the fire, holding out his hands to the warmth.

He must have put the matchbox down somewhere and he must have left it open, because he suddenly became aware that Arianwen was climbing up the back of the armchair. When she reached the top she swung down to the arm, leaving a silver thread behind her. Up she went to the top again, and then down, her silk glistening in the firelight. Now the spider was swinging and spinning back and forth across the chair so fast that Gwyn could only see a spark, shooting over an ever-widening sheet of silver.

'A cobweb!' he breathed.

And yet it was not a cobweb. There was someone there. Someone was sitting where the cobweb should have been. A girl with long pale hair and smiling eyes: Bethan, sitting just as she used to sit, with her legs tucked under her, one hand resting on the arm of the chair, the other supporting her chin as she gazed into the fire. And still Arianwen spun, tracing the girl's face, her fingers and her hair, until every feature became so clear Gwyn felt he could have touched the girl.

The tiny spider entwined the silk on one last corner and then ceased her feverish activity. She waited, just above the girl's head, allowing Gwyn to contemplate her creation without interruption.

Was the girl an illusion? An image on a silver screen? No, she was more than that. Gwyn could see the impression her elbow made on the arm of the chair, the fibres in her skirt, the lines on her slim, pale hand.

Only Bethan had ever sat thus. Only Bethan had gazed into the fire in such a way. But his sister was dark, her cheeks were rosy, her skin tanned golden by the wind. This girl was fragile and so silver-pale she might have been made of gossamer.

'Bethan?' Gwyn whispered, and he stretched out his hand towards the girl.

A ripple spread across the shining image, as water

40

moves when a stone pierces the surface, but Gwyn did not notice a cool draught entering the kitchen as the door began to open.

'Bethan?' he said again.

The figure shivered violently as the door swung wider, and then the light went on. The girl in the cobweb hovered momentarily and gradually began to fragment and to fade until Gwyn was left staring into an empty chair. His hand dropped to his side.

'Gwyn! What are you doing, love? What are you staring at?' His mother came round the chair and looked down at him, frowning anxiously.

Gwyn found that speech was not within his power, part of his strength seemed to have evaporated with the girl.

'Who were you talking to? Why were you sitting in the dark?' Concern caused Mrs Griffiths to speak sharply.

Her son swallowed but failed to utter a sound. He stared up at her helplessly.

'Stop it, Gwyn! Stop looking at me like that! Get up! Say something!' His mother shook his shoulders and pulled him to his feet.

He stumbled over to the table and sat down, trying desperately to drag himself away from the image in the cobweb. The girl had smiled at him before she vanished, and he knew that she was real.

Mrs Griffiths ignored him now, busying herself about the stove, shovelling in coal, warming up the soup. By the time the meal was ready and sat steaming in a bowl before him, he had recovered enough to say, 'Thanks, Mam!'

42

'Perhaps you can tell me what you were doing, then?' his mother persisted, calmer now that she had done something practical.

'I was just cold, Mam. It's nice by the stove when the door is open. I sort of . . . dozed . . . couldn't wake up.' Gwyn tried to explain away something his mother would neither believe, nor understand.

'Well, you're a funny one. I would have been here but I wanted to pickle some of those tomatoes and I had to run down to Betty Lloyd for sugar.' Mrs Griffiths chattered on, somewhat nervously Gwyn thought, while he sat passively, trying to make appropriate remarks in the few gaps that her commentary allowed.

His father's return from the workshop brought Gwyn to life. 'Don't sit down, Da!' he cried, leaping towards the armchair.

'What on earth? What's got into you, boy?' Mr Griffiths was taken by surprise.

'It's a matchbox,' Gwyn explained. 'In the chair. I don't want it squashed.'

'What's so special about a matchbox?'

'There's something in it, a particular sort of insect,' stammered Gwyn. 'For school,' he added, 'It's important, see?'

His father shook the cushions irritably. 'Nothing there,' he said and sat down heavily in the armchair.

'Here's a matchbox,' said Mrs Griffiths, 'on the floor.' She opened the box, 'but there's nothing in it.'

'Oh heck!' Gwyn moaned.

'What sort of insect was it, love? Perhaps we can find it for you?' His mother was always eager to help where school was concerned.

'A spider,' Gwyn said.

'Oh, Gwyn,' moaned Mrs Griffiths, 'not spiders. I've just cleaned this house from top to bottom. I can't abide cobwebs.'

'Spiders eat flies,' Gwyn retorted.

'There are no flies in this house,' thundered Mr Griffiths, 'and when you've found your "particular" spider, you keep it in that box. If I find it anywhere near my dinner, I'll squash it with my fist, school or no school!'

'You're a mean old . . . man!' cried Gwyn.

Mrs Griffiths gave an anguished sigh, and her husband stood up. But Gwyn fled before another word could be spoken. He climbed up to his bedroom and nothing followed, not even a shout.

He had turned on the light as soon as he entered the room, so he was not immediately aware of the glow coming from the open top drawer. He walked over to the window to draw the curtains and looked down to see Arianwen sitting on the whistle. Incredibly, she must have pulled the whistle from beneath the yellow scarf. But, on consideration, Gwyn realized it was a small feat for a creature who had just conjured a girl into her web. And what of the girl now? Had she been mere gossamer after all, a trick of the firelight on a silver cobweb?

'Why couldn't you stay where you were?' Gwyn inquired of the spider. 'You caused me a bit of bother just now!'

Arianwen moved slowly to the end of the whistle and it occurred to Gwyn that she had selected it for some special purpose.

'Now?' he asked in a whisper.

Arianwen crawled off the whistle.

Gwyn picked it up and held it to his lips. It was cracked and only a thin sound came from it. He shrugged and opened the window. Arianwen climbed out of the drawer and swung herself on to his sleeve.

'But there's no wind,' he said softly, and he held his arm up to the open window. 'See, no wind at all.'

The spider crawled on to the window frame and ran up to the top. When she reached the centre she let herself drop on a shining thread until she hung just above Gwyn's head. A tiny lantern glowing against the black sky.

Gwyn had been wrong. There was a wind, for now the spider was swaying in the open window and he could feel a breath of ice-cold air on his face.

'Shall I say something,' he mused. 'What shall I say?'

Then, without any hesitation he called, 'Gwydion! Gwydion! I am Gwydion! I am Math and Gilfaethwy!'

Even as he said the words, the breeze became an icy blast, rattling the window and tugging at his hair. He stepped back, amazed by the sudden violence in the air.

Arianwen spun crazily on her silver thread and the wind swooped into the room, tearing the whistle from Gwyn's hand and whisking it out through the open window.

Now the sound of the wind was deafening; terrifying too, for where a moment before, the land

45

had lain tranquil in the frosty silence, there was now an uproar; a moaning, groaning and screaming in the trees that was almost unearthly. Sheep on the mountain cried out in alarm and ran for shelter, and down in the yard the dog began to howl as though his very soul was threatened. Gwyn heard his father step outside to calm the dog. 'It's a damn peculiar kind of wind, though,' he heard him say.

Something shot into the bedroom and dropped, with a crack, on to the bare floorboards. It was a pipe of some sort: slim and silver like a snake. Gwyn stared at it apprehensively, then he slowly bent and picked it up. It was silky smooth and had an almost living radiance about it, as though it had no need of human hands to shine and polish it. Tiny, delicate lines encircled it: a beautiful pattern of knots and spirals; shapes that he had seen on a gravestone somewhere, and framing the pictures in one of Nain's old books.

Almost fearfully, he put the pipe to his lips, but he did not play it. He felt that it had not come for that purpose. He sat on the bed and ran his fingers over the delicate pattern.

The window stopped rattling and the wind dropped to a whisper. The land was quiet and still again. Arianwen left her post and ran into the drawer.

Gwyn laid the pipe on his bedside table and went to shut the window. He decided that he was too tired to speculate on the evening's events until he was lying down. He turned off the light, undressed and got into bed.

But he had awakened something that would not

sleep and now he was to be allowed no rest.

For a few moments Gwyn closed his eyes. When he opened them he saw that Arianwen had spun hundreds of tiny threads across the wall opposite his bed. They were so fine, so close, that they resembled a vast screen. Still she spun, swinging faster and faster across the wall, climbing, falling and weaving, not one thread at a time but a multitude. Soon the entire wall was covered, but the spider was not satisfied. She began to thread her way along the wall beside Gwyn's bed; over the door, over the cupboard, until the furniture was entirely covered with her irresistible flow of silk.

Gwyn was not watching Arianwen now. Something was happening in the web before him. He had the sensation that he was being drawn into the web, deeper and deeper, faster and faster. He was plunging into black silent space. A myriad of tiny coloured fragments burst and scattered in front of him, and then nothing for minutes that seemed like hours. Then the moving sensation began to slow until he felt that he was suspended in the air above an extraordinary scene.

A city was rising through clouds of iridescent snow. First a tower, tall and white, surmounted by a belfry of finely carved ice; within the belfry a gleaming silver bell. Beneath the tower there were buildings, all of them white, all of them round and beautiful, with shining dome-like roofs and oval windows latticed with a delicate network of silver – like cobwebs.

Beyond the houses there lay a vast expanse of snow, and surrounding the snow, mountains,

47

brilliant under the sun, or was it the moon hanging there, a huge sphere glowing in the dark sky?

Until that moment the city had been silent but suddenly the bell in the white tower began to sway and then it rang, and Gwyn could hear it, clear and sweet over the snow. Children emerged from the houses; children with pale faces and silvery hair, chattering, laughing and singing. They were in the snowfields now, calling to each other in high melodious voices. Was this where the pale girl in the web had come from?

Suddenly another voice called. His mother was climbing the stairs. 'Is that you, Gwyn? Are you awake? Was that a bell I heard?'

The white world shivered and began to fade until only the voices were left, singing softly in the dark.

The door handle rattled and Mrs Griffiths came into the room. For a moment she stood in the doorway, silhouetted against the landing light. She was trying to tear something out of her hair. At length she turned on the light and gave a gasp. 'Ugh! It's a cobweb,' she exclaimed, 'a filthy cobweb!' For her the silky threads did not glitter, they appeared merely as a dusty nuisance. 'Gwyn, how many spiders have you got up here?'

'Only one, Mam,' he replied.

'I can hear singing. Have you got your radio on? It's so late.'

'I haven't got the radio on, Mam.'

'What is it then?'

'I don't know, Mam.' Gwyn was now as bemused as his mother.

The sound seemed to be coming from beside him. But there was nothing there, only the pipe. The city, the children and even the vast cobwebs, were gone.

Gwyn picked up the pipe and put it to his ear. The voices were there, inside the pipe. He almost dropped it in his astonishment. So they had sent him a pipe to hear the things that he saw, maybe millions of miles away. The sound grew softer and was gone.

'Whatever's that? Where did you get it?' asked Mrs Griffiths, approaching the bed.

Gwyn decided to keep the voices to himself. 'It's a pipe, Mam. Nain gave it to me.'

'Oh! That's all.' She dismissed the pipe as though it was a trivial bit of tin. 'Try and get some sleep now, love, or you'll never be up for the bus.' She bent and kissed him.

'I'll be up, Mam,' Gwyn assured her.

His mother went to the door and turned out the light. 'That singing must have come from the Lloyds, they're always late to bed,' she muttered as she went downstairs. 'It's the cold. Funny how sound travels when it's cold.'

Gwyn slept deeply but woke soon after dawn and felt for the pipe under his pillow. He drew it out and listened. The pipe was silent. It did not even look as bright, as magical as it had in the night. Gwyn was not disappointed. A magician cannot always be at work.

He dressed and went downstairs before his parents were awake; had eaten his breakfast and fed the chickens by the time his father came downstairs to put the kettle on.

49

'What's got into you, then?' Mr Griffiths inquired when Gwyn sprang through the kitchen door.

'Just woke up early. It's a grand day, Dad!' Gwyn said.

This statement received no reply, nor was one expected. The silences that sometimes yawned between father and son created an unbearable emptiness that neither seemed able to overcome. But they had become accustomed to the situation, and if they could not entirely avoid it, accepted it as best they could. It was usually Gwyn who fled from his father's company, but on this occasion he was preoccupied and it was his father who left, to milk the cows.

A few moments later Mrs Griffiths shuffled down the stairs in torn slippers, still tying her apron strings. She was irritated to find herself the last one down. 'Why didn't someone call me,' she complained.

'It's not late, Mam,' Gwyn reassured her, 'and I've had my breakfast.'

His mother began to bang and clatter about the kitchen nervously. Gwyn retreated from the noise and went into the garden.

The sun was full up now; he could feel the warmth of it on his face. The last leaves had fallen during the wild wind of the night before and bedecked the garden with splashes of red and gold. A mist hung in the valley, even obscuring his grandmother's cottage, and Gwyn was glad that he lived in high country, where the air and the sky always seemed brighter.

At eight o'clock he began to walk down towards the main road. The school bus stopped at the end of the lane at twenty minutes past eight every morning, and did not wait for stragglers. It took Gwyn all of twenty minutes to reach the bus stop. For half a mile the route he took was little more than a steep track, rutted by the giant wheels of his father's tractor and the hooves of sheep and cattle. He had to leap over puddles, mounds of mud and fallen leaves. Only when he had passed his grandmother's cottage did his passage become easier. Here the track levelled off a little, the bends were less sharp and something resembling a lane began to emerge. By the time it had reached the Lloyds' farmhouse the track had become a respectable size, tarmac-ed and wide enough for two passing cars.

The Lloyds had just erupted through their gate, all seven of them, arguing, chattering and swinging their bags. Mrs Lloyd stood behind the gate, while little Iolo clasped her skirt through the bars, weeping bitterly.

'Stop it, Iolo. Be a good boy. Nerys, take his hand,' Mrs Lloyd implored her oldest child.

'Mam! Mam! Mam!' wailed Iolo, kicking his sister away.

'Mam can't come, don't be silly, Iolo! Alun, help Nerys. Hold his other hand.'

Alun obeyed. Avoiding the vicious thrusts of his youngest brother's boot, he seized Iolo's hand and swung him off his feet. Then he began to run down the lane while the little boy still clung to his neck, shrieking like a demon. The other Lloyds, thinking this great sport for the morning, followed close behind, whooping and yelling.

51

Gwyn envied them the noise, the arguments, even the crying. He came upon a similar scene every morning and it never failed to make him feel separate and alone. Sometimes he would hang behind, just watching, reluctant to intrude.

Today, however, Gwyn had something to announce. Today he did not feel alone. Different, yes, but not awkward and excluded.

'Alun! Alun!' he shouted. 'I've got news for you.'

Alun swung around, lowering Iolo to the ground, and the other Lloyds looked up at Gwyn as he came flying down the lane.

'Go on,' said Alun. 'What news?'

'I'm a magician,' cried Gwyn. 'A magician.' And he ran past them all, his arms outstretched triumphantly, his satchel banging on his back.

'A magician,' scoffed Alun. 'You're mad, Gwyn Griffiths, that's what you are,' and forgetting his duty, left Iolo on the lane and gave furious chase.

'Mad! Mad!' echoed Siôn and Gareth, following Alun's example.

'Mad! Mad!' cried Iolo excitedly, as he raced down the lane, away from Mam and his tears.

Soon there were four boys, tearing neck and neck, down the lane, and one not far behind; all shouting, 'Mad! Mad! Mad!' except for Gwyn, and he was laughing too much to say anything.

But the three girls, Nerys, Nia and Kate, always impressed by their dark neighbour, stood quite still and murmured, 'A magician?'

4.
The
Silver
Ship

Nain had warned him that he would be alone, but Gwyn had not realized what that would mean. After all, he had felt himself to be alone since Bethan went, but there had always been Alun when he needed company on the mountain or in the woods, to share a book or a game, to lend a sympathetic ear to confidences.

And for Alun the need had been as great. Gwyn was the one with an empty house and a quiet space to think and play in. And Gwyn was the clever one; the one to help with homework. It was Gwyn who had taught Alun to read. On winter evenings the two boys were seldom apart. Gwyn had never envisaged a time without Alun's friendship and perhaps, if he had kept silent, that time would never have come. But it never occurred to Gwyn that Alun would find it impossible to believe him. He felt that he only had to find the right words in order to convince his friend, and on the homeward journey, that same afternoon, he once again brought up the subject of magicians.

Iolo always raced ahead when they got off the school bus. The older children, however, were not so keen to run uphill. They lingered on the lane, Siôn and Gareth arguing, the girls collecting wild flowers or coloured leaves. Alun and Gwyn always brought up the rear.

'Have you heard of Math, Lord of Gwynedd?' Gwyn began innocently.

'Of course; he's in the old Welsh stories. Dad talks about them,' Alun replied.

'And Gwydion?'

'Yes, and how he made a ship from seaweed,' Alun's interest had been aroused.

'I'd forgotten, Dad never talks. But Nain reminded me; she's got more books than I've seen anywhere, except in the library.'

'Your Nain's a bit batty isn't she?' Alun had always been a little suspicious of Gwyn's grandmother.

'No! She's not batty! She knows a lot,' Gwyn replied. 'She knew about me; about my being a magician!'

'Now I know she's batty. And you are too,' Alun said good-naturedly.

Gwyn stopped quite still. His words came slow and quiet, not at all in the way he had intended. 'I'm not mad. Things happened last night. I think I made them happen. I wasn't dreaming. I saw my sister, or someone like my sister. Nain said Math and Gwydion were my ancestors . . . and that I have inherited . . . ' he could not finish for his friend had begun to laugh.

54

'They're in stories. They're not real people. You can't be descended from a story.'

'You don't know,' Gwyn began to gabble desperately. 'I can make the wind come. I saw another planet last night, very close. It was white and the buildings were white, and there was a tower with a silver bell, there were children, and this is the most fantastic part, I could hear them in a pipe that came from . . .'

'You're mad! You're lying!' Alun cried bitterly. 'Why are you lying? No one can see planets that close, they're millions and millions and millions of miles away!' And he fled from Gwyn still crying, 'Liar! Liar! Liar!'

'How d'you know,, Alun Lloyd?' Gwyn called relentlessly. 'You don't know anything, you don't. You're ignorant! I know what I know. And I know what I've seen!'

He had gone too far. He realized that before Alun sprang through his gate and followed his brothers up the path to the house, slamming the door behind him, to emphasise his distate for Gwyn's conversation.

Gwyn was alone on the lane with Nerys, Nia and Kate. The three girls had lost interest in their posies and were staring at Gwyn in dismay. He could not bring himself to speak to them, and so passed by in an awkward silence.

Half a mile further on he reached his grandmother's cottage and, knowing she was the only person in the world who would believe him, unceremoniously burst in upon her. He was astonished at what he saw.

Nain had sewn up the red velvet dress. She was wearing it; standing in the centre of her room like some exotic bird, surrounded as she was, by her flowering plants and gaudy paraphernalia. She had something shining on her forehead, huge rings on her fingers and, round her waist, a wide bronze chain.

'Nain!' said Gwyn, amazed. 'Where are you going?'

'I'm staying here,' his grandmother replied. 'This is my castle; I have to defend it.'

She was talking in riddles again. Gwyn decided to come straight to the point. 'Nain, I had something else from the wind last night: a silver pipe, and there were voices in it, from far away.'

'Ah,' said Nain. 'Even when men whispered, Math could hear them; he could hear voices beyond any mortal ear! The pipe is from him!'

'And something happened,' Gwyn went on, 'in Arianwen's web!'

As he spoke his grandmother began to move about her room, but Gwyn knew she was attending to his story, and when he mentioned the girl in the web, she hovered before a huge gilt-framed mirror at the back of the room and said softly, 'Gwydion Gwyn, you will soon have your heart's desire!'

'My heart's desire?' said Gwyn. 'I believe I am a magician but I am not strong yet. I don't know if these things are happening to me because I have the power, or if they would have happened to anyone.'

'You've forgotten the legends, haven't you, poor boy?' said Nain. 'I used to read them to you long ago, but your father stopped all that when Bethan went; he

56

stopped all the fun, all the joy. But he couldn't stop you, could he? Because you are who you are! Now I'll read you something.'

In spite of the multitude of books scattered about the room, his grandmother always knew exactly where to find the one she needed. From beneath a blue china dog, supporting a lopsided lampshade, she withdrew a huge black book, its leather cover scarred with age.

'The legends,' she purred, stroking the battered spine. It looked so awesome and so old Gwyn half expected a cloud of bats to fly out when his grandmother opened it.

She furled the train of her velvet dress around her legs, settled herself on a pile of cushions and beckoned to him.

Gwyn peered at the book over his grandmother's shoulder. 'It's in old Welsh,' he complained, 'I can't understand it.'

'Huh!' she sighed. 'I forgot. Listen, I'll translate. "At dawn rose Gwydion, the magician, before the cock crowed, and he summoned to him his power and his magic, and he went to the sea and found dulse and seaweed, and he held it close and spoke to it, then he cast it out over the sea, and there appeared the most marvellous ship . . .".' She turned the next few pages hurriedly, anxious to find the words that would convey to Gwyn that she wanted. 'Ah, here,' she exclaimed. 'Now you will understand. "Then Gwydion's son subdued the land and ruled over it prosperously, and thereafter he became Lord over Gwynedd!" ' She closed the book triumphantly.

'Well?' said Gwyn. 'I don't think I understand,

yet.'

'He was our ancestor, that Lord of Gwynedd,' said Nain, 'and so, it follows, was Gwydion.'

'But they're in a story, Nain.' In spite of himself Gwyn found he was repeating Alun's words. 'They're not real people.'

'Not real?' Nain rose tall and proud, out of her chair. 'They're our ancestors,' she said, glaring at Gwyn, and she slammed the book down upon others piled on a table beside her.

Gwyn winced as a cloud of dust flew into his face. A tiny jug tottered precariously beside the books, happily coming to rest before it reached the edge of the table.

'But how do you know, Nain?' he quietly persisted.

'How do I know? How do I know? Listen!' Nain settled back on to the cushions and drew Gwyn down beside her. 'My great-great-grandmother told me. She was a hundred years old and I was ten, and I believed her. And now I'll tell you something I've never told anyone, not even your father. She was a witch, my great-great-grandmother. She gave me the seaweed and the brooch and the whistle. "Keep it for you-know-who", she said, and I did know who.'

'And the broken horse?'

Nain frowned. 'I am afraid of that horse,' she said thoughtfully. 'I tried to burn it once, but I couldn't. It was still there when the fire died, black and grinning at me. I believe it is a dreadful thing, and she thought so too, my great-great-grandmother. She tied a label on it, "Dim hon! Not this!" for it must

58

never be used, ever. It must be kept safe; locked away; tight, tight, tight. It is old and evil.'

'I'll keep it safe, Nain. But what about the scarf? She didn't give you the scarf, your great-great-grandmother?'

'No, not the scarf. That was my idea. I found it on the mountain, the morning after Bethan went; but I didn't tell a soul. What would have been the use? I kept it for you.'

'Why for me?'

'Can't you guess? I knew you would need it.'

'And are you a witch too, Nain?' Gwyn ventured.

'No,' Nain shook her head regretfully. 'I haven't the power, I've tried, but it hasn't come to me.'

'And how do you know it has come to me?'

'Ah, I knew when you were born. It was All Hallows Day, don't forget, the beginning of the Celtic New Year. Such a bright dawn it was; all the birds in the world were singing. Like bells wasn't it? Bells ringing in the air. Your father came flying down the lane, 'The baby's on the way, Mam,' he cried. He was so anxious, so excited. By the time we got back to the house you were nearly in this world. And when you came and I saw your eyes, so bright, I knew. And little Bethan knew too, although she was only four. She was such a strange one, so knowing yet so wild, sometimes I thought she was hardly of this world; but how she loved you. And your da, so proud he was. What a morning!'

'He doesn't even like me now,' Gwyn murmured.

'No, and that's what we have to change, isn't it?' Nain said gently.

Gwyn buried his face in his hands. 'Oh, I don't know! I don't know!' he cried. 'How can a spider and a pipe help me? And what has another world to do with Bethan? I've just had a row with my best friend. He wouldn't believe me.'

'I warned you never to betray your secret,' Nain admonished him. 'Never abuse your power. You must be alone if you are to achieve your heart's desire.'

'What's the use of magic if no one knows about it?' Gwyn exclaimed irritably, 'and how do I get my heart's desire?'

'You know very well,' Nain replied unhelpfully. 'Think about the scarf. Think about using it. And now you'd better leave me, and eat the supper that is growing cold on your mother's table.'

The room had become dark without their noticing it. The fire had almost died and the few remaining embers glowed like tiny jewels in the grate. Gwyn was unwilling to leave his grandmother, he wanted to talk on into the night. But Nain was not of the same mind, it seemed. She lit a lamp and began to pace about her room, moving books and ornaments in a disturbed and thoughtless manner, as though she was trying either to forget or to remember something.

Gwyn pulled himself up from the pile of cushions and moved to the door. 'Good night then, Nain!' he said.

The tall figure, all red and gold in the lamplight, did not even turn towards him. But when he reluctantly slipped out into the night, words came singing after him: '*Cysgwch yn dawel*, Gwydion Gwyn!
60

Sleep quietly!'

When he got home the table was bare.

'Did your grandmother give you a meal?' his mother inquired, guessing where he had been.

'No,' said Gwyn. 'I forgot to ask.'

Mrs Griffiths smiled. 'What a one you are!' She gave him a plate of stew kept warm on the stove.

Gwyn could not finish the meal and went upstairs early, muttering about homework.

He did not sleep quietly. It was a strange, wild night. The restless apple tree beneath his window disturbed him. He dreamt of Nain, tall for ten years, in a red dress, her black curls tied with a scarlet ribbon. She was listening to her great-great-grandmother, an old woman, a witch with long grey hair and wrinkled hands clasped in her dark lap, where a piece of seaweed lay, all soft and shining, as though it was still moving in water, not stranded on the knees of an old, old woman.

Gwyn gasped. He sat up, stiff and terrified. He felt for the bedside light and turned it on.

Arianwen was sitting on the silver pipe. Gwyn lifted the pipe until it was close to his face. He stared at the spider and the pipe, willing them to work for him. But they did not respond. He laid them carefully on the bedside table, and got out of bed.

His black watch told him that it was four o'clock; not yet dawn. He dressed and opened his top drawer. It was time for the seaweed. Yet he took out Bethan's yellow scarf and, without knowing why, wrapped it slowly round his neck, pressing it to his face as he did

61

so, and inhaling, once again, the musty sweet smell of roses. He closed his eyes and, for a moment, almost thought that he was close to an answer. But he had forgotten the question. It was something his grandmother had said: something about using the scarf. Try as he might to order his mind, he felt the answer and the question slipping away from him, until he was left with only the tangible effects: the scarf and the dry dusty stick of seaweed.

Gwyn tucked the seaweed into the pocket of his anorak and went downstairs, letting himself out of the back door into the yard.

There was a pale light in the sky but the birds were still at rest. The only sounds came from sheep moving on the hard mountain earth, and frosty hedgerows shivering in the cold air.

He did not ascend the mountain this time, but wandered northwards, through the lower slopes, seeking the breeze that came from the sea. Here the land was steep and barren. There were few sheep, no trees and no farms. Gigantic rocks thrust their way through the earth and torrents of ice-cold water tumbled over the stones. Gwyn longed for the comfort of a wall to cling to. The wide, dark space of empty land and sky threatened to sweep him away and swallow him. One step missed, he thought, and he would slip into nowhere.

And then he smelt the sea. Moonlight became dawn and colours appeared on the mountain. He was approaching the gentler western slopes. He started to climb upwards, gradually, field by field, keeping close to the stone walls, so that the breeze that had now veered into a wailing north-east wind, should not confuse his steps.

Gwyn had passed the fields and was standing in the centre of a steep stretch of bracken when it happened; when the thing in his pocket began to move and slide through his fingers, causing him to withdraw his hand and regard the soft purple fronds of what had, a few moments before, been a dried-up piece of seaweed. The transformation was unbelievable. Gwyn held the plant out before him and the slippery petal-like shapes flapped in the wind like a hovering bird. And then it was gone; the wind blew it out of his hand and out to sea. And all the birds above and below him awoke and called out; the grey sky was pierced with light and in that moment Gwyn knew what he had to do.

He took off the yellow scarf and flung it out to the sky, calling his sister's name again and again, over the wind, over the brightening land and the upturned faces of startled sheep.

Then, from the west, where it was still dark, where the water was still black under the heavy clouds, there came a light, tiny at first, but growing as it fell towards the sea. It was a cool light, soft and silver and, as it came closer, Gwyn could make out the shape of a billowing sail, and the bows of a great ship. But the ship was not upon the sea, it was in the air above it, rising all the time, until it was opposite to him and approaching the mountain.

A wave of ice-cold air suddenly hit Gwyn's body, throwing him back into the bracken, and as he lay there, shocked and staring upwards, the huge hull of

63

the silver ship passed right over him, and he could see fragments of ice, like sparks, falling away from it. He could see patterns of flowers and strange creatures engraved in the silver, and then the ice was in his eyes and he had to close them, and curl himself into a ball, shaking with the pain of bitter cold that enveloped him.

A dull thud shook the ground: something scraped across the rocks and filled the air with a sigh.

Gwyn lay, hidden in the bracken, for a long time; cold, curled-up tight, with eyes closed, too frightened and amazed to move and when he finally stood up, the cold, cold air was gone. He looked behind him, around and above him, but the mountain was empty. There was snow on the bracken and in one flat field beyond the bracken, but no sign of a ship of any kind. Yet he had seen one, heard one, felt the bitter cold of its passage through the air.

Gwyn began to run. Now that it was light, he had no difficulty in finding his way across the northern slopes. Soon he was back in familiar fields, but when he came to within sight of Tŷ Bryn he paused a moment then kept on running, down the track, past his gate, past his grandmother's cottage, until he reached the Lloyds' farmhouse. He flung open the gate, rushed up the path and, ignoring the bell, beat upon the door with his fists, shouting, 'Alun! Alun! Come quick! I want to tell you something! Now! Now! Now!'

Within the house someone shouted angrily, it must have been Mr Lloyd. Then footsteps could be heard, pattering on the stairs and approaching down the passage.

64

The front door was opened and Mrs Lloyd stood there, in a pink dressing-gown, with rollers in her hair, her face all red and shiny.

'Whatever is it, Gwyn Griffiths?' she said. 'Accident or fire?'

'No fire, Mrs Lloyd. I want Alun. I have to tell him something. It's urgent!'

'No fire, no accident,' snapped Mrs Lloyd. 'Then what are you doing here? We've not had breakfast. Why can't it wait till school?'

'Because it's just happened!' Gwyn stamped his foot impatiently. 'I've got to see Alun.'

Mrs Lloyd was angry. She was about to send Gwyn away, but something about the boy, standing tense and dark against the dawn clouds, made her hesitate. 'Alun! You'd better come down,' she called. 'It's Gwyn Griffiths. I don't know what it's about, but you'd better come.'

'Shut that door,' Mr Lloyd shouted from above. 'I can feel the cold up here.'

'Come inside and wait!' Mrs Lloyd pulled Gwyn into the house and shut the door. 'I don't know – you've got a nerve these days, you boys.'

She shuffled away into the kitchen, leaving Gwyn alone in the shadows by the door. It was cold in the Lloyds' house. The narrow passage was crammed with bicycles and boots, and coats half-hanging on hooks; it was carpeted with odd gloves, with felt-tip pens, comics and broken toys, and there were two pairs of muddy jeans hanging on the bannisters.

Alun appeared at the top of the stairs, in pyjamas that were too small. He was trying to reduce the

66

draughty gap round his stomach with one hand, while rubbing his eyes with the other. 'What is it?' he asked sleepily.

'Come down here,' Gwyn whispered. 'Come closer.'

Alun trudged reluctantly down the stairs and approached Gwyn. 'Go on, then,' he said.

Gwyn took a breath. He tried to choose the right words, so that Alun would believe what he said. 'I've been on the mountain. I couldn't sleep, so I went for a look at the sea . . .'

'In ᵤe dark?' Alun was impressed. 'You're brave. I couldn't do that.'

'There was a moon. It was quite bright really,' Gwyn paused. 'Anyway, while I was there I . . . I . . .'

'Go on!' Alun yawned and clutched his stomach, thinking of warm porridge.

'Well – you've got to believe me.' Gwyn hesitated dramatically, 'I saw a spaceship!' He waited for a response, but none came.

'What?' Alun said at last.

'I saw a ship – fall out of space – it came right over the sea – it was silver and had a sort of sail – and it was cold, ever so cold, I couldn't breathe with the cold of it. I had to lie all curled up, it hurt so much. And when I got up – it had gone!'

Alun remained silent; he stared at his bare toes and scratched his head.

'Do you believe me? Tell me?' Gwyn demanded.

There was no reply.

'You don't believe me, do you?' Gwyn cried.

'Why? Why? Why?'

'Sssssh! They'll hear!' Alun said.

'So what?'

'They think you're a loony already.'

'Do you? D'you think I'm a loony?' Gwyn asked fiercely. 'I did see a ship. Why don't you believe me?'

'I donno. It sounds impossible – a sail an' all. Sounds silly. Spaceships aren't like that.'

Gwyn felt defeated. Somehow he had used the wrong words. He would never make Alun believe, not like this, standing in a cold passage before breakfast. 'Well, don't believe me then,' he said, 'but don't tell either, will you? Don't tell anyone else.'

'OK! OK!' said Alun. 'You'd better go. Your mam'll be worried!'

'I'll go!' Gwyn opened the door and stepped down into the porch, but before Alun could shut him out, he said again, 'You won't tell what I said, will you? It's important!'

Alun was so relieved at having rid himself of Gwyn's disturbing presence, he did not notice the urgency in his friend's voice. 'OK!' he said. 'I've got to shut the door now, I'm freezing!'

He was to remember Gwyn's words – too late!

5.
Eirlys

Alun did tell. He did not mean to hurt or ridicule Gwyn, and he only told one person. But that was enough.

The one person Alun told was Gary Pritchard. Gary Pritchard told his gang: Merfyn Jones, Dewi Davis and Brian Roberts. Dewi Davis was the biggest tease in the school and within two days everyone in Pendewi Primary had heard about Gwyn Griffiths and his 'spaceship'.

Little whispering groups were formed in the playground; there were murmurings in the canteen and children watched while Gwyn ate in silence, staring steadily at his plate of chips so that he should not meet their eyes; girls giggled in the cloakroom and even five-year-olds nudged each other when he passed.

And Gwyn made it easy for them all. He never denied that he had seen a silver ship, nor did he try to explain or defend his story. He withdrew. He went to school, did his work, sat alone in the playground and spoke to no one. He came home, fed the hens and ate his tea. He tried to respond to his mother's probing chatter without giving too much away for he felt he had to protect her. He did not want her to know that his friends thought him mad. Mrs Griffiths sensed that something was wrong and was hurt and offended that her son could not confide in her; he had never shut her out before.

And then, one evening, Alun called. He had tried, in vain, to talk to Gwyn during their walks home from the bus, but since the gossiping began Gwyn had taken pains to avoid his old friend. He had run all the way home, passing the Lloyds on the lane, so that he should not hear them if they laughed.

Mrs Griffiths was pleased to see Alun. Perhaps he knew something. She drew him into the kitchen saying, 'Look who's here! We haven't seen you for a bit, Alun. Take your coat off!'

'No!' Gwyn leapt up and pushed Alun back into the passage, slamming the kitchen door behind him. 'What d'you want?' he asked suspiciously.

'Just a chat,' said Alun nervously.

'What's there to chat about?'

'About the things you said: about the spaceship, an' that,' Alun replied, fingering the buttons on his anorak.

'You don't believe, and you told,' Gwyn said coldly.

'I know, I know and I'm sorry. I just wanted to talk about it.' Alun sounded desperate.

'You want to spread more funny stories, I s'pose?'

'No . . . no,' Alun said. 'I just wanted to . . .'

70

'You can shove off,' said Gwyn: he opened the front door and pushed Alun out on to the porch. He caught a glimpse of Alun's white face under the porch lantern, and shut the door. 'I'm busy,' he called through the door, 'so don't bother me again.'

And he was busy, he and Arianwen. Every night she spun a web in the corner of Gwyn's attic bedroom, between the end of the sloping ceiling and the cupboard, and there would always be something there, in the web. A tiny, faraway landscape, white and shining; strange trees with icy leaves; a lake, or was it a sea? with ice-floes bobbing on the water and a silver ship with sails like cobwebs, gliding over the surface.

And when he ran his fingers over the silver pipe he could hear waves breaking on the shore; he could hear icicles singing when the wind blew through the trees, and children's voices calling over the snow. And he knew, beyond any shadow of a doubt, that he was hearing sounds from another world.

Once Arianwen spun a larger cobweb again, covering an entire wall. The white tower appeared and the same houses. Children came out to play in the square beneath the tower. Pale children with wonderfully serene faces, not shouting as earth-bound children would have done, but calling in soft, musical voices. It began to snow and suddenly they all stood still and turned to look in the same direction. They looked right into the web; they looked at Gwyn and they smiled, and then they waved. It was as though someone had said, 'Look, children! He's watching you! Wave to him!' And their bright eyes were so

71

inviting Gwyn felt a longing to be with them, to be touched and soothed by them.

But who had told the children to turn? Gwyn realized he had never seen an adult in the webs, never heard an adult voice. Who was looking after the faraway children? Perhaps they had just seen the 'thing' that was sending the pictures down to Arianwen's web. A satellite perhaps, or a ship, another star, or another spider, whirling round in space, and they had turned to wave to it.

A few weeks before the end of term three new children appeared at Pendewi Primary. They were children from the city, two boys from poor families who had no room for them, and a girl, an orphan it was said. They had all been put into the care of Mr and Mrs Herbert, a warm-hearted couple with four girls, a large farmhouse and an eagerness to foster children less fortunate than their own.

John, Eirlys and Dafydd were officially entering the school the following term, but had been allowed three weeks of settling in before the Christmas holidays. Miss Pugh, the headmistress, was a little put out. She had expected only two children, eight-year old boys, to put in a class where there was still space for at least five more. There were thirty children in Gwyn's class, where Eirlys would have to go. Mr James, their teacher, a rather fastidious man, was already complaining that he could feel the children breathing on him. He gave Eirlys a tiny table right at the back of the class, where no one seemed to notice her.

72

In the excitement of Christmas preparations some of the children forgot about Gwyn and his 'stories'. But for Gary Pritchard and his gang, baiting Gwyn Griffiths was still more entertaining than anything else they could think of, especially when they saw a flicker of anger beginning to appear in their victim's dark eyes.

And then, one Monday, Dewi Davis went too far. It was a bright, cold day. Snow had fallen in the night, clean white snow that was kicked and muddied by children running into school. But the snow fell again during the first lesson and, as luck would have it, stopped just before the first break, and the children were presented with a beautiful white playground in which to slide and snowball.

Dewi Davis never could resist a snowball, just as he could never resist shoving girls with white socks into puddles, or putting worms down the backs of the squeamish. He took a lot of trouble with Gwyn's snowball; patting and shaping it until it was rock-hard and as big as his own head, then he followed Gwyn round the playground, while the latter, deep in thought, made patterns in the snow with his feet.

Soon Dewi had an audience. Children drew back and watched expectantly while Gwyn trudged, unaware, through the snow. Dewi stopped about three metres behind Gwyn, and called, in his slow lisping voice, ''Ullo, Mr Magic. Seen any spaceships lately?'

Gwyn began to turn, but before he could see Dewi, the huge snowball hit him on the side of the face and a pain seared through his ear into his head.

Girls gasped and some giggled. Boys shouted and laughed, and someone said, 'Go on, get him!'

Gwyn turned a full half-circle and stared at Dewi Davis, stared at his fat silly face, and the grin on his thick pink lips, and he wanted to hurt him. He brought up his clenched right fist and thrust it out towards Dewi, opening his fingers wide as he did so, and a low hiss came from within him, hardly belonging to him, and not his voice at all, but more like a wild animal.

There was nothing in Gwyn's hand, no stone, no snow, but something came out of his hand and hit Dewi in the middle of his face. He saw Dewi's nose grow and darken to purple, and saw anguish and amazement on Dewi's fat face. Only he and Dewi knew that there had been nothing in his hand.

Then, suddenly, the rest of the gang were upon Gwyn. Someone hit him in the face, someone punched his stomach, his hair was tugged, his arms jerked backwards until he screamed, and then his legs were pulled from under him and he crashed on to the ground.

Everyone stopped shouting: they stared at Gwyn, motionless in the mud and snow. And then the bell went and, almost simultaneously, Dewi Davis began to scream for attention. The children drifted away while Mr James ran to Dewi and helped him from the playground, he never noticed Gwyn lying in a corner.

The whole of Gwyn's body ached, but his head hurt most of all. He could not get up and did not want to. There was blood on the snow beside him and his lip felt swollen and sticky. The playground was empty, and he wondered if he would have to lie there all day. Perhaps the snow would fall again and no one would see him until it was time to go home. He managed to pull himself up until he was kneeling on all fours, but it was an effort and he could not get any further because something in his back hurt whenever he moved.

And then he saw that he was not alone. Someone was standing on the other side of the playground. Someone in grey with long, fair hair and a blue hat. It was Eirlys. The girl began to walk towards Gwyn; she walked slowly, as though she was approaching a creature she did not wish to alarm. When she reached Gwyn she bent down and put her arms beneath his and round his body. Then, without a word, she began to lift him to his feet. She was very frail and Gwyn could not understand where her strength came from. Her hair, beneath his hands, was so soft it was like touching water, and her face, now close to his, was almost as pale as the snow. He had never really looked at her before and realized, with a shock, that he knew her. He had seen her somewhere but could not remember where.

They walked across the playground together, still without speaking, his arm resting on her shoulders, her arm round his waist, and although his legs ached he tried not to stumble or lean too heavily on the girl. When they reached the school door, Eirlys withdrew her arm and then took his hand from her shoulder. Her fingers were ice-cold and Gwyn gasped when she touched his hand.

'What is it?' she asked.

'You're so cold,' Gwyn replied.

Eirlys smiled; her eyes were greeny-blue, like arctic water; it was as though they had once been another colour, but that other colour had been washed away.

When they got to the classroom Gwyn told Mr James that he had slipped in the snow. Eirlys said nothing. Mr James nodded. 'Get on with your work now,' he said.

Eirlys and Gwyn went to their desks. Everyone stared. Dewi Davis was still holding his nose, and Gwyn remembered what he had done. All through the next lesson, through the pain in his head, he kept thinking of what he had done to Dewi Davis. He had hit him with magic. Something had come out of his hand and flown into Dewi's face, something that had come to him from Gwydion, the magician, and from Gwydion's son, who had once ruled Gwynedd. And it was the same thing that had turned the seaweed into a ship, the brooch into a spider and the whistle into a silver pipe. These last three, he realized, had merely been waiting for him to release them; they had been there all the time, just waiting for his call. But when he had hit Dewi Davis, he had done it by himself; he had wanted to hurt Dewi, wanted to smash his silly, cruel face, and he had done it, not with a stone nor with his fist but with his will and the power that had come from Gwydion. If he could do that, what could he not do?

While Gwyn dreamt over his desk he was unaware that Eirlys was watching him. But Alun Lloyd noticed and he wondered why the girl gazed at Gwyn with her aquamarine eyes. He was uneasy about the

76

things that were happening.

During the day Gwyn's aches and pains receded and he was able to hobble to the school bus unaided; when he got off the bus, however, he could not run up the lane as he had been doing, and he felt trapped for Alun was lingering behind the rest of his family, watching him.

'You OK?' Alun asked Gwyn.

'Yes, I'm OK'

'D'you want me to walk up with you?'

'No,' Gwyn replied. 'I said I was all right, didn't I?'

'Are you sure?' Alun persisted. He turned to face Gwyn and began to walk up the hill backwards.

'They didn't hurt me that bad,' Gwyn said angrily. 'I just can't walk that fast.'

'I s'pose she's going to help you?' Alun said. He was still walking backwards and looking at someone behind Gwyn.

'Who?'

'Her!' Alun nodded in the direction of the main road and then turned and ran up the lane.

Gwyn glanced over his shoulder to see what Alun had meant. Eirlys was walking up towards him.

'What are you doing?' Gwyn shouted. 'You don't get off here?'

The girl just smiled and kept coming.

'You'll be in trouble! How're you going to get home?'

'I'll walk,' said Eirlys.

'Oh heck!' cried Gwyn.

'Don't worry!' The girl continued her approach

and Gwyn waited, unable to turn his back on her.

'It'll be all right,' the girl said when she was beside him. 'I'll just come home with you. You might need someone, all those bruises.' She tapped his arm and began to precede him up the hill.

When they turned a bend and Nain's cottage suddenly came into view, Eirlys stopped and stared at the building.

'My grandmother lives there,' Gwyn said.

'Does she?' Eirlys spoke the words not as a question, but as a response that was expected of her.

She passed the cottage slowly, trailing her fingers along the top of the stone wall, so that sprays of snow flew out on to her sleeve, but she never took her eyes off the light in Nain's downstairs window.

Gwyn was tempted to take the girl in to see his grandmother, but it was getting dark and they still had to pass the furrows of snow that had drifted into the narrow track further on. He wondered how on earth Eirlys was going to get home. 'What will Mrs . . . What's-'er name say, when you're not on the bus?' he asked.

'Mrs Herbert? She's kind. She'll understand,' Eirlys replied.

They held hands when they reached the snowdrifts, Gwyn leading the girl to higher ground at the edge of the track, and once again he gasped at the icy touch of her fingers, and when Eirlys laughed the sound was familiar to him.

She was reluctant to come into the farmhouse, and when Gwyn insisted, she approached it cautiously with a puzzled frown on her face, and every now and

then she would look away from the house and up to where the mountain should have been, but where, now, only a moving white mist could be seen.

'Come on,' said Gwyn. 'Mam'll give you a cup of tea.'

He opened the front door and called into the kitchen, 'I'm back, Mam. Sorry I'm late; had a bit of trouble with the snow.'

'I thought you would,' came the reply.

His mother was stirring something on the stove when he went into the kitchen. She turned to speak to him but instead cried out, 'Your face! What's happened?'

'I had a bit of a fight, it's not anything, really!' Gwyn said.

His father got up from the chair by the kitchen table, where he had been mending some electrical equipment; he was about to be angry, but then he saw Eirlys standing in the doorway. 'Who's this?' he asked.

'Eirlys!' said Gwyn. 'She helped me. She walked up from the bus with me, to see I was all right.'

'That was kind of you, Eirlys,' said Mrs Griffiths. 'Take your coat off and have a bit of a warm. I'll make a pot of tea.'

She began to help Gwyn with his anorak, exclaiming all the time at the state of his muddy clothes and the bruises on his face.

Eirlys came into the room and took off her hat and coat. She drew a chair up to the table and sat down opposite Mr Griffiths. He just stood there, staring at her, while his big hands groped for the tiny brass

80

screws that had escaped him and now spun out across the table.

The girl caught one of the screws and stretched across to put it safe into his hand. Gwyn heard the sharp intake of breath as his father felt the girl's icy fingers, and he laughed. 'She's cold-blooded, isn't she, Dad?' he said.

Mr Griffiths did not reply. He sat down and began his work again. Mrs Griffiths poured the tea and brought a fruit cake out of the larder. They discussed the snow and the school and the fight. Mrs Griffiths asked how and why the fight had begun and, although Gwyn could not give a satisfactory explanation, Mr Griffiths did not say a word, he did not even seem to be listening to them, but every now and then he would look up and stare at Eirlys.

When it was dark Mrs Griffiths expressed concern for the girl. 'You'd better ring your mam, she'll be worrying,' she said.

'She hasn't got a mam,' Gwyn answered for the girl. 'She's living with the Herberts.'

'Oh, you poor love.' Mrs Griffiths shook her head sympathetically.

'They're lovely,' said Eirlys brightly, 'so kind. They won't mind. They'll fetch me; they said they always would if I wanted, and it's not far.'

'No need for that.' Mr Griffiths suddenly stood up. 'I'll take you in the Landrover.'

Gwyn was amazed. His father never usually offered lifts. 'You're honoured,' he whispered to Eirlys as Mr Griffiths strode out of the back door.

By the time Eirlys had gathered up her hat and coat

and her school bag, the deep throbbing of the Landrover's engine could be heard out in the lane.

'Good-bye,' said Eirlys. She walked up to Mrs Griffiths and kissed her. Mrs Griffiths was startled; she looked as though she had seen a ghost.

She remained in the kitchen while Gwyn and the girl walked down to the gate. The door of the Landrover was open and Mr Griffiths was standing beside it. 'You'll have to get in this side and climb over,' he told Eirlys, 'the snow's deep the other side.'

Gwyn had never known his father to be so considerate to a child.

Eirlys stepped out into the lane but before she could climb into the Landrover, Mr Griffiths' arms were round her, helping her up. For a second the two shadowy figures became one and, for some reason, Gwyn felt that he did not belong to the scene. He looked away to where the frozen hedgerows glittered in the glare of the headlights.

Inside the house the telephone began to ring. Then the Landrover's wheels spun into movement and Gwyn had to back away from the sprays of wet snow. It was too late to shout 'good-bye'.

He turned to go back into the house and saw his mother standing in the porch. 'Mrs Davis, Tŷ Coch, was on the 'phone,' she said gravely. 'She wants to talk to us tomorrow. It's about Dewi's nose!'

6.
A
Drowning

We've left Dewi with his auntie,' said Mrs Davis.

Dewi had many aunties. Gwyn wondered which one had the pleasure of his company, and if Dewi was to be envied or pitied.

The Davises had come to 'thrash out the problem of the nose', as Mr Davis put it.

It was six o'clock. The tea had only just been cleared away and Gwyn's stomach was already grumbling. They were sitting round the kitchen table: Mr and Mrs Davis, Gwyn and his parents – as though they were about to embark on an evening of cards or some other light-hearted entertainment, not something as serious as Dewi's nose.

'The problem, as I see it,' began Mrs Davis, 'is, who's lying?'

'Gary Pritchard, Merfyn Jones *and* Brian Roberts, all say that they think they saw Gwyn throw a stone,' said Mr Davis solemnly. 'Now, this is a very serious business.'

'Very dangerous too,' added Mrs Davis.

'That goes without saying, Gladys,' Mr Davis coughed. 'Now, the situation is,' he paused dramatically, 'what's to be done about it?'

'How . . . er, how bad is the nose?' Mrs Griffiths asked.

'Very bad,' replied Mrs Davis indignantly. 'How bad d'you think your nose would be if it had been hit by a rock?'

'Now wait a minute!' Mr Griffiths entered the conversation with a roar. 'First it's a stone, now it's a rock, and we haven't yet established whether *anything* was thrown. Perhaps Dewi bumped his nose, we haven't heard his explanation.'

'That's the problem.' Mr Davis banged his fist on the table. 'Dewi says he did bump his nose, but the other boys say Gwyn hit him with a stone.'

'Dewi's frightened of him, see!' Mrs Davis pointed an accusing finger at Gwyn. 'He's afraid your boy'll do something worse to him if he tells.'

'Bloody nonsense!' Mr Griffiths stood up, his chair scraping on the tiled floor. 'Let's hear your side of it, Gwyn?'

Gwyn looked up. He was unused to having his father defend him. He felt that he could take on any number of Davises now. 'I didn't throw a stone,' he said.

'There!' Mr and Mrs Davis spoke simultaneously.

Mr Griffiths sat down and the two sets of parents eyed each other wordlessly.

'He's lying of course,' Mr Davis said, at last.

'He ought to be punished,' added his wife. 'The headmistress should be told.'

'It's a pity they don't thrash kids these days,' growled Mr Davis.

This time it was Mr Griffiths who banged the table. Gwyn got up and began to pace about the room while the adults all talked at once. He had a tremendous desire to do something dramatic and the knowledge that he probably could, made the temptation almost unbearable. What should he do though? Box Mr Davis's ears from a distance of three metres? Pull Mrs Davis's hair? The possibilities were endless. And then he remembered Nain's warning. He must not abuse his power. It must be used only when there was something that he truly needed to do.

'It's not as if your son is normal,' he heard Mrs Davis say. 'Everyone's been talking about his being *peculiar,* if you know what I mean. Ask any of the children.'

For the first time his parents seemed unable to reply. Mrs Griffiths looked so miserable that Gwyn could hardly bear it. She had known for days that something was wrong, and now she was going to hear about his 'stories'.

'It seems,' went on Mrs Davis, 'that Gwyn has been saying some very *peculiar* things, if you know what I mean. And why? If you ask me your son's not normal.'

Gwyn had to stop her. Contemplating the generous curves that overflowed the narrow kitchen chair supporting Mrs Davis, his eyes alighted upon a large expanse of flesh, just above the knee, that her too-tight skirt could not cover. He flexed his fingers, then pressed his thumb and forefinger together, tight,

tight, tight!

Mrs Davis screamed. She glared at Mr Griffiths and then asked haughtily, 'Have you got a dog?'

The two men frowned at her, for the distraction, and then frowned at each other, while Mrs Griffiths said, 'Yes, he's in the barn!'

'A cat?' Mrs Davis inquired hopefully.

'A black tom,' Mrs Griffiths nodded towards a dark form sitting on the sill, outside the kitchen window. 'We call him Long John,' she went on, 'because he lost a leg on the road when he was just a kitten; it's wonderful what vets can do these days.'

Mrs Davis glanced at Long John then quickly looked away, her cyclamen-pink lips contorted with distaste. 'I think we'll go,' she said, and stood up.

Her husband looked at her but did not move.

'Get up, Bryn!' Mrs Davis commanded. 'I want to go!'

Mr Davis followed his wife out of the kitchen with a bemused expression on his face. He could not understand why the interview had ended so abruptly, and wondered if the situation had been resolved without his being aware of it.

The Griffithses were as perplexed as he. They silently followed their unwelcome guests to the front door, and there the whole unpleasant business might have ended, had not Mrs Davis been heard to mutter darkly, 'Someone pinched my thigh!'

Mrs Griffiths gasped, her husband roared, 'What?' But Mr Davis, having opened the front door, thrust his wife through it, before she could cause the affair to deteriorate further. He then leapt quickly after her and the wind parted the two families by slamming the door.

Mr and Mrs Griffiths retreated into the kitchen and slumped battle-weary beside the table. And then the humour of the situation overcame them and they began to laugh with relief.

'Thanks for sticking up for me, Dad,' said Gwyn, when his parents had recovered. He felt awkward and not at all sure that he had done the right thing in the end.

'If you say you're innocent, that's all I need to know,' said Mr Griffiths gruffly.

Gwyn looked hard at his father; he could not understand his change of attitude. A week ago he would neither have been believed nor defended. In all probability he would have been sentenced to a weekend in his room and a meal of bread and water. 'I'd better get on with my homework,' he said shyly.

He was about to leave the room when his father suddenly said, 'Is that girl coming again, then?'

'What girl?' Gwyn asked.

'You know what girl. The one that was here yesterday. I can always run her home if,' his father hesitated and then added diffidently, 'if she wants to come.'

'I don't suppose she will,' said Gwyn. 'She's a girl. She only came because I was hurt.'

'Oh, that was it?'

Gwyn thought he could detect something almost like regret in his father's voice. What had come over Mr Griffiths? It was quite disturbing. It had nothing to do with him, Gwyn was sure of that. He knew, instinctively, that he could not, should not, use his power to influence thought. The pinch had been satisfactory though.

He remembered that his father's mood had changed when Eirlys appeared. If that was the case, then she must come again, if only to keep his father happy. And so, although it was against his principles to have

girls at Tŷ Bryn, the following day he asked Eirlys if she could come to the farm on Saturday.

'Of course,' Eirlys replied, and her eyes shone with pleasure.

'Mam and Dad want it,' said Gwyn, by way of explanation, 'and . . . and so do I, of course!'

The weather changed. December brought sun instead of snow. The wind was warm and smelled of damp leaves and over-ripe apples.

Gwyn took Eirlys on his mountain and she saw it in sunshine where before she had only glimpsed it at dusk, through a mist of snow. She saw the colours that he loved, the buzzards hunting low over the fields, and rosy clouds drifting above the plateau. He had not realized that he would enjoy the company of a girl. But then Eirlys was not like other girls.

They leapt, and sometimes slipped, upon wet stones in the tumbling streams; they ran, arms-outstretched, along the drystone walls, scattering the sheep that dozed there, and they chased crows that hopped, like black thieves, behind the leafless trees. And somehow Gwyn's father always seemed to be there, watching them from a distance, or walking nearby with his dog and his blackthorn stick, listening to their voices. And after tea he began to whistle in his workshop, and Gwyn realized he did not recognize the sound; even his mother looked up, astonished, from her ironing.

In the evening, while it was still light enough to see the trees, the children walked in the orchard and Gwyn told Eirlys about Nain and the five gifts; about the power that had come to him from Gwydion and

90

how he had hit Dewi Davis without a stone. He told her about the silver ship that had caused all his trouble at school and, unlike Alun, Eirlys believed him and did not think it strange that a ship had fallen out of the sky. Even so, Gwyn did not speak of the snow spider. He was still wary of confiding too much. 'I'll take you to see my grandmother,' he told the girl. Nain would know whether he could tell Eirlys about the cobwebs.

Later, he asked his parents if Eirlys could come again, so that they could visit Nain.

'Why can't she stay the night?' Mr Griffiths suggested. 'She can sleep in Bethan's room.'

'No!' cried Mrs Griffiths, and then more quietly. 'It's . . . it's just that the room isn't ready!'

Nothing more was said just then, but when Mr Griffiths had returned from his journey to the Herberts he suddenly said, 'Shall we ask the girl for Christmas? She can stay a day or two, and there'll be time to get the room ready.'

'No!' his wife said again. 'No! It's my Bethan's room.'

'But she isn't here, Mam,' Gwyn said gently.

'It's waiting for her, isn't it?' his mother reproached him.

'But Eirlys could sleep there,' Gwyn persisted. 'The room *is* ready – I looked in. The bed is made, and the patchwork quilt on it: the cupboards are shiny and all the dolls are there, it's such a waste!'

'Yes, all the dolls are there!' cried Mrs Griffiths. She sank into a chair and bent her head, covering her face with her hands. 'You don't seem to care, any more, either of you. It's my daughter's room, my Bethan's: her bed, her dolls, her place.'

Her husband and her son stood watching her, sad and helpless. How could they tell her that it did not matter if Bethan was not with them, because now there was Eirlys.

'We won't discuss it now,' said Mr Griffiths. 'But I've already agreed to fetch the girl tomorrow. Be kind while she's here. She's an orphan remember?'

'I won't upset her,' Mrs Griffiths said. 'I'm sorry for her, she's just not my Bethan.'

When Gwyn took Eirlys to visit his grandmother the following afternoon, Nain was waiting by the gate. She had dressed carefully for the occasion, in an emerald green dress and scarlet stockings; round her neck she wore a rope of grass green beads, long enough to touch the silver buckle on her belt, and from each ear a tiny golden cage swung, with a silver bird tinkling inside it.

Eirlys was most impressed. 'How beautiful you look,' she said, and won Nain's heart.

Gwyn noticed that his grandmother could not take her eyes off the girl. She watched her every move, hungrily, like a bright-eyed cat might watch a bird. 'Eirlys!' she murmured, 'that's Welsh for snowdrop. So we have a snowflower among us!'

After they had sipped their flowery tea, and eaten cake that tasted of cinnamon and rosemary, Gwyn told his grandmother about the ship, and Dewi Davis's nose, while Eirlys wandered round the room, touching the china, the beads and the plants;

studying pictures in the dusty books and tying coloured scarves around her head.

Nain was not surprised to hear about the silver ship. She merely nodded and said, 'Ah, yes!' But now that her prophesies for Gwyn were coming true, she found it almost too gratifying to bear. 'You have nearly reached what you wanted, Gwydion Gwyn,' she said. 'But be careful! Don't do anything foolish!'

'Shall I tell Eirlys about the spider?' Gwyn asked his grandmother. 'Should she know about the cobwebs and that other world?'

'Of course,' said Nain. 'Though I believe she knows already.'

They left the cottage before dark. Nain followed them to the gate and as they set off up the track she called again, 'Be careful!'

Gwyn was not listening to his grandmother; he had begun to tell Eirlys about the spider. He realized that he had not seen Arianwen for several days and wondered where she was.

When they got back to the farmhouse, Mrs Griffiths was upstairs, sewing the hem on her new bedroom curtains. Her husband was cleaning the Landrover. He had used it to transport a new batch of pullets from the Lloyds that morning, and they had made more of a mess than he had bargained for.

Gwyn told Eirlys to wait in the kitchen while he fetched the pipe and the spider from his attic room. When he returned she was sitting in the armchair by the stove. The light was fading but a tiny slither of winter sun had crept through the swaying branches of the apple tree, and into the kitchen window. The light glimmered on the girl in the armchair and Gwyn had to stop and take a breath before he said, 'You are the girl in the web, Eirlys!'

'Am I?' she said.

'Yes, it was you! I knew it all the time, but I couldn't see how . . . You're like my sister, too. Where have you come from Eirlys?'

The girl just smiled her inscrutable smile and asked, 'Where is the spider?'

'I don't know,' he replied. 'I looked in the drawer, on top of the cupboard and under the bed. I couldn't find her.'

Eirlys looked concerned. 'Where can she be?' she asked.

Gwyn shrugged. 'I don't know, She's been gone before, but only for a day. I haven't seen her for nearly a week.'

His father called through the front door, 'Time to go, Eirlys. Are you ready?'

Eirlys stood up. 'You must find the spider, Gwyn,' she said. 'She's precious! She will make it possible for you to see whatever you want, and when I . . . '

'When you what?' Gwyn demanded.

'I can't say, just yet,' Eirlys replied. And then she had disappeared into the passage and run out of the house before Gwyn had time to think of another question.

He watched the lights of the Landrover flickering on the lane before he climbed up to his room again. This time he shook the curtains, felt under the carpet and, beginning to panic, emptied the contents of every drawer upon the floor. Arianwen was not there.

94

He went down to the kitchen to see his mother. 'Have you seen that spider?' he inquired.

'I've seen too many spiders,' Mrs Griffiths replied. She was rolling pastry on the kitchen table and did not look up when she spoke.

'But have you seen my own, particular, spider?'

'I saw one, yes. It could have been the one.' Mrs Griffiths inexorably rolled and rolled the pastry and did not look up. 'It was different,' she went on, 'a sort of grey.'

'Silver!' Gwyn corrected her. 'Where was it?'

'Here. On the curtain.'

'Did you catch it?'

'Yes! You know I can't abide cobwebs.' Mrs Griffiths had finished the pastry, but still she did not look up.

'What did you do with it?'

'I put it down the drain,' his mother said flatly. 'Drowned it!'

Gwyn was speechless. He could not believe what he had heard. His mother had to be joking. He stared at her, hoping for a smile and a teasing word, but she kept tearing little pieces away from the pastry and would not look at him.

And then Gwyn found himself screaming, 'Drowned? Drowned? You can't have!'

'Well, I did!' At last his mother faced him. 'You know I don't like spiders. Why did you keep it so long?' She could not explain to Gwyn that she was afraid, not only of the spider, but of the strange girl who could not be her daughter, yet seemed so like her, and who was beginning to take her daughter's place.

'You don't understand,' Gwyn cried. 'You foolish woman. You don't know what you've done.' He ran to the kitchen sink. 'Did you put it down here? Where does the drain go to?'

'The septic tank,' Mrs Griffiths said defiantly. Guilt was making her angry. 'And you can't look there. Nothing can live in that stuff. The spider's dead.'

7.
The
Broken
Horse

'No! No! No!' Gwyn rushed out of the kitchen and up to his room. He regarded the dark places where cobwebs had sparkled with snow from that other world. The room seemed unbearably empty without them. He flung himself on to the bed and tried to tell himself that Arianwen had not gone for ever. Surely he had the power to bring her back?

But he had nothing left for the wind. All Nain's gifts had been used up: the brooch, the whistle, the seaweed and the scarf. Only one thing remained – the broken horse.

Gwyn got up and went over to the chest-of-drawers. He tried to open the top drawer but it appeared to have stuck. He shook it and the silver pipe rolled off the top. He bent to pick it up and, as he touched it, a sound came from it, like whispering or the sea.

He ignored the sound and left the pipe on his bed while he continuted to wrestle with the drawer. It suddenly burst open and almost fell out with the force that Gwyn had exerted on it.

The black horse lay within; it was alone and broken; grotesque without ears and a tail. Its lips were parted as if in pain and Gwyn was overwhelmed by a feeling of pity. He took the horse out of the drawer and examined it closely. '*Dim hon!*' he murmured, reading again the tiny scrap of yellowing paper tied to its neck. 'Not this! Why "Not this"? This is all I have!'

From the bed the pipe whispered, 'Not this! Not this! Not this!'

But Gwyn was not listening.

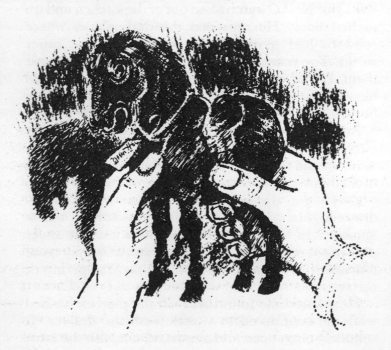

The following morning Gwyn woke up with a sore throat and a cold.

'You'd better stay indoors,' his mother told him over breakfast. 'No use getting worse or spreading your germs.'

Gwyn was about to remark that other people carried germs about, but thought better of it. He would not mind missing a day of school and if, by some miracle, Arianwen should have escaped the septic tank, she would fare better if she had a friend near at hand.

'I'm not staying in bed!' he said sulkily. He had not forgiven his mother.

'I didn't say in bed,' she retorted.

'I don't want to stay indoors either.'

'Please yourself! I'm only thinking of your good!'

Mr Griffiths did not seem to be aware of the acrimony flying round the breakfast table. He took himself off to the milking-shed, still whistling.

Gwyn went up to the attic and put on his anorak. The sun was shining and the air was warm. He went downstairs and out through the back door into the yard. To the left of the yard a row of barns formed a right angle with a long cowshed directly opposite the back door. To the right, a stone wall completed the enclosure. Within the wall a wide gate led on to the mountain track, and somewhere in the field beyond that gate lay the septic tank.

Gwyn wandered towards the gate, climbed over it and jumped down into the field.

A circle of hawthorn trees surrounded the area where the septic tank lay, buried under half a metre of earth. The trees were ancient, their grey branches scarred with deep fissures. It always came as a surprise when white blossom appeared on them in spring. Sheep had ambled round the thorn trees and nibbled the grass smooth. Not even a thistle had been left to give shelter to a small stray creature.

Gwyn stood at the edge of the circle and contemplated the place where Arianwen may have ended her journey from the kitchen sink. He imagined her silver body whirling in a tide of black greasy water, and he was filled with helpless rage.

Thrusting his hands deep into his pockets, he stepped away from the hawthorn circle and began to stroll up the mountain. As the track wound upward, so the field beside it sloped gently down towards the valley until, a mile beyond the farmhouse on a sharp bend, there occurred a sheer drop of ten metres between the track and the field below. Here Gwyn stopped, where a low stone wall gave some protection for the unwary. There was something hard in his right pocket; he withdrew his hand and found that he was holding the broken horse. He must have slipped it into his pocket by accident, the night before.

He stared at the poor, broken thing, and then looked back at the farmhouse. A wreath of smoke streamed from the chimney into the blue sky. A blackbird sang in the orchard, and he could see his mother hanging out the washing. A breeze had set the pillowslips flying and a pink curtain flapped from an upstairs window. It was such a peaceful, ordinary scene. And then his gaze fell upon the ring of thorn trees and he hated the morning for being beautiful while Arianwen was dying in the dark.

Gwyn swung out his right hand, and hesitated. The horse seemed to be staring at him with its wild lidless eyes, inviting him to set it free; its maimed mouth was grinning in anticipation. All at once Gwyn felt afraid of what he was about to do, but his grasp had slackened and, in that moment, a gust of wind tore the horse away and his hand tightened on empty air. The wind carried the tiny object over a flock of sheep that neither saw nor cared about it, but some of the animals raised their heads when the boy above them cried out, 'Go! Go then, and bring her back to me if you can! Arianwen! Arianwen! Arianwen!'

The broken horse vanished from sight and, as it did so, a low moan rumbled through the air. A black cloud passed across the sun and the white sheep became grey.

Gwyn turned away to continue his walk, but after he had taken a few paces it began to rain, only a few drops at first, and then suddenly it was as if a cloud had burst above and water poured down upon his head in torrents. He began to run back down the track and by the time he reached the house the rain had become a hailstorm. His mother was bundling the wet washing back into the kitchen, and he took an armful from her, fearing that it was he who had brought the storm upon them.

And storm it was. Sudden, frightening and ferocious. It beat upon the windows and tore into the barn roofs, causing the cattle to shift and grumble in their stalls. It shook the gates until they opened and

101

terrified sheep poured into the garden and the yard. The hens shrieked and flapped battered soaking wings, as they ran to the hen-house. And once there they did not stop their noise but added their voices to the terrible discord of the other animals.

The sky turned inky black and Mrs Griffiths put the lights on in the house, but the power failed and they were left in the dark, surrounded by the sounds of distressed creatures that they could not help.

Mr Griffiths burst through the back door, his big boots shiny with mud.

'The track's like a river,' he exclaimed. 'I've never seen anything like it.'

'What is it, Ivor?' whispered his wife. 'It was such a beautiful day.'

'Just a storm,' Mr Griffiths tried to sound calm. 'It'll blow itself out eventually.'

Will it? Gwyn thought. Have I done this?

They lit a candle and sat round the table drinking tea. Mrs Griffiths seemed the only one capable of speech. 'Whatever's happened?' she kept murmuring. 'It's like the end of the world. And Gwyn with a cold, too.'

The storm abated a little in the afternoon. The hail turned to rain again and they were able to attend to the animals. But the air still cracked and rumbled and the dog was too terrified to work effectively. Gwyn and his father had a hard time driving the sheep out of the garden and through torrents of running mud, to the field.

They managed to get the ewes into an open barn, where they remained, anxious but subdued.

'They'll lose their lambs if it goes on like this,' said Mr Griffiths.

The yard had become a whirlpool and they had to use a torch to find their way safely to the cowsheds. The cows were in a state of panic. They trembled and twisted, bellowing mournfully. In the torchlight, the whites of their eyes bulged in their black faces and though they were full of milk they refused to be touched.

Mr Griffiths loved his black cows. He loved to be close to them and he still milked by hand, ignoring the cold electric apparatus other farmers preferred. He stood in the cowshed suffering with his animals, dismayed by their condition.

'What is it?' he muttered. 'It can't be the storm. I've never seen them like this.'

'Leave them till later, Dad,' Gwyn suggested. 'They'll calm down when the wind dies.'

'It's like the devil's in there,' said his father, closing the big door on his cattle.

They waded back to the kitchen door, leaving their sodden macs and boots in the narrow porch outside. A cloud of water followed them into the room but, for once, Mrs Griffiths did not seem concerned. She was looking out of the window on the opposite side of the room. 'I'm thinking about Nain,' she said. 'The lane is like a river, her front door rattles even in a breeze and you never fixed her roof in spring, like you said you would, Ivor.'

'I'll go and see her in a bit.' Her husband sighed and sank into a chair.

'I'll go,' Gwyn offered. He wondered how Alun

and the other Lloyds had fared in the storm.

The Lloyds were already at home. Fearing that her little ones would be soaked if they had to walk up the lane, Mrs Lloyd had fetched her family by car; and just as well, for Iolo was mad with fear; he hated thunder.

Alun was in the room he shared with his brothers. He was standing by the window, watching the rain while the twins argued on the floor behind him. Alun enjoyed a storm; he relished the noise and the violence. He gazed at the contortions of the trees, hoping that one might fall. And then he saw something.

Someone was out in the storm. Someone small and alone: a pale shape, moving slowly against the wind and the water.

The figure stopped opposite the Lloyds' gate, on the other side of the lane. Alun saw a face, white in the light from the window, looking up at him, and he knew who it was. Her hood had fallen back and her soaking hair hung in ash-coloured strands over her hunched shoulders. She was holding one arm across her chest and looked frightened and exhausted.

Alun quickly drew the curtains and turned away from the window.

'What is it?' asked Gareth. 'What did you see out there? You look funny.'

'I didn't see nothing,' Alun replied. 'Only the storm.'

'Looks like you saw a ghost, to me,' said Siôn.

104

Gwyn was on the front porch, drawing on his boots. His mother helped him with his mac, buttoning it tightly at the neck.

'Don't be long, now,' she said. 'Just pop in and see if your grandmother needs anything. Come straight back or your cold'll get worse.'

'It's gone,' said Gwyn. 'The water's washed it away,' and he tried to laugh, but the sound stuck in his throat.

He ran down the side of the track where the ground was higher, leaping from island to island, his torch beamed on the lane ahead to ensure that the rivulets of mud had not encroached upon the remaining patches of dry land.

When he reached his grandmother's cottage the rain suddenly stopped and, beneath the clouds, an eerie yellow light crept across the horizon. The dripping trees stood black against the sky and the only sounds came from innumerable streams gushing down the mountainside.

There was no light in Nain's cottage. Gwyn knocked but there was no reply. He opened the door and looked in. His grandmother's room was cold and dark. There was something dreadfully wrong about the place, an oppressive stillness that frightened him. He turned on the light and saw what it was.

Beneath a grey veil of ashes, Nain's treasures lay in ruins. Pictures hung at crazy angles round the room, and once-bright scarves dropped in colourless shreds. The canary lay motionless at the bottom of its cage, and all about the floor were fragments of glass, books ripped and spoiled, shattered beads and dying plants.

Some terrible element had crushed and abused everything in the room that was a part of his grandmother. Every object that she had chosen, nurtured and loved, had been destroyed.

Beside the dead fire from where the flying ashes had scattered, Nain sat huddled in a chair. She seemed older, smaller than before. There were ashes in her black hair and her face was grey.

Gwyn stepped slowly over the broken possessions until he stood beside his grandmother. 'What has happened, Nain?' he asked. 'What has been here?'

Nain looked up at him and her black eyes narrowed. 'You know very well, Gwydion Gwyn,' she said. 'You know and I know what you have done. You mad, bad magician!'

'What have I done, Nain?' Even as he asked the question, Gwyn knew what the answer would be.

'You let it go! My great-great-grandmother trusted me, and I trusted you. You have failed us, Gwydion Gwyn!'

'You mean the broken horse, don't you?' Gwyn cried defiantly. 'Well, say so then! Speak its name! It was all I had. Arianwen has gone, drowned perhaps, and I had to get her back. Eirlys said I must!'

'But why the horse? Why the horse?' Nain rose out of her chair and her voice rose with her. 'Didn't I tell you to keep it safe? Never to let it go? The spider would have returned to you. A creature like that could never die. She belongs to you and you can get her when you want to, if you really try.'

'I didn't know,' said Gwyn. 'And I didn't mean to let the horse go. The wind took it. What is it anyway,

107

that I have released? And how can I stop it?'

'Only you can find that out, Gwydion Gwyn,' his grandmother replied. 'And I am afraid for you. It is a strong and dreadful thing that you must capture!'

'But didn't you see it? It was here. Why did it do this to your room?'

'Ah!' Nain sank back into her chair. 'I tried to stop it, see. When I heard that noise in the air, and all the birds stopped singing; when the hail began to batter the land and the trees trembled, then I knew what you had done. So I went to my great-great-grandmother's books and I tried to find out how to stop it.' Her voice sank to a whisper. 'I burnt leaves in a bowl, and some bones and berries, and I began to sing. But *it* knew, didn't it? *It* knew what I was doing and it came in through the door and knocked me down. It smashed my bowl and blew out the fire. So angry it was. It roared round the room and broke everything in its way, and then it went!'

'And didn't you see *anything*?'

'Nothing! It was in the wind, wasn't it?'

Gwyn was silent. He was terrified of the thing that he had to face, but determined to make reparation. 'I'll help you clean up, Nain,' he said.

'Leave it to me!' she snapped. 'They'll be needing you at home.'

But Gwyn refused to go until he had helped his grandmother to sweep the debris from the floor. They gathered the dying plants and put them in water, dusted the furniture and straightened the pictures. Gwyn picked up the torn pages and replaced them in the books, before his grandmother tenderly arranged
108

them into piles again. He sifted out the broken china and she put it in order, ready for glueing. After a while the room began to come to life again. But the canary still lay quiet at the bottom of its cage, its neck bent and its eyes closed.

'*It* could do this?' Gwyn asked, staring at the broken bird.

'*It* could do worse,' Nain replied. 'Go on now! And take this.' From beneath the cushion on which she had been sitting, she withdrew the black book. 'I kept one thing safe, you see,' she said. 'I knew you would need it.'

It was dark when he left the cottage. The water was not so deep and the thunder had rolled away, but there was a strange turbulence in the air that disturbed him.

He was relieved to see that the lights had come on again in the farmhouse. It looked safe and welcoming. His father met him at the door, 'Did you see the girl?' he asked.

Before Gwyn could reply his mother said, 'Why were you so long? What happened?'

'I had to help Nain,' he explained, and would have said more if his father had not interrupted again.

'Did you see the girl?' he demanded anxiously.

'The girl? Eirlys? No, I didn't see her,' Gwyn said.

'Where is she then?' His father sprang past him and strode across the lawn to where the Landrover waited in its shed.

'The Herberts rang,' he shouted. 'They said she left two hours ago. Slipped out of the house into the storm. Came to see if you were well, they thought, because you weren't at school!'

He disappeared into the shed and the Landrover burst into life. It crashed down on to the track and rocked and roared its way through the mud.

Two hours? Gwyn thought. And in the storm. Can she have fallen somewhere and I didn't see?

In the kitchen his mother had laid four soup bowls on the table. 'Your dad'll find her,' she said, when she saw Gwyn's worried frown.

Gwyn was not so sure. There was that 'thing' in the air. That awful 'something' that had destroyed Nain's room.

They heard the Landrover returning only minutes later and Gwyn ran to open the front door. His father was already beside the vehicle. The door was swinging wide and he was gathering something into his arms; something grey that was streaked with mud.

Mr Griffiths walked through the gate and up the garden path, and as he came within the arc of light thrown out by the porch lantern, they saw the grey bundle. The girl's pale hair was black with mud, her white face covered with smudges of brown, and she had lost her shoes.

Gwyn held his breath. He realized that he had known the girl for a long, long time. What a dull magician he was, indeed, not to have understood, just because her hair was pale and her face white.

'I found her in the lane,' said Mr Griffiths, 'just beside the Lloyds' wall. I can't think how they didn't see her. She's unconscious, the cold probably, but I can't see any broken bones.'

110

'I'll ring Doctor Vaughan.' Mrs Griffiths ran to the telephone in the kitchen.

'She's staying here, Glenys,' her husband called after her. 'In Bethan's room. I'm not having them take her from us.'

He carried the girl upstairs, and Gwyn followed, mopping at the drips with a paper handkerchief. When Mrs Griffiths had finished with the telephone she ran up and covered the pillow with a towel, then they gently removed the sodden grey coat and laid Eirlys on the bed.

They stood around the bed and, without saying a word, without even looking at each other, they knew that they had all seen the girl lying on the bright quilt. They had seen her there before, long ago. They knew that Bethan had come back.

'You go and have your tea. I'll stay with her.' Mr Griffiths drew a chair up to the bed.

Gwyn did not move.

'Don't worry, lad,' his father said. 'It's all over now.'

Gwyn knew that it was not. He could not eat. He took the torch down to the gate to watch for the doctor's car, and saw something black lying there, beside the hedge, all huddled in the mud.

Gwyn bent down and picked up poor Long John's limp body. The black cat's eyes were closed, his nose was full of earth. His three good legs had let him down at last, and he had drowned, unable to escape the malice of the storm.

'Who d'you think you are, you THING?' Gwyn screamed into the night. 'I'll get you! Just you wait!'

8.
The
Trap

The doctor came late. He had many visits to make that night. Other mysterious accidents had occurred: falls, burns and near-drownings.

When he had finished listening through his stethoscope he held the girl's wrist for a long time, feeling her pulse. Something puzzled him. She reminded him of someone he had seen in the same house, in that very room, only the other had been dark with golden skin. 'It seems you have recovered,' said Doctor Vaughan. 'But you had better stay where you are for a day or two.'

'Watch her!' the doctor told Mrs Griffiths before he went. 'She's well, but her pulse is so weak I can hardly feel it; it's almost as though – no one was there.'

Gwyn was allowed into the girl's room the following morning. It was still dark and the bedside light was on. She was sitting up in one of Bethan's old nightdresses. Her hair had been washed and looked paler than ever.

It's strange she hasn't grown, thought Gwyn. Now we are the same size.

She was gazing round at all the things that made the room peculiarly Bethan's place: a group of rag dolls on the dressing-table in faded cotton dresses, a picture of bluebells on the wall, a yellow dress in a plastic cover, still hanging on the back of the door, and the blue and pink forget-me-not curtains that Bethan had chosen.

They did not refer to the past, just then. They talked about the *thing* that had come hurtling out of the storm to throw her down into the mud, the terror of the animals, Nain's devastated room and poor Long John.

'And it's my fault,' said Gwyn. 'I know it is. I gave something to the wind that I should not have given. An old, old broken horse. I was told to keep it safe, never to let it go, but I did. I wanted Arianwen back and I thought it was the only way.'

'It seems to me,' she said, 'that if you are to stop the *thing,* you have to get its name, discover what it is.'

'How can I do that,' Gwyn asked. 'It could be one of a million names, like Rumpelstiltskin, and we can't wait that long. Who knows what damage *it* may do while we're searching for a name.'

She rested her chin upon her hand, like Bethan used to do, and said slowly, 'If you are your namesake; if you are Gwydion, the magician from a legend, perhaps the broken horse is from a legend too. Perhaps a demon from a true story was trapped inside the broken horse by magic, to keep its evil

114

locked up, safe, away from the world.'

Gwyn frowned. It seemed to make sense. It had felt so very old, that broken horse.

All at once the girl leaned forward and said quietly. 'There was another gift wasn't there? Nain gave you five; you have only told me about four of them!'

Gwyn looked hard at the girl in Bethan's bed, and then he said, 'A yellow scarf: your scarf, to bring you back!'

They grinned at each other and Gwyn felt as though all the heavy air that he'd been holding tight inside himself, was flowing out of him and he could breathe again. He had so many questions to ask and did not know which to choose. 'Where have you been, Bethan?' he said at last.

'I'm not Bethan,' she replied. 'I might have been Bethan once, but now I'm Eirlys. I'll never be Bethan again. I've been out there!' She inclined her head, indicating a slither of darkness dividing the forget-me-not curtains.

'On the mountain?'

'No.' She seemed reluctant to continue and then said, 'Out there! Further than the mountain! Further than the sky!'

'How?'

'It will be hard for you to believe.'

'Go on; I know what it's like when people don't believe you. Tell me about the night you went to find the black ewe.'

It was several minutes before Eirlys spoke again. Gwyn waited patiently while she searched for words to tell him what few people would believe.

115

'I wasn't frightened,' she said slowly. 'It was exciting out there with the rain shining in the torchlight. I had a feeling that something was going to happen. Something that I'd always wanted, but never understood. I couldn't find the black ewe. I called and called. You gave her a name, remember? Berry! Because her wool was purply-black, like dark fruit. I had to go higher and higher, and it began to get cold. I'd forgotten my gloves and my fingers felt so stiff I could hardly hold the torch. I wanted to rest and warm my hands in my pockets but I couldn't

116

because of the torch. And then I saw Berry; she was standing by that big rock, just past the last field, where it's quite flat, except for the rock. I called to her and I put out my hands – and I dropped the torch. It was so black. I tried to move in the dark, but I fell. I rolled and rolled, I don't know how far, then I managed to grab a tuft of grass and stop myself.'

The girl stopped speaking and stroked the patchwork quilt, spreading her fingers out, as though she wanted to feel her way back to a place where she had once belonged.

'I thought I was going to die,' she went on, dreamily, 'either from cold, or falling, or the wet. And then I saw a light, far away. There weren't any stars. The light came close and all around it the storm shone like a rainbow. I saw a sail and dancing creatures on a silver ship, just like you did. And I wanted to touch it, I wanted, so much, to be with it . . .'

'And then?' Gwyn begged.

'They took me in!'

'Who took you in?'

'The children. Only they're not really children, they're quite old, and very wise. But they have never grown – like me. They took me to that other world. The place you saw in the web!'

'And Berry?'

'Berry was there too. She knew her name but her fleece was silvery-grey instead of black. And my hair was pale and so was my skin. And I never grew, and nor did she.'

'Is it a good place?'

'Yes, it is.'

'Why did you come back?'

'You called me, didn't you? At first your calls were very faint, and then, when Nain gave you the gifts, your voice became so loud we couldn't ignore it. We sent the spider because you wanted to see me. She was all we had. That's how I could see you, back here – in cobwebs!'

'Cobwebs?' said Gwyn. 'You mean there are more spiders? And you use them like . . . like television?'

Eirlys looked pityingly at him. 'Not television,' she said. 'Our cobwebs are far more wonderful than that.'

'Tell me more about the place out there. Could I go there?'

This time Eirlys ignored his question. 'Find Arianwen!' she said.

'But how? Mam drowned her. She's out there, under the ground. I've nothing left, no gifts to get her back. And I don't know the words.'

Eirlys stared at him. 'You're a magician,' she said. 'You're Gwydion Gwyn. You can get her back. Try!'

Gwyn felt ashamed. Under the compelling gaze of those arctic eyes, he left the chair beside the bed and slipped silently out of the room.

He went downstairs and pulled on his boots. The rain had stopped and there was nothing to remind him that he would need a coat. He opened the front door, and closed it noiselessly, behind him. Within seconds he was standing outside the circle of hawthorn trees. There was something heavy in the air, forcing the grey, twisted branches to bend towards the earth, thus discouraging any passage beneath them.

Gwyn hesitated. Was it possible that even the trees were possessed? He stepped quickly into the circle and gasped as a thorn tore into his shoulder.

The sodden ground was beginning to freeze and a white mist hung low over the grass. There was someone or something else within the circle. He could feel it, drawing him back towards the thorn trees. In order to resist it he had to fling himself to the ground and crawl towards the centre.

Once there, Gwyn did not know what to do. He tried to remember how he had felt when he had hit Dewi Davis, but this was different. Something was distracting him, tugging his mind away from what he wanted to do. He lay his head on the freezing earth and listened, but all he could hear was the air above him, crackling like an angry firework. And then he too began to get angry. A deep hatred of the thing that had killed Long John boiled up inside him. He pushed and pushed against it with his mind, until he felt it falling away, and he had a clear space in his head. He closed his eyes and thought of the bricks beneath the earth, the water from the kitchen sink within the bricks, the spider in the water. He brought up his hands, to rest beside his head, thrust downwards, and felt himself plunging through the earth, down, down, down!

Mrs Griffiths had come into the bedroom with a glass of milk. She gave the drink to Eirlys and then walked over to the window. 'It's snowing again,' she said.

'What a start to the winter.'

'I love the snow,' said Eirlys.

'I know!' Mrs Griffiths smiled, and then something through the window, caught her eye. 'Someone's out there,' she said, 'lying on the ground, and in the snow. Is it Gwyn?'

She opened the window to call to her son but suddenly a shaft of lightning pierced the snow and, with a deafening crack, hit the ground just where Gwyn lay. Mrs Griffiths screamed and fell to the floor. Eirlys, who had run to her, was the only one to see what happened within the circle of thorn trees.

She saw the ground sparkle and shake and Gwyn, arms outstretched, tossing like a bird in the wind. She saw his hands glowing in the snow, and the earth beneath them crack and a shower of glittering icicles fly up and festoon the trees like tinsel. And in one of the trees something shone brighter than a star, and she knew that Arianwen was safe.

Only then did Eirlys run to fetch a cold flannel. She laid it on Mrs Griffiths' head and gently stroked her hair.

Mrs Griffiths opened her eyes. 'It's you,' she said, and she took the girl's hand. 'What happened? I felt queer, and so afraid.'

'It's the snow,' Eirlys replied. 'It's the whiteness. It makes you feel queer sometimes.'

Mrs Griffiths sat up, still keeping the girl's hand clasped in hers. 'It's so good to have you here,' she said.

They stayed quite still for a moment: the girl kneeling beside the woman, calm and silent, until

120

Mrs Griffiths suddenly got to her feet exclaiming, 'What a nurse I am. It's you who's supposed to be the patient. Back to bed now or the doctor will be telling me off!'

She had just tucked the girl's blankets in again, when Gwyn appeared in the doorway. He was wet with snow and smiling triumphantly.

'Gwyn! Was that you out there?' his mother asked. 'Lying in the snow? Are you mad?'

'No, not mad – a magician!' he replied.

Mrs Griffiths made a clicking noise with her tongue. 'I don't know,' she said. 'Sometimes I wonder if Mrs Davis wasn't right about you.'

'Can I talk to Eirlys for a bit?'

'You ought to be in school,' his mother said, 'but seeing as you aren't, yes, you can have a chat. Change your clothes first, mind, and dry your hair!'

Gwyn retreated. When he returned, dry, to the bedroom, he was carrying his grandmother's black book. 'I've got Arianwen,' he said, and he held out his hand, allowing the silver spider to crawl on to the patchwork quilt. 'I had to fight for her; something was trying to stop me.'

'I saw,' said Eirlys. 'You *are* a magician, Gwyn!'

Gwyn was gratified, yet a little embarrassed. 'I've been looking at Nain's book,' he told the girl, 'and I can read it. I never thought I could.'

'Read it to me then, and we'll try and find the demon in the broken horse!'

Gwyn sat on the bed and began to read the old Welsh legends, translating as he went. It was not an easy task, but the more he read, the more fluent he

121

became and Eirlys heard again the stories that she half-remembered, from the time when Nain had sat where Gwyn was sitting now, and would talk on and on, until she slept.

She heard about kings and princes, magicians and giants, and even the knights of King Arthur, but nowhere could Gwyn find a broken horse.

'Read about Princess Branwen,' Eirlys said. 'There are horses in that legend, I remember. It used to make my cry, but I've forgotten it.'

Gwyn began the story of Branwen. Before he had read two pages he suddenly stopped and said quietly, 'I have found it. But it is too terrible to read aloud. I can't read it!'

'Tell me,' said Eirlys.

'I can't!' Gwyn stared at the page; there were tears in his eyes.

'Tell me!' she insisted.

'You'll hate it,' said Gwyn, and then he read, ' "Efnisien, Branwen's brother, came upon the King of Ireland's horses. 'Whose horses are these?' he asked. 'They belong to the King of Ireland,' said the soldiers, 'he has come to marry your sister, Branwen.' And Efnisien screamed, 'No one asked me. No one asked my consent. She shall not marry the King of Ireland!' And he drew his sword and, filled with rage and hatred, he cut off the horses' ears and their tails, their eyelids and their lips, until they screamed with pain, and no one could touch them!'' '

Silence filled the room and Gwyn said, 'You're sorry now, I told you!'

'No!' Eirlys had drawn the quilt around her neck.

'We had to know. Perhaps that mad prince never died, but became locked in the broken horse because of what he'd done!'

'Nain tried to burn the horse, but she couldn't,' said Gwyn.

'It couldn't be destroyed so it was given to the magicians to keep safe,' Eirlys suggested. 'They were the most powerful men in the land in those days!' She paused and then said, 'Well, you know who you have to catch!'

'I know his name, but I can't see him. How do I know where he is?'

'He's on the mountain, for sure. You'll be able to feel him. And you have Arianwen to help you!'

Gwyn went to the window and drew the curtains wide. It was light now and snowflakes were flying past the window; some would linger in their journey and dance gently up and down against the pane, before drifting on to the apple tree below.

'Perhaps you'd better wait,' said Eirlys, when she saw the snow. 'There'll be a blizzard on the mountain.'

'No! I daren't wait. Something will happen if I don't stop him now. I won't go far. I know what to do. Tell Mam I've gone to see Nain.'

Mrs Griffiths was in the kitchen when Gwyn slipped downstairs, put on his mac and boots and, for the second time that morning, crept out of the house.

He realized, as soon as he was through the door, that he would not get far. Eirlys was right. There was a blizzard on the mountain. The wind and snow lashed his face and he had to screw up his eyes and

123

look down at his boots in order to make any headway. But he knew the way, and he knew what he had to do.

When he arrived at the stone wall from where he had flung the broken horse, he took Arianwen from his pocket and held her out into the snow. She clung to his hand for a moment, bracing herself against the wind.

'Go!' Gwyn whispered. And then words came to him that he had never known and did not understand, and he began to chant.

The spider rolled off Gwyn's hand and drifted up into the snow. He watched her, shining silver, amongst the white flakes, and then he had to shut his eyes against the blizzard. When he opened them the spider had gone, and already the wind had slackened. There was a sudden stillness as the mountain held its breath. Clouds of snow began to gather on the summit; they intensified and rolled downwards in a vast, ever-thickening ice-cold wave. In a few seconds Gwyn could hardly see his hands. He felt for the stone wall and found instead, something smooth and tall – a pillar of ice!

And then Gwyn ran. Or rather threw himself, snow-blind and stumbling, down the track and away from his spell. Arianwen had begun to spin!

At that moment, someone was knocking on the farmhouse door. Mrs Griffiths, when she opened it, found Alun Lloyd on the doorstep.

'It is Alun, isn't it?' she asked, for the boy was muffled up to his eyes in a thick red scarf.

'Yes,' Alun mumbled through the scarf.

'You've not gone to school, then?'

'No school,' the reply was just audible. 'No bus – blizzard – where's Gwyn?'

'Stamp the snow off those boots and come in!' said Mrs Griffiths. She took the boy's anorak and shook it outside before closing the door. 'Gwyn's upstairs with the girl,' she went on. 'Poor little thing had an accident yesterday. She's in bed!'

'I heard,' muttered Alun. 'Can I go up?'

''Course love. First door on the left. Don't stay too long, mind. She's still a bit . . .'

Alun had sprung up the stairs before Mrs Griffiths could finish her sentence. He opened the door and saw only the girl. She was sitting up in bed, reading a book.

'Where's Gwyn?' Alun asked.

'With his grandmother,' the girl replied.

'No he's not. I've been there!'

The two children stared at each other across the patterned quilt.

Alun decided to put his question another way. 'Is he in the house? Won't he see me?'

The girl regarded him gravely and he had to look away from her strange, greeny-blue gaze. He did not like her eyes; they made him feel cold.

'OK. You're not going to tell, are you? I'm sorry about – about your falling down an' that, an' I came to say so.' He glanced briefly at her pale face, then quickly averted his eyes again. 'But I want to tell Gwyn about it. I want to talk to him, see? An' I'm going to find him. I don't care if it takes – for ever!'

Alun turned swiftly and ran out of the room.

A few seconds later Mrs Griffiths heard the front door slam and called out, 'Was that Alun? Why didn't he stop?' Receiving no reply, she returned to her washing, still unaware that Gwyn was not in the house.

Outside, Alun saw footsteps in the snow, and began to follow them.

Gwyn returned only minutes later and, having quietly divested himself of snow-soaked garments, crept barefoot up to the bedroom.

'It's done!' he told Eirlys. 'The spell's begun!'

'Your friend was here!' she said.

'Alun? What did he want?'

'To see you! He was angry!'

'Where has he gone?' Gwyn began to feel a terrible apprehension overwhelming him.

'I think he went on to the mountain,' Eirlys replied with equal consternation.

'I didn't see him. He must have missed the track!'

'He'll get lost!'

'Trapped!' cried Gwyn. 'Trapped and frozen!' He tore down the stairs and out into the snow, forgetting, in his panic, to put on his boots, or his mac, or to shut the front door. He called his friend's name, again and again as he ran, until he was hoarse. The snow had become a fog, still and heavy, like a blanket, smothering any sound.

He found his way, with difficulty, to the place where he had touched the pillar of ice. There was another beside it now, and another and another; they rose higher than he could reach and too close to pass

126

through. A wall of ice! Gwyn beat upon the wall, he kicked it, tore at it with his fingers, all the while calling Alun's name in his feeble croaking voice, and then he slid to the ground, defeated by his own spell.

9.
Return

Gwyn's mother was waiting for him when he stumbled home. 'You left the door open,' she accused him. 'Whatever have you been doing? Where's Alun?'

Gwyn could not tell her. The trap had been set and now there was nothing anyone could do until Arianwen had finished her work. Besides Alun might have gone home; they had no proof that he was on the mountain. 'I think he's gone home,' Gwyn told his mother.

But later that day, when Mr Lloyd arrived, searching for his eldest son, Gwyn admitted, 'Yes! Alun was here,' and, 'Yes! He might have gone on to the mountain. But I didn't know. I didn't know for sure!'

Then Mrs Lloyd, who had followed her husband with little Iolo, rounded on Gwyn and vented all her anger and her fear upon him. 'He was your friend,' she cried. 'He came to look for you! Why didn't you go after him? Why didn't you say? Don't you remember how it was when your sister went? It's
128

been four hours now! Don't you care? Don't you care about anyone, Gwyn Griffiths? You're not normal, you aren't! Not a normal boy at all!'

Little Iolo began to scream and Gwyn's fingers ached with the desire to hurt. But he could not use his power because he knew the woman was terribly afraid. How could she know that he was suffering as much as she? He left the kitchen and went up to his room.

He could see nothing out of his window, the fog was so dense. He knew he had to protect Alun, but how? And then he remembered something Nain had said about those long-ago magicians. 'They could turn men into eagles!' Why could he not turn Alun into a bird – a small bird – white so that it should not be seen against the snow.

He scanned the room for something that had belonged to Alun and saw, on his bookshelf, an old paperback on boats that his friend had lent him. It hardly seemed appropriate but it would have to do. He took the book to the window and held it very tight; he closed his eyes and tried to see Alun, tried to remember every feature of his friend: his blue eyes and his freckles, and his short red fingers with the nails all bitten. And then he thought of a bird, a small white bird, and put the picture of the bird that was in his mind over the blue eyes, the freckled nose and the tufty fair hair of his friend, until the bird and the boy seemed to become one.

Gwyn did not know how long he stood by the window. He was not aware of any sound until the search party began to arrive. The grapevine in

Pendewi worked fast; sometimes people even sensed the news before they heard it. Ten men set off to look for Alun Lloyd, and later Mrs Griffiths and another wife, followed them.

The search did not last long. Gwyn heard them return: the defeated stamping of boots in the snow; grave, deep voices and the kettle whistling on and on and on!

Hunger and curiosity drove him downstairs. The kitchen was so crowded he could not find a chair, nor reach the bread bin. He managed to sneak a plate of biscuits from the table, and retreated with it to the door, where he leaned and listened, waiting for someone to mention the mountain and whatever it was that Arianwen had built there.

They were all talking at once, yet avoiding what they wanted to say. They were adults and did not know how to discuss something that was impossible, something they did not understand.

There were pools of water on the kitchen floor, mingling with crushed biscuits and cigarette ash. Iolo was under the table, snivelling, but everyone had become accustomed to the sound and was ignoring him. And Gwyn remembered that other search, four years ago, when he had sat under the table and cried, because his sister was lost.

And then the words that he wanted to hear began to creep out towards him.

'Did you feel it?' 'Bloody peculiar!' 'Like a net!' 'A cloud?' 'No, not that!' 'Ice!' 'A frozen cloud?' 'More like a wall!' 'Never heard of anything like it!' 'Call the police!' 'What can they do?' 'Can't see a bloody thing out there!' 'Searchlights?'

Gwyn sidled out of the door and carried his plate of biscuits upstairs. He heard the police arrive and the girl, being the last person to see Alun, was called down to speak to them.

Everybody stopped talking when she came in. They drew back and gazed at the frail, white-faced child, so insubstantial and fairy-like in her white nightdress and borrowed grey shawl. They were all thinking about that other time, in the same farm-house, when they had come to search for a girl like this one, so very like this one; only the other had been dark and rosy-cheeked, and they had never found her. They bent their heads, straining to hear the words the girl spoke so softly. And when she had done they all began to sigh and murmur about mists and mountains, and P.C. Perkins had to rub out half his notes. He was new to the area, just up from the city, and he felt a stranger among these superstitious and excitable farmers; their melodious voices conveyed nothing but confusion to him.

He went out, all the same, with his partner, P.C. Price, and they walked up the track for a bit, to find out what they could. They returned before long, and drove away without a word.

It'll be in the papers, thought Gwyn. They'll call it a phenomenon, and then they'll forget about it!

The searchers departed in ones and twos. 'We'll be back in the morning!' they called. 'We'll find him!'

The Lloyds were the last to leave. Iolo had fallen asleep in his father's arms, but now Mrs Lloyd was crying.

It was such a long, long night. Gwyn could not sleep. He sat on the edge of his bed and stared at the window. Eirlys came up and kept him company. They did not speak but her presence was comforting. Just as she was about to go a sound came from the mountain; a long, wailing sigh!

'Did you hear that?' Gwyn whispered.

'Was it the wind?' she asked.

'No, not the wind!'

The sound came again. Louder this time. Such an anguished, melancholy howl. It crept down Gwyn's spine and made him shiver.

'It's like a wild animal,' said Eirlys.

'Trapped!' he added.

The howling gradually died away and Eirlys returned to her bed. But, later that night, it came again, louder and more terrible than ever, though it seemed to be only Gwyn who heard it. It got in to his head and he had to rock back and forth to endure the sound. He knew who it was, of course, and agonized over what it might do to Alun, if it found him.

And then he became aware that the sound was in the room; it was in the silver pipe, lying on the bedside table.

Gwyn jumped out of bed, seized the pipe and ran with it across the room, thrusting it into his drawer and slamming the drawer tight after it. But to his horror, the voice within the drawer seemed merely to intensify; it got louder and louder until the whole chest vibrated with the sound.

Gwyn put his hands over his ears and stumbled backwards to the bed. He knows about the pipe,

Gwyn thought. He's using it to fight me. But he won't get out! He won't! He won't! He won't! Arianwen and I are too strong for him!

It ended at last. Gwyn lay back, exhausted, and fell asleep on top of the bedclothes.

He was awakened by another sound; a muffled, intermittent tapping on his window. Someone was throwing snowballs.

He went to the window, opened it and looked out. There was a shadowy figure beside the apple tree, but he could not make out any of its features. 'Who's there?' he called.

'Alun!' came the reply.

Gwyn ran down and opened the front door.

Alun was standing in the porch. He was pale, but certainly not frozen. He was holding something small and dark in his hand and he had an odd, vacant expression in his eyes, as though he was not sure why or how he had come to be there. He stepped into the house and, when the door had been closed behind him, wordlessly followed Gwyn into the kitchen, where he laid the thing that he had been holding on the kitchen table. It was the broken horse!

Gwyn stared at it. 'Where've you been?' he asked gently.

'Out there!' Alun jerked his head towards the window.

'I know, out there,' said Gwyn, 'but where?'

Alun wiped his nose on the sleeve of his anorak. He did not seem inclined to answer any more questions.

'Better take some of that off,' said Gwyn, nodding at his friend's soaking clothes.

133

Alun removed his anorak, his boots and his socks, and then he sank on to a kitchen chair and wiped his nose, this time on his shirt-cuff.

'Wish you could tell me about it!' Gwyn bit his lip. He realized that it was no use trying to force Alun to talk. He would have to wait until his friend was ready.

'Aw heck!' Alun scratched his head. 'I donno. It's all so peculiar, like. I don't really understand what happened. I was following your footsteps in that blizzard, and I got lost. So I turned round to come back – an' I couldn't. There was something there, like bars: ice-cold they were, but hard as anything. At first it was all cloudy, an' I couldn't see, but then it got brighter and brighter and I saw what I was caught in. It was a sort of cage, bars all round in a pattern, like a . . . like a . . . '

'Cobweb?' Gwyn suggested.

'Phew!' Alun looked hard at Gwyn. 'You know, don't you? It's damn funny though. All those things you said; they were true, weren't they?'

'Yes, they were true!'

'Well, I s'pose you know about the man, then?'

'What man?' Gwyn stepped closer. 'Was there a man in there with you?'

'A kind of man. He scared me. He had red hair and he was dressed all in kind of bright stuff: jewellery an' that, with a cloak an' a gold belt with a big sword in it. An' he was beating at the bars with his fists, tearing at them, banging his head on them, an' yelling. I was scared, I can tell you. But he didn't see me. It sounds funny but I felt very small and kind of . . . like I had

134

something round me, very warm and soft. Anyway he kept on an' on at those bars for hours and hours. I fell asleep, and when I woke up he was still at it: moaning an' crying, an' then something awful happened!'

Gwyn waited. He could hardly bear the suspense but he dared not ask a question.

'He began to disappear,' Alun continued, 'just shrank, sort of faded away, and so did the bars of ice, until there was nothing left there, except . . . '

'Except what?'

'That!' Alun pointed to the broken horse.

Gwyn looked at it, lying on its side, black and disfigured. Poor thing! he thought. You want, so much, to get out: but I can never, never let you. It was all over, and suddenly he felt very tired.

There were sounds from above and Gwyn said, 'They've been looking for you: your dad and mine.'

'I bet!' said Alun.

'And Mr Davis came, and Gary Pritchard's dad, and Mr Ellis and Mr Jones, Tŷ Gwyn, and people I can't remember. Even Mrs Pritchard came, and she and my mam went out to look. And your mam was here with Iolo, I don't know why she brought him, he was making such a racket.'

'He always does,' Alun nodded sympathetically.

Mrs Griffiths came into the kitchen and gasped at the sight of Alun, sitting there, so rosy and cheerful, but before she could utter a word the doorbell rang. The Lloyds had returned to resume their search.

Mrs Griffiths ran to open the door. 'He's back,' she cried. 'He's safe, your Alun. Good as new and nothing wrong with him, as far as I can see.'

'Where? Where?' Mrs Lloyd tore into the kitchen and flung herself upon her son.

'Come on, Mam. I'm OK,' came Alun's muffled voice from beneath his mother.

'What happened? Where've you been? They went to search. We thought you'd freeze!'

'I stayed where I was, didn't I?' Alun said, wriggling. 'I didn't want to get lost, did I? I got behind some rocks – in a sort of cave. It was quite warm, really.'

Mrs Lloyd began to wrap up her boy like a baby, though the mist had gone and the sky was brightening. She bundled him out into the passage talking non-stop and nervously, to her husband and Mrs Griffiths. And while she spoke, Alun looked back at Gwyn and said, 'I found this out there, as well,' and he put something cool into Gwyn's hand – the snow spider.

Gwyn curled his fingers round the spider as Alun whispered hoarsely, 'Don't tell about . . . about what I said, will you?'

'I won't tell!' Gwyn grinned. 'One loony's enough!'

Alun grinned back and gave the thumbs-up sign, before his mother whisked him through the door.

Mr Griffiths had his way and Eirlys stayed for Christmas. It was the sort of Christmas one always remembers. The trees were iced with snow and the sun came out to make the mountain sparkle. The biggest Christmas tree they had ever seen at Tŷ Bryn, was put into the front room, and decorated with lights
136

like candles, with silver stars and home-made sweets wrapped in coloured paper.

A log fire was lit and they all played Monopoly and Scrabble, and even made up games, so as to prolong the fun. Mrs Griffiths played carols on the out-of-tune piano with damp hammers, and it did not matter that the soloists were sometimes out of tune too. The children were allowed to drink punch which made them giggle at Nain, who had drunk too much and looked like a Christmas tree herself, all bedecked in coloured beads and bangles.

Just before they went to bed, Eirlys looked out of the window at the white, moonlit mountain and said, 'It reminds me of home!' Only Gwyn heard her. He knew that she was not talking about Wales and it occurred to him, for the first time, that she might not stay with them for ever.

On New Year's Day, the children decided to walk in the fields. It was a cold day and, while the girl waited in the garden, Gwyn ran up to fetch the gloves his father had given him for Christmas. They were blue and silver, lined with fur, and Gwyn cherished them even more than his black watch.

When he opened his drawer he saw Arianwen and the silver pipe. They looked so innocent, who would guess what they could do? One that had travelled a million miles or more, the other from somewhere in the distant past. They would always be with him now, he knew that. As he turned away the pipe whispered something; it sounded like, 'Don't go!' Gwyn smiled and drew on his gloves, 'I'm not going anywhere!' he said.

His parents were outside, in the garden, with Eirlys. They were standing by the gate, talking quietly while they stared up at the mountain. They did not see Gwyn when he came out, nor hear him close the front door.

'I have to go soon,' he heard Eirlys say. 'I have to go back to where I came from.'

His parents did not speak immediately. They seemed to have been frozen by her remark, and then Mrs Griffiths put her hand out and gently tucked the girl's hair into her hood, saying, 'Do you have to go, Eirlys? Can't you stay?'

Eirlys shook her head.

'Were you happy there, where you came from?' Mr Griffiths asked.

'Oh, yes! Very happy!'

They did not ask where she lived; they did not seem to want to know. And then Gwyn broke into their thoughts. 'Come on,' he cried, 'I'll race you to the trees!' and he ran past them, through the open gate.

Eirlys followed, and they ran to the circle of hawthorn trees, where Gwyn had released Arianwen. The snow had melted and the grass was smooth and green. There was nothing to show that the earth had shaken or that icicles had flown from it, like stars.

'Why couldn't she escape without my help?' Gwyn thought aloud. 'She has her own power.'

'She has nothing without you,' said Eirlys. 'She needs your thoughts to help her.'

'She's just an ordinary spider, then?'

'Oh, no! No creature from my place is a common-or-garden thing!'

138

My place! There it was again. 'Are you leaving here?' He put the question cautiously.

'Today!' she answered.

'What? So soon? You can't!'

'They are coming for me!' She looked up at the sky. 'Even with your magic, I only had until today.'

'Do you want to go?'

'Oooooh, yes!' Her reply came like a deep contented sigh.

'But Mam and Dad?'

'They understand. I said I had to go back to where I came from.'

Gwyn nodded. 'They wouldn't want to know the truth,' he said.

'I think they do know. But they're too old now to be able to talk about it.'

'And they don't mind you going?'

She shook her head and smiled at him. 'It'll be all right now between you and Dad. He knows I'm safe. That's all he wanted.'

'And the Herberts?'

'I'm just a number that got muddled up. They think I've gone already.'

They had begun to walk up the track without his really being aware of it. When they had passed the first bend and the farm had disappeared from sight, Gwyn suddenly stopped to look at a kestrel hanging motionless in the air. Cloud shadows raced across the snow-capped mountains beyond the bird, and a lorry, piled with golden hay, made its way slowly across the green fields below.

'Won't you miss all this?' Gwyn asked.

'No!' she said. 'I like it where I'm going.'

He noticed the cold before he saw anything, 'I don't think I'll come any further,' he said.

'Come on! Just for a bit, to keep me company!' She took his hand.

Her fingers seemed colder than ever, but he allowed himself to be led away from the track and through the fields of sheep. And then he saw the light, glinting now and then, through the billows of a great, grey cloud. And he felt an icy breeze on his face.

'You go on,' he said. 'I'm staying here!' He tried to pull his hand away, but she would not let him. They were approaching the flat field where Bethan had gone to rescue the black ewe, four years before.

'Let me go!' cried Gwyn.

Her fingers tightened on his wrist. He twisted and turned but her grip was like steel, her strength irresistible. He could see the ship now, falling slowly through the clouds, the great sail swelling, the dancing creatures sparkling on the hull. Icy fragments spun earthwards, and terrified sheep swung away from the field and scattered in a great wave past the children.

'Let me go!' Gwyn begged.

'Come with me!' Her soft voice floated above the moan of the wind, 'Come!'

'No!' Gwyn screamed. 'I want to stay. No! No! No! Leave me!'

'Come!' She looked back at him and smiled, but her fingers bit deeper into his wrist. 'Please!' she sighed. 'I need you, Gwyn. We need you – out there!'

'No!' Gwyn began to shake, and through his tears,

140

saw the ship as a huge, glittering cloud behind the girl's pale shape. Then a voice inside him suddenly burst out, 'Gwydion lives HERE!' and he tore from her grasp and flung himself to the ground.

He lay there, with his eyes closed, nursing his aching hand, and when the bitter cold and all the threatening sounds had vanished, he got up and saw something where Eirlys had been – the yellow scarf, frozen into the snow, and the seaweed beside it. He picked them up and put the seaweed into his pocket, but the scarf was stiff with frost, like a strange, twisted stick.

He wandered slowly through the fields until he came to the track and there, on the last bend, he found Alun standing by the drystone wall.

'What's that?' Alun asked.

'Someone's scarf,' said Gwyn. 'Look, it's still frozen!'

'Where's the girl?'

'She's gone!'

'Phew!' said Alun.

They walked back to the farm in comfortable silence. Mr Griffiths was standing in the porch when they arrived, 'She's gone, then?' he said.

'Yes!' Gwyn replied. And then, before his father could turn away, he said, 'I'm not going, Dad. I'm not ever going!'

'I know!' Mr Griffiths smiled, 'And I'm glad of that, Gwyn! Very glad!'

They went into the house. A house that was not empty any more.

Emlyn's Moon

For my mother

Contents

1
The Boy
from the
Chapel

'Don't go into Llewelyn's chapel!' they told Nia. 'No good will come of it. Something happened there!' But Nia disobeyed. If she hadn't, nothing would have changed. She'd still be plain Nia, dull Nia, Nia who couldn't do anything!

It all began on the day they left Tŷ Llŷr. The children, tucked between boxes in the back of the Landrover, were waiting for their mother to lock up. Nia was propped on a rolled mattress at the open end of the car. She was gazing at a red geranium in the kitchen window, the only bright thing left. And then the flower was lifted out of the dark window by unseen hands. It reappeared in the doorway, perched upon a pile of towels in her mother's arms.

'I nearly forgot it!' Mrs Lloyd beamed over the geranium.

Nia wished she *had* forgotten the flower; just for a day or two. At least there would have been something left alive in Tŷ Llŷr. If a house could look forlorn, then that's how Tŷ Llŷr seemed to her: curtains gone from the windows, the farmyard bare and tidy, and a stillness so unnatural it almost hurt. A stray feather drifted in the sunlight, the

11

only reminder that chickens had once inhabited the yard. It was May but the ewes and their lambs had gone, and the only sounds came from bees in the giant sycamore tree.

Even the children in the Landrover were silent. Leaving their home had ceased to be an exciting idea; suddenly it had become a rather shocking reality.

Mrs Lloyd climbed up to sit beside her husband. The engine started. The spell was broken. An excited shouting and chattering broke out.

Nia was the only one to look back and see the boy beneath the sycamore. He was standing so close to the shadowy tree-trunk that she could barely make out his shape. But she knew it was Gwyn Griffiths by the mass of dark hair and the way he stood, hands in pockets, so very still and thoughtful. No other boy could do that.

Nia nudged her brother, wedged in beside her. 'Look, Alun! There's Gwyn!'

There was so much noise, so much movement amongst the seven children packed tightly together between boxes and cases, that Alun neither felt nor heard Nia, so she raised her own hand and waved, rather tentatively.

The boy beneath the tree responded.

'He's waving, Alun!' Nia shouted above the rumpus.

'What? Who?'

'Gwyn!'

'Oh!'

'He's come to say "goodbye", Alun! Quick!'

Alun leant over his sister, accidentally knocking the sheep-dog's nose with his elbow. Fly yelped, the Landrover lurched round a bend and Alun was flung backwards on top of his twin brothers. Siôn and Gareth were too happy to grumble.

Gwyn Griffiths disappeared from sight.

The Landrover rattled on, down the mountain, gathering speed as the lane became steeper, and the chatter in the back increased to an hysterical crescendo of excitement; Catrin even broke into song.

Mr Lloyd joined in, humming gustily. He'd done it at last; broken free of the farm that his ailing father-in-law had begged him to take over. Iestyn Lloyd was a small, dark man, his face as weather-tanned as any hill-farmer, but he was too fond of his food and a good pint to stay as fit as he should, too gregarious to enjoy the solitary existence that suited his neighbour, Ivor Griffiths, so well. But he had tried, no one could say he hadn't. For fifteen years he'd struggled with hard mountain earth, with ewes trapped in snow and lambs lost, and he had failed. He would never make a good farmer, his heart wasn't in it, and with another child on the way, he had to find some way of earning a decent living. When the butcher's shop in Pendewi came up for sale, it was like an answer to Iestyn's prayers. He'd been an apprentice butcher, it was what he knew, what he could do best. He would succeed this time. He'd sold his stock and all his land to Ivor Griffiths, who had a magic touch when it came to animals, and a way of knowing the land that only a born farmer could have.

No one wanted the farmhouse though. No one wanted ancient Tŷ Llŷr, with its crumbling chimney, its family of bats, and the plum trees that curled their way under the wavy roof.

'Mae hen wlad fy nhadau yn annwyl i mi,' sang Mr Lloyd, breaking out in a rare exhibition of patriotism, as he cheerfully sped away from the things that Nia loved.

Fly, the sheep-dog, rolled her eyes and gazed imploringly at Nia. The dog, at least, felt as apprehensive as she.

13

There was nothing in Pendewi for Nia. She had neither the talents nor the aspirations of her brothers and sisters. In Pendewi there was a library for Nerys to browse in every day, if she wished. For Catrin, a music teacher only two doors away, and a disco on Saturdays. For the boys, shops stuffed with comics and bubblegum, with batteries and nails, glue and string. There they would all be, crammed into their little rooms above the shop, reading and singing, building, hammering and chewing, while the plums turned from green to gold in the orchard at Tŷ Llŷr, and strangers put them into baskets and carried them away.

No one would notice the wild Welsh poppies that Nia had nurtured in little places by the stream, or see the white roses behind the farmhouse. The garden would become a carpet of petals and then, when the wind came, the petals would scatter over the mountain like snow. And no one seemed to care, not even Mrs Lloyd, preoccupied as she was with thoughts of the baby who would come in summer, when the plums were turning gold.

Gwyn Griffiths' sister had loved flowers, but she had vanished on the mountain, no one knew how.

'I wish you had waved to Gwyn!' Nia said to Alun, but she spoke half to herself, and did not expect him to hear.

The Landrover slowed down before turning into the main road. Summer visitors had begun to arrive and the road was busy. Mr Lloyd swung in behind a caravan, and there they stayed, unable to pass the clumsy vehicle, and travelling so slowly that Nia could count the primroses on the verge.

At the top of the hill leading down into Pendewi, the caravan stopped without warning. Mr Lloyd jammed on his brakes and leant out of the window, mouthing oaths

14

about visitors and caravans; he could see the owner in the driving seat of his smart red car, unconcernedly reading a map. Mr Lloyd banged his fist on the horn. The children pressed forward, anticipating a row, all except for Nia, who had noticed something far more interesting.

The Landrover had stopped beside the old chapel; the chapel that wasn't a chapel now, but a home for someone. The gate and the iron railings had been painted pink and gold; the door was blue with big golden flowers on it and bright curtains framed the long windows. When Nia stood up she could see down into the room beyond the window. A boy in green trousers lay sprawled across a rug; he was doing something with his hands, making something, but Nia couldn't see what it was. Curious, she leant further out, but as she did so the Landrover suddenly jerked forward. Nia screamed and clutched wildly at the air, trying to keep her balance.

The boy in the chapel looked up in surprise, and then grinned at Nia's predicament, before Alun caught the back of her jersey and pulled her to safety.

'What on earth were you doing?' Nerys, the eldest, inquired tetchily. She felt responsible for incidents in the back of the Landrover.

'I was just looking,' Nia replied.

'Looking at what?'

'Just into the chapel. I saw Emlyn Llewelyn from school. I didn't know he lived there!'

'Course he does,' said Alun. 'Him and his dad. It's a bad place that!'

'Who says?'

'Gwyn says!'

'Why?'

'Something happened there, didn't it?' Alun said

15

world-wearily.

'What happened?' Nia persisted.

'I donno; something bad! It's all wrong that place. No one goes there!'

'It's beautiful!' Nia protested. 'And I like Emlyn.'

'You don't know, do you?' Alun said in a grim and rather condescending manner.

Nia was silent. Why had she defended Emlyn? She hardly knew him. He was in Alun's class and nearly two years older than herself. She wished she had been able to see further into his strange home.

Outside Pendewi the caravan turned left on to the sea road, and the Landrover continued on, down into the little market town.

Sunshine flooded the High Street. The trees were in blossom and Saturday shoppers in bright spring clothes, bustled in and out of the narrow grey-tiled houses. It wasn't such a bad place after all, Nia thought.

The Lloyds parked outside a tall black and white building at the furthest end of the town. There was a huge blue van in front of them, with removal men in grey overalls munching sandwiches in the cabin. The furniture was all in place.

There were two entrances; one that led into a shop furbished with red carcases and neat trays of sliced meat; the other, a very private-looking black door with a brass number 6 on it.

The family went into their new home through the black and private door, leaving it open to allow warmth and light into the dark house.

Mr Lloyd persuaded the reluctant and grumbling Fly down a long passage to the back garden. Mrs Lloyd sank into a sunny chair by the door; she was still carrying the

16

red geranium.

The four boys clattered noisily up the stairs and along the creaking and uncarpeted landing, eager to break into boxes that had been withheld for weeks; to find ancient and beloved toys and strew them across floorboards of unfamiliar rooms and make them theirs, their fortress and their home.

Nerys, Nia and Catrin stood before their mother, flushed and still pretty in her flowery smock.

'Well, I think it's upstairs first, girls. When the clothes are in the drawers and the beds are made, we'll have a cup of tea.'

Nia followed her older sisters upstairs. Nerys and Catrin disappeared into a room overlooking the High Street. Nia glimpsed a wide sunlit window before the door was closed against her.

Opposite her sisters' room, Siôn, Gareth and Alun had already extended their territory. A wooden railway track snaked through their open door, and along the landing. Nia side-stepped, too late! She tripped and a red engine flew across the floor.

'Watch it!' the twins sang out. 'Nia-can't-do-nothing! Nia-in-the-middle! Nia's got a funny tooth, and her nose goes squiggle, squiggle!'

Nia was fed up with the twins' new rhyme, but she couldn't think of a suitably clever retort. It was all true, of course, that was the worst of it. They'd got her, pinned her down like a butterfly on a board, only she was more of a moth; a very ordinary brown moth who wasn't good at anything except screwing up her nose when she didn't understand. A moth in the middle; with two butterfly sisters and an older brother who could mend anything; with two younger brothers who could stand on their heads, and an even younger one who got by just because he was the youngest, and had curls.

She retrieved the red engine and put it into Siôn's hand. 'It's Iolo's engine, anyway,' she said.

The twins allowed Nia to escape without further aggravation. She continued down the corridor until she reached two open doors at the end. To her left, the bathroom, bright with sunlight and frosted glass. Iolo was playing with something in the basin; little waves of soapy water were spilling over on to the floor.

Let someone else find the puddle! Leaving Iolo in peace Nia turned to the room on her right; the room she was to share with Iolo. There were no spaces left for her in her sisters' room and none for Iolo in his brothers'. They would have to put up with each other for the time being. As they had grown in size and number, the Lloyd children had become used to an annual re-arrangen.ent of bedrooms. If the new baby was a girl, Nia would share her bright little room at the top of the house, if not, Iolo would move in with the new brother and Nia would stay here, in this small, shadowy room, that had an old and unused air about it.

The window looked out on to the back garden, a garden in shadow with hardly a blade of grass. There was the river to look at though, splashing over bleached pebbles beyond the garden wall. And, on the other side of the river, Morgan-the-Smithy's long black barn with blue sparks lighting the windows, and Morgan and his sons singing in green boilersuits

Next year there would be flowers growing by the river. Nia fumbled in her pockets and brought out a tiny paper parcel. She carefully unfolded the paper and laid on the floor a part of Tŷ Llŷr: honesty seeds in their flat, silvery

18

shells, tiny black poppy and campion seeds, all mixed together, so that when she sowed them next spring, the meagre little patch below would be splashed with orange and purple and pink.

'What's that?' Iolo had finished with boats and stood dripping in the doorway.

'Seeds,' Nia replied. 'You'd better dry yourself and the floor, or you'll get a row.'

'I can't find a towel,' Iolo explained.

Nia could hear her mother moving about in the room above them. 'I'll look downstairs for you; Mam had them in the hall.'

'I need something to eat too,' Iolo informed her.

'I'll see.'

Nia tucked her precious seeds back into a pocket and went downstairs.

Sunlight was streaming through a semi-circle of stained-glass above the front door. The hall was lined with a clutter of cases, bags and upturned chairs, but in the centre there was only one thing; a box, *the* box! Nia recognised it; it contained Mam's clothes from twenty years before; dresses that were too tight, but too full of memories to throw away; shoes too flimsy, beads too bright for a mother of seven. It was like a gift, wrapped in the glowing colours from the stained-glass window. A gift for Nia-can't-do-nothing, who could now become Nia-can-do-anything!

Forgetting Iolo and towels, Nia knelt beside the box and began to pick at the string that held it shut. The string fell off and she opened the box. Almost reverently she began to lift out the contents and lay them on the floor.

There were shouts from above and around Nia but, amazingly, no one came into the hall. Catrin had found

19

the piano and was practising her scales. Fly was whining somewhere.

'Someone take the dog out!' Mr Lloyd shouted from the shop.

No one answered.

Nia had found a violet dress, patterned with pink and white flowers. She stood up and slipped it over her head. The hem touched the ground. She knelt again and scrabbled in the box, trying to find the thing she needed. There it was – a wide-brimmed red straw hat. And now she could feel the little paper bundles of beads and shoes at the bottom of the box. She drew out a rope of big silver shells and a pair of pink shoes with stars on them.

Nia kicked off her trainers and stepped into the pink shoes; the violet dress covered them; she would trip. The silver shells would have to become a belt. They encircled her waist perfectly, not a shell too long. Nia hitched the dress a few inches over the shell-belt, just enough to reveal the shoes. She was almost ready.

The finishing touch was a long string of multi-coloured beads wound once, twice, three times round her neck.

20

Catrin moved on from Mendelssohn to Mozart and Fly's distant whine became a long, low howl.

'Someone take that poor dog for a walk,' Mrs Lloyd pleaded from a box-lined room upstairs.

'I'll go,' answered Nia.

'Don't let her off the lead; she's not used to the town,' came a voice muffled by mounds of linen. 'And don't go into any shops.'

'I won't!'

'Poor thing! She can't stay here much longer.' The rest of Mrs Lloyd's words were drowned by Fly's howl of agreement.

Nia tottered down the passage and opened the back door. Four stone steps led down into the yard. Fly was tied to the rail beside the steps, with just enough lead to allow her to stretch out, head on paws, in a tiny patch of sunlight that had managed to creep round the house. The dog leapt up when she saw Nia, and barked joyfully.

'Sssh!' Nia knew her father would not approve of her outfit if he saw her. She began to untie Fly's lead, all the while eyeing the long room that extended into the yard beyond the rest of the house; the hateful room that held all those dead and dreadful things. Through the tiny window she glimpsed a red carcase, swinging where her father had just hung it. Mr Lloyd was whistling; happy among his sides of beef, his lamb chops and purple pigs' livers. Poor dead, dismembered creatures. It was enough to put you off meat forever.

'Ugh!' Nia could even smell them.

Fly, free at last, bounded up the steps, dragging Nia behind her. They flew down the passage and through the hall, Fly scattering discarded cardboard and all the rubbish of removal, Nia sliding and tripping in the outsize pink shoes.

Nerys appeared at the top of the stairs, alerted by the commotion. 'Nia, what are you . . . ?'

But Nia had opened the front door and leapt through it before her sister had time to take in her appearance.

Fly began to live up to her name; her paws barely touched the ground as she tore joyfully up the street.

The pink shoes hadn't a chance; first one flew off and then the other. Nia dared not stop to retrieve them for fear of choking Fly. Clasping the red hat to her head with her free hand, she careered after the dog, darting between startled shoppers and shouts of 'Watch it!', 'Mind the pram!', 'Where are you going, girl?', 'Good God, what's she doing?'.

Not a very favourable first appearance, Nia thought.

Fly bounded on, back towards Tŷ Llŷr and the mountain fields. The road became steeper and, at the end of the town, the dog stopped and stared mournfully up the hill, her sides heaving and her long tongue hanging out like a wet flag.

Nia dropped down beside Fly, in worse shape than the dog. They sat side by side on the hot paving stones, gasping and panting. Nia felt as though she'd spent a month in the desert. She closed her eyes and leant against Fly's woolly neck. When she opened them again a few moments later, she found herself looking at a shop window, and at a boy moving past the window and into the shop; he was a tall boy with thick brown-gold hair and green trousers – the boy from the chapel.

Afterwards, Nia could never remember whether it was thirst or curiosity that lead her to follow him. Whatever it was, she forgot all the rules, all the warnings about sheep-dogs in shops, and followed Emlyn Llewelyn through the

22

door.

The wide back of a woman in brown obliterated most of the counter. The wide woman was whispering to the shopkeeper, a man in red braces and a grubby shirt, who seemed more interested in gossip than business. Nia had time to contemplate the rows of sweets and biscuits before making a decision. She spied cans of fruit juice on the highest shelf. On the other side of the shop, Emlyn Llewelyn was bending over tubes of glue.

'Yes?' The shopkeeper was staring suspiciously at Nia.

The wide woman had rolled back, propping herself up on the counter; she was staring at Nia's bare feet.

Nia tried to smile but instead screwed up her nose.

'I want a drink, please!' she said quickly.

'Get what you want then. Can you reach?'

'I think so.' Nervous of the disapproving glances Nia thoughtlessly let the loop of Fly's lead slip down her arm, and reached for a can of orange juice. Just as her fingertips touched the can, two more customers entered the shop. Fly panicked; she leapt away from the shelves growling anxiously. Nia was jerked backwards, her heel caught in the hem of the violet dress and she tumbled to the floor, followed by a pile of cans. Suddenly the whole top shelf became possessed. Cans and bottles tottered and clinked and began to roll towards her. There was nothing Nia could do to halt that dreadful and inexorable shower of cans. Some fell on top of her, some crashed to the ground and others were caught by a darting figure in green trousers. She was aware of the shopkeeper hopping up and down beside her, kicking out at the barking Fly and screaming, 'Who's going to pay? Look at the shop!' and low voices murmuring, 'It shouldn't be allowed!', 'She's no shoes!', 'And look at the hat!', 'What's her mam

24

thinking of?', 'Get the dog out!', 'No shoes! No shoes!'.

And then a boy's voice said, 'It isn't a crime, having no shoes!' and Emlyn Llewelyn stepped forward, holding Fly tight by the collar. 'Only two cans are damaged,' he said, 'and we'll buy those. Come on!' He tapped Nia on the shoulder and held out his free hand.

Nia looked up. Emlyn had never spoken to her before; he had golden eyes, like a lion.

'Come on!' commanded Emlyn Llewelyn.

Nia put her hand in his and he helped her to her feet.

'You'd better hold your dog,' he said, 'and pull your dress up or you'll trip again.'

Nia obeyed and Emlyn placed a pile of coins on the counter. Then he strode out of the shop, dragging Nia with him.

'I owe you for the drink,' said Nia when the door had been closed against reproachful mutterings.

'That's OK!' Emlyn said. 'Are you all right?'

'Yes,' Nia lied. Her shins ached where the cans had hit them. 'But I'm thirsty.'

'Have it on me,' Emlyn held out a can. 'Dog looks thirsty too. It's a nice dog. What's its name?'

'Fly,' Nia replied, 'and it's a she.' She opened the can and tipped it to her lips, gulping and coughing as the fizzy drink trickled down her throat.

Emlyn watched her for a moment, politely refraining from mentioning the splutters, then he asked, 'Why don't you bring Fly up to my place and give her a drink?'

'I don't think I'd better,' Nia said. 'I must find Mam's shoes. They fell off when I was running, and they've got stars on them.'

'OK!' Emlyn accepted her refusal almost too fast, as though he expected it. He kicked the ground with the heel

25

of his sandal and looked away from her.

And suddenly Nia remembered what Alun had said about the chapel. 'Nobody goes there – something happened – it's no good!' and she suddenly found herself saying, 'All right! I'll come, just for a bit!'

She could see that Emlyn was more than pleased, but trying hard not to show it. 'Good!' he said. 'Can I take the dog?'

Nia handed him Fly's lead. 'I wanted to see inside your place,' she said.

Emlyn grinned. 'I thought I recognised you, spying on us. You're Alun's sister, aren't you? You look different in all that stuff. I wasn't sure.'

Nia giggled. 'I nearly fell out, didn't I?'

'What's going on? How is it you're in jeans one minute and then beads and a funny hat?'

'We've moved,' said Nia. ' "Moved with the times!" That's what my dad says.'

They began to walk up the hill. Fly too hot and thirsty now to run, and Emlyn striding out faster than the dog. Nia had to take little running-hopping steps in order to keep up with the boy and to avoid loose stones on the ground.

Once a van passed on the other side of the road, its engine coughing as it strained up the hill, and Fly rushed at it barking furiously, just as she used to do when strangers passed Tŷ Llŷr.

'She doesn't like cars and that sort of thing,' Nia explained breathlessly. 'She wants to go home, like me. Only it isn't home any more; the farm, I mean, where we come from.'

'Where did you come from?'

'Tŷ Llŷr, on the mountain. Dad didn't like it, the work

was too rough; sheep kept dying and that in the winter, and Mam said the house was too small with another baby coming, but you'd have thought she'd want to stay, being as it was her home all her life, she was even born there. Nobody wanted to stay except me and Fly. I planted flowers there, see. I like to watch things grow and all the colours.'

'Are there a lot of you?' Emlyn inquired. He was gazing intently at Fly and, for a moment, Nia wondered if he really wanted an answer.

'Seven!' she replied. 'Seven children, that is, and I'm in the middle, right in the very middle. Nerys is the oldest, she's clever and quite pretty, but Catrin is beautiful. She called herself Kate last year, she thought it sounded more romantic but now she's Catrin again; she plays the piano and her hair is – oh . . . ' Nia sighed, 'all pale yellow and floating, like . . . like ash trees.'

Emlyn looked at her with interest but he said nothing and Nia began to wonder if she'd talked too much. She'd never been able to express herself before and couldn't think how it had come about. They walked on in silence until they reached the pink and gold railings of the chapel and all at once Nia began to feel afraid. Fly was apprehensive too; she kept making worried rumbling noises in her throat.

It was too bright: the painted door, the coloured curtains; it was like the house of gingerbread that had tempted Hansel and Gretel, and look what had become of them! 'Something happened in that place, something bad . . . ' Alun's words kept repeating themselves in her head, but Emlyn had taken her hand and was drawing her up the steps to the door!

2
A
Promise
– Broken

The blue door opened and Nia was pitched into
Wonderland. Astonished and enchanted, she forgot her
fear and murmured, 'Oh! I didn't know! I didn't know!'

From floor to ceiling the walls of the chapel had been
covered with bright paintings. Patterns of trees and fields
jostled with fantastic flowers, with faces that Nia knew,
and some that she did not. Coloured birds swooped
through clouds and rainbows and a boy with gold-brown
hair tumbled in the corn, swung from green branches and
slept beside a stream.

'I can see you,' said Nia quietly. 'You and your life.
Who did it?'

'My dad,' said Emlyn, not proud, but pleased that she
was impressed.

Above her, huge coloured butterflies floated on
glittering threads from the vaulted ceiling, and all about
the room wonderful wooden beasts gazed out with brilliant
painted eyes.

'And did he make these?' Nia nodded at the beasts and
the butterflies.

'All of it!' Emlyn closed the door. The butterflies
shivered in the draught and the whole ceiling spun and

shone.

Was this why everyone avoided the chapel? Just because it was extraordinary. There were no demons here.

Sunlight, pouring through the long windows, dazzled Nia and she dared not move for fear of stumbling on a treasure. Something large and dark stooped at the far end of the chapel, but she could not make out what kind of creature it was for its outline was blurred against the glare. And then it began to move. It rose and rose until its long shadow almost touched her feet.

A tall man in a black boiler suit was approaching; his hair a lion's mane, his eyes golden, like Emlyn's. A large hand clasped Nia's and a deep voice asked, in Welsh, 'Beth ydi'ch enw chi?'

'Her name is Nia,' Emlyn answered for the speechless girl, 'and her dog wants a drink!'

'Dog?' Mr Llewelyn dropped Nia's hand and regarded the bewildered Fly peering round Emlyn's legs. 'Good God, boy! I told you not to bring dogs in here. He'll wreck my work!'

'I'll take it out, Dad. And it's a *she*; her name is Fly.'

'Fly, is it? Well, remove Fly and give her a drink from the trough.'

'And can I let her loose in the field, Dad?'

'Ask the lady,' boomed Mr Llewelyn. 'It's her dog.'

Nia nodded.

'Let the dog loose, Emlyn boy. And I will entertain your visitor. Here, lady, have a seat!'

Abandoned by the boy and the dog, Nia perched uncertainly on the edge of the cane chair that Emlyn's father drew out for her.

'And now, before tea,' Idris Llewelyn's dark presence loomed over Nia, 'may I make a small sketch of you, Nia?

29

So splendid in your beads, and with silver shells all round your waist! And, ah, what a hat!'

Nia had a great desire to break out of the cane chair, but she could not. There was something reassuring about the kindly wooden beasts, the painted landscapes and the bright butterfly ceiling. So she curled herself tighter into the chair, while Mr Llewelyn pulled a stool beneath the north window and took up a large sketch pad.

Cocooned in soft cushions, Nia relaxed and let her eyes explore the chapel. In a corner by the door she noticed a truckle bed covered with a striped blanket; Emlyn's place, she decided. There were piles of books under the bed and, beside it, small wooden animals, some perfect and some whose heads and legs were still encased in uncarved blocks of wood. There were empty tubes of glue, pieces of string, scraps of paper, a penknife and a magnifying glass, but no Lego, no model cars, not a toy of any sort.

At the other end of the chapel a huge brass bedstead protruded from behind a wicker screen. It was an ancient bed with wonderful knobs and decorations, some scratched and some repainted; its satin cover was patterned with splashes of red and green and gold, the sort of transport you would need for a very special dream. And then Nia noticed something that made her fingers tighten. Her tiny intake of breath caused Mr Llewelyn to glance at her face but he said nothing.

Nia quickly looked away from the thing that had disturbed her, but when the artist looked back at his work, she found herself gazing at the bed again. The hem of the beautiful bedcover was scarred by a long black mark. Some of the coloured threads had been severed at the edge, and hung in uneven sooty strands. It was a small thing but ugly and, somehow, alarming.

30

She decided to count the piles of rugs that were scattered on the bare floorboards, each one a different size, a different colour.

Mr Llewelyn, a pencil in his mouth, smiled and said, 'We've been wanderers, you see. Our collection was gathered from every part of the world, but now we must stay put while Emlyn goes to school.'

'And will you go away again, when Emlyn has grown?' Nia asked.

Mr Llewelyn was silent for a while, dabbing at his sketchbook, and then he muttered, almost to himself, 'Perhaps . . . one day . . . '

Emlyn came in and placed a kettle on a rusty gas stove in a corner. There was an ancient sink beside the stove, with cupboards above and below it. A teapot appeared, and three blue mugs. Everything you could need in one room, Nia thought. Just as it should be.

'Can we take the tea outside, Da, to keep Fly company?' Emlyn asked.

'Why not?' said Mr Llewelyn. He closed his sketchbook and put it on a table beside him. 'I'm not showing you yourself yet, Lady-with-the-Violet-Dress, because it's not finished. And you must come again, with your hat and your beads.'

'I could wear Mam's shoes,' said Nia eagerly, 'they've got stars on them.'

'Why not? Why not?' Mr Llewelyn laughed, very deep and loud, and helped her out of the chair.

They all went outside and sipped their tea at the back of the chapel, where a steep field of wild flowers stretched down and down to the river.

'Oh!' cried Nia joyfully. 'You can see the mountain from here; you could see Tŷ Llŷr too, if it wasn't for the

31

trees.'

'Ah, that mountain,' murmured Mr Llewelyn. 'You know Tŷ Bryn and Emlyn's cousin then?'

'Cousin?' Nia repeated, turning to Emlyn. 'Whose cousin are you?'

Emlyn did not reply. He picked up a stick and threw it for Fly.

'Gwyn Griffiths is his cousin,' said Mr Llewelyn. 'Their mothers were sisters, but you wouldn't know it. We're down here, and they're on the mountain, and there's a world between us.'

They all turned to look at the mountain as he spoke, and in that very second an extraordinary thing happened. A huge, shining cloud appeared from nowhere, right above the mountain and although the sun still shone, everything went very, very cold, and an icy gust blew Nia's hat on to the grass.

No one referred to the cloud, they just watched it, settling slowly on to the mountain. Emlyn went to fetch a tin of biscuits. They ate them all except one which they gave to Fly, who had begun to whine. And Nia became aware that hours, not minutes had passed. The sun was low, there were shoes to find, explanations to make up. She jumped up, rubbing her cold arms and crying, 'I must go. I'll get a row!'

'I'll come with you,' said Emlyn, grabbing Fly's collar.

'Yes, go with her, boy! And don't forget the hat.' Mr Llewelyn squashed the big hat down over Nia's ears and led them round to the front of the chapel.

As the children passed through the pink and gold gate, Mr Llewelyn exclaimed, 'By heck, it's cold. What's happened?'

'It's like a spell,' said Emlyn, laughing. 'Let's run

33

before we turn to stone.'

They scampered down the hill, Fly bounding beside
them, forgetting where she was going, just happy to be
running, and Emlyn shouted, breathless, 'Would your
dad sell Fly to me? If I could get the money?'

'Don't know!' Nia called back. 'She's a sheep-dog, see,
and valuable they say. My dad wants £30 at least. We
can't keep her, that's sure. Anyway, what about your
dad?'

'I can talk him round. I know I can!'

'Oooow!' Nia's bare toes had met something sharp and
painful. She sat on the grass and examined her foot. It was
extremely dirty but there was no blood to be seen.

'You all right?' Emlyn crouched beside her.

Fly began to bark.

'No blood,' said Nia. 'But I think I'll walk now and let
the spell get me, if it can.'

They sauntered on until they reached the shop where it
had all begun. It was closed and the street was empty.
Emlyn said, 'I won't come any further. They might not
like it, your mam and dad!'

'Why not?'

'Because they're from the mountain.'

'So?'

'I'll tell you one day.'

'What were you doing when I looked into the chapel?'

'Making an animal,' Emlyn grinned. 'That's why I
came to the shop, for glue; the tail broke off.'

'What sort of animal?'

'It doesn't matter, just an animal. About the dog. I've
got some money saved and I think Dad'll lend me the rest.
I'll let you know at school on Monday. Promise not to let
them sell Fly till then!'

34

'I promise,' said Nia, never dreaming that she could break her promise.

'Thanks!' Emlyn passed Fly's lead to her and turned to go.

'Emlyn?' Nia had remembered something that had been worrying her. 'Where's your mam?'

He stopped and stood quite still with his back to her. Nia thought he wasn't going to reply and wished she hadn't asked the question.

But Emlyn turned and, looking past her at the distant clouds, said, 'Mam? She's in the moon, isn't she?' And then he ran back up the hill, only stopping when Nia couldn't reach him, even with a word.

She didn't shout, 'That can't be true!' for with Emlyn, she felt, anything could be true.

She began to walk down the deserted street, peering in doorways, behind trees, post boxes and a telephone kiosk. The star-spangled shoes were nowhere to be seen.

Ivor Griffiths' Landrover was parked in the road outside Number 6, and Nia hoped his presence would occupy her parents' attention while she slipped unnoticed into the house.

But it was not to be.

'Nia Lloyd! What on earth? Where've you been, I'd like to know?' Her mother was in the hall, her face white and angry, and her pretty smock covered in dust. 'If I didn't know you better I'd have had the police out. Nerys went looking and found my best shoes in the gutter!'

'But you don't wear them now,' Nia said quietly.

Mrs Lloyd stamped her foot. 'That's not the point, is it?'

Mr Lloyd emerged from the kitchen mumbling, 'What's this? What's this? Close the door, it's gone cold!'

He was closely followed by Ivor Griffiths and three boys with jam on their faces, eager to witness a scolding.

Confined in the dark hall, Fly began to growl.

'Good God, girl! What d'you think you're doing in that stuff?' Mr Lloyd seized Fly's lead. 'Where've you been, all got up like a . . . like a prize cake!'

Iolo and the twins began to giggle, but Nia lifting her head, said, 'I think I look quite nice, really. Anyway Emlyn Llewelyn's dad thought I did!'

'What? You haven't been up there?'

'It's beautiful!'

All at once her parents, and even Ivor Griffiths, began to chatter low and nervously. They were upset, Nia could feel it. They didn't want to alarm her but their restraint was far more frightening. Her mother gently removed the red hat and the beads, and started to undo the shell-belt, all the while murmuring, 'You won't go there again, love, will you? It's best not to! Promise you won't!'

Nia nodded. She was shivering and wriggling her nose because she couldn't understand them, but she was careful not to make a promise. She knew she would go to the chapel again, whatever they said.

'You do as Mam says!' Mr Griffiths added his advice in a grave and gravelly voice.

Taking her assent for granted, her father and Mr Griffiths retreated to the kitchen, herding Fly and the boys before them.

Nia stepped out of the violet dress and her mother gathered it up, with the beads and the belt. 'I'm going to put these away now, my love,' she said, 'and I don't want you to wear them again for a bit.'

'Even in the house?' Nia asked, dismayed.

'No, your dad doesn't like it!'

'But, Mam . . . '

'I'm putting them away,' Mrs Lloyd said firmly. 'No more dressing-up for a while,' and she whisked her bright bundle up the stairs.

'Where are you taking them, Mam?' Nia cried frantically, leaping after her mother, two steps at a time. 'I may need them.'

'No, you won't!' Her mother was already far above her, on the narrow stairs that led to the third floor and her own bedroom. 'Wash your hands and go and have your tea!'

A door slammed.

Alone on the landing, Nia clenched her fists with frustration and cried, 'Oh! Oh! Oh!'

Alun came out of his room, followed by Gwyn Griffiths. 'Did you get a row?' Alun asked with some sympathy.

'A bit!' said Nia staring at Gwyn Griffiths. She was surprised to see him so soon after the move from Tŷ Llŷr.

'I came with Dad!' Gwyn returned Nia's stare. 'To help unpack and that!'

Nia did not believe him. Upset as she was, she noticed a conspiratorial air about the boys. Gwyn had come to see Alun about something; and it must be very important, and secret.

'Gwyn brought a cake from his mam,' Alun said. 'It's great! Go and have some!'

Nia was not put off the scent. Something unusual had happened; Gwyn looked so tense. 'Come with me!' she said.

Alun was about to refuse, but Gwyn nudged him and said, 'We've had our tea, but we'll eat some more,' and he led the way downstairs

Nerys and Catrin were doing the washing-up when they went into the kitchen. The crockery had been unpacked

37

but not put away and waited in precarious piles around the room.

'You don't deserve cake, Nia Lloyd' said Nerys. 'A lot of bother you've caused today. It isn't as if we didn't have enough to do, without going looking for you.'

'Nia-can't-do-nothing! Nia-in-the . . . ' the twins began.

'Now then! Now then!' Mr Lloyd intervened. 'It's all over. Come for some more is it, boys? Sit down, then. By golly, your wife bakes a grand cake, Ivor!'

'She does indeed!' Mr Griffiths agreed. He wasn't a man given to long speeches but on the subject of his wife's talent he was always more than generous. 'She's a grand cook, Glenys is; she can bake anything, never fails; wins prizes at Pendewi show every year.'

'Every year,' Mr Lloyd repeated, on cue.

'And so would our mam if she wasn't washing all day,' said loyal Catrin, placing a large slice of sponge cake on Nia's plate. 'Aren't you cold, just in a T-shirt, Nia? Your arms are blue.'

Nia shook her head, her mouth full of cake. She was cold but cake was more important than cardigans.

'What's happened to the weather?' grumbled Mr Lloyd. 'There'll be a frost tonight I shouldn't wonder, and it was so hot today.'

If Nia hadn't been looking to see if Alun's slice of cake was larger than her own, she wouldn't have noticed his expression; as it was she was just in time to see him lift his eyebrows, very slightly, and glance at Gwyn and she suddenly remembered the terrible cold, nearly two years ago, just after Gwyn had come flying down the lane past Tŷ Llŷr, shouting that he was a magician. No one believed him, of course and, for a while even Alun wouldn't speak to him. And then everything went wrong. A great storm had blown up from nowhere. Sheep had died and Alun had got lost on the mountain – it had disappeared in a cloud of snow; no one could get through. It was a phenomenon they said, but they didn't talk about it much. Alun had been found and after that he believed Gwyn. But Nia had always believed, right from the beginning, and when she looked at Gwyn she could feel the excitement in him, half-afraid, half-yearning, and she knew something would happen again, quite soon.

'I saw your cousin today, Gwyn!' she said brightly.

Gwyn frowned at his plate. 'Which cousin?'

'Emlyn Llewelyn,' Nia said.

Gwyn looked at his father, who was staring at him. 'Who says he's my cousin?'

'Mr Llewelyn.'

'What's so special about seeing Emlyn, he lives here, doesn't he?' Alun said accusingly. Nia got the impression that he was trying to defend Gwyn.

'I just thought . . .'

Before she could finish her sentence Mrs Lloyd sang out from the hall, 'Bath, Iolo! Come on!' and bustled in, carrying a bundle of clean clothes.

'Why me first?' Iolo complained, just as he always did.

'You're the youngest! You're the youngest!' the twins chanted, just as they always did.

'Just imagine,' said Catrin. 'You'll be first in the new bath, Iolo!'

That did it.

'Can we get in too?' Changing their tune, the twins rushed out after Iolo and their mother, and the room immediately became a little larger.

'We'd better get going, Gwyn.' Mr Griffiths stood up

and tapped his son on the shoulder. 'We haven't fed the animals.'

'I'll get the dog!' said Mr Lloyd.

Nia thought nothing of her father's words until she heard Fly barking, and then she jumped up crying, 'Dog? You're not taking our dog?'

'She's a good dog,' said Mr Griffiths, 'and not happy here. She'll be better at our place.'

'No! No!' Nia ran into the hall. 'You never said, Dad. You never told me.'

'What's got into you, girl?' her father retorted impatiently. Fly was sitting by the door, ready to go, all neat and alert, like someone going to a new school. 'Mr Griffiths agreed to take the dog if I couldn't find another buyer,' Mr Lloyd went on. 'She can't stay here, can she? No sheep, no field; she's as miserable as sin!'

'But I did find a buyer, Dad! I did! I did!'

'And who is that?'

'Emlyn Llewelyn!'

'Don't be daft, Nia! Fly's a sheep-dog, a good one, too; she needs sheep and a farm.'

'But I promised! I promised!' Nia sobbed. 'I can't break my promise, he'll never forgive me.'

Through her tears she saw her father pass Fly's lead to Mr Griffiths; the door opened; the man and the dog stepped out.

Gwyn Griffiths, following his father, looked back, concerned by Nia's outburst. 'You can come and see her,' he said kindly.

'It's not me that wants to, is it?' Nia snapped.

It wasn't the black door that closed then, it was the bright blue door, with golden flowers on it. How could she go back now? They wouldn't want her without the beads and the violet dress. They wouldn't want her without Fly.

'Everything's gone,' she wailed at the door, though her words were meant for her family. 'I've got nothing left! Nothing, nothing, nothing!'

'Course you have, my love,' said her mother from the stairs. 'You've got us, and you've got a nice new home!'

Mam didn't understand!

3

The Woman in the Moon

'It won't do, will it, Nia Lloyd?'

Mr James slammed Nia's exercise book on to her desk. 'Do you call that writing? My eyes ache with the searching, searching for a word I can read!'

Nia regarded her messy indecipherable letters. It was the best she could do.

'You'd better buck up, girl, or it's back to the nursery class for you, isn't it?' Mr James turned away to silence, with a stare, the sniggering that had broken out behind him. He had taken an aspirin to soothe his toothache but any relief he might have expected had been destroyed by the sight of Nia Lloyd's attempt at writing. It was worse than her reading. Was there nothing she could do? Perhaps his long-cherished Project would stir some latent talent in the poor girl.

Mr James, his shoulders significantly braced, his chest puffed out with promise, strolled back to the front of the classroom, where he swung round on his heel and, smiling through swollen gums, delivered his long-awaited announcement.

'And now for the Project!' Mr James exhaled with optimism. 'I want all of you, *all* of you,' he fixed Nia with a cold blue eye, 'to do for me, a piece of work on our glorious little patch of Wales; our town and environment. Write a story!' He flourished with his left hand. 'Draw a picture, make a painting, compose a song!' Here, several flourishes with his right hand sent papers flying from his desk. Undeterred and in full steam now, Mr James pounded to his climax, 'And at the end of term, we'll have an exhibition, a bit of a show, in the library, for everyone to see.'

If she had dared, Nia would have rested her head on her desk in despair. She could already feel the humiliation that was bound to come when her inevitably messy work was exposed to the world. Mr James was watching her while he rattled on about mountains and monuments, about the Celtic magicians, Gwydion, Math and Gilfaethwy and the heroes of Wales. Nia could not attend to his words. She could neither paint nor draw, her writing was a mess, and she had absolutely no musical talent. Why could he not leave her in peace?

The bell went and she left the classroom with Gwyneth Bowen.

'What are you going to do, Nia?' Gwyneth was full of the Project. There were not many things that Gwyneth could not do. She was Nia's friend, and also her tormentor.

'Don't know,' Nia mumbled.

'It's a pity you can't draw,' Gwyneth said, as they strolled on to the playground. 'It's easier than writing. I'm going to write a story and illustrate it.'

'I expect it will be the best,' Nia said humbly. 'Your work usually is.'

'Yes,' Gwyneth agreed, 'but this time it's going to be fantastic, even for me.'

43

'Well done,' Nia said prematurely. She had noticed a boy detach himself from a group and look in her direction. Emlyn Llewelyn was coming towards them. She had an overwhelming desire to flee from the conversation that would end either with her lying, or with Emlyn turning his back on her for ever. She wanted, so much, to talk to him, and she wanted, above all, to go back to the chapel.

'Hullo, Nia!' Emlyn's voice was casual but his eyes were anxious. 'Did you talk to your dad?'

'Yes!' That, at least, was true!

'What did he say?'

'He . . . he isn't sure.'

'What are you talking about?' Gwyneth disapproved of Emlyn; she didn't know why, unless it was because her mother did, and he didn't go on school trips or wear the special school T-shirt.

'A dog,' Nia explained. 'Emlyn's going to buy our sheep-dog.'

'You can't keep a sheep-dog,' said Gwyneth scornfully. 'You haven't got sheep.'

'We've a field,' Emlyn said quietly.

'Huh!' Gwyneth sauntered away to join more congenial friends.

'Will you come and see us after school?' Emlyn asked. 'Dad wants to finish your portrait, and can you bring Fly?'

'Mam's taken the clothes. She doesn't want me to wear them again.'

'Doesn't matter. Just bring the dog!' Emlyn ran off and was lost in the crowded playground before Nia could reply.

She spent the rest of her break alone. She sauntered round the playground perimeter, pausing to gaze at games that did not interest her. Her mind was racing. How could

44

she get away to the chapel again? Would Emlyn discover her lie too soon? Would Gwyn Griffiths tell? No, he never spoke to Emlyn. And why was that? Why?

Nia was quite incapable of concentrating on the afternoon activities. Fortunately she was blessed with an hour of singing practice, when she could move her mouth in appropriate directions without making a sound, something that did not require a great deal of effort on her part for she was, by now, quite practised at it.

At home her abstraction went unnoticed. There was still so much to be done. So many pieces to fit into new places. The ancient dark furniture, which had seemed so much a part of Tŷ Llŷr, looked awkward and overpowering here. Cupboards obscured windows, tables protruded through doorways, jam-jars mounted the stairs like sentinels – no walk-in larder here – no room for pickled damsons and plum jam at Number 6.

The old dresser seemed to occupy more than half the kitchen. It regarded the family with sadness and disapproval as they sat, squashed in their chairs, beneath its dark brooding presence. But none of them would have been prepared to do without it, for hadn't it been made by Mam's great-great-grandfather Llŷr, a hundred and fifty years ago?

When Nia had helped with the washing-up she informed her mother she was 'going to see Gwyneth for a bit'.

'Which Gwyneth?' Mrs Lloyd inquired.

'Her mam's Mrs Bowen that sells the wool and buttons and stuff like that,' Nia said happily, for this part was all true. 'She said I could go and visit any time. Gwyneth doesn't get on too well with her brother, see, and it'll be nice for her to have company like me!'

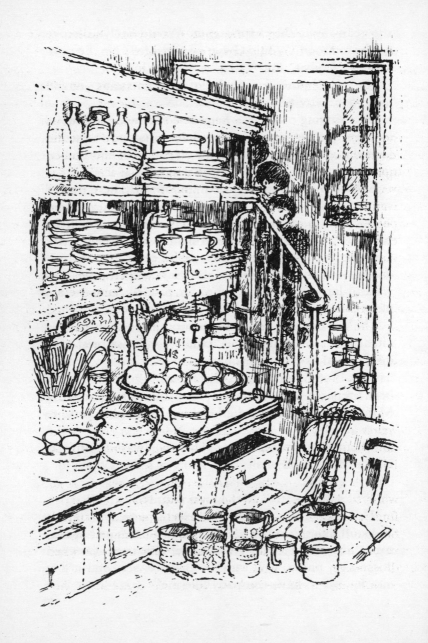

'You're not going to the chapel, are you?' Suddenly doubtful, Mrs Lloyd looked at her daughter.

'Why would I? Fly's gone.'

'Go and fetch your anorak then, the evenings are still cool. And don't be long.'

Nia dashed up to her room, grabbed her anorak from its hook, and ran back to the landing. Here, however, she did not descend the stairs, but slipped off her shoes and tiptoed up to the third floor. The door that stood open before her revealed a room bursting with boxes; the new nursery, waiting to be decorated. Nia opened the second door and peeped into her parents' room. It was filled with their enormous bed. How the bed had reached its lofty, inaccessible position she could not imagine, but there it was, huge and magnificent, with its patterned posts and patchwork cover, taking up all but a few centimetres between the wardrobe and the wall. If she stood on the bed she would be able to reach the tiny scrap of violet that her mother had failed to conceal behind a row of jars on top of the wardrobe.

Nia withdrew her head and listened to the house: Catrin practising scales in the front room; the boys making explosive noises in the throes of a war game; her parents watching television in the kitchen. Nerys had gone to the library, open late on Mondays. There was no one to spy on Nia.

She leapt upon the big bed and stretched upwards. A jar wobbled dangerously and then was still. Nia extended two fingers between the jars; she could feel a piece of material. She gave a little tug; the jars rattled. She tugged again, very gently, and the violet dress slithered past the jars and dropped on to her head.

Nia jumped off the bed and thrust the dress inside her

anorak which she zipped up to her neck. Then she half-ran, half-slithered down the steep and shiny wooden staircase. Pausing on the landing to step into her shoes, she confidently tip-tapped down the second flight of stairs.

She was about to open the front door when her father came out of the kitchen. 'You still here, girl?' he asked, glancing out of the kitchen at her bulging anorak.

'Couldn't find my anorak.' Nia answered.

'Don't go into Llewelyn's chapel, girl,' Mr Lloyd said earnestly. 'No good will come of it.'

'But why, Dad? What's the matter with it?' Nia had to ask.

'Something happened there, didn't it?'

Before Nia could question him further, Mr Lloyd had escaped into his shop.

She opened the front door and stepped out into the quiet street. Bowen's Wool Shop was only three doors away, next to the house where tiny Miss Olwen Oliver turned truants into choirboys, and skinny girls into stars of the opera. Nia decided she would visit Gwyneth, just for a moment, so that if she was questioned later, she could truthfully answer that she had seen her friend.

Gwyneth was not at home and there was no answer to Nia's insistent knocking. She would have to risk a lie.

There was a light in the chapel, but Nia's first timid knock went unheard and, reluctant to intrude, she climbed on to the lowest rung of the pink and gold railings and peeped into the window. Emlyn was kneeling on the floor beside an oil-lamp; he was absorbed in one of his animals, in an attitude of such repose he might have been a statue himself. The only movement came from a small knife in his hand, that flashed now and then, in the lamplight. Mr Llewelyn was nowhere to be seen.

Nia stepped down from the railings, climbed the steps that led to the blue door, and knocked again. The door was opened, a few seconds later, by Emlyn. He seemed pleased to see her. 'What did your dad say about the dog?' he asked.

'He's thinking about it.'

'Good.' Emlyn held the door wider to let her pass.

Nia looked uncertainly at the figure, hunched by a window before his easel.

'Don't worry about him,' Emlyn drew her in and closed the door. 'He's in a bad mood. Work's not going well.' He spoke as though his father were not aware of them.

Nia decided to adopt Emlyn's attitude. 'What's he painting?'

'I don't know – patterns. Someone commissioned it, someone from London. So we'll have a feast when it's finished. They're paying a thousand pounds. I'll get new trainers.'

Nia regarded the worn straps of leather stretched across Emlyn's bare toes. She had thought that he wore sandals from choice. 'Will you have roast beef for your feast?' she asked. 'There's beef hanging in our place, and pigs, all slit open with the blood dripping out.'

A look of horror passed over Emlyn's face. Nia realized how grim her words must have sounded. She hadn't meant to shock; she just wanted to voice her disapproval of Mr Lloyd's new trade.

'We don't eat meat!' Emlyn said.

'I don't like it either,' Nia said quickly. 'It smells, doesn't it?' she added for good measure. 'But I have to eat it, Dad being a butcher an' that.'

Emlyn looked relieved. Nia could not be held responsible for the food that was forced upon her.

'Pwy sydd yna?' The Welsh words came low and weary through the darkening chapel. Nia had almost forgotten Mr Llewelyn.

'It's Nia!' Emlyn said. 'The girl with the dog.' He crouched back on to the floor and picked up his knife.

'Ble mae'r ci? Where is the dog?'

'I – I couldn't bring her today,' Nia grasped for words that would not utterly condemn her when her treachery was discovered.

'And where are the pink shoes that you promised with stardust on them?' Mr Llewelyn's dark features were not fierce. He seemed more like a tired but kindly beast, ambling towards her through his jungle of exotic animals.

'Mam hid them,' Nia said, 'and the hat and the beads. I've brought the dress though.' She unzipped her anorak and proudly displayed her loot.

'It's too dark now,' Emlyn's father sighed and looked over her head. 'What a sky. Like slate it is'

They don't want me, Nia thought; don't need me without the dog. The dress is not enough.

'Have some soup! It's ready!' Emlyn, absorbed in his carving, seemed to make the invitation as a matter of course, rather than a genuine desire for her company.

Undeterred by his indifference, Nia said, 'Yes, please!' and just in case she seemed too eager, 'I didn't have much tea; it was ham, see!'

Mr Llewelyn went to the stove and poured three bowls of soup. It was hot and thick, and rather too green for Nia's liking, but she decided she could get used to it.

They sat cross-legged on the floor to drink their soup, even Mr Llewelyn, and it didn't matter that no one spoke. They didn't grasp for words, search for a subject with which to entertain each other; and Nia felt so comfortable
50

in the silence, she began to wonder at her contentment, and in wondering broke the spell and remembered the Project. She began to cough and couldn't stop until Mr Llewelyn patted her on the back. Even then she still gulped for air, red in the face and breathless.

'Hold on, girl. I'll get you some water!' Emlyn's father went to the sink.

'It isn't just the soup, is it?' Emlyn looked hard at her. 'Something came into your mind to spoil the taste. It does that with me, sometimes. What was the thing that made you cough?'

Nia sipped the water that was handed to her, and while Mr Llewelyn knelt to give them slivers of coarse brown bread, she said, 'It's the Project, Mr James's Project!' And, with a sigh, she unburdened herself and told her hosts of all her problems with Mr James and his desire to exhibit the classroom's work on their environment.

'He's a real pain, that Mr James,' Emlyn remarked sympathetically. 'He's always on about exhibitions; can't leave you alone. I'm glad I'm in Miss Powell's class now.'

'I'm hopeless,' said Nia wistfully. 'They'll all laugh whatever I do. Nia-can't-do-nothing, that's what my brothers call me.'

Mr Llewelyn threw back his head and roared with laughter.

'It's not funny,' Nia said, offended.

'It is, you know.' Mr Llewelyn was still chuckling, but seeing the children's reproachful glances added, 'Not you, though, Nia. It doesn't make sense, you see, Nia-can't-do-nothing. If Nia *can't* do nothing, then Nia *can* do something, see!'

Nia thought she saw, but knowing that her brothers used bad grammar didn't solve her problem.

And then Emlyn repeated, 'Nia-*can*-do-something; everyone can do something!'

'Not me!' Nia said gloomily.

'Don't be so pessimistic. You grow flowers, you said. You can see colours, feel them. I know you can.'

'What d'you do at home, girl?' asked Mr Llewelyn, inspired by his son's enthusiasm. 'Can you knit, make things? What d'you do to help your mam?'

'I darn the socks,' Nia said doubtfully. 'I'm quite good at that, actually!'

'There you are then,' said Mr Llewelyn. 'Sew a picture, make fields and mountains from cloth and cotton.'

'Something silver for the river, tinsel maybe, and wool for the clouds,' Emlyn went on eagerly.

'And flowers,' said Nia. 'Mam's got dusters, bright yellow, and old sheets cut up for rags, but still white as anything. Perhaps I can do it.'

'Of course you can, girl. You've got imagination.' Mr Llewelyn leapt to his feet, and gathered up their empty soup bowls. 'I'll find you a piece of canvas, big enough for a masterpiece, and you can sew your shapes to it.'

He dropped the bowls into the sink and began to search among the empty frames and unfinished paintings that leant against the wall, six or seven deep. Suddenly, in the shifting and searching, one of Emlyn's paintings appeared. Nia found herself looking at a woman hanging in the moon; not hanging, perhaps, but stretching up against the lower half of a crescent, as one might do when clinging to a fairground creature on a roundabout. Her hair was black and her long pale dress floated out and round the moon like a cloud. Nia knew who it was, but all the same she asked, 'Who is that?'

And Emlyn answered, as she knew he would, 'It's my

mam!'

'Did you do it?'

'Yes, I did; after she went, two years ago.'

Nia wanted to ask about the moon and why the woman was hanging there, but the painting vanished under another and Mr Llewelyn stepped towards them with a long roll of something. He held one end and unfurled two metres of dusty canvas, filling the air with tiny lamplit particles that glowed and drifted round their heads.

'Here it is then; the background for your picture, Nia.' Mr Llewelyn laid the canvas beside her and stepped away.

'But it's so big!' Nia exclaimed.

'A masterpiece must be large,' he replied. 'I have a feeling about this canvas,' Emlyn's father went on. 'I think you will find yourself here. But keep it out of sight until it is complete. It must be yours, all yours. If you need help, ask us; no one else. And one day, we will see here the true and special Nia!'

'Thank you!' Nia stood up and stared uncertainly at the huge rectangle at her feet.

'Well, take it, girl!' commanded Idris Llewelyn. 'Roll it up and conceal it somewhere about you.'

'But the dress; I can't hide them both in my anorak.'

'Leave the dress here,' Emlyn suggested, 'and fetch it when you bring the dog. Will it be soon?'

'I expect so.' Nia wished he hadn't mentioned Fly. She was taking their gift under false pretences. She knelt and folded the canvas, tucking it guiltily into her anorak, like a thief who knows he is observed but has gone too far to save himself.

'You look so glum, girl,' Mr Llewelyn remarked. 'Cheer up! This is the beginning. Can you use an iron?'

Nia nodded and got to her feet.

'Iron the creases out of your canvas when no one is about, and then hide it; right?'

'I'll do that,' said Nia. 'I'd better go now, and thank you for the soup and . . . and everything.'

'Damn the sky!' Mr Llewelyn was, once again, preoccupied with his own work. 'The light is going and I should have had another two hours.'

Emlyn followed Nia out of the chapel and began to accompany her down the hill.

'I'll be all right,' Nia said.

'I'll come anyway,' he replied and fell into step beside her.

'What's your mam's name?' Nia asked, hoping to forestall any inquiries about Fly.

'Elinor,' he said.

'That's a beautiful name. Why do you think she's in the moon?'

'She told me!'

And then, without any prompting, Emlyn began to tell Nia of the night his mother left; of the howling wind that tore slates from the chapel roof and sent them banging against the windows; the baby crying and his father roaring in the dark, because there were no lights. 'But I could see them both,' Emlyn said softly, 'the moon was so bright, and my mam was walking up and down and round the wooden animals, pushing at them, like she hated them. I fell asleep while they were still rowing and then, much later, she woke me. She said she was taking the baby and leaving my dad; she wanted me to go with her, but I said no. I couldn't leave my dad, could I? And then she said something. ". . . Yr Hanner Lleuad", the half moon, that's all I heard because of the wind; so I painted her in the moon, in a crescent moon, because that's what she said.
54

But I never told my dad why and he never asked.'

They were no longer walking, but now and again placing one foot in front of the other, until, at last, they stopped moving altogether and Nia said, 'She just went, like that, in the middle of the night?'

'She just went,' he replied.

Nia felt he had left something out, perhaps the most important thing of all; but she had no right to ask any more questions, for she had broken her promise and, even now, when she knew he had probably confided more to her than to anyone, she could not bring herself to tell him the truth about Fly.

The sky was, indeed, like slate; heavy and damp, it pressed all around them, holding the shape of fields and mountains fixed and dark in the distance. Emlyn looked away to a lamplit window at the top of the hill. 'I stood on my bed after she'd gone,' he said, 'and I looked out of the window. There was a Landrover in the road, and a man beside it.'

Nia gasped. 'D'you know who it was?' she asked.

'Yes,' said Emlyn. 'I knew him all right. It was Mr Griffiths, Gwyn's dad. He took my mother away.'

Nia looked hard into his eyes, willing him to smile and tell her that it was not so, not Gwyn's father, but the gaze he steadfastly returned was so grave and so sad that she had to believe him. And then, all at once, he burst out, 'They blame him; blame my dad for driving my mam away. But it's all a lie. She went, didn't she? She didn't have to go. My dad gave her a home, with pictures on the wall and a butterfly ceiling for her baby. She didn't have to go. And they blame me too, for staying. "A boy should go with his mother," they said, but I couldn't, could I? Couldn't leave my dad?'

Emlyn who had seemed so confident, was shaking his head from side to side like a sleepless child, and Nia knew that her answer really mattered. Could she manage, just for once to get it right? 'No,' she said calmly, 'you couldn't leave your dad; he'd be alone.'

Emlyn smiled, almost apologetically, and Nia knew that she had chosen her words wisely.

'I'll come all the way with you tonight,' Emlyn said. 'There are spooks in the air.'

They laughed and then they ran; ran all the way to Number 6, where Emlyn held his nose and made hideous faces at the butcher's dark and empty window, and Nia giggled as she rang the bell. Someone had latched the door. Nerys opened it with a book in one hand. 'I saw your friend Gwyneth in the library,' she said.

'Yes, her dad let me in and I waited!' Nia decided that Gwyneth's father was not likely to frequent libraries. 'We had a great time. Gwyneth's got a new doll's house.'

'She's spoiled,' said Nerys. Her spectacles had slipped to the end of her nose and she didn't see Emlyn, dancing in the street, thumbs in his ears and feet turned out like Charlie Chaplin. 'What're you grinning at, idiot?'

'Nothing,' Nia replied. She followed her sister into the house and turned to give Emlyn a secret signal of farewell.

Emlyn had stopped dancing. He was staring into the hall, listening to the cheerful sounds beyond: the singing, shouting and laughter. He reminded Nia of a hungry, golden-eyed animal, searching for warmth.

She hated closing the door.

4
A
Fight

It was a cold night. The grey clouds drifted south and the moon sailed out, bright and startling from behind the mountains. Falling through frosted glass, it filled the yellow bathroom with soft light and Nia, sleepless with impatience, knew that she had found a safe and secret place to do her work.

Iolo was not easily disturbed from sleep; his face was pressed against his blue monster and his breathing was calm and even as his sister crawled beneath her bed to retrieve the canvas from its hiding place. Nevertheless she tiptoed through the door and dared not shut it tight behind her.

Beside the bath, in the brightest patch of moonlight, Nia spread her canvas and gazed at it. She had managed to iron it in the tiny upstairs room, on the board her mother had left unattended while she ran Iolo's bath. Nia stroked the rough surface and screwed up her eyes, silently demanding the canvas to show her where and how to begin. A huge rectangle of dull brown stared back at her, giving no advice, no encouragement.

Once again, the hateful and familiar feeling of hopelessness began to overwhelm Nia. She sank back on her heels, numb with disappointment. She was not what they thought after all. She could not see shapes and colours where they did not exist. She was not gifted with imagination. The Llewelyns had burdened her with a talent she did not possess. They expected too much.

Motionless, she crouched on the cold floor until the church clock struck twice. The lonely, hollow sound made her shiver. It was time to put away the masterpiece that would never be.

A wisp of cloud passed across the moon; the long dress of a lady in the sky. A shadow covered the canvas like a ghost and, when it had gone, a faint shape appeared beside Nia's cold hand where it touched the frayed edge. The pale form gathered strength and colour, it became a roof, dark grey, with a chimney in the centre. Another roof emerged beside the first, dark red this one, with a curl of smoke drifting from the chimney-pot. The lower edge of the canvas began to fill with imaginary shapes and colours. Nia was so excited she ran to the bedroom, crashing the door back against Iolo's toy box. The rhythm of her brother's quiet breathing changed, but he did not wake.

Nia opened a cupboard and took out her sewing basket. She found a large needle, scissors, and a ball of soft grey wool. Terrified that the picture in her mind would evaporate before she could commit it to canvas, she rushed back to the bathroom, slipped on the shiny floor, and crashed into a stool, sending it spinning into the bath. In the silent house, the noise seemed deafening. For a whole minute Nia waited, frozen, against the wall. When she had assured herself that she had not woken her family she knelt beside her canvas and began to thread the needle. This done, she made three tiny stitches in the material. She paused to consider, then made a long stitch, then a curve.

Nia teased the wool with the sharp end of her needle and pale grey, drifting smoke appeared.

'Oh!' she sighed, surprised and delighted by her achievement.

'Nia?'

Someone had been disturbed after all. Catrin stood in the open doorway.

'Can't you sleep?'

It was too late to hide the canvas. 'Something woke me!' Nia said.

'What's that on the floor?'

'Nothing – just a piece of stuff I found; I'm . . . I'm sewing on it. Please don't tell.'

'I won't tell, but you'd better go to bed now or you'll never wake up in the morning.' Kind Catrin never scolded.

Nia smiled and rolled up her work. She had begun. Nothing mattered now. The smoke was there and it would remain. Tomorrow there would be a chimney and a roof and perhaps pink blossom on a tree. 'I'll sleep now,' she said happily.

Catrin followed Nia to her room and smoothed the pillow. 'You're a funny one,' she said as Nia climbed into bed.

'I'm glad it wasn't Nerys who found me,' Nia whispered.

'I bet you are!' Catrin began to tidy the rumpled sheets. Before she had finished, Nia was asleep.

There began a week of feverish activity for Nia. Scraps of cotton, corduroy and velvet were begged from her mother and retrieved from rag-bags, boxes and bottom drawers. Christmas paper, tinsel and ribbons were carefully

acquired from friends and neighbours. Gwyneth Bowen
came up trumps and donated a whole box of shop-soiled
wool and her mother's tired satin petticoat. She didn't
even ask what they were for.

All these precious bits Nia hoarded, mouse-like, in
plastic bags beneath her bed. And no one guessed, no one
asked, no one wanted to know what she was up to!

Luckily Mrs Lloyd had never been a great one for
'doing out' bedrooms, and the hoard grew undisturbed,
until there was scarcely enough room for the canvas which
Nia rolled with great care every night, after she had
smoothed bits of material, snipped loose threads and
ensured that glue was dry.

She forgot about Fly and her broken promise. Her mind
was filled with the colour and complexion of the world
about her; the intensity of shadows, shades of the sky, the
brilliance of flowers and curving shapes of trees. She was
completely enthralled by her new occupation, though she
managed to chat to Gwyneth and play hopscotch while
counting windows.

And then, one day, when the canvas lay safe and secret
under her bed, already half-filled with patches, Nia was
forced to remember Fly. She was standing in the middle of
the playground, gazing up, through half-closed eyes, at a
giant yew in the churchyard beyond the school wall.

She was hardly aware of the activity about her, until
someone began to approach and Emlyn Llewelyn broke
through a hazy foreground.

I can ask him about the yew, she thought; he'll know if
it's green or black. But when she had made sense of his
expression she realized that she could ask him nothing. He
had discovered her treachery.

When he knew he had Nia's attention, Emlyn stood

very still; his golden eyes were dangerous and his words quiet and cold.

'Why didn't you tell me about the dog?'

'I didn't know . . . I wasn't sure, I . . . I couldn't . . .'

'You promised!'

Nia shook her head hopelessly. 'My dad did it. I told him about . . . about you, wanting the dog an' all, but it was too late!'

'You let *them* have it, and you never told me!' Emlyn's voice began to rise.

A crowd of children, sensing conflict, gathered closer.

'Why Gwyn Griffiths? Why not me? You knew I wanted the dog. You knew how much I wanted her.'

Nia looked away from him. She had been prepared for anger; it was his humiliation that she could not endure.

'Look at me,' Emlyn cried, and, turning, Nia saw his hand go to his pocket and pull out a strip of leather. 'I even bought a lead. Stupid, wasn't it? A lead and no dog. I don't need it now, do I?'

Emlyn raised his arm. For a moment the strip of leather hung innocently from his hand and then, suddenly, it came snaking towards Nia as she stood awaiting her punishment.

But someone stepped in front of her and Nia heard gasps of horror and delight as the hard leather struck Gwyn Griffiths in the face. An angry red mark appeared on his cheek and he walked towards Emlyn, holding the lead tight in his hand.

Emlyn stood his ground for a moment, angry and unrepentant, then he turned and ran.

Gwyn pursued him slowly at first, but as Emlyn approached the low playground wall, Gwyn gathered speed. Emlyn flung himself at the wall and tumbled over

61

into the narrow lane between the churchyard and the playground. Gwyn followed only seconds after, and Nia found that she was running too, knowing that whatever was going to happen would be her fault.

'Nia Lloyd, where are you going?' called Miss Powell, on duty by the climbing frame and more concerned with death-defying five-year-olds than Nia Lloyd's flight. She hadn't even noticed the boys.

'You'll catch it when you get back!' someone called as Nia fell, breathless, into the stony lane.

She caught sight of Gwyn turning on to the path that led to the churchyard and stumbled after him. Her mind was racing her feet and they would not obey her. She could not keep her balance; twice she tripped and crashed on to the stones. 'You'll catch it!' warned the sing-song voices, Gwyneth Bowen's louder than the rest.

Nia reached a swinging wrought-iron gate. The voices faded. She hesitated. Beyond lay the graveyard; not her favourite place. It was dark with ancient trees; a place where long ago, before any church was built, men had prayed to gods other than the one she knew.

She braced herself and passed through the gate. A shroud of trees enveloped her as she walked down the avenue, soft with moss and weeds. She watched and listened for signs of battle, but there were none. Perhaps the two boys had parted without a fight, yet she could not believe it.

There were five yews in the churchyard, all of them a thousand years old, so it was said, and Nia could believe it. Their hollow trunks were scarred and dusty, their branches of dark needles bent and cracked. Mysterious trees, sacred and poisonous.

She left the path and allowed herself to be drawn further

out into the maze of older graves; into a place inhabited by
phantoms whose names could not be read, and where the
yews trailed damp fingers over decaying stones. The
feeling of unseen and mysterious power never left her, and
she wondered why Emlyn had chosen such a retreat.

On a patch of dead ground, beneath the furthest,
darkest tree, Nia saw the boys. Or rather she saw one
form, circling slowly. They were closed in combat, their
tangled arms embracing, their legs hardly moving. The
black head tight against the brown and their bodies
pushing, unremittingly, one against the other. And then
one boy broke free, Emlyn, and he began to beat his
adversary with desperate and deadly fists.

Gwyn reeled back, defending himself with upraised
arms. Emlyn was the taller and more powerful boy, but

Nia sensed a strength about Gwyn that could withstand
and even overcome the other. And she remembered that
strange time two years ago, when Gwyn had inflicted a
terrible injury on fat Dewi Davis, no one knew how. They
said a stone had been thrown and broken Dewi's nose, but
Nia had seen no stone; she believed Gwyn had a power
that could not be named; once, he had called himself a
magician.

The magician was kneeling now, shielding his head with
his hands. Emlyn seized him by the shoulders and would
have thrown him over, but something happened. The
kneeling boy seemed to lose his shape, or change it.

Emlyn stepped back, his eyes fixed on Gwyn, utterly
astonished; and he kept on stepping back until he was
almost lost in the gloom beneath the tree. And when he

stopped moving the two boys were frozen in a great bowl of nothingness where no birds sang, no leaves fell, and even dust was motionless. And Nia was standing on the very edge, breathing, but only just. She wanted to scream, but something was strangling sound.

Then Gwyn stood up, his arms raised, fingers stretched wide, like a cat spreading its claws. A boy who was not a boy, but a part of the magic in the sacred yews and of the ageless shadows beneath them. All the dark power that still dwelt in the graveyard seemed to have gathered into his hands.

And then he let it go. His arms dropped to his sides, and something fell away from him, an unseen mantle that he had borrowed from the air in a moment of need.

Emlyn, released, sprang forward and felled his enemy with one blow.

He ran past Nia, scarcely seeing her. The victor. But his face showed repentance and when he reached the path, she thought she heard a sob.

Gwyn got to his feet, rubbing his head. An ordinary boy who had been hurt, but Nia still felt in awe of him. She walked towards him, meaning to thank him for defending her, but instead she asked, 'Why did you let him beat you?'

'He's stronger,' Gwyn said.

'No he isn't! You can do things to the air. It's frightening!'

Gwyn gave her a sly look, the sort of look he usually reserved for Alun. She felt privileged.

'Emlyn had to win,' was all he said.

Nia understood. 'He is your cousin, isn't he?' She looked sideways at him.

Gwyn sighed. 'Yes, he's my cousin. But he hates me,

and it isn't just the dog.' He closed his eyes and rubbed his forehead. 'There's something wrong between our families.'

'Your father stole his mother!' Nia said quietly.

'That's not true!' he sounded angry, but astonished at the solution to an old and painful puzzle. 'It can't be true . . . ' his voice trailed off and then he added softly, 'I didn't know. Why didn't he tell me?' and then again, 'It's not true!'

Nia was glad that he hadn't known; hadn't been part of the plot. 'It is true,' she said. 'The way Emlyn told it to me . . . he couldn't have made it up!'

They began to walk towards the church, their feet making no sound on the damp yew needles.

'My dad's secretive,' Gwyn murmured, 'he's deep, but he always has a reason. Where did he take Emlyn's mam then?'

'Emlyn says she's in the moon.'

Gwyn didn't laugh, he just said, 'She was my Auntie Elinor. She was beautiful and very special to Bethan.'

'Your sister?'

'Yes; she went . . .'

Nia thought he was going to tell her where, but he continued, ' . . . nearly five years ago. Disappeared. And then my Auntie Elinor,' Gwyn was almost speaking to himself. 'They'd just come back from somewhere, the Llewelyns; France, I think it was. Emlyn was born out there, I didn't know him. Bethan really took to Elinor, they used to plant seeds together, and pick wild flowers and press them in a book. Then, in November, Bethan went, just after Halloween. We didn't see much of the Llewelyns after that. Dad was, well, sick or something. And soon after, Auntie Elinor went away and Dad told me

66

my Uncle Idris was wicked and I was never to speak to him or Emlyn again, they weren't relations any more.'

'Emlyn isn't wicked!' Nia said.

Gwyn shrugged. 'I've gone to the same school,' he said, 'and I've sat in the same room, and since then I've never spoken to him till today.'

'Did you speak today?'

Gwyn frowned. 'No,' he said, surprised by his answer. 'But we fought and that's like speaking, in a way.'

'It was my fault, all of it!' Nia said.

'No it wasn't. I had to defend you, and myself. I had to pay him back for being mad, he expected it.'

They were on the path now, and leaving the trees. The playground was near but unusually quiet. They had almost reached the churchyard gate when Nia found the courage to ask, 'Gwyn, you told us once that you were a magician. Are you one?'

He sighed, thrust his hands deep into his pockets and looked up at the sky. 'Yes,' he said, 'but don't talk about it. It's not always an advantage, being a magician! I have to hide it. It's getting stronger in me, and sometimes I'm afraid I'll get it wrong; do something, in a moment, without thinking, and then . . . !'

Fearing he had said too much, Gwyn waited for a scornful response. None came. Remembering what had happened beneath the yew, Nia was overawed, and did not know what to say. But instinct told her that Gwyn's power would never hurt Emlyn again.

Beside the gate they saw the dog's lead, where Gwyn had dropped it. He picked it up. 'What shall I do with this?' he muttered.

'Keep it,' Nia said. 'Perhaps you can give it back one day.'

Gwyn put the lead in his pocket. 'Fly might have pups,' he said thoughtfully.

They emerged into sunlight and Nia saw clearly the red stripe across Gwyn's cheek where the leather had lashed it.

'Does your face hurt?' she asked.

'Not much!'

'What are you going to say about the mark?'

'I'll say I had a fight with Nia Lloyd and she beat me!' He laughed and then he ran down the lane away from her.

They soon discovered why the playground was so quiet. In spite of Miss Powell's vigilance, the climbing frame had claimed a victim: one of the Lloyd twins, Gareth, lay moaning on the ground.

5
The
Curtain

Iolo rushed to Nia, when he saw her. 'Where've you been? I wanted you. Gareth's hurt!' he cried.

Before Nia could reply, Siôn was pulling at her skirt and yelling, 'Where've you been? Gareth's had an accident!'

'I can see that,' Nia said sharply. 'I wasn't far away – I'm here now. What happened?'

'He was balancing,' Siôn said proudly. 'It was great. Right on top he was! Miss Powell yelled at him to come down. He'd have been all right if she hadn't yelled.'

Miss Powell was in a bit of a state. She seemed unable to decide whether to scold, comfort or assist the stricken boy. Then Mr James arrived and took control of the situation. He gently felt all Gareth's limbs, picked him up and carried him into the school.

A crowd of children respectfully made way for the patient's relatives. Alun, Nia, Siôn and Iolo, wearing suitably funereal expressions, followed Mr James and their brother. Nia wished that Nerys and Catrin were with them, and not half a mile away at the High School.

Doctor Vaughan arrived and only minutes later, Mrs Lloyd. Gareth was whisked off to hospital, accompanied by his mother. The other Lloyds returned to their separate classrooms, amid sympathetic murmurs from their friends.

'Is it fatal?' Gwyneth inquired in a solemn whisper.

Nia did not deign to reply.

The anxiety that she betrayed when she returned home was misinterpreted by her mother.

Mrs Lloyd had left the hospital, reassured that broken limbs were all the rage for eight-year-old boys.

'Don't fret, cariad. It's only a broken leg. It'll soon mend,' she said when Nia, tears springing to her eyes, had misplaced a glass and let it smash on to the tiled kitchen floor.

Nia felt guilty. Her thoughts were not with Gareth. Emlyn hadn't returned to school that afternoon. Where had he gone and why? He had won a fight, but she could not forget the desolate look on his face when he had passed her, and she could not forget the way Gwyn Griffiths had frozen life in the dim space under the yews, or the red mark on his cheek that should have been on hers.

When she took her canvas to the bathroom that night, there was no moon. The street lamp was bright enough but her picture looked somehow dead in artificial light. She found green corduroy for the yew trees, but couldn't remember their shape, and there was not enough of Alun's old grey socks to make a church.

'I can't do it! I can't do it!' She muttered angrily at the canvas. Nia-can't-do-nothing, who had been absent for a week, was peering over her shoulder, clutching at her hands. She needed to see Emlyn and his father, to ask for their advice and encouragement. Would they ever speak to her again?

When she replaced the canvas under her bed she had not added one stitch to it. Nor did she add any the following

70

night. Emlyn had not been in school.

On the third evening after Gareth's accident, Nia slipped into the boys' bedroom when it was empty, and took a new grey sock from Gareth's drawer.

'He'll only need one now,' she told herself.

That night she tried to cut it into the shape of a church. The frayed pieces stretched and fell apart. Nia sat in the bathroom, glaring at her unfinished collage, remembering that Gareth had not lost a leg but merely broken one. She snipped the grey sock into tiny shreds and flushed them down the lavatory.

'There's something in the toilet,' Nerys complained next morning at breakfast. 'It's grey and it won't flush away.'

'Worms!' said Siôn with relish.

'You're a worm, worm!' Nerys retorted.

'It's a rag – just a rag,' Nia said quickly. 'All cut up.'

'Oh, Nia!' Mrs Lloyd, distracted from scraping burnt toast into the pedal bin, let her foot slip and sooty crumbs flew everywhere. 'Now look what you've made me do. I've told you not to throw things down the toilet.'

Nia wondered if there'd be a hole in the toast after her mother's attack. 'I thought it would go down if I cut it up,' she said meekly.

'Now then, girl. You know better than that. We don't want trouble with the drains again,' said Mr Lloyd, scrubbing his butcher's fingers extra hygienically in the sink.

Emlyn was in school for the first time since the fight. He wouldn't even look in Nia's direction.

She decided to postpone making the church and concentrate on trees, but she didn't know how to make blossom. And then she remembered something.

Catrin had a music lesson after school that evening, with Miss Olwen Oliver, always called Olwen to distinguish her from her sister Enid Oliver who ran the bakery and took boarders.

'Can I come with you to Miss Olwen Oliver?' Nia asked her sister.

'Whatever for?'

'I like listening to you play.'

Nia had tried music lessons but had proved unmusical, as Miss Oliver put it.

'What a good idea!' Mrs Lloyd said brightly. Perhaps they had started Nia on a musical career too early. Perhaps, after all, she had talent. 'I'm sure Miss Olwen Oliver wouldn't mind. Nia could sit quietly at the back of the room: it's such a big room, you wouldn't even notice her.'

'Well . . . ' Catrin's blue eyes widened uncertainly.

'Please?' Nia begged.

Gentle Catrin was persuaded.

Ten minutes later Nia found herself sitting exactly where she wanted: at the end of Miss Oliver's long chair-lined music room. The chairs were all of a different size and age, acquired on separate occasions as Miss Oliver's fame and fortune progressed; very few were comfortable. The faded, floral wallpaper was bare except for black-framed certificates and photographs of successful music students at local Eisteddfodau. Apart from the two black pianos and a smell of fish, that was it.

The fish smell was a mystery. Miss Oliver was not even a Roman Catholic and, as far as anyone knew, did hardly enough shopping to keep a bird alive. She was a tiny woman, her face a triangle of carved ivory, with pointed nose and chin, and deep-set black eyes. Her hair, plaited

and coiled neatly into the nape of her neck, had been white for so long even *she* could barely remember what colour it had been. All these features paled into insignificance behind Miss Olwen Oliver's truly magnificent eyebrows; long, black and shaggy, they dominated her every expression, controlled every situation, disciplined every six-foot chorister. No one crossed swords with Miss Oliver's eyebrows, if they could help it.

Nia had no intention of taking up piano lessons again; the experience had been far too painful.

Miss Oliver had welcomed her in with a rather predatory gleam, and allowed her to choose a chair. 'Not too close to the piano, now, or it'll be a distraction for Catrin, who is to take an examination soon, isn't she?'

So Nia chose a chair beside the window, as far from the
piano as possible. There was a lace curtain in the window,
real lace, a beautiful creamy white, like plum blossom.
The scalloped hem of the curtain hung a good ten
centimetres below the window!

Nia took a pair of tiny sewing scissors out of her skirt
pocket. Catrin and her teacher were concentrating on
Mozart. It was a very beautiful sonata; it reminded Nia of
the music Catrin had played at Tŷ Llŷr. Nia had made her
dolls dance under the window where the plum trees made
green patches on the thick white wall.

Snip! Snip! Snip! She had severed half the hem of the
lace curtain. It was all she needed but the other half looked
odd now. She cut to the end of the hem, taking her time
and carefully following the curves in the lace. How

beautifully the patterns parted, how prettily the scalloped hem brushed the window-sill. She'd done Miss Oliver a favour. Nia slipped the strip of deliciously soft lace into her pocket.

Catrin's music lessons always ended with a small display by Miss Oliver, just to show that, whatever level of excellence her pupils had attained, there was still a long way to go before perfection was achieved.

Almost on cue, Catrin's friend, Mary McGoohan rang the bell on the last note of Miss Oliver's final flourish.

'Shall I open the door for you?' Nia offered.

'There's a kind girl,' tiny Miss Oliver turned and gave a neat smile. 'Perhaps you'd like to have lessons again, Nia?'

'Perhaps.' Nia didn't linger. She was out of the music room and opening the front door before Miss Oliver had closed her trim lips.

'I thought you'd given up the piano, Nia?' said Mary McGoohan.

'I have!' Nia leapt past her and would have run to Number 6 but, remembering to appear calm, waited for Catrin and walked sedately beside her.

Catrin always sang after her music lesson; her voice was very sweet and soothing. There was no one Nia would rather be with. Catrin was restful and undemanding. One day she would be a star, Nia was sure of that; she was tall and golden, like the girl in a picture on the library wall, painted by a fifteenth-century Italian. Catrin was understanding, she never asked questions. Today, however, she did.

'Are you sleeping better now, Nia?'

'Oh yes!' They had reached Number 6. 'That is, more or less,' Nia said cautiously. She opened the black and private door, rushed across the hall and up the stairs to her room.

Iolo's cars were coming for her in single file across the floor, Iolo behind them, making appropriate revving noises. 'Where've you been?' he muttered through the revs.

'Music lesson!' Nia replied. She had expected him to be watching television. Now she couldn't hide the lace in her scrap bags. She stood as close as she could to the chest of drawers, opened the top drawer a fraction and took the lace from her pocket.

'What're you doing?'

'Getting a hanky,' Nia said irritably. She had never known Iolo to be so interested in her movements.

From the bottom of the stairs, Nerys called, 'Tea!' and Iolo, always eager to have first choice of whatever was on the table, leapt up and ran out of the room.

Nia tucked the stolen lace under a pile of white socks and followed him.

It was cold roast beef for tea: Sunday left-overs. Mrs Lloyd put a slice on Nia's plate. The meat stared up at Nia; it was pink in the middle and Nia found herself saying, 'No thanks!'

'What?' her mother didn't seem to understand.

'I don't want any meat, thank you,' Nia said.

'Are you ill, cariad?' Mrs Lloyd's children had never turned down cold roast beef before.

'No, I'm not ill, I'm a vegetarian!' Nia pushed her plate away.

'What?' Her mother stared at her stupidly, her mouth hanging open like a fish.

'I'm a vegetarian,' Nia repeated. '*I don't like meat!*'

The silence that followed reminded her of the time

Uncle Maldwyn and Auntie Ann had died, he under his tractor and she an hour later of heart failure. They were nearly eighty but it had still been a shock. Being a vegetarian was surely not so shocking?

The boys began to giggle; Catrin looked embarrassed; Nerys had a sort of 'I told you so' expression on her face. And then the atmosphere dissolved abruptly as a menacing rumble crescendoed from the end of the table and Mr Lloyd leapt up roaring, 'By God . . . By God, girl. We'll have no vegetarians here. Meat's my trade!' Here his voice accidentally slipped into a higher register and he had to bang the table to emphasise his words. 'Meat! Meat! Meat! Meat!' he squeaked.

Alun's restrained giggle went inwards and he snorted, piggily. Siôn choked on his orange juice and Iolo laughed out loud.

Nia hunched herself over the table, too close to the pink-tinged slice of meat. She couldn't foresee how it would all end, and then the doorbell rang, precipitating her into an even worse situation.

Somehow she knew the identity of their visitor even before her mother opened the front door, and when she heard Miss Oliver's shrill accusations her heart sank.

Mrs Lloyd called Nia into the hall. Her nose was twitching uncontrollably when she left the table and went to face the music.

'Why?'

'Why? Why? Why?' That was all the two women seemed capable of uttering.

And Nia couldn't reply. She couldn't explain why she had severed the beautiful creamy hem from the lace curtain.

The music teacher was in the hall now, her words

coming fast and hysterical. Her tight figure, a tiny rod of pent-up fury. She was literally hopping.

Mr Lloyd came out of the kitchen and the boys filled the open doorway behind him. Nerys spread her arms and blocked their passage. Catrin, anxious and bewildered, appeared beside her sister.

Nia backed to the stairs. Someone had told her to fetch the lace. Invisible mending had been mentioned. Punishments were suggested. Abject apologies were made. Nia knew all this though she scarcely heard the words through the dull ache in her head. And then she remembered something. She stood on the second stair and said, 'It was like trees!'

The three adults stared at her.

'What?' said Mr Lloyd at last. 'What did you say, girl?'

'Trees!' Nia repeated in a small voice. 'It was like blossom, you see. And I needed it!'

'Needed it?' Her father was roaring now.

More words, loud and angry, were coming at her like bullets and she fled up to her room. She took the lovely lace from her drawer and brushed it against her cheek. Even now, even when it was the cause of all the wrathful sounds beneath, she was reluctant to part with it. But she took it downstairs and held it out to Miss Oliver.

'What do you say, girl?' her father muttered.

'I say I'm sorry,' Nia said.

'And are you? Are you?' Miss Oliver's beetle eyebrows closed above her nose.

'Yes!' Nia murmured dutifully, and abandoned her parents to a task that was beyond her.

A phrase of her father's rose distinctly above the apologetic noises that she left behind; a description of herself. 'She's always been a problem but, I don't know

78

she seems to be getting worse . . . going up to that chapel
. . . cutting up new socks, we think . . . '

Nia closed her bedroom door and went to the window.
She watched the sparks in Morgan-the-Smithy's window.
She listened to his sons singing as though there was
nothing in the whole wide world to worry about.

She was not sorry for herself and regretted nothing but
the trouble she might have caused Catrin. She had
forgotten Catrin when she had cut Miss Oliver's lace,
forgotten that poor Catrin would have to face Miss Oliver
every week, remembering Nia's crime.

Nia opened her drawer and took out the tiny packet of
seeds: honesty, campion and poppy. She let them roll over
her palm while she remembered the garden at Tŷ Llŷr: the
brilliance of the poppies and the soft whiteness of the plum
trees in spring.

Later, when her mother came into the room, Nia was
still sitting on her bed, clasping the seeds.

Mrs Lloyd sat on Iolo's bed, facing her daughter. She
picked up Iolo's woolly blue monster and smoothed its
hair. She seemed to be waiting for a word to come from
somewhere to bring them closer but when that did not
happen, she got up and sat beside Nia on her bed. She was
breathing rather fast and the baby under her smock looked
very round and almost unreal. Nia was just wondering if
the baby would come soon when her mother asked, 'Is it
the baby, my love?'

'Baby?' Nia turned to her in surprise.

'Are you worried about us having another baby?'

'Oh no! I'm very pleased. I'm sure I'll like it,' Nia said,
as enthusiastically as she could.

'Is it Tŷ Llŷr then? Would you like to go back?'

'That's impossible.'

'No, it isn't, actually! We've had an idea, see. You know it's half term next week? Well, Alun's going to stay with Gwyn and Mrs Griffiths suggested that you should go too, and Iolo.'

Banished! But what a lucky banishment! 'Up to Tŷ Bryn?' Nia could scarcely believe it.

'Would you like that?'

'They don't mind?'

'Of course not. Mrs Griffiths asked specially; she wanted to help me out. I'm going to be so busy with Gareth and his leg when he comes home from hospital.'

Alun was a frequent overnight guest at the Griffiths' farmhouse, but Nia had never stayed. She had a sneaking feeling that it was her mother who had begged a favour, to keep her out of trouble. She did not care how the situation had come about. She would be going back to the mountain again. She could walk down to Tŷ Llŷr and care for her garden. 'What about punishment?' she asked. Surely life could not be so pleasant, not after what she had done.

'No pocket money for a month, your father says! We'll have to pay Mrs Bowen for invisible mending.' Mrs Lloyd sounded almost apologetic. 'And . . . and could you keep from being a vegetarian while you're with the Griffithses. We'll discuss it when you come home.'

'There's nothing to discuss, I just am one,' Nia said. 'But I can be tactful, you know!'

The lace was never mentioned again and Catrin, such a talented pianist and singer, was never reproached for her sister's crime. Prodigies are sensitive and Miss Oliver knew that any deterioration in her favourite pupil's performance would only reflect badly on herself.

6

Cold Flowers

Mr Griffiths came to collect Alun, Nia and Iolo the following Saturday afternoon.

Iolo wanted to take two toy boxes, but having been persuaded that Gwyn would happily share his possessions, took only his blue monster.

Nia rolled her canvas in brown paper and tucked a small bag of scraps into a holdall that already contained a muddle of sweaters, socks and underwear.

'What've you got there girl? Not a rolling pin? My wife's fussy about her pastry!' Mr Griffiths laughed at his own joke as no one else seemed inclined to do so.

'It's my work,' Nia explained gravely. 'Something I have to do for school.'

'I see.' Mr Griffiths was a little disconcerted by Nia's sober expression. He was aware of her crime and hoped she wasn't going to be a problem.

Alun was already in the Landrover, chatting eagerly to Gwyn. He glanced resentfully at Nia and Iolo when they climbed in beside him. He had never had to share Gwyn with anyone, and regarded the Griffiths' home as his own, and a refuge from his siblings.

Left-behind Lloyds spilled out of the door on to the

81

pavement, waving and shouting instructions as the Landrover pulled away from the kerb, even Gareth with his plastered leg and Mr Lloyd in his striped butcher's apron and funny white hat. Nia wished her father had stayed indoors.

She had to take deep breaths in order to contain her excitement as the Landrover changed gear and began to ascend the hill out of Pendewi. And then they passed the chapel. She was sitting with her back to it, but she could not resist turning to look into the windows. There was no one there.

Mr Griffiths drove fast; he resented every minute away from his farm. Gwyn called his father 'demon-driver' and Nia wondered if the name implied talents other than fast driving. He had, after all, fathered a magician.

They were swinging up a familiar lane now. It rose steep and twisting between hedges sprinkled with hawthorn stars and green buds that would soon be honeysuckle. The windows were open and Nia inhaled the indescribable scent of new growth, of earth disturbed by movement and the sun. Beside the hedge golden celandine were opening and the brook glittered with melting mountain snow. There were crows and curlews tilting in the air and everywhere the great and mysterious rushing of bright grass towards the sky.

'There's Tŷ Llŷr!' Gwyn said.

'Tŷ Llŷr! Tŷ Llŷr!' shouted Iolo.

And Nia smiled, light-headed now and incapable of speech. She glimpsed white blossom, a deserted yard and two pigeons on a window sill. Later, she would come and leave a stale crust that Mrs Griffiths would surely give her.

They passed the white cottage where Gwyn's strange grandmother lived, with tall plants in every window and a garden full of herbs. Round another bend and then the Landrover was bouncing off the lane and up the stone track beside Tŷ Bryn, a farmhouse much neater than Tŷ Llŷr; the porch freshly painted, the path free of weeds, and flowers beside the stone walls, confined in neat pebble-edged borders.

Gwyn's mother was waiting by the front door; a shy woman with soft brown hair and eyes to match. She never said much but she had always been kind. She took Iolo's bundle and would have taken both of Nia's, but Nia clung to her roll of canvas and said she was quite strong enough to carry her bag, thank you!

Inside the house, everywhere was clean and tidy, warm and bright. Wherever we live, us Lloyds, it will never be as neat as this, Nia thought. And yet this was where a magician lived.

Gwyn and Alun raced up two flights of stairs to Gwyn's attic room, where they would sleep side by side and share their private thoughts, once again.

Nia and Iolo followed Mrs Griffiths at a more respectful pace, Iolo chewing his monster's arm and looking apprehensive.

They were shown into a room where forget-me-not curtains fluttered in a window and three rag dolls with faded cheeks and button eyes sat on a white dressing-table. Dolls that looked as though they had been loved once but now were all forlorn because the person who had loved them had left them.

'It was my Bethan's room, Gwyn's sister, you know,' Mrs Griffiths explained, while Nia stared at the dolls.

Nia was to sleep in a bed covered in bright patchwork, Iolo on a mattress beside her.

'Can I go now?' said Iolo, more interested in the

outdoors than in bedrooms.

'Of course,' Mrs Griffiths smiled. 'I'll unpack your things, Iolo. We'll put your monster on the bed, shall we? There are white rabbits in the orchard.'

'Aww!' Iolo rushed out. He wouldn't leave his monster though.

'Are they wild?' Nia asked.

'Wild?' Mrs Griffiths looked confused.

'The rabbits!' Nia had a vision of Iolo chasing thistledown.

'Oh, no!' Mrs Griffiths laughed. 'They're in a hutch. We couldn't have them out and eating our lettuces, could we?'

'I suppose not,' Nia said solemnly. 'I'll unpack Iolo's

things. I'd like to.'

'Well, if you want.' Mrs Griffiths hesitated. 'I'll go back to my cooking. I'm not used to cooking for so many. I hope I get it right, cariad.'

Nia liked that. She liked the word 'cariad'. It made her feel at home. 'I expect you will,' she said, with a smile she had been told was the best part of her.

Quite unexpectedly Mrs Griffiths put her arms round Nia and hugged her quickly. 'It's good to have a girl in the house,' she said.

Nia, taken by surprise, murmured, 'I'll try . . . ' but did not know how to finish the sentence, and said instead, 'Could I go down to Tŷ Llŷr and see my garden?'

'Well, of course, cariad.' Mrs Griffiths, a neat plastic-aproned housewife again, rushed out. 'And visit Gwyn's Nain,' she called from the stairs. 'She'd be pleased to see you.'

Gwyn's grandmother doesn't know me, Nia thought. 'And I'm not going into that poky planty place alone,' she said to the rag dolls.

The dolls looked sympathetic. They watched Nia unpack her bag and open a drawer in the dressing-table. A dry sweet smell wafted out: roses! Nia opened the wardrobe. There were clothes inside: another girl's clothes; a yellow skirt, a grey coat and a blue dress with flowers on it. She began to remember someone: a girl with dark hair and eyes very like herself; a girl in a blue dress picking flowers in the lane. The wardrobe smelt of roses too.

Bethan's room softly enclosed her, settled smoothly and easily around her, as though she fitted exactly into a space in the dust that had been occupied, only a moment before, by someone else.

Nia unpacked Iolo's bag and began to lay his clothes in the second drawer, but seeing her reflection in the mirror, paused to loosen her long plaits of dark hair. The girl that now looked out at her belonged in a room with forget-me-not curtains, and the scent of roses. The rag dolls smiled with approval.

She closed the drawer, took one happy look around the room that was to be hers for a week, and went downstairs.

The boys were in the orchard, gathered round a pen where two white rabbits leapt enthusiastically about a pile of fresh dandelion leaves.

Fly bounded out of nowhere, greeting Nia with a display of delighted barking and rolling.

'I'm going to Tŷ Llŷr,' Nia called. She was glad no one responded. She wanted the place to herself. Fly was keen to accompany her though. 'Stay,' said Nia, rather too severely. 'You're Gwyn's dog now.'

She ran all the way, only slowing her pace when she passed Gwyn's grandmother in her garden. The old woman was leaning on a hoe, peering at a patch of earth.

'Bore da,' said Nia, knowing that the older Mrs Griffiths preferred to hear Welsh.

Mrs Griffiths looked up, her thoughts still with the patch of earth or whatever it was that should or should not be growing there. She wore a big straw hat squashed down over black curls. Her eyes could not be seen.

Receiving no reply to what she had considered a polite greeting, Nia ran on to Tŷ Llŷr. She didn't linger in the yard where the ghosts of hens gathered into awful emptiness. She didn't peep into the windows where rooms that she had known would be slowly dying. She ran straight to her wild garden by the stream – and received a great surprise.

Someone had been there. The earth round her poppies was brown and freshly turned; no weeds to strangle the orange gold flowers. And how they had flourished! Divided and replanted they covered the ground in huge brilliant clusters.

'Oh!' Nia cried. 'Who did it?'

Beyond the poppies where thick rushes crept up the bank, someone had built a low stone wall, three layers deep, to keep the weeds at bay, and here and there blue forget-me-nots grew, like tiny pieces of reflected sky.

There was nothing for Nia to do but sit beside her flowers and watch the water.

'I'll forget the church and those old yews,' she muttered, thinking of her canvas, 'and I'll make Tŷ Llŷr and my garden.' She wondered if she could persuade Mrs Griffiths to find yellow cloth. She had a feeling she would be offered a duster.

Happier now, and confident, she walked back to the house and risked a quick peep in her old home. She chose a window overhung with the blossom of two ancient plum trees that curved towards each other from either side. Ghosts of absent furniture stood against the walls; pale shapes on the stained and lived-in wallpaper: a cupboard, a dresser, a silent piano. The only three-dimensional furnishing now was a neat pile of torn paper in a corner. Home for a mouse!

As she stepped away from the window she almost trod on the soldier: a small knitted soldier with a red coat, a stripe of yellow buttons and a tall black hat. Not a Lloyd toy; she knew every one of those. Nia slipped the soldier into her pocket.

The two wood pigeons, bold as brass, were pecking in the yard. If Mr Butcher Lloyd had been there, he would have run for his gun. 'Wood pigeons are a pest,' he would say. 'They'll get my seed.' If Mr Lloyd had been there, the pigeons would have left. But this year they would nest in the sycamore tree and there might be four or five pigeons living at Tŷ Llŷr. Nia wished she had remembered the crust.

She wandered out of the yard, closing the big gate out of habit, though now there was no reason to do so.

Nain Griffiths was standing by her garden wall when Nia passed, as though she had been waiting. She was wearing a purple cardigan so bright it was almost shouting and there were pearly pink parrots swinging from her ears.

'Hello!' said Nia, over the wall.

'Bore da, Nia,' returned Gwyn's grandmother.

'You know?' said Nia, astonished.

'I know my neighbours, don't I?' said old Mrs Griffiths.

'But you knew which one I was; you knew I was Nia. Nobody ever knows me, I'm in the middle, see!'

'Well, I know you, don't I?' The dark and wrinkled face came closer; pink birds quivering under grey-black curls. 'I don't know any of the others, but I know you!'

'Oh!' Nia stepped back, but not to be outdone she asked, 'Have you been weeding my garden?'

'Weeding?'

'Yes. I've got poppies by the stream and someone has been caring for them, doing some gardening there. Was it you?'

'Don't you think I've got enough to do?' Gwyn's grandmother heaved a forkful of stringy weeds above the gate. A shower of mud and leaves flew into the air, some landing on Nia's head.

'Sorry!' said Nia. 'It was just a guess.' It was not she who should have apologized she thought, but it was quite evident that old Mrs Griffiths did not regret showering her with mud. Nia began to run up the lane.

'Pob hwyl!' Nain Griffiths called after her. 'Come and see me soon.'

'Same to you!' Nia shouted without turning. She didn't think she would call on Gwyn's grandmother again, if she could help it.

After lunch, which was shepherd's pie and much better than Nia expected, the boys announced that they were going to walk up the mountain.

'And what about Nia?' Mr Griffiths could have been smiling under his heavy moustache, it was difficult to tell.

'I might, that is I . . . ' Nia hesitated.

'Going to help muck out the hens, are you, then?'

'Well . . . ' Nia began. 'Someone's been in the garden at Tŷ Llŷr,' she said changing the subject. 'Caring for my plants; building a little wall an' that.'

Mr Griffiths gaped speechlessly at Nia. It was as if she had said there were wolves in the wood.

Mrs Griffiths was washing up. She didn't see her husband's face. 'I'm afraid I've no time for other people's gardens,' she said. 'Perhaps it was Nain?'

'No,' said Nia. 'I asked her.' She was fascinated by Mr Griffiths' discomfort.

Shifting away from Nia's disturbing scrutiny, Mr Griffiths left the kitchen without a word and went out into the yard.

'Perhaps it was Gwyn?' Nia persisted.

'Gwyn's no gardener,' Mrs Griffiths replied. 'His sister was though!' She suddenly dropped a pan and became quite still, her shoulders hunched and her hands motionless in the soapy water. Nia couldn't see her expression, but her voice changed pitch and she said,

89

'Why don't you run along now and follow the boys.'

Nia went. Why had her garden caused such a stir?

The boys were wandering up the mountain track, surrounded by ewes and their fat, excitable lambs. The air was full of noisy bleating; Iolo was happily echoing the sounds; he'd abandoned his woolly monster at last.

Nia did not catch up with the boys; she did not intend to. They passed the stone wall where the track rose away from the field and disappeared from sight.

Nia left the track and walked on through the field. She could hear the boys above her, climbing now and shouting to each other.

Nia was in Griffiths' land, but she knew it well. The mountain had belonged to her mother's family, the Llŷrs, and their sheep, for as long as anyone could remember. Her feet fitted well into the hard slanting land. She wandered south, towards the sun, while the voices above her became lost in the chorus of sheep and streams.

She had been walking for a mile up and down, still in the same landscape, when she came upon a place she could not remember: a valley lay below her, where blossom floated like a cloud among darker trees; an orchard of palest pink apple blossom swept like a crescent moon round a low cottage with a mossy green roof and smoke drifting from the chimney. Perhaps she had never been there in spring; never looked down into the valley; it was the blossom that had made her look.

Nia began to walk down into the trees. The ground became steeper and she was suddenly precipitated into a rushing, sliding descent. Breathless and frightened she caught hold of a branch and saw a path, narrow but well-trodden, that wound between the trees. Someone often came this way. But there was no place for a car or a vehicle

90

of any kind.

On the path her pace became more dignified. She had time to observe the land before her. The wood was ancient: oak and ash trees, their branches dappled with the pale green of leaves not fully grown; delicate rowan and bushy hazel and, now and then, a holly tree, shining dark and dangerous in the distance. And then Nia was in the orchard. The sun was high, sparkling through the bright canopy of blossom. But Nia was cold! She was walking through flowers; tall and dense they covered the ground beneath the apple trees. They were white flowers, huge blooms, like stars on tall stems; their leaves broad spears of emerald.

Nia bent to pick a flower and gasped; it was like touching ice!

7

A Visit
to Nain
Griffiths

Holding the flower cautiously by the stem, Nia moved through the orchard. The cold began to penetrate her shoes and socks, it moved up her body and she began to shiver. She might have been walking through a field of snow.

She emerged from the orchard and came into a garden where the low cottage stood surrounded by wild flowers. It seemed to be utterly deserted. Lost. The silence was profound. Yet smoke still drifted from the chimney.

All at once Nia became aware that she was trespassing; that this was a very secret and private place. She turned back into the orchard and began to run. She ran from the silence and the cold white flowers.

Stumbling over brambles and loose rocks that seemed, suddenly, to have invaded the well-trodden path, Nia began to make her way out of the valley. The valley, it appeared, was reluctant to let her go. It tried to halt her progress with stones that slid beneath her feet, with wet and slippery stalks, twigs that caught in her loose hair and thorns that scratched her face. She threaded the white flower into her hair, freeing her hands to protect her face. The ground was surely steeper than it had been on her

93

descent. Nia began to panic. She could see a misty rim of trees at the top of the valley and climbed towards them, but in doing so lost the path. The quiet wood closed in upon her, a damp blanket of decaying leaves smothered her feet and, tired and uncertain, she stopped moving. 'Nerys would say a poem,' she muttered aloud. 'Catrin would sing! But Nia-can't-do-nothing. Nia is trapped!'

'Nia *can* do something!' admonished Idris Llewelyn who had assumed the shape of a broad oak.

Pulling her feet through the leaves, Nia ran towards a bank and climbed upwards, hand over hand, until she burst through bushes of sweet-smelling elderflower, and fell into a field where sheep stared anxiously at her sudden and violent arrival.

'All right, so I was scared,' Nia said to her audience, 'but I didn't notice any of *you* down there!'

The sheep regarded her, unblinking. A few spoke back, and then they frightened themselves into a wild and disorganized retreat.

'Who's scared now?' Nia called after them and laughed. She felt safe out in the rough sunlit field, and ran happily, all the way back to the farmhouse.

The boys were already there. Their muddy boots were in the porch.

'They're up in Gwyn's room!' Mrs Griffiths told Nia.

She climbed the stairs quickly, reluctant to intrude on male territory but eager to discuss her adventure.

'Where've you been?' Alun asked suspiciously when Nia walked in on them. 'We called and called!'

'Just walking,' she replied. 'I haven't done nothing that I shouldn't've!'

Alun looked relieved. 'Gwyn's rabbits are expecting,' he said. 'We can have some of the babies and keep them in

94

a hutch out in the yard at Number 6.'

'Dad would kill them!' The words spilled out; she still resented Alun's first question.

The boys looked appalled.

'He never . . . ' Alun said at last.

'He would!' Nia couldn't stop herself. 'It's his trade now. He'd chop off their heads and hang them in his window.'

'You're mean, Nia,' Iolo cried. 'Our dad 'ud never kill white rabbits. They'd be ours; our pets!'

'What's that?' Gwyn was staring at the white flower, hanging in Nia's hair. She had forgotten it.

'I found it in a valley,' she said, 'a valley I never noticed before, with an orchard and a stone cottage.'

Gwyn came over and took the flower out of her hair. No one but Nia heard his quiet gasp as he touched it. 'It's cold,' he said.

'And it shines,' Alun remarked. 'It's like those luminous stars on your watch, Gwyn.'

Gwyn cupped his hands round the starlike petals. He gazed at the flower, saying nothing. The others looked down into the dark cradle of Gwyn's hands. Each petal glowed like a Christmas-tree lantern.

'Awww!' Iolo exclaimed. 'It's beeee-autiful!'

'There are lots of them in the valley,' Nia said. 'Thousands. Can I have it now?'

Gwyn held the flower out to her. 'There are some in our garden too,' he said thoughtfully. 'But they're not so big and they don't shine. My sister planted them.'

Mrs Griffiths called them to tea and they tumbled out of Gwyn's attic room, down the twelve ladder steps that led from it, across the narrow landing and then on down the conventional and carpeted staircase. The mountain air

95

had made them hungry.

They crowded expectantly round the long kitchen table where plates of fruit cake and sandwiches had been laid on a white cloth.

'May I have a glass?' Nia asked Mrs Griffiths. 'It's for my flower. Look!'

'Well, well I never! It's beautiful, Nia. Where did you find it?'

'In a valley,' Nia replied, 'with an orchard and a little cottage. There were hundreds of them.'

Mr Griffiths, already drinking tea at the table, looked up. 'I wouldn't go there, girl!' he said sternly.

'Why not?' Nia couldn't stop herself.

'Because I say not, that's why!' Gwyn's father barked out.

The children, subdued, sat down and began their tea.

Mrs Griffiths put Nia's flower in a tall glass and placed it on the table, but after the meal Nia took it up to her room and stood it on the dressing-table beside the rag dolls. They brightened in its presence, as though the dust of four years had been swept off their raggedy faces and pretty cotton clothes.

The Griffiths family went early to bed. Nia lay in her new room listening to Gwyn's parents moving about on the other side of the passage. She heard Gwyn and Alun murmuring in their attic. Iolo fell asleep on his mattress beside her.

Nia couldn't close her eyes. The pale flower glowed in the dark, its reflection in the mirror sent points of light dancing into the room. Why were so many places forbidden? First the Llewelyn's chapel, now the orchard valley, and it all came back to solitary, taciturn Mr Griffiths.

96

Wide awake, she crept to the window and drew back the forget-me-not curtains. The round shadow of the earth almost obliterated the moon, only a tiny slither was left, hanging like a sickle among the myriads of distant stars.

Nia turned on her bedside light. Undisturbed, Iolo slept soundly in shadow on the other side of her bed. She took her canvas from a rose-scented drawer and rolled it out. One corner insisted on curling upwards so she set the rag dolls on the offending place and spread glue across the top of the canvas. She took a length of dark blue velvet from her rag-bag, cut it to shape and pressed it on to the glue. A midnight sky! She dotted the velvet with glue and shook Christmas glitter on to the dots. The glitter clustered in bright constellations, just as she wanted. Bethan's dolls looked on with interest.

Nia worked well. She cut green for the grass, violet, black and brown for the trees and their shadows, and grey for the drystone walls; purple for foxgloves and yellow for buttercups, but there was nothing in her bag that would do for her special orange-gold poppies.

When she turned off her light and climbed into bed, the multicoloured cockerel was crowing from his roost.

Nia tackled the problem of the poppies after breakfast next morning. Mrs Griffiths was kneading dough on the kitchen table.

'Have you got a piece of cloth, orangey-gold, like the poppies at Tŷ Llŷr?'

'What for, cariad?'

'My work,' Nia replied. She felt it unnecessary to give any more information.

'I see,' Mrs Griffiths seemed to find Nia's answer adequate. She rinsed her floury fingers under the tap and went to a cupboard.

97

'There's all sorts in here.' She pulled out a large box and set it on the kitchen table. The box was stuffed with pieces of torn shirts, holey socks and even underwear. Mrs Griffiths held up a faded T-shirt.

Nia shook her head. 'It has to be like the poppies.'

'Well, that's all there is. You could dye something, I suppose. Go and see Gwyn's grandmother; she knows all about dye, she does it with flowers and herbs.'

'No. I don't want to go there, thanks!'

'Why ever not!' Mrs Griffiths seemed disconcerted by Nia's candour.

'She's peculiar-like, isn't she? Gwyn's Nain? And I don't fancy going in that dark old place with all those plants poking in at me.'

Mrs Griffiths laughed. 'What a girl you are, Nia Lloyd!' She went to the door and called, 'Gwyn, come here. I want you to take Nia down to see Nain.'

Gwyn came rattling down the stairs. Alun and Iolo followed, less enthusiastically

'What's it about?' Gwyn asked.

Mrs Griffiths put the T-shirt into Nia's hands. 'Nia has to dye something. Nain will show her how.'

'Aw heck,' moaned Alun. 'We don't have to go, do we?'

'I don't want to,' Iolo added nervously, from behind his brother.

'There'd be no room in there for you two, anyway,' Gwyn assured him. 'We won't be long.' He was about to rush out of the front door when he suddenly stopped and said to Nia, 'Bring the flower!'

Grateful, Nia ran up to the bedroom and took the white flower out of the glass. Was it her imagination, or had the flower grown in the night? She took it downstairs and gave
98

it to Gwyn. He frowned at it, puzzled, and then said, 'Come on!'

They left Alun and Iolo in the lane, playing with Fly. The young sheep-dog seemed to have forgotten her nightmare at Number 6. Her barks were joyful here. Nia thought of Emlyn.

But Gwyn had other things on his mind. He was staring at the flower, gingerly touching the icy petals with his forefinger.

They walked in silence until they reached a white gate with the name 'Coed Melyn' – the yellow wood – painted in green upon it.

Nia stopped, twisting the T-shirt in her hands.

'She won't bite!' Gwyn grinned.

'Won't she?' Nia followed Gwyn through the gate and up a cinder path bordered with tall, fragrant flowers. The door was opened before they had reached it and Gwyn's grandmother stood on her step, dressed all in red, with a gold belt round her waist and rings on every finger.

'Has your prince come then, Nain?' Gwyn asked his grandmother.

'Not yet! Not yet!' The old woman giggled at their private joke. 'Who's this, then?' She poked a finger at Nia.

'You know who I am!' Nia said fiercely. 'You said you knew.'

'Just testing!' Nain Griffiths laid her ringed fingers on Nia's arm and drew her into the room beyond.

It was not as bad as Nia expected. Dark, yes, but colourful, and the plants that lived there jostled with ropes of beads, painted pottery, ancient jewelled boxes, ostrich feathers and exotic shawls. You could hardly see the furniture beneath. Such splendours could not be appreciated by a quick peep through a window, and that was all that Nia had ventured until today.

'Take a seat and I'll bring you rosehip syrup,' Nain commanded and disappeared behind a screen.

The only seats were patchwork cushions on the floor. A black hen slept in the armchair. The children sat down, and Nia found she had settled beside a white cat in a glass box. Her nose began its nervous twitching.

Nain Griffiths reappeared and gave the children mugs of warm rosy liquid. Nia sipped suspiciously, but it was very good.

'Look at this, Nain,' Gwyn said, offering her the white flower. 'Feel the petals!'

Nain Griffiths took the flower. She sniffed it, touched it, gasped and regarded it with her head on one side, as though listening for a message from the ground. 'Well, I don't know,' she murmured. 'It's not of this earth, child. It doesn't belong here!' and she darted a look at Gwyn, so fierce and full of meaning, Nia was quite shaken.

'What is it?' she asked.

They looked at her, Gwyn and his grandmother and then Gwyn said, 'Two years ago my sister came back. I called her with . . . ' he hesitated, looked at his hands and then at his grandmother who nodded approvingly, '. . . with the power I inherited from my ancestors.'

'From the dead?' Nia whispered.

'She's not dead!' Gwyn's black eyes were fathomless. 'She's out there.' He looked towards chinks of sky behind red flowers in the window; somehow Nia knew that he meant to indicate a place beyond the sky. 'They took her,' he went on, 'things that look like children but aren't human. Icy things that smile and sing and make you want to be with them. Bethan wanted to go and they took her.

100

She's happy there, she said.'

'Where?' Nia's throat was dry and the question came out in a frightened croak.

'On a planet of ice, where everything is covered in snow. She'd changed her name and she was cold and pale, even the colour in her eyes had been washed away.'

'How did you call her?' Nia found a small tight voice. Gwyn seemed to have brought frost into the room.

'I had her scarf,' he smiled slyly, the way a wizard might, 'and I gave it to the wind. Do you know about Gwydion, the magician, and the seaweed?'

'He made a ship,' she said, and because she almost knew what Gwyn was going to tell her, added, 'out of seaweed.'

'Gwydion lived in these mountains,' Gwyn said. 'Sometimes I think he's still here inside me.' He looked at his fingers; long, sinewy fingers, too long for a boy. 'Nain gave me seaweed for my birthday.' He glanced at his grandmother, tall and crimson, her eyes fixed on her grandson, reliving with him the moment when the strange inherited power had awakened in him. 'I threw my seaweed from the mountain and a ship fell out of space. It was silver and there were icicles clinging to it. The cold of it hurt my eyes, hurt all of me and I could barely see. It brought my sister back.'

Nia stared at Gwyn and at his young-old hands. She had seen his power in the churchyard. 'Where is Bethan now?' she asked softly.

'She went back.'

'How?'

'On the ship. Alun knows.'

'Alun?' How had Alun managed to keep a secret like that? And then Nia remembered the time he had been lost in snow on the mountain but had miraculously survived. Gwyn had saved him, somehow, with the power that no one believed in. 'At school they teased you,' she said.

'Children are cruel,' Nain muttered, 'when they don't believe.'

Nia had no such difficulty. 'It was very cold the day we moved from Tŷ Llŷr,' she went on. 'It came suddenly. Was it the ship? Did you call your sister again?'

'No. I didn't call. There's something I don't understand,' said Gwyn. 'Perhaps it has to do with the flower.'

Nain brought the flower close to her face. Shadows appeared on her strange, lined features. She was beautiful, Nia realised, in a way that rocks and trees and ancient polished things were beautiful.

They sipped their sweet drink for a while and then Nia said, 'You used your power on Emlyn Llewelyn.'

'What?' said Nain Griffiths. 'What's this I hear, Gwydion Gwyn? Did you abuse your power, then?'

'No, Nain,' Gwyn cried. 'I never hurt him. I had to stop him for a while. He was angry, unreasonable.' And he told Nain about Nia and Fly, about the dog's lead and the fight in the churchyard. 'But I let him win, Nain,' he finished. 'I knew I had to do that!'

'That may be,' said Nain, 'but it's not right what your father and the town have done to Emlyn Llewelyn.'

Nia had never heard anyone put Emlyn's point of view. 'Why?' she asked.

'They're ignorant,' Nain said scathingly. 'Idris Llewelyn is an artist, trying to do his best, making things beautiful. And there is his wife, Gwyn's aunt, leaving her husband and her own boy just because she hasn't got electricity!'

102

Gwyn jumped up. 'She couldn't live in that old chapel. She wanted a proper home for her baby. Uncle Idris was cruel and wicked, Dad says.'

'Emlyn stayed,' Nia said quietly.

'He should have gone with his mam, he should!' Gwyn retorted.

'Emlyn stayed because he knows what's right He's loyal and he's brave and you and he should be friends, Gwydion Gwyn, and not fighting in a sacred place, where you know the power is all on your side!' Nain's tone was not unkind but Gwyn turned from her resentfully as she passed him and whisked the T-shirt out of Nia's hands. 'Now let us see what we can do with this!' she said.

'How did you know?' asked Nia, astonished.

'I can't imagine you would visit me just for pleasure, Nia Loyd,' Nain teased.

Nia did not answer that question. 'I wanted to make some orange cloth,' she confessed. 'It's for my work. I want to make it the colour of Welsh poppies – my own special poppies by the stream at Tŷ Llŷr. Gwyn's mam said you could do it.'

Nain beckoned Nia out behind the yellow screen into her kitchen. Nia followed cautiously. She watched Nain Griffiths take a large enamel pot from the wall, fill it with water and set it on her stove. 'First, onion skins,' Nain muttered and pulled six onions from a neatly plaited string hanging from the low-beamed ceiling. 'Peel them!' she commanded, handing Nia the onions.

Nia put them on the table and began to dig her nails into the crackling skins; her eyes smarted and as she looked up to wipe the tears away, she heard the front door bang and Gwyn's footsteps running up the lane.

'Don't cry,' Nain Griffiths chuckled. 'He's a sensitive

boy but he'll come round. And you needn't be afraid of me!'

'It's the onions,' said Nia, annoyed by the tears. 'And I'm not afraid.'

The hours that then sped by seemed more like five minutes. Nia stood by while Gwyn's grandmother stirred a boiling liquid of onion skins and lichen until it turned golden. Into this bubbling, syrupy water she dropped the faded T-shirt which had first been washed by Nia in the sink. They then took turns with the stirring, using a wooden spoon as long as Nia's arm, and while they stirred Nain told Nia about the boy who had just left them. About the line of magic that stretched back through her family to
104

a time when princes and magicians ruled Wales, and the people that Nia had thought were only part of a story became as real to her as the mountain beyond Nain's door. She saw a time and place where enchantment was a necessity, the life-blood of an ancient people, who had changed and grown through invasion and suppression, still keeping a small piece of magic inside themselves until, once every century perhaps, it bubbled out and a witch was burned or driven to secrecy, like Gwyn Griffiths.

'And you have it, too, Nia Lloyd!' said Nain, breaking into Nia's thoughts.

'Me?' she exclaimed, amazed. 'But I'm no one. I'm in the middle. I can't do nothing!'

'What's this, then?' Nain lifted a spoonful of golden liquid and let it trickle back into the pot. 'Turning white cloth to gold, isn't it? And aren't you a Llŷr, whose ancestors once ruled Britain. There's a little bit of power left inside you, Nia Lloyd, if you look for it!'

The shirt was pulled out and hung, steaming from the huge spoon, darker by several shades. It was thrust under cold water, squeezed and put on the stove to dry, while Nain and Nia nibbled biscuits made of oats and berries.

'You'll have to leave the cloth with me for a day or two, for the dye to set,' Nain told Nia. 'But you'll come again, won't you, if you need more colours?'

'Oh, I will,' Nia replied fervently.

When she left Coed Melyn she was older by far more than a few hours. And she was stronger, strong enough, perhaps, to bring together two boys who had been divided by a silly quarrel that had nothing to do with them.

8
The
Wrong
Reflection

Nia kept her own company for the rest of the holiday. She did not mention Emlyn again. The days were warm and dry; days for the boys to help with fence-mending, stone-wall building and sheep dipping, and for playing barefoot in the streams when their work was done.

Nia was excused farm duties and allowed to work in Bethan's room. Through the open window the boys' cheerful voices were companionable and undemanding. She worked well. The canvas began to come to life.

Nain Griffiths came to the house one day, holding a piece of bright cloth, as gloriously golden-orange as a bouquet of poppies. And that night Nia cut her poppies to shape and sewed them neatly in place, beside a stream of silver tinsel and blue forget-me-nots that had once been Mrs Bowen's satin underwear.

By the end of the week Nia had recovered her confidence sufficiently to believe that she could, after all, visit the Llewelyns again. She would say she had come to fetch the violet dress and Mr Llewelyn would welcome her in and finish her portrait. Emlyn would have to forgive her.

Happily absorbed in future plans, Nia left Tŷ Bryn believing that her canvas could be a masterpiece; and that her friendship with Emlyn would surely be renewed.

As she said 'goodbye' to Mrs Griffiths she told her, 'It's the best holiday I ever had, anywhere!' And she meant it.

Mrs Griffiths seemed sad at their departure. 'We don't see enough of girls up here,' she said wistfully. 'Come again, cariad!'

'If you'll have me,' Nia beamed.

Gwyn was nowhere to be seen. She hoped he didn't regret the secrets he had confided.

Nain Griffiths was standing by her gate when the Landrover bounced past. She was wearing a dress she had dipped in the bowl of Nia's poppy-gold dye. She did a little dance and blew a kiss. Nia had to laugh. She knelt on the seat and leant out of the window. 'You're a poppy!' she cried, and waved until the bright figure was out of sight.

'She's batty, Gwyn's grandmother!' Alun remarked.

'She's not! She's fantastic!' Nia leapt down and glared at Alun. 'I think she's a great lady, would have been a queen, probably, if the Anglo-Saxons hadn't come, and all that lot!'

All at once Mr Griffiths began to roar with laughter. He couldn't stop. It was such an unusual sound to come from him; the children stared at his shaking back in perplexity and Alun couldn't decide who was the most mad, his sister or his best friend's relations.

Number 6 seemed unbearably dark and muddled after the clear mountain light. There were sheets and shirts mounded on chairs, waiting to be ironed. Stained butcher's aprons were piled by the washing-machine. Gareth, with his autographed white leg, was, somehow, everywhere, moaning because he 'couldn't sit down nowhere!' He'd tried putting his foot on a chair and smashed a lens in Nerys's spectacles.

Nerys was in a horrendous mood. Her new hairdo had gone wrong: mousy spikes framed her long face and she regarded everything with a slit-eyed furious glance. Siôn was fed up with Gareth's moaning and even calm Catrin was thumping out Mozart like she was massaging a footballer.

Nia had brought her white flower, the stem wrapped carefully in damp tissue. To save bothering her mother she put the flower in her blue tooth-mug and set it on the window sill. It looked as bright and as fresh as ever.

Mrs Lloyd had forgotten that she would have three extra for tea and it was Sunday, so she couldn't run to the shops.

'I don't need cake,' Nia informed them. 'I want to go and see Gwyneth. I've got to ask her something about school. Can I go now?'

'Well, seeing as it's about school . . . !' Mrs Lloyd gratefully cut the remaining piece of fruit cake into eight neat slices.

Nia squeezed between the dresser and her brothers on their bench, happily relinquishing fruit cake in order to escape.

'Won't be long!' she called confidently from the hall.

Outside she did not feel so sure of herself. The walk up to the chapel seemed longer than usual, but she did not have to knock. Idris Llewelyn was painting silver leaves beneath the gold flowers on his door. 'I hadn't finished,' he told Nia, 'but it's done now. Do you approve?'

Nia nodded and followed him into the chapel. Emlyn was sitting on the floor with a book; he did not look at her.

'Well, get up, boy, and welcome your visitor,' said Mr Llewelyn. He prodded his son gently with a sandalled foot. 'Had a bit of trouble with you, Nia, and his cousin, I heard: about the dog!'

'It wasn't my fault,' Nia blurted out. 'Dad sold it to Mr Griffiths. I tried to stop him. But I couldn't . . . couldn't tell you. I was a coward!'

'Not a coward, just cautious. And Emlyn is contrite! Aren't you, boy? He came to see you in the holiday.'

'Did you?' Nia looked at Emlyn in surprise. She perched herself on a cushion beside him, but he still refused to respond. He hasn't forgiven me; he never will, she thought.

'You weren't there,' he said at last, and still without looking at her. 'That sister of yours opened the door. The one with specs. I'm sorry but I can't stand her.'

'I know what you mean,' Nia said. Now and again there were good reasons for being disloyal. 'Did she say something spiteful? They didn't want me to come here again. They sent me away, up to Gwyn Griffiths' place, with Alun and Iolo. I'd been in trouble, see!'

'Trouble?' Mr Llewelyn sounded concerned.

'I thought everyone would know by now. Miss Olwen Oliver is famous for her gossip.'

'We haven't seen no one,' Emlyn murmured. 'No one comes here.'

'Tell us your trouble, girl.' Mr Llewelyn put his silvery brush into a jar of spirit and sat on an extraordinarily large upturned bucket.

'The first thing was,' Nia began, 'I said I was a vegetarian.'

Emlyn looked up.

'Well that didn't go down too well, Dad being a butcher. The next thing happened because I wanted something for blossom and I couldn't think what, so I . . . so I . . .'

'Go on,' Emlyn said, with a spark of interest.

'So I cut a piece of lace from Miss Olwen Oliver's curtain. I did that before being a vegetarian, but they didn't know,' Nia said in a rush. 'I didn't think it would notice, well, it *didn't* notice, but she saw, didn't she? And, aw heck, there was so much trouble.' She sighed and rolled her eyes towards the ceiling, remembering the horror of it all.

When she dared to observe the effect her confession had made, she found that Mr Llewelyn's very white teeth were showing through the mass of brown hair on his face. He was smiling, and then he was laughing, and Emlyn with him.

'But it was a terrible thing I did,' Nia reproached them.

'It was! It was!' agreed Mr Llewelyn. 'Excuse us! Why didn't you come to us, cariad bach? We can give you lace and anything you need for your masterpiece.' He strode to a wooden box beneath one of the long windows and flung it open. 'Look!' he exclaimed. 'Lace and cotton, feathers and pretty things!' He held up a dress, the palest of pink cotton embossed with white flowers. 'Blossom! Don't you agree?'

The children stood, simultaneously. Emlyn was staring at his father and at the dress.

'What d'you think, Emlyn? Shall I give this to Nia for her work?' His words were somehow more than a question. Nia had the feeling that, perhaps, he was trying to lay a ghost.

Emlyn was still gazing at the dress. He screwed up his face, like someone with toothache. 'I don't mind,' he said at last.

'No anorak to hide it in today,' observed Mr Llewelyn. 'Will you dare to say you got the dress from us?'

'I'll say it was from Gwyneth Bowen. I'm always getting

110

wool and stuff out of her mam's shop. They'll believe me.'

'Nia Lloyd, you have criminal tendencies,' Idris Llewelyn remarked, with half a smile.

'No, I never . . . ' she began, but the big man laughed again and bundled the dress into her arms.

'Will you stay for tea?' he asked.

Nia hesitated. She dared not risk trouble on her first day at home. 'I'll come tomorrow,' she said.

When she left, Emlyn followed her out on to the road but no further. He sat on the chapel steps and when she turned back to wave he would not look at her; his chin was cupped in his hands and he was staring out at distant, empty mountains.

He hasn't forgiven me, Nia thought. But he will, he must!

Everything at Number 6 had simmered down, by the time Nia returned. The boys were by the river examining something dead on the bank, while the three big Morgan brothers shouted fishy information across the water. The river was low and so was the sun. The water sparkled gold over smooth stones and bare feet.

'What's that?' Iolo poked a wet finger at the dress in Nia's arms.

'Don't!' she sprang back. 'It's for my work.'

'Oh!' He fished a handkerchief from his pocket and a matchbox came tumbling out and fell into a shallow pool at his feet. 'Aw, no!' he cried, retrieving the damp box. 'Nia, take it inside for me, will you?'

'What is it?'

'A spider! I found it at Gwyn's place. It's special, like silver!'

Nia took the box and left them to decide the identity of the dead fish. She passed the window of her father's 'cold

111

room'; told herself not to look in, but did. The sight was even more gory than she had imagined. Her father was removing unimaginable things from something lying on a bloody slab – and he was whistling!

She ran up to her room where curiosity prompted her to open Iolo's matchbox. The spider was, indeed, special: very tiny, silvery and, like the white flower, it seemed to glow.

She put the box on the chest of drawers, slightly open so that the spider could breathe or spin, or do anything a spider should do.

The boys would be in the river for hours, she could tell. There was no one to bother her. She knelt down and spread the dress on the floor. It was almost too beautiful to cut but someone had already done that. The hem had been unevenly severed, slashed, hastily, as though with a knife.

The sight was, somehow, rather shocking. Nia scissored away the painful gashes, neatening the wound, tidying the sad, pale dress. She put the severed strands into a rag-bag and then, almost by accident, found herself slipping the dress over her head. The cuffs of the long full sleeves covered her fingers, the high collar tickled her neck, very softly.

She smoothed the dress close to her body, over her skirt and crumpled shirt. It concealed everything but her trainers. Elinor Llewelyn must have been tall and slim.

Nia wished she could see herself. A mirror had been promised once. Catrin and Nerys had a mirror in their room that reached to the ground, but Nerys was probably there reading.

Sometimes a hint of a reflection would emerge from the wardrobe's shiny doors. Today, to Nia's amazement, there was more than a hint. A huge circle of shimmering silver hung over the doors: a cobweb, spun so fine, so close, that it resembled a mirror. How it had come there, and when, Nia could not imagine but it must have been the work of Iolo's spider for there it was, at the very top, swinging on an inch of gossamer.

The window was open and the web was blown into a slow, deep movement, like a wave. Nia waited for it to calm. She could already see the pink dress and dark hair above it, like someone lying under clear water. Gradually, features began to appear, large dark eyes, a pale face and lips, parted in a scream. The face that looked out at Nia was not hers

Nia screamed, and went on screaming. She gasped for air, terrified and trembling.

'Nia, what is it?' Catrin stood behind her, clasping her shoulders.

'Not me! It's not me!' sobbed Nia. 'Not my face!' She pointed to where a dark woman's features had replaced her own, but the shining cobweb had broken loose. A cloud of silvery threads streamed out towards them, and drifted through the open window.

9
Children
after
Midnight

Later, when Nia had recovered and Mam sat reading by her bed, the spider crawled over the carved pattern at the top of the wardrobe. The tiny creature mesmerized her, but when her mother anxiously inquired whether Nia was 'seeing things' again, she replied, 'It's nothing. I was thinking!'

They had not understood, of course, and Nia had no intention of trying to explain what she had seen. Her scream had not been a call for help. It had just burst out of her at the sight of something unnatural. She had experienced the same sensation in the churchyard, when Gwyn Griffiths had interrupted time, but he'd stolen her breath as well so she had not been able to cry out.

Was it coincidence that her mother was reading of Welsh magicians; magicians who had also been soldiers, kings and princes. Could Gwyn bring them, even here, in safely terraced Number 6?

She did not doubt that Gwyn was responsible for the mysterious cobweb, and for the spider that was now moving so gracefully over carved wooden flowers. Mrs Lloyd's quiet voice drifted on, soothing herself as well as her children. She seemed almost to be talking to the baby inside her, Nia thought.

The white flower on the window sill began to glow as the sky behind it deepened into a gloomy twilight. Iolo fell asleep. He couldn't see the spider he had taken from Gwyn Griffiths, hadn't seen the magic he had stolen.

'Nos da, cariad,' Mrs Lloyd bent and kissed her daughter.

'Good night, Mam!'

'Better now?'

'Yes, Mam. I'm sorry to be a nuisance.'

'You can go back to Tŷ Llŷr again, you know, for a visit. It isn't far.'

'No, Mam.' Nia smiled and closed her eyes. She had just had a wonderful idea.

Her mother drew the curtains, carefully moving the flower as she did so. 'Trust you to find a strange plant,' she muttered. 'Never seen anything like it.'

After school next day, Nia left Gwyneth Bowen at the school gates, the latter still half-way through a recital of her hamster's holiday misadventures.

'You are rude, Nia Lloyd,' Gwyneth called after her. 'You don't care about animals, do you? You don't care if Gethin put my Sandy in the freezer, do you? You're callous, you are!'

'So's Gethin,' Nia shouted back. She had spied Emlyn Llewelyn striding up through the town, always the first to leave school.

Nia tore after him, twisting herself into her back-pack and her jacket. She gave up trying to wear them and carried them in a bundle before her.

'Hold on! Emlyn, wait! *Please* wait! *Wait!*' she cried, almost tripping on the trailing bag strap.

Emlyn stopped; he looked back, unsmiling, until Nia

116

caught up with him.

'I've got something for you,' she said, 'in my bag. And I want to tell you something about the dress you gave me!'

Emlyn began to stride out again.

Nia had to take little running steps in order to keep up with him. 'Hang on! Don't go so fast!' she exclamed breathlessly.

'Are you coming back with me then?' he asked, slowing his pace a fraction.

'I'll come up to the chapel, but I'd better not come in!' She gulped for air. 'I had a bit of bother yesterday.'

'You're always having a bit of bother,' he remarked, but he slowed down sufficiently for her to heave her bag on to her shoulders. They were on the bridge now and the river obliterated all the town sounds.

'Emlyn,' she said. 'I think I saw your mam last night.'

'You what?' He stood quite still, trying to determine her expression, then he shook his head and resumed his frantic pacing.

When he had crossed the bridge, however, he did not continue up the hill to home but leapt down a steep bank, where nettles and brambles had been previously attacked to allow a narrow, safe passage to the river bank.

Nia followed, less adroitly, and found herself, with scratched hands and a dusty skirt, sitting beside Emlyn on the river bank. Before them the wide river snaked into the sunlight; behind and all about them, tall reeds concealed their presence from all but a moorhen, stepping daintily over shining stones.

They sat silently contemplating the water until Emlyn said, 'Go on, then!'

'Iolo had a spider in' a matchbox.' Nia frowned, wondering if she had begun at the wrong place. 'The box

117

got wet down by the river; he gave it to me to look after.' She ploughed on. 'It belonged to Gwyn Griffiths really. You know about Gwyn Griffiths, don't you?'

'Huh!' was all Emlyn said.

'I mean, I know you know him,' Nia floundered. 'But he's not like other boys, you know that, don't you? Because of what happened in the churchyard.' She glanced at Emlyn but he gave her no encouragement.

'Well, this spider, it was like silver and it sort of glowed. I put the box down somewhere in my bedroom and then I . . . well, I hope you don't mind, but I put on your mam's dress. The one your dad gave me yesterday, like blossom. It was your mam's, wasn't it?'

Emlyn nodded.

'The spider had made this cobweb, like a mirror it was – shining.' Nia stared out at the water remembering the glimmering shapes in the web. 'An' I could see my reflection in it; only it wasn't me, it was your mother, I'm sure it was. She had long dark hair, see, and big dark eyes and . . .'

'Don't!' Emlyn jumped up and crashed his way through the dense, dry reeds, then he swung round and came back to her. He stood looking down at her, with his hands in his pockets and said quietly, 'I didn't finish about the night my mam went. I didn't tell you all of it.'

'I know,' Nia said, and waited.

Emlyn crouched beside her. He spoke quietly and unemotionally. 'She was wearing that dress, because it was their wedding anniversary. It was all so good at the beginning; they had wine and gave me some, and they danced in the field, to some music on the old wind-up gramophone. But then it all went wrong.' He gritted his teeth, biting on a puzzle that still tormented him. 'There

118

was this wind, like I said, come up from nowhere. It made such a racket and the baby was crying and crying. It got dark and my mam was going on about the baby an' how we shouldn't be living in a place so small and cold and with no electricity. And my dad got mad; he shouted at her to "shut up" and she yelled back and pushed at one of the wooden animals, and somehow it must have knocked the heater over, because the next thing I saw, it was lying on its side and Mam was screaming with flames all round her, but Dad pulled the bedclothes off and wrapped her up in them, and put the fire out!'

'Was she burnt?'

Emlyn shrugged. 'Not much. Not badly. Dad saved her, see. But that wasn't the end of it. I went to sleep for a bit, and so did Dad I suppose, because when I woke up I saw him running into the field in his pyjamas. I got out of bed and followed him.' He took a deep breath which he expelled in a long sigh. His next words were spoken to the water, low and stiltingly. 'My mam was there right at the top of the bank, where the field goes down and down to the river. She'd got a big pile of my dad's paintings, heaped like a Guy Fawkes' bonfire, an' she'd poured paraffin on them, you could smell it, and she'd set them alight. She was throwing them into the river on a long branch, all flames: little bits were flying up into the sky. All Dad's work: all burning! And my mam was yelling she'd go mad if she stayed here. But we reckoned she was mad already.'

It all made sense now. The warnings. The fear and the suspicion in Pendewi. A fire and a mother driven mad. Flames in the air and in the river. 'Have you forgiven her?' Nia asked.

'Of course I have.' He hugged his knees and almost smiled, remembering, perhaps, a happier time, when his

119

mother had worn the dress in a sunny place, far away from damp green Wales. 'She's waiting for me, maybe, in that moon she went to, wondering why I haven't come to her. Someone knows where she is, but they're not telling.'

Nia took Iolo's matchbox from her bag and opened it a little. 'There's something special about this spider,' she said. 'It belonged to Gwyn; but he's got Fly. You should have this!' She put the box into Emlyn's hand.

He regarded the box. 'Can't take a spider for a walk!' he remarked.

'No, but perhaps . . . perhaps you'll see your mam in a web, like I did.'

He didn't reject her suggestion, but he stared at her very hard and put the box in his pocket.

Nia got to her feet. 'I'd better go now,' she said. 'I missed the cake yesterday.'

She scrambled up the bank, but Emlyn didn't follow and, when she looked back from the bridge, nothing moved beside the slowly misting river.

There was *bara brith* for tea, everyone's favourite; moist, fruity and delicious. Two whole loaves were consumed at a sitting.

Nia couldn't sleep afterwards. She took her canvas to the bathroom and began to cut a mountain out of mottled grey leather: her mother's gloves, once smart and best, now torn and marked from holding baskets and babies' hands. Something called her to the window, not a sound, but a feeling, somehow, that something was taking place outside that she should see.

The frosted glass distorted form and colour in the street. Things changed but had no features. She slid the window up a fraction, and knelt down to peer through the gap. Nothing.

She pulled the window further, widening the gap enough to put her head out. Nothing in the street. But up on the bridge something moved, pale yellow in the deadening glare of the street lights, but probably white. Small creatures crossing the bridge: children, no bigger than herself, for the stones of the bridge wall came shoulder high.

Children out later than midnight! One, two, three, four, five! Nia counted them. Boys or girls? She couldn't tell. They were too far away, their heads concealed in hoods or scarves. Were they the 'things' Gwyn had talked of: the icy creatures who had taken his sister? They were on the hill now, walking to where a lamp still burned in the chapel window.

She slid the window down, careless of its rattle, rolled up her canvas and ran back to bed. She was trembling and for comfort clutched Iolo's blue monster which had fallen from his arms.

It was all wrong out there. Something terrible had happened. Something unstoppable. Should she run to Emlyn? No, they would stop her, take her. Nia folded herself over the soft woolly monster and screwed up her eyes. She found herself humming, low and monotonously, her head beneath the blankets, trying to blot out what she had seen, telling herself that there were no unearthly children moving towards the chapel.

When she fell asleep at last, it was to dream of herself, almost a baby, playing in the earth near the gate at Tŷ Llŷr. The soil was soft in her hands. She was poking little seeds into the ground, planting and playing. Someone was singing in the lane, and when she looked up she saw a woman with dark hair and a girl beside her, equally dark, holding white flowers, like stars.

122

The girl knelt beside Nia and laid the flowers on the ground. She took the seeds and planted them in a neat row under the sycamore, where the gate would not disturb them. Her dark hair brushed the earth. She was smiling as she worked, and she smelt of roses.

But you can't dream the smell of roses. Was it a memory?

Next morning a dusting of frost outlined the roofs and railings in Pendewi. The frost did not sparkle: there was no sun. Tiny beads of moisture hung in the air, motionless and cold. Damp penetrated the childrens' clothes: sleeves clung: shoes slipped. Beside the school gates, violet and yellow irises leaned forlornly, their petals turned to icy paper.

The climate in Pendewi had slipped.

The day had no shape. Within the school a cycle of learning and playing took place, while outside nothing changed. And when the children went home, afternoon seemed like cold, grey dawn.

Emlyn was not hurrying as he usually did. Nia had to wait for him to fall into step beside her. He seemed to have difficulty in finding his direction, though it only lay forward. He wandered from side to side, jostled by other children, uninterested and dreamy. The street was almost deserted by the time they reached Number 6.

'Did you . . . did you see anything last night?' Nia ventured, uncertain as to whether Emlyn was even aware of her.

He turned to look at her. The moist air made his face glossy. It looked like a face full of tears. He said nothing.

'The spider?' she gently reminded him. 'Did you see a

123

cobweb?'

He seemed to find speech an effort, but at last he said, 'Yes!'

'And did you see anything?' She dared not mention his mother's name. The climate seemed to forbid it.

He stared at her, thoughtfully, then shrugged.

'Tell me, please!'

He shook his head. 'No, I can't,' he said. He turned away but Nia caught at his sleeve.

'Please tell me,' she begged. 'Did you see your mam?'

He hesitated and then said, 'I saw her . . . but I still don't know where she is. There was more in the web. It made me want . . . I can't tell you what I saw!' He shook her off and drew away.

Rejected, Nia swung round and opened the black door, passed through it and slammed it behind her.

It could have been a stranger out there, not Emlyn who was always full of life and sometimes anger. Was it the children? What had he seen in the web, that was tugging at his mind? Would they lead him out of this world to see his mother?

Nia was too distracted to work on her collage that night, and the following day brought her no comfort. Emlyn was more remote than ever. As the days passed he seemed to fade. He was not eating, she could tell; he had become two sizes thinner than his clothes.

Taking a chance, one evening, Nia ran up to the chapel after tea. 'Just going to see Gwyneth,' she called to the voices scattered about Number 6, and didn't wait for an interrogation.

Idris Llewelyn was alone, applying giant splodges of yellow to a huge canvas. 'Emlyn's not here,' he informed Nia. 'Been off in the evenings lately. Thought he'd been with you.'

'No, he hasn't! I'm worried, Mr Llewelyn. Emlyn doesn't seem . . . right, if you know what I mean.'

'He doesn't, does he?' The painter sighed and scrubbed his brush on the sleeve of his black boiler suit.

'What d'you think's the matter, then?' She tried to get his attention by sidling round behind his canvas and tapping her foot.

He took up another brush. 'I wouldn't know, would I?'

'Well, you ought to!' Nia said. 'You ought to be worried. I am!'

'Look, girl!' He flung his brush on to a paint-spattered chair beside him. 'I am worried. I'm worried about this,' he jabbed a finger at his canvas. 'It's for an exhibition, see, and it's not ready!'

It hadn't occurred to Nia that adults had exhibitions, too. She shuffled away from him. Mr Llewelyn was obviously too preoccupied to notice the change in his son.

She left the chapel and returned to the town slowly, surveying hills and woods: watching for a boy who might be walking alone. But Emlyn Llewelyn was hidden with a mysterious someone or something who was slowly extinguishing him.

10
Orchard
of the
Moon

Only one person could help. She would have to make a confession, but in secret, somewhere where Gwyn Griffiths would listen and advise.

The cold mist shifted to the mountain. Next morning Gwyn's black hair glistened in the sun that had appeared to cheer the flowers in Pendewi.

'Is it cold up there, on the mountain?' Nia asked, surprising Gwyn and Alun as they talked together in the playground before school.

'It's cold!' Gwyn affirmed.

And I bet you know why, she thought. The boys were being conspiratorial again.

'I found something of yours,' she said. 'Iolo found it, really. A spider.'

Gwyn's reaction was more than she had hoped for. 'Where?' he demanded. 'Where is it?'

'At home, in a matchbox,' she lied. She had to get him to Number 6, somehow, in order to confide her problem.

'Come back with us, tonight,' Alun suggested. 'You can pick it up from there. Your dad'll fetch you after, won't he?'

'You've got it safe, then?' Gwyn asked.

'Oh yes!'

Emlyn Llewelyn passed just then. He looked in their direction. Gwyn returned his cousin's vacant stare: he seemed perturbed by Emlyn's appearance. Something passed between them, silently, an understanding that even Alun did not share.

Later, after school, Gwyn went home with the Lloyds.

Mrs Lloyd was not surprised, but quickly rang Gwyn's mother to ask if he should not stay for tea; she had barely enough sausages for her family.

Gwyn and Alun followed Nia to her room. Iolo was safely munching afternoon crisps in front of the television.

'Well, where is it then, and what has it been doing?'

Gwyn scanned the room, stepping over boxes and toys.

Nia shut the door and leant against it. She would have to hold Gwyn until she had wrung a promise from him. She did not know whether he would help his cousin.

'It's not here,' she said flatly.

Gwyn swung round.

'Aw, no!' Alun sank on to Nia's bed. 'What the heck are you up to, Nia?'

'I gave it to Emlyn Llewelyn!'

Understanding dawned in Gwyn. 'Why?' he asked.

'Because it's special, isn't it? Because it made a cobweb, there,' she pointed at the wardrobe, 'shiny-like, and I saw a woman in it, Emlyn's mother. I was wearing her dress, and . . .' Gwyn's expression was beginning to alarm her, 'so I gave the spider to Emlyn because you've got Fly and he's got nothing, and . . . and . . .' she clung to the door handle. Words were slipping out of her unevenly and too fast, but she couldn't check them. 'I thought he needed to see his mam but . . . it's all gone wrong, hasn't it? Something's swallowing him up, trying to take him . . .

127

there were children on the bridge after midnight, five of them going to the chapel, they were very pale and . . . '

'When?' Gwyn's dark eyes seemed to burn.

'Four days ago.'

'What? You stupid girl, why didn't you tell me?' Gwyn looked older than any boy she had known. She could feel another presence standing there. It made her limp. 'We must go there – stop them – if we're able!' Gwyn commanded.

'Where?' she cried. 'Who?'

'To the chapel!' He didn't answer her second question.

'They won't let her,' Alun said. 'They've forbidden it.'

'We'll see!' Gwyn took Nia by the shoulders and moved her out of his way. He opened the door. 'Get the dress!' he commanded, and was gone.

Alun, following his friend, looked back into the room and scolded, 'Why can't you do anything right?' He slammed the door behind him.

Muffled voices slipped between the sounds of Catrin's piano and a television presenter: Gwyn's voice and her father's, arguing.

Nia knelt beside her bed. She drew the pale blossomy dress into the light, then pulled the rolled canvas towards her. She laid it flat. Once she had thought it would be a masterpiece, but it was nothing, just a few scraps of coloured stuff, stitched and glued. It would never be finished.

She got to her feet and took her scissors from the drawer, then knelt again. 'Nia-can't-do-nothing,' she told the poppies that Nain Griffiths had dyed with such care. 'Nia is wicked, yes, and stupid. Nia's getting worse. Cut! Cut! Cut! Cutting Miss Oliver's lace, cutting socks! Cut your work, Nia Lloyd! It's back to the nursery class with you!

You'll never finish! Never!'

The small, sharp scissors glinted. She began to cut where she had started; where grey smoke drifted from a chimney. Cut! Cut! Cut!

'Don't!' Gwyn Griffiths was there, glaring at her from the door. 'Stupid girl! Don't!'

Nia was bewildered. She sat back. Her scissors dropped on to the canvas. 'How did you know?'

'I know! I'm nosy, see! I like to know things. Leave it: it's a masterpiece. Roll it up, quick!' Gwyn was a boy again, almost. 'Emlyn needs us. Cutting won't help, will it? Will it?' His voice changed with the questions, became that older, wiser voice, full of authority.

'No!' Stunned, Nia rolled up her canvas.

'Hurry!'

'Where are we going?'

'To the chapel.'

'Do they know: Mam and Dad?'

'They know. I've fixed it. Come on, and bring the dress!'

Was he all-powerful? Nia pushed her canvas into the secret darkness beneath her bed, picked up the dress and followed Gwyn.

Down the stairs, across the hall, through the front door, making no effort to tread lightly. The piano shrilled, the television blared, and Mr and Mrs Lloyd sat in the kitchen, bemused. That Gwyn Griffiths! He had a way of making you do things – Good God, what were children coming to?

Gwyn closed the black door against the Lloyd's mixed-bag of noises. 'It's OK,' he said. 'Don't look so downcast. And hurry!' He began to run and Nia pursued him, past Miss Oliver's grey house where unlucky lace curtains concealed someone murdering Mendelssohn; past the other chapel where Mary McGoohan was accompanying herself on the organ; past Police Constable Jones, who was humming in the street. The town was in good voice today, while Nia's throat was tight with apprehension.

How could Gwyn run up a hill so steep? They were out of the town now with all the singing sounds behind them. Nia stopped, gasping for air.

'Come on!' Gwyn commanded and she ran again, clutching the blossom dress, too breathless to wonder what the boy-magician wanted. He was on the chapel steps; she could hear him banging on the blue and gold door and then he vanished through it.

Nia reached the chapel, expecting to hear Idris Llewelyn shouting at his nephew. But there were no sounds. She peered inside. Gwyn was standing beside a wooden beast with a fiery orange mane, a unicorn with vacant yellow eyes. 'I had forgotten,' he said. 'I came here, once, when we were friends.' He seemed to have lost, momentarily, the resolve which had brought him to the place.

'Gwyn, what shall we do?' she asked.

'Arianwen's here,' he said.

'Arianwen?' Nia saw no one.

'Come in and close the door!'

'But . . .'

'Do it!'

Nia obeyed. She went over to Gwyn who was holding something. She saw the snow spider glowing in the palm of his hand. 'I call her Arianwen,' he said, 'white-silver. She came in the snow, from another world. My sister sent her.'

'I don't understand,' Nia said.

'But you will believe me, won't you, if I try to tell you?'

130

'I'll believe!'

He sat on the painter's chair, while she nervously paced round the wooden animals, listening for approaching footsteps, but hearing only Gwyn.

'Two years ago, nearly, just after my ninth birthday, I threw an old brooch into the wind. Nain told me to. It was a very ancient brooch, twisted and patterned, silver and bronze; it came from Nain's great-great-grandmother. They say she was a witch. I threw it from the mountain where Bethan disappeared. Snow fell afterwards and in the snow on my shoulder I found Arianwen.'

Nia gazed at the tiny creature that had lived in her room for a while.

'She came from that other planet,' Gwyn went on, 'and in her webs she showed me the place where my sister lives now. And I saw the pale children who took her away.'

'On the bridge!' Nia cried. 'They're here, aren't they?'

Gwyn didn't answer her. 'There's something I never told anyone,' he said. 'Bethan tried to take me back with her and part of me wanted to go, but I belong here, I feel like I've got roots going very deep, down into the time when there were magicians where we live now.'

'Emlyn hasn't,' Nia said. 'Emlyn hasn't got anything. He'll want to go.'

'So we must find his mother and then he'll have something, won't he?'

Nia nodded, knowing that Gwyn was going to ask something of her. 'Your auntie, Elinor, she isn't out there, is she?'

'No, she's still here and my dad knows where, but I can't ask him. He thinks he's saved her, see. He doesn't know Emlyn like we do.'

'So, what must I do?'

'Put on the dress!'

'Over my clothes?'

'Over your clothes. Don't be afraid.'

'What if someone comes?'

'Do it!' he said solemnly. 'Arianwen shows us what she thinks we should see, whether it's hours or years or miles away. Time and distance, they're all the same to her.'

Nia slipped the dress over her head. Nothing could interfere with what she and Gwyn were about to do. She felt the cool silky stuff sliding against her skin. If there was a place for spells then it was surely here. The beasts and butterflies, the long windows and the many-coloured paintings began to drift out of her vision; a boy with brown hair looked down, smiling, from beside a river, and then he was gone behind a shining, widening screen of gossamer. Gwyn's spider was spinning; climbing and falling, weaving and swinging across the wall beside Emlyn's bed.

'Hold tight! Stay very still! Don't run, even if there's pain!' Distance or time had come between her and the voice but the words, though faint, held her fast. She could see the dress now, in the web that was a mirror; she could see the face that wasn't hers, and the dark hair. She felt unaccountably sad. Beside her a baby cried, on and on, above the clamour of the wind. She was angry now and shouting, pushing out at the thing that had made her angry.

'What am I doing? Where am I going? Who am I? Gwyn?' She called, and again, 'Gwyn, where are you?'

And the old, wise voice replied, 'Stay, Nia! Don't run!'

Flames crept into the web; guttering gold streaks flared into silver; dazzling scarlet fingers caught at the dress and leapt up at her face.

133

'Help me!' she screamed. 'I hate you!' she shouted to someone she couldn't see.

'Don't move, Nia!'

But she couldn't help herself. While small, frightened Nia clung to the space in which she existed, her reflection fled through dark fields carrying a baby. She ran along familiar paths, down into a valley where moonlight made strange shapes and shadows, towards small, ancient trees that bent under a canopy of blossom; an orchard planted in a crescent – like the moon!

'Where are you going, Nia?'

'I'm going to the moon,' she cried. 'Of course, the moon! The orchard of the moon! That's where she is – Perllan yr hanner Lleuad; those were her words, but Emlyn only heard her say 'half-moon'. Elinor Llewelyn is in the valley where the cold flowers grow!'

'Come out then, Nia! Step back, towards my voice!'

But Nia couldn't move. She was caught in the web. A silly fly bound by strands of the past and another person's life. The spell was too powerful, she couldn't break out.

'Nia! Nia!' The voice was nearer, its power increasing.

Nia held her breath, leant backwards and took one laboured step away from the mirror. As she did so, the glittering glass rippled like the sea and tore apart. Branches of blossom drifted up through the sky of butterflies, fragmenting into tiny flakes that melted to nothing.

She felt a hand on her shoulder; someone tapping gently.

When she turned she saw a face as old and as tired as she felt. Gwyn looked utterly exhausted.

'It's as though we've been asleep,' she said.

'Not me. I've never worked so hard,' he replied. 'And

134

we can't rest now. There's more to do.'

'Yes,' she said meekly.

She stepped out of the dress and laid it on Emlyn's bed
while Gwyn took his spider from the bedpost, where it had
come to rest.

'We must go to my aunt now,' he said, 'and make her
come back to her family before it's too late.'

Gwyn opened the chapel door and almost walked into
Idris Llewelyn who stood there, angry at finding strangers
in his home, astonished to see who they were. 'Beth wyt 'in
eiseau, Gwyn Griffiths?' he asked coldly. 'What do you
want?'

11

Soldiers at Dusk

'We are looking for your wife,' Gwyn said.

'You won't find her here!' Idris Llewelyn took a step towards Gwyn. His fists were clenched.

Gwyn stood his ground. 'I know, and it's wrong,' he said. 'She should be here and she will.'

'And who are you, boy, to think that you can reconcile people who were torn apart by your own family?'

Nia saw arrogance flare up in Gwyn but he resisted the temptation to tell who and what he really was. 'I'm going to do what you should have done, long ago, for Emlyn,' he said. 'You never bothered even to search for your wife, so proud you are, Idris Llewelyn!'

To Nia's horror, the painter laughed. It was not a happy sound. On his face Nia saw a loss that was too unbearable to speak of. She plucked at Gwyn's arm, hoping to stem any more unpleasant truths that he might fling out. But Gwyn had not finished.

'You're going to lose Emlyn, too,' he said. 'Where is he now?'

Idris Llewelyn wasn't laughing when he answered. 'He's been gone all night!' And turning to Nia, he said, 'I'm worried, girl, like you. Find him for me, will you?

You're the . . . '

He could not say what he intended, for they were interrupted by the screech of brakes. Gwyn's father glared out from his Landrover. He could see the children standing inside the open door, beyond Idris Llewelyn. 'What're you doing there, boy?' he shouted.

Idris swung round. The two men looked at each other, but said nothing.

Gwyn ran past his uncle and Nia followed. They climbed into the back of the Landrover while the engine was still throbbing, but as they drove off Nia called to the lonely man on the chapel steps, 'I'll find him, Mr Llewelyn. I promise I will!'

Gwyn's father accelerated away from the chapel. The Landrover roared up the hill. He committed a crime here, Nia thought: kidnapping, of a sort, and he doesn't like visiting the scene of his crime.

Mr Griffiths was not in a mood for questions it seemed. He drove fast and remained silent. When they reached Tŷ Bryn, however, and the children climbed out, he suddenly asked, 'What's Nia Lloyd doing here, then?'

'She's come for tea,' Gwyn airily replied. 'We're going up the mountain first to look for something.'

Did his father guess? If so, he gave no sign. 'What were you doing in that – place?' He couldn't bring himself to say the name.

'They're relations,' Gwyn retorted. 'Everyone needs relations!'

He took Nia's hand and led her back on to the lane that wound and narrowed between thick hedges until it became a sheep track in an open field.

'I'm going to run now,' Gwyn warned her. 'Can you keep it up?'

Nia nodded. His urgency inspired her. 'I'll probably race you,' she said.

They took off and ran side by side, away from the track and across the steep field where their feet twisted into unaccustomed angles on the hard, listing land.

Gwyn drew ahead and reached the valley before her. He waited until she was beside him again and they looked down into Half Moon Orchard. Frost had snapped at the blossoms and petals were drifting from the bare branches on to the white flowers beneath.

'They're so bright,' Nia said. 'You could see them from miles in the air.'

'Even further,' muttered Gwyn. '*They* have seen them.'

They began to walk down into the valley, through the oak wood and through the flowers that had grown knee-high, turning the atmosphere above them into arctic air.

And there was the stone cottage, with a light in the window and wood smoke curving from the chimney.

Gwyn marched up to the door and knocked. Elinor Llewelyn opened it: she stared at Gwyn for a moment, then smiled, relieved to recognise her visitor. 'Gwyn!' she said. 'Your father told you, then?'

'My father told me nothing,' Gwyn answered. 'Can we come in?'

The woman hesitated. She had not seen Nia at first. 'Who is this?' She had become nervous, her hand plucking at a string of beads round her neck.

'It's Nia Lloyd from Tŷ Llŷr. You remember!'

Elinor Llewelyn relaxed. 'I thought it might be . . . '

'Bethan?' Gwyn said. 'No. She's gone!'

'Of course!' His aunt stood back while they passed her into a dark room that was sparsely furnished, clean and tidy: a fire burned in a small black grate. The floorboards

138

were polished, the rug thin and frayed. A boy of two or three played on a bench beside the window.

'This is Geraint,' she said, and the boy ran and hid his face in her skirt. 'He doesn't see many people,' she explained. 'Will you sit down? I've got orange juice, I think, and . . . and biscuits.'

Her voice was ordinary, light and pleasant, and her face was not as beautiful as the reflection Nia had come to know. This woman looked older, her hair greyer, her eyes deeper and ringed with blue shadows.

'If it wasn't for your father, I wouldn't see a soul,' she went on. 'I don't go out much, see. I can't since . . . '

'It must be lonely,' Nia said, looking at Emlyn's little brother.

'Well . . . I suppose . . . but . . .' again the woman seemed unable to form a sentence. She backed away to a tall green cupboard where she found mugs and orange juice, and a tin of biscuits.

The children took her offerings and sat side by side on the bench amongst Geraint's toys.

'I think you'll have to come out soon, Auntie Elinor,' Gwyn said.

'Come out?' She didn't sit with them but paced nervously beside the fire while little Geraint still clung to her.

'For Emlyn's sake,' Gwyn said. 'Your other son. He needs to see you. Something is happening to him. They will take him away.'

'Take him? But his father is good to him? Ivor, your father, tells me what I need to know. He tells me they're well, my husband and my son. And . . . and I could never go back to them, now . . . I don't like going out.'

'Are you ill, Auntie Elinor?' Gwyn asked, carefully.

139

'Ill? Yes!' she replied. 'Since the fire, you see. I feel safe
here. Your father brings me all I want. And your mam,
Glenys, she brings my pills and clothes and toys for
Geraint, little things you didn't need, Gwyn.'

Nia suddenly remembered the knitted woollen soldier
she had found at Tŷ Llŷr.

'Mam said she'd taken them to Oxfam,' Gwyn said,
almost to himself.

'Oh we do go out, you know,' Elinor went on, 'early
when no one's about, don't we, Geraint? Sometimes we
walk to the top of the track. Ivor picks us up in the
Landrover. But we never go to Pendewi. I could never go
there again, never. They know what's best for me, don't
they?' She began to bite her nails and Nia was reminded of
Alun who used to do that when he was angry and only
eight years old. He'd grown out of the habit long ago.

The children stared at Elinor Llewelyn in dismay. She
appeared to have an illness that couldn't be named. Could
such a frightened and sick person help anyone?

'Who planted those flowers?' Gwyn asked, hoping to
jolt his aunt away from memories that distressed her.

'Oh those? A girl.' Elinor brightened visibly. 'Such a
lovely girl, like Bethan, only fair. She stumbled in here one
winter time, when Geraint was a baby. It was quite
wonderful. There'd been a heavy fall of snow and we
hadn't seen a soul for weeks but there she was, smiling in
at the window. I brought her in, of course, but she didn't
seem to feel the cold. Such a funny child; we talked about
flowers, I don't know why, and trees, the things that I
shared with Bethan.' She was calm now, recalling happier
times. 'Before the girl left,' she went on, 'she gave me
some seeds. ''Plant them under the trees when the snow
has gone,'' she said, ''and next year you will have flowers

in your orchard, flowers like stars, and then we can always find you." '

Nia felt Gwyn tense beside her. He put his hand on hers, whether to alert her or comfort himself she couldn't tell, but his taut fingers pressed so hard she almost cried out.

'What was her name?' he asked.

'Eirlys!' His aunt was smiling now. 'I remember because it's the Welsh for snowdrop and she came in the snow.'

Gwyn jumped up, pulling Nia with him. 'We have to go now,' he told his aunt, 'and if Emlyn comes here, tell him to wait for us!'

'Emlyn? Oh no! He won't. You mustn't tell him!' The woman instantly became anxious again.

'Don't you want to see him?' Nia asked accusingly.

'I do! do! I wanted to go back for him so many times. But he knew where I was and he never came. Besides Idris would have made me stay and I couldn't. You're only children. You don't understand what it's like, wanting something but being afraid. The pills help me to forget, and it's best like that.'

Nia began to wish she had never found Elinor Llewelyn. But she had reason to thank her. She pulled the knitted woollen soldier out of her pocket. 'Geraint must have dropped this in my garden,' she said, 'when you went to look after my poppies.'

Elinor took the soldier. 'So he did!' She smiled. 'Thank you, Nia. There was no one there, so I took it on myself to do a bit of gardening. It was sad to see lovely Tŷ Llŷr so empty and alone.'

Gwyn was already hovering impatiently outside the door. Nia joined him and they began to run, calling 'Goodbye' to Elinor Llewelyn, though she had already closed the door.

They ran through the cold flowers and up the path, and this time Nia did not panic, because Gwyn knew the way. He had been there before, when the cottage was deserted, but never since his aunt had lived there. 'Dad told me it wasn't safe,' Gwyn said. 'I didn't think to ask why. I just never bothered to come and look.'

When Nia climbed out of the valley, Gwyn had increased the distance between them. He was leaping ahead like a wild animal, but when the farmhouse was in sight he stopped and waited for her.

Nia caught up with him and as they walked down the track together she asked, 'Is your aunt mad then, Gwyn? To run away from her own family, to want to forget them?'

He shook his head. 'It was the baby,' he said. 'Mam told me that mothers do strange things when they are frightened and have a baby. It's protection, like animals and birds. Even our old hens go mad if you touch their chicks.'

'They don't stay mad,' Nia remarked, 'when the chicks are grown.'

'No. Then it's something I can't explain. My dad went mad when Bethan disappeared. Perhaps that's why he took special care of Auntie Elinor: he understood. He didn't get better until . . . ' Gwyn began to run again.

'Until what?' Nia tried to keep up though her legs and her ribs were aching.

'Until she came back. Until Eirlys came. I'm scared, Nia,' he confessed, 'about the flowers she planted.'

'She?' Nia was confused.

'Don't you understand? Bethan was Eirlys!'

She stood quite still. Pieces of a jigsaw began to move

143

closer It was like glimpsing a picture through spaces in a cloud. 'Bethan?' she breathed.

Gwyn stopped too. He looked at her. 'She must have had seeds with her, in her pocket, when they took her to that other place, and when she came back she brought the seeds with her, only they had changed, like she had. Things that grow in the dark, they're pale. Bethan meant no harm; she only wanted to find her way back to Perllan yr hanner Lleuad. But *they'll* see them, the others, it's like a landmark, shouting at them, and they'll go there, where it's safe and quiet, and they'll wait and take someone, a child, they only take children.'

'But they're here already!'

'Only five, you said. There'll be more, many more.'

'We must tell someone. Get help.'

'You can't explain things like this,' Gwyn said. 'I know; I've tried. It's too hard for people to understand.'

'What must we do?'

'There were three of us once,' he muttered. 'We're stronger together.' He was looking into a space above her head, and then, becoming aware of her scrutiny, he said, 'Wait, and think!'

They went into the farmhouse and Mrs Griffiths, so happy to see Nia again, did not ask why she was there, but spread the table with hard-boiled eggs and salad and a newly-baked malt loaf and chocolate cake. Nia did her best to do justice to such treats, but her stomach refused to accept more than a few mouthfuls.

'What is it, cariad? Are you going down with something? How are they at home?' Mrs Griffiths asked, concerned for her favourite visitor.

'Gareth's OK. His leg gets in the way, though,' Nia said. 'And Mam's that tired. I expect it's the sponge I had

144

for dinner. I'll feel better soon. Can I take some cake home with me?' She was glad Nerys was not there, to glare at her for asking such a question.

'Of course! You might have to wait a bit, though. Gwyn's dad wants to do some fencing on the lane before dark, those Tŷ Llŷr lambs keep getting out.'

'Dad never did his fences proper,' Nia said, and then, because she'd been disloyal, added, 'He's good at butchering, though. He's great at that; people come for miles!'

'That's nice, isn't it?' Mrs Griffiths smiled uncertainly.

The children helped to clear the table and then went to see Gwyn's white rabbits in the orchard. They were in separate hutches now. Gwyn lifted a hinged door above the female's sleeping quarters and Nia, crouched beside him, saw a bed of soft fur. 'It's where the babies will be born,' he told her, 'but we don't dare look for a while, or she'll eat them. They go peculiar-like when they give birth.'

'Like your Auntie Elinor,' Nia said.

'A bit like that.'

It was much darker than usual for an early summer evening; and cold. The rabbits wouldn't eat their supper of favourite weeds. They sat rigid on their hind legs, alert and anxious. The birds had fallen silent and even the chorus of ever-hungry lambs had died to an intermittent plaintive bleat.

Something rippled through the air, not a breeze, but more like a shock wave: a sound like silent screaming.

Gwyn stood up. 'Aw heck!' he said quietly. 'Aw heck, Nia. It's happening.' He clutched his thick hair with both hands.

'What?' she asked, frightened by his attitude.

'The children are here, and I didn't call. I didn't make the ship; the seaweed is safe in my drawer. They've come for someone, like they came for Bethan. Can't you feel it?'

Nia didn't need to answer. Cold and dread had caused her to wrap her arms tight about herself.

They stood staring helplessly at each other and then a movement by the gate broke the tension and Nain Griffiths came towards them, tall under the apple trees, and dressed in forest green.

'I heard children in the lane,' she said, 'and I thought it was you.'

'We're here,' Gwyn said. 'We've been here all the time.'

'I saw a boy,' Nain went on, 'and he was alone. But there were others in the woods beside him. I heard them laughing.'

'Emlyn knows,' Nia whispered. 'He knows where his mam is. They're taking him there.'

'And the others will be waiting!' Gwyn's voice cracked and then he was seizing Nia's hand, dragging her through the orchard, up the path and through the gate. 'Tell them we've gone to look for someone,' he shouted to his grandmother as they pounded towards the field.

Their race, this time, was desperate. Nia felt as though the earth was rocking upside down. They ran on dark rolling clouds in an icy stream of air. The only warmth in the whole world was caught between her hand and Gwyn's, and then he let go of her and, as he drew ahead, she lost him in a mist of freezing vapour.

Her feet and instinct took her to the place, and on the woodland path she caught up with Gwyn as he stood waiting for her. He was watching Emlyn Llewelyn walking toward the Orchard of the Half Moon, and the cottage

146

where his mother was.

Emlyn would soon be with his mam. Nia sighed with relief. She let herself sink on to the path and sat there, relaxed and almost happy. Gwyn took several paces away from her. Something about the set of his shoulders, the way he moved, would not let her rest. When she stood again she was petrified by the prospect before her.

There were children crowding into the cottage garden: pale, graceful children; hundreds: they moved in from the trees like streams of thistledown, murmuring softly, their voices gentle as rain.

'They are ancient,' Gwyn said. 'But only in wisdom. Their bones are not brittle. They will not die – unless they are afraid. I know this!'

Nia knew that Emlyn had forgotten his mother. He could only see the children, so beautiful, almost translucent in the dusk.

'They'll take him, Gwyn,' she wanted to cry, but even had she been capable, Gwyn wouldn't have heard her: he had gone and something else was where he should have been: a frosty tree stump: a man kneeling under a cloak that reflected all the bright shades in the sky, and hair silver with sunlight.

There were words in the air, rising and falling like insistent, monotonous music. Names perhaps: Math, Lord of Gwynedd, Gwydion and Gilfaethwy. Names in the air, sung like a sacrament.

And once again, as in the churchyard, time held back and nothing moved, except the flowers, and they were growing. And Nia saw, or maybe dreamt, that from the flowers two men came: soldiers or princes, the way they used to be, with gold at their throats, and round their naked arms; with broad shining swords and patterned shields that gleamed like fire.

They dipped their swords, once, twice, as in a rite, together, and where fiery bronze touched the earth, flames came leaping round them.

If nothing else was real, the fire was. Nia could feel the heat on her face. But Emlyn wasn't moving. Fear or the children seemed to paralyse him and he would soon be engulfed by flames.

'Help him, Nia!' It was Gwyn's voice. He was beside her, tugging her hand. 'He's remembering.'

Nia couldn't move.

'I can't do it alone, Nia!'

The fire was white hot.

'It's an illusion, Nia. It won't hurt you. But I can't keep it!'

'No!' she shrank back.

'We must hold him, or he will go. I am losing myself . . .'

'I can't do nothing,' she moaned.

'We're in this together, Nia Lloyd!' the voice hissed in her ear, so close that she felt it in her head; she sprang away from it and ran with one boy, down towards the other who now seemed less substantial than the flames.

But she grasped one hand in both of hers, while Gwyn took the other, and they held and pulled him.

The fire spat and stank. It licked their feet and clothes like a hungry beast. And Emlyn was rooted in the ground, heavy as oak.

They pulled him until Nia thought that if her body didn't burn it would surely break, and then, slowly, he came with them.

Beyond the tall soldiers, Nia could see the children, pressing together, terrified by something that should not exist either in their world, or in the place they had invaded. They turned and screamed through the trees.

A mist of swimming white shapes escaped out on to the mountain and gathered into a cloud of snow: it seemed to shake the earth as it rose into the sky.

Before she fell, Nia thought she saw a billowing sail and a silver prow with dancing creatures on it passing overhead.

12
A
Masterpiece

They were all in the kitchen at Tŷ Bryn. Nia hardly remembered how they had come there.

It had been dark in Perllan yr Hanner Lleuad, and there had been a wind. They had gone to find Emlyn, she and Gwyn, but the world had rocked and they had fallen, all three, down together to the place where Emlyn's mother lived.

An earth tremor, Gwyn's father called it.

But the bruises on Nia's hands were red, like burns. Her father was there, without his butcher's apron, and he was stroking her head like he used to do, when she was a very little girl.

She couldn't see Gwyn.

Emlyn was there, on the big settle beside his own mother, who held him like she never wanted to let him go, and Geraint was sitting on Idris Llewelyn's knee.

But Nia couldn't see Gwyn.

Gwyn's father was there, grim by the stove. He had known where the children would be when Idris Llewelyn came banging on his door, and summer lightning shattered the sky.

Gwyn wasn't there.

Mrs Griffiths was pouring tea by the kitchen table. It was she who had carried Nia out of the valley. She had gone with her husband and Idris Llewelyn, under a sky as green as a field of spells. And they had found the children, dazed and bruised, with Elinor Llewelyn crying beside them. The wind had torn her roof away.

'Where is Gwyn?' Nia cried.

They all looked at her and Gwyn's mother said gently, 'He's resting, cariad.'

'Let me see him!'

'He's asleep!'

She didn't believe them. 'I want to see him!' she demanded.

So Mrs Griffiths took Nia into the front room and she saw Gwyn lying in a big armchair with a blanket over him. His eyes were closed and his face, beneath the cloud of black hair, looked like paper.

'The doctor's coming soon,' Mrs Griffiths told her. 'He'll put Gwyn right; he must!'

It seemed then that, not only Nia's voice, but her whole body yelled, 'He's not asleep!' And tears spilled out in a wave that left her breathless. She wiped them away again and again; as though they had no business there, when there were so many things to consider.

Mr Griffiths gripped her shoulders. 'He's not gone, girl,' he said. 'We'll get him right. Come away, now.'

As he drew her into the passage, the front door opened and Nain Griffiths stood there, in a cloak that shone darkly, like crow feathers.

'Give me my boy!' she said.

Without a word, Mr Griffiths went and lifted his son out of the chair. He put Gwyn, wrapped in the blanket, into Nain's arms, and although he was ten years old, his

151

grandmother carried him into the night, as if he was nothing but a shadow.

Summer came swiftly after the storm: a scorching summer of cloudless skies and hours of sunshine that stretched from early dawn till long after bedtime.

Morgan-the-Smithy and his three sons worked shirtless out of doors. Nia watched them in the evenings, splashing themselves cool in the river, singing and swearing cheerfully at each other.

Six weeks went by and in those weeks so many things happened it was as if a train had thundered through the valley, throwing out goodwill like birthday parcels.

Idris Llewelyn sold his yellow-patterned painting to a gallery in London; they wanted more if he could do them. They took his photo for the papers, with his wife and his two sons. How proud he was in his black boiler suit, holding a cheque for a thousand pounds.

Emlyn came back to school, quite his old self again, only now he was, 'that Emlyn whose dad sells paintings', and children queued up to talk to him.

Elinor Llewelyn left the cottage in Half Moon Orchard; she couldn't stay for her roof had fallen in. She and Geraint went to live in the Griffiths' farmhouse. She saw Emlyn and her husband every day, but nothing would persuade her to move back to the chapel. This unsatisfactory situation might have continued, had not help arrived from quite an unexpected quarter.

One afternoon Mr Lloyd came out of his shop, hot and a little irritable. It wasn't easy trying to sell meat from the window and keep it cool. His impatient family waited for their tea while he scrupulously scrubbed his hands in the sink, and then he said, in an off-hand way, 'Would Idris

Llewelyn think of living in Tŷ Llŷr? His wife would go there, I'm sure. There'd be no money involved – well not much – no one else wants it, and it'll fall down if it's empty longer. He can keep his chapel, just for work.'

Nia ran and hugged him, bloody apron and all.

'Hold on, girl,' he laughed. 'They haven't agreed. And it'll need a fair bit of work doing on it.'

Of course they did agree. Elinor had always loved Tŷ Llŷr, and Idris could turn his hand to any sort of building.

He and Ivor Griffiths, reconciled at last, spent a night in The Red Dragon inn, with Iestyn Lloyd, to seal the buying of Tŷ Llŷr. It was a night the town never forgot. They called it Llewelyn's night, for he was like a returning prince, now that he had a house and a wife, two fine sons and money in the bank. Pendewi Male Voice Choir was there, and you could hear the singing all the way to the sea.

But Nia remembered it because it was the night she finished her picture. She took the tiny pieces she had cut from the hem of Elinor Llewelyn's dress and sewed them in a half-circle on the side of the mountain, and beneath them she glued clusters of silver glitter, so that they appeared to reflect the stars in her midnight sky.

It was finished – yet incomplete.

She could have asked Emlyn's advice: he was an acceptable visitor now, and she could have taken it to Idris Llewelyn in his chapel studio, to ask what was missing. But she waited until Gwyn Griffiths had recovered.

He came to visit them a week after Llewelyn's night. He was still pale, but his grandmother's herbs had brought him to life. If it was shock that he had suffered from, as his father said it was, then why did his eyes look so weary and why did he stumble on the stairs? Nia knew that it was exhaustion, that he'd put too much of himself into the spell

153

that had brought ghosts back to Wales, to save his cousin.

After tea, when the other boys were playing in the river, Nia took Gwyn indoors to see her work.

She laid it out on the floor of her room and sat back, watching him.

Gwyn knelt beside the canvas. He observed it solemnly, while Nia waited anxiously.

'It's beautiful, Nia!' he said at last. 'It's a masterpiece. It's magic . . . '

'But,' she said anxiously, 'something's missing, isn't it?'

Gwyn frowned. 'No. Not really, it's only . . . there's no one there: no people: only birds and sheep.'

'Oh!' She gazed at the canvas for a moment. 'People change,' she said. 'They go and they die!'

Gwyn looked at her. 'In a way,' he said. Then he left her and went to join Alun by the river.

When he had gone she cut the shape of a girl out of her mother's shell-grey tights, and put it where the starry flowers grew in Perllan yr Hanner Lleuad. And in the oak wood she put a starling's feather: it could have been a holly tree or a shining cloak. Beyond the feather she glued strips of brown silk sprinkled with gold glitter, and in the centre of each strip, a silver circle, like the shield of a soldier, a prince – or a magician!

Her landscape was complete.

The following day the children in Standard Three had to submit their Project work.

They were all in the Assembly Hall, Miss Powell and the older children from Standard Four as well, brought in to help Mr James with his judging. The long table at the end of the hall was filling with papers, books and models. Gwyneth Bowen's story was three exercise books long,

154

and her illustrations drew sighs of envy and admiration.

Then it was Nia's turn. She handed Mr James her long roll of canvas and he looked at her apprehensively before unrolling it. For a second Nia panicked. It was the wrong way up. They wouldn't understand. Then Miss Powell caught the other end and they held it up, two metres of it, high enough for everyone to see.

It went dead quiet and Nia's nose began to itch, though it hadn't done so for nearly a month, and she felt Gwyneth Bowen glaring at her.

There was sunlight in the hall. The stars, streams and flowers glittered. Nia had never seen her picture from a distance. She could hardly believe it was she who had put those brilliant colours and shapes together.

'Nia Lloyd, did anyone help you with this?' Mr James asked, astonished and disbelieving.

'No, sir!' Nia tried to say, but her throat had gone dry and the words came out as a guilty sort of cough.

Then, from the back of the room, Emlyn Llewelyn shouted, 'Nia did it herself, sir. I know. You can ask my dad. And don't you ever say she didn't!'

Everyone looked at him and then at Nia who felt very hot, and Mr James was too taken aback to make an issue of the impudence. 'Well!' he said, and, 'By heck, this is a helluva . . . '

He didn't realize he was swearing until everyone began to laugh and he felt Miss Powell staring at him.

'I think this is it, children, don't you?' he said, remembering his dignity. 'A masterpiece! We'll hang it right in the middle! Pride of place! Llongyfarchiadau, Nia Lloyd! Congratulations! By heck, this is something for the papers!'

Then everyone was clapping and stamping and

shouting, 'Hooray!' and banging Nia on the back. And when she left the Assembly Hall she knew she would never be Nia-can't-do-nothing again.

She went up to Llewelyn's chapel that evening. It was the last night that it would be a home and although the painter would come to work there, it would never be quite the same again.

The Griffiths family were there. The boys were kicking a ball round the field, little Geraint following Emlyn and screaming with delight. The parents watched and murmured to each other.

Nia stepped up on to the railings and looked over. She couldn't go in. They were all together now, one family, but not hers. She clung to the railings and watched them for a long time. They never saw her. She had brought them together, just as she'd always intended.

She stepped down into the road and became aware that someone was shouting her name.

Alun was running up the hill. 'It's come, Nia! The baby! Mam wants you!' he called.

Nia flew down towards him but Emlyn must have seen her. He came out on to the road and shouted, 'Nia! You'll come to Tŷ Llŷr, won't you? There's going to be loads of plums and the flowers are yours, they always will be!'

But she was too breathless to reply or turn to him. There were so many thoughts racing through her mind, above all the sudden realization that she wasn't in the middle any more.

If she was a little apprehensive ascending the last flight of stairs, she forgot everything when she found her family, crushed into the few spaces round the huge bed.

The boys were sitting on it, her sisters leaning on one side, and Mr Lloyd on the other.

156

Mrs Bennett, the midwife, was in the only chair. The baby had come that quick she was still breathless from bicycling two miles and running up three flights of stairs, and she overweight and old enough to retire.

'Come and see your sister, Nia,' Mrs Lloyd said. 'Beautul, she is! And so like you!'

'Give her a name, girl!' Mr Lloyd drew her closer to the bed, where the baby lay in her mother's arms.

'It's your turn, Nia, to name the baby!' Catrin reminded her.

Nia approached, self-conscious and diffident. The baby looked solemnly out of her knitted white cocoon: her eyes were round and dark as berries. There was only one name for a baby like that.

'Let's call her Bethan!' Nia said.

The Chestnut Soldier

For Myfanwy

Contents

Chapter

1

The Prince did not come entirely unannounced! There were messages. They slipped through the air and kindled Gwyn's fingers; the joints ached, things fell out of his grasp and he knew something was on its way.

They had nearly finished the barn; it only needed a few extra nails on the roof to secure it against the wild winds that were bound to come, and planks to fit for the lambing pens; that was Gwyn's task; he had never been much of a carpenter and today he was proving to be a disaster. But he could not pretend that cold or damp was causing his clumsiness. A huge September sun glared across the mountains, burning the breeze. The air was stifling!

Gwyn hated hammering on such a day. Sounds seemed to sweep, unimpeded, into every secret place, and with his father on the roof banging away at corrugated iron, the clamour was deafening.

'Aww!' Gwyn dropped his hammer on to a bucket of nails and thrust his fist against his mouth.

'What've you done, boy?' Ivor Griffiths called from his perch.

'Hammered my thumb, didn't I?'

'You need specs!'

'Take after you then, don't I?' It was a family joke, Ivor's spectacles. They were always streaked with mud, or lost.

1

Gwyn could see them now, balanced on a pile of planks.

'Is it bad?' his father asked.

'Mmm!' Pain began to get the better of Gwyn; the numbing ache aggravated by a bruised and bleeding thumbnail.

'Better go and see Mam,' his father suggested. 'You're no good wounded, are you?'

'No, Dad!' Gwyn slid a chisel into his pocket, wondering why he felt compelled to do this. Perhaps something at home needed his attention. He didn't know, then, what it would be.

He stuck his thumb in his mouth and jogged down the mountain track towards the farmhouse. In spite of the urgency he could not resist a look back at the barn. It would be a grand shelter for the ewes; something to be proud of, for they'd done it all themselves; he and his dad, his cousin Emlyn and Uncle Idris. It was a family affair.

'Idiot!' Gwyn told himself. 'There's nothing here.' It was such a bright and beautiful day. He could see it all from his high field and all was well. Nothing threatened from the valley, where trees glowed with early autumn colour. There were no phantoms hiding in the mountains that stretched calm and splendid under an empty sky. But the warning in his hands could not be ignored.

He was tired of magic, of intuition and the unnatural power that rippled through him sometimes. Once, he'd been tall for his age. But in four years he'd hardly grown. Now information slipped in and out of his mind too swiftly for him to make sense of it. In class he dreamed, wondered about the distance between stars instead of trees, drew crescents where he should have made straight lines, forgot his English and wrote Welsh poetry that no one understood.

Perhaps soon, he thought, when I am thirteen, the wizard in me will fade away and I will grow and be like an average boy. To be average was Gwyn's greatest wish.

Bending his head over his injured thumb, Gwyn began to

run, really hard this time, so that the stitch in his side would distract him from the painful little hints of bad tidings.

His mother was in the kitchen, baking for the school fête. Her face glowed pink, with triumph or the unnatural temperature, Gwyn couldn't guess which. The long table was mounded with extravagantly decorated cakes and the stove was still roaring. Mrs Griffiths had a reputation to maintain. Her cooking won prizes. Two sticky flypapers hung above the table, diverting insects from chocolate sponges, iced buns, jammy gâteaux and waves of *bara brith*. The papers buzzed with dead and dying creatures.

'Duw! It's hot in here, Mam!' Gwyn exclaimed. 'How can you stand it?'

'I've got to, haven't I?' Mrs Griffiths mopped her flushed cheeks with a damp tissue. 'Your dad's not shifted the muck from the yard and if I open the window there'll be stench and bluebottles all through the house. I don't know how the wasps get in, the sly things!'

'Dad's still on the barn. He's nearly done. It's going to be just grand, Mam!'

'I know! I know! What've you done then?' she eyed Gwyn's bloody thumb.

'Hammered my nail, didn't I?' Gwyn grinned sheepishly.

'You're not going to tell me it was the cold made you clumsy?'

'Naw! It was the sun, made my eyes water.' It was a pretty lame excuse since he'd been inside the barn, but it would have to do. He gave up all attempt at bravery and grimaced. 'It hurts, Mam!'

'Come on then, let's put it under the cold tap!' His mother took his hand.

The water was icy. It calmed the pain in his thumb but now his fingers tingled unbearably. Something needed to be done, but what? 'That's enough! I'm O.K.!' He pulled his hand away.

3

'It's still bleeding, Gwyn. I'll have to bandage it.' His mother brought a first-aid box from the cupboard by the sink. 'Tch! I've no wide plasters. Hold still!'

Gwyn hopped from foot to foot. Things took so long when you needed to be finished with them.

'What's your hurry, boy?' His mother spread yellow cream on to the torn nail and began to wrap it up. 'Anyone would think there was a time bomb here!'

Perhaps there is, of a sort, Gwyn thought.

The bandage swelled into a giant grub.

His father peered in through the window. He tapped a pane. 'I'm off to Pendewi, Gwyn. Want to come.?'

'I...well...' Was it here, or was it there that he was needed?

'Make up your mind, boy. I'm late as it is!' Mr Griffiths vanished.

'Go on, Gwyn. Go and have a chat with Alun.' His mother pushed him gently away.

The landrover hustled noisily from the lane.

Gwyn hovered by the door. 'O.K.,' he said and rushed through it. He needed to talk to someone.

As he flung himself into the seat beside his father, he realised it was not Alun he wanted to see, but Nia, Alun's sister.

Alun was a good friend and would be, probably, forever, but he drew away from magic and all talk of it. Only Nia understood. Only she had glimpsed events beyond the world that surrounded her, and welcomed spells as naturally as she did spring flowers.

The journey to Pendewi took twenty minutes. It would have taken ten if the lane had not been so steep. The town was only five miles away. But the Griffiths' farm was the highest on the mountain. It lay at the end of a track that was hardly more than a twisting channel carved into the rock. Even in the landrover, progress was slow until they reached the main road. Then it was a few minutes of racing with

4

coast-bound cars and caravans, over a bridge and down into the town.

Traffic between the Lloyds and the Griffithses was frequent. They had been neighbours until the mountain drove the Lloyds down to the valley. Its pitiless winters had almost done for Iestyn Lloyd, father of eight. Such a man must be master of his home so he had left farming and sold his old house to Gwyn's Uncle Idris. Now Iestyn was a butcher in Pendewi and doing very nicely. But five miles and a different way of life could not interrupt a friendship which was as constant as time.

The Lloyds lived at Number Six, the High Street. Their tall terraced house had two doors, one blue for the shop, the other black for the family. Gwyn and his father went into the shop. Iestyn was placing chickens on to shiny trays in the window. 'Alun's not here,' he told Gwyn. 'Gone swimming with the twins.'

'Doesn't matter,' Gwyn said.

'Wife's out too, showing the baby off again!' Iestyn gave a smug wink.

'I'll go and see Nia!'

Leaving the men to discuss the price of lamb, Gwyn turned through a door that led into the house beyond; the Lloyds' living quarters.

It was a rare, quiet moment in a house that held eight children.

Gwyn walked down the passage to the open back door, but he did not step into what they called the garden: a small square of dry grass confined by, ivy-covered walls and the back of the house. In one wall a glass pane revealed scarlet carcasses hanging in the butcher's room. And beside the low wall that held the garden back from the river, Nia had planted bright flowers, almost, it seemed, as a distraction from the lifeless gaudy things behind her father's window.

Today, however, the distraction came from elsewhere. The boys had made a hammock and slung it between the

5

branches of next door's apple tree. They had joined rope and twine and their mother's rags into a bright lattice, and where the rags were knotted, thin strips of colour floated like tiny breeze-blown flags.

Catrin was lying in the hammock while Iolo, who was eight, gently set the swing in motion.

Catrin was sixteen; she had cornflower blue eyes and abundant yellow hair. Gwyn thought her, probably, the most beautiful girl in Wales. Lately he had found it difficult to talk to her. He did not even come up to her shoulder.

Catrin turned and waved. She looked like a princess, swinging in a basket of silk ribbons.

'I'm looking for Nia,' Gwyn mumbled and stepped back into the passage. He could hear voices at the top of the house, Nerys and Nia arguing.

He walked to the bottom of the stairs but decided against interrupting.

The shouting subsided. A door slammed.

Gwyn sank on to the only seat in the hall; a low oak box where outgrown boots and shoes waited for the next child to find and approve them.

The hall was cool and shady. Gwyn expected to be soothed, but if anything his agitation increased.

Could it be here, the menace that was troubling his hands? Surely nothing could invade this cosy house. It was too crammed with children, it was barricaded with noise, constant movement and the smell of washing. Could a demon slip through a swinging door or slide on a draught beneath loose windows? And if so, where could it hide? None of the small low-beamed rooms was empty for long.

Gwyn hummed tunelessly.

And then, from the top of a bookcase the telephone shrilled. He stared at the instrument, vibrating on its perch, hoping that someone would come to put it out of its misery. Perhaps he should answer it? Take a message. But he found

6

that he couldn't touch it. He was about to escape through the front door when Iolo bounded in exclaiming, 'Is it for me? I bet it is! My friend said he'd call.'

Perhaps Iolo was too eager, for the receiver slipped out of his hand and swung on its black cord, back and forth across the dusty books. For some reason Iolo couldn't touch it either. He shrank from it as a voice called from the instrument, 'Who is there? Who is there?' And Nia ran down the stairs.

Taking in the scene she stepped towards the telephone ready for conversation but suddenly she recoiled. And still the receiver swung on its shiny cord, impelled by nothing, unless it was the voice tumbling through it.

All three watched it, helplessly, until it came to rest and then words spilled towards the reluctant children, clear and strong: a man's voice deep and anxious, 'Who is there? Who is there?'

It was only a voice but, somehow, as potent as electricity, and Gwyn was reminded of a black snake he'd heard of, very small and unremarkable, but with enough venom in its fangs to kill an army.

He clasped his hands and leant over them as little stabs of pain shot through his fingers right up to his elbows.

'What've you done to your thumb?' Nia inquired, glad to find a reason for ignoring the voice.

'Been clumsy again,' he said.

Catrin came into the hall. 'What's the matter with you three?' she asked. 'There's someone on the phone,' and without waiting for them to reply she took the receiver and soothed, 'Catrin Lloyd here! Who is it you want?' Her hair was all tangled gold from the swing.

'Catrin?' Gwyn could hear the voice. 'Ah, Catrin,' and it seemed to sigh. 'It's Evan here. Your cousin, Evan Llŷr!'

'Evan Llŷr!' Catrin repeated the name, frowning.

'You remember me?'

'I…I remember…'

7

'I don't believe you do.' Here, a deep laugh. 'It's been ten years, you were a little child.'

'I was six.'

'How many of you are there now?'

'Eight.'

'Eight?' There was an exclamation and a sentence inaudible to the listeners, except the words, 'and you're the eldest?'

'No, there's Nerys.'

The voice softened, its words maddeningly muffled.

'You're coming here?' Catrin said.

Gwyn didn't like the way she pulled at her tangled curls, as though the voice was watching her.

'No, Mam's not at home...I'll tell her... Evan Llŷr is on his way...Oh, you'll be welcome, sure...' Catrin's free hand was at her throat, the other gripped the receiver.

They were only words, ordinary, pleasant words spoken far away but they slid through the air like a spell.

Gwyn wanted to shout, 'Leave it! Run, before he catches you!'

'Goodbye, now!' Catrin replaced the receiver. Her cheeks were pink. It could have been the heat. 'You're a funny lot, you are,' she said. 'Why didn't you answer the poor man?'

'It wasn't for us,' Nia said, illogically.

'You can take messages, can't you?'

Nia chewed her lip but was not put down. 'Not that sort,' she muttered.

'Sometimes you're very silly!' Catrin swung away and ran up the stairs. Her feet were bare and her swirling skirt made mysterious shadows on her long golden legs.

Gwyn, watching Catrin, knew that Nia was watching him. He had never heard the sisters quarrel. Nia had come off badly. Nerys could scold, and did, often. Catrin was always kind.

Remembering the scene, weeks later, Gwyn wondered if that was when the strife began.

Iolo ran back outside, leaving Gwyn and Nia alone. Nia was troubled and Gwyn didn't know how to comfort her. He had wanted to see her but the disembodied voice had confused him and he couldn't remember his purpose.

'I wish I could grow,' he suddenly confided.

'Grow?' Nia said, as though the word had no meaning.

'You can't say you haven't noticed. Alun's much taller than me now.'

'Alun's taller than everyone.'

'Sometimes I think I'll never grow again,' Gwyn rambled on, almost to himself. 'I'll be a dwarfish sort of man, thoughts ramshackling in my brain beside the magic and never getting clear of it.'

'You'll grow,' Nia said. It sounded automatic. She was still not herself.

'You coming, boy?' His father emerged through a door from the butcher's shop. He was carrying a joint of meat, several red-stained bags and the Lloyds' evening paper.

'Yes, Dad!' Gwyn levered himself up from the chest. The tingling in his hands had eased. All at once he realized it was he who had, somehow, prevented Nia and Iolo from touching the telephone, and he didn't know why. But whoever he is, this Evan Llŷr, Gwyn thought, he has already reached Catrin and I can't match that.

He followed his father to the front door but before leaving he turned to Nia and asked, 'Are you all right?' He spoke softly, not wishing to call attention to his concern for the girl.

Nia nodded and replied, 'Mind your fingers.'

He knew she was not referring to his injured thumb. She understood. Nia, too, experienced irrational stabs of fear.

At least they had each other.

Something had invaded the house. They didn't know what it was, but it still smouldered there.

Mr Griffiths did not drive straight home. He pulled up where the mountain lane began to twist through arches of yellowing ash trees. The landrover lurched on to a bank that had become part of the crumbling wall it supported. Beyond the wall a cottage could be glimpsed, through a jungle of giant shrubs and plants.

'I've got Nain's bacon here,' Mr Griffiths said, 'Coming in to see her?'

'No,' Gwyn replied.

'What's wrong, boy? Why d'you keep avoiding your grandmother? What's the trouble between you?'

'No trouble, Dad.' Gwyn drew himself into the back of the seat. 'I don't want to go in.'

'Don't hurt her! It's not much to ask, a quick visit, only take five minutes.' Mr Griffiths opened the door and looked hopefully at his son. 'You were once so close, Gwyn, but you haven't visited her for weeks.'

'No need to tell her I'm here,' Gwyn said.

His father left him in peace. Gwyn watched him gradually disappear into the ocean of plants. You couldn't see the front door any more.

Ashamed and angry with himself, Gwyn huddled down into his seat. His grandmother had a peephole through the plants, he knew, because once he'd been on the other side of her narrow window and seen his father herding his black cows up the lane.

He couldn't go in there any more. Nain asked too much of him. Four years ago, on his ninth birthday, his grandmother had given him five gifts that had changed his life. For with the gifts had come the knowledge that he was a descendant of Gwydion, the magician, and inheritor of his power. Gwydion, who sent messages like fire in his fingers, who drew a force from him that could even search the stars.

Once Gwyn had been so triumphant, so proud of his talent; but being different led to loneliness. He had to watch himself, to curb his anger for fear of hurting. Being extraordinary was not a happy state.

But wrapped in her dark herbal-scented house, Nain

always wanted more from him. Her own great-great-grandmother had been a witch, but she herself hadn't the power, so she wanted his, even when there was nothing to be done. She couldn't see that it was stunting him – Nain was as tall as her own front door.

One of those birthday gifts was a small carving of a mutilated horse that Gwyn must never use, nor leave where it might tempt a stranger to set it free, for it held the spirit of a demon prince. Gwyn's fingers burned again and he exclaimed aloud in surprise, wondering why he remembered the Lloyds' telephone when he thought of the broken horse, and why he heard the disembodied voice crying 'Who is there?'

Mr Griffiths appeared at the gate. He looked grim. When he had climbed in beside Gwyn he said, 'She knew you were here. It's cruel not to see her.'

'I'm sorry!' He could not explain the reason to his father. Gwyn remained in his mute huddle.

His silence infuriated his father. 'I won't force you, Gwyn, you know that,' Mr Griffiths spoke quietly at first and then he suddenly railed, 'but, by God, you're a mean-spirited little beast.'

And you're a terror for losing your temper, Gwyn thought, but he said nothing.

Mr Griffiths wrenched the handbrake free and jabbed at the ignition. The landrover rocked off the bank and roared up the lane, its occupants cleft into an unwelcome quarrel.

The kitchen table was laid for tea when they reached home. Tins, bowls and messy ingredients had vanished.

'A genius you are, Glenys,' Ivor Griffiths told his wife.

Rows of cakes in plastic packaging were stacked on the dresser, neat as soldiers on parade.

'Wow!' breathed Gwyn. 'You'll break a record with this lot.'

His mother beamed and poured the tea so Gwyn couldn't

11

be unkind and run upstairs just then. He knew now why he'd slipped a chisel into his pocket.

His father relaxed after his meal. He sat in his big armchair and read Iestyn Lloyd's newspaper.

Gwyn went up to his room. He stared at the rug beside his bed for a full minute, then he rolled it up, revealing five dusty floorboards. The centre board had been replaced, long ago by three short planks, one only half a metre long. The nails securing this board were obvious and shiny; they were only four years old. The others, scattered across the floor, brown and invisible, were more than two hundred.

Gwyn eased his chisel into a narrow gap at one end of the short board, and began to lever it up, wondering, as he worked, why he was invading the hiding place. Was it only for reassurance? The thing that he'd imprisoned there four years ago could surely not have escaped.

It was easier than he had imagined. Two nails suddenly snapped free, then the others. The board was loose. Gently, Gwyn lifted it away.

Dust covered the hidden object in a thin grey film but did not conceal it. He experienced a tiny jolt of fear, but forced himself to bring into the light a small four-legged wooden creature.

He blew the dust away and it drifted into the warm air, some settling on his hands. It was smaller than he remembered and even more hideous; a mockery of a horse, with severed ears and tail, blank lidless eyes and teeth bared forever in what could only be despair.

And Gwyn felt pity as he had four years before and a longing to do what he must never do, to set the captured demon free and take away its pain. But the injunction still remained on a scrap of dappled paper tied to the creature's neck, 'Dim hon! Not this!' scrawled in a witch's hand.

If he'd been rational then, he'd have replaced the horse in that safest of hiding places, but panic and his aching fingers distracted him, caused him to hover about the room, rumbling in drawers and cupboards. At length he chose a beam set high into the back wall but protruding twenty centimetres from it; a narrow shelf where he kept his most precious possessions.

He climbed on to the bed and pushed the horse between a lump of glittering quartz and a crowd of pearly shells. The other gifts were there too; the yellow scarf, folded tight; a dry stick of seaweed and the pipe that his ancestors had flung to Gwyn through time so that he might hear voices inaudible to other mortals. Once, he'd heard a sound he wished he could forget.

The last gift was resting in a tiny circle of gossamer at the end of the beam; Arianwen, the spider, sent by his lost sister from another world, in exchange for an ancient metal brooch.

'What d'you think, Arianwen?' Gwyn spread his fingers invitingly along the beam. 'Will I grow? Is the magic shrinking me? I'm tired of it, see. It hurts. I don't want it any more!'

The spider crept towards him and, as she moved into deep shadow beneath the beam, a cloud of glowing particles spiralled round her.

Gwyn took her into his hand. 'There,' he said. 'I didn't mean it!' She was part of the magic and he would never reject her. He could hardly feel her, but the coolness of her silvery body soothed his tingling fingers.

Gently he dropped her on to the broken horse. 'Guard it for a while,' he said. 'I don't know what to do.'

But the little spider ran away from the dark creature and Gwyn couldn't blame her. Something writhed in there, someone glared out from the dead eyes: a mad, imprisoned prince. But what had it to do with that lost voice clutching at Catrin through a telephone receiver?

Gwyn stepped away and jumped off his bed. 'I'm not sleeping with you there,' he told the horse. 'I'll move you later.' He left the room, closing the door tight.

13

Behind the horse's terrible injuries, someone smiled to himself. He had waited for two thousand years; what did a few days matter? The man he had summoned was drawing closer.

Chapter
2

Catrin withheld the message. It was the beginning of a time when she was to keep more and more of herself away from her family.

It isn't my message, Nia thought. It isn't mine to pass on. Perhaps there was no telephone call. She didn't want to think about the lost voice stealing into the house and catching at her sister. If she had answered the phone the message and the voice would have been hers, but Gwyn Griffiths had come between her and Evan Llŷr. She knew it was Gwyn, sitting there, bent over his fingers like the wizard he was. He had done it before. She knew the feeling now; he had stopped her from doing things, saved her! He hadn't stopped Catrin though!

When the letter came, two days later, Mrs Lloyd was unprepared and quite flustered at the news. 'Evan Llŷr!' she exclaimed over the buzz of eight children munching breakfast. Her voice had such an unnatural ring it managed to penetrate the noise and even to subdue it.

'Who is Evan Llŷr, Mam?' Nerys asked.

'Your cousin!'

'Our cousins are girls,' said Gareth, grimacing.

'Rotten girls,' Sîon repeated, always derisive where the opposite sex were concerned.

15

'He says he telephoned,' Mrs Lloyd went on, ignoring the twins. 'Gave someone a message!'

'I forgot,' said Catrin, vigorously buttering her toast. 'I'm sorry.'

You didn't forget, Nia thought. You wanted to keep it all to yourself, Catrin Lloyd.

'He wants to come … dear, dear…I wish I'd known…well, of course,' Mrs Lloyd brought the letter closer to her face.

Nia leant over the table for the butter dish and peered into Catrin's face.

'Don't look at me like that,' Catrin said sharply. 'I forgot. Why didn't you remind me?'

'It wasn't my message and anyway, how was I to know you'd keep it to yourself?'

'Oh, no… and he's been wounded!' Mrs Lloyd announced.

'Wounded?' The twins looked up.

'Yes, wounded. He's a soldier, didn't I tell you?'

'A soldier?' Three boys brightened at the word.

'I can hardly read this bit…' Mrs Lloyd ran her fingers through uncombed morning curls.

Nia abandoned her breakfast and ran behind her mother. It was strange to read the hand that belonged to that deep disturbing voice. Gwyn wasn't there, this time, to keep Evan Llŷr from reaching her.

The letter was written in black ink. At the top of the paper the words sprawled huge and forceful towards the right hand margin, but after a few sentences the character of the writing changed, it dwindled as though the writer had lost confidence; either the ink was not flowing or the pen hardly touching the paper. And through and about the uneven, hesitant pattern of lines, Nia caught something of the unknown cousin behind them and was, at the same time, entranced and infinitely saddened. The words at the end could hardly

16

be deciphered: 'Forgive me; if you've no room, I'll go elsewhere.'

'No 'Love from', ' Nerys remarked. 'Do we really know this man?'

'Anyone would think he was a stranger,' muttered her mother. 'Of course we know him, though it's been ten years, and of course he can come. There's a bit of space in Iolo's room.' Then she dropped the letter on the table and exclaimed, 'Oh, but he wants peace and it's such a tiny room. He must have a place to himself.'

'Iolo can come in with Bethan and me,' Nia offered.

'No!' moaned Iolo.

'Please, cariad. I'm sure it won't be for long,' Mrs Lloyd gave Iolo one of her special winning smiles. 'It'll be nice, three quiet ones together!'

'And three noisy down below,' said Nia. She wouldn't have shared her room with Alun or the twins.

'It's half past eight,' Mr Lloyd informed his children from the kitchen door. 'You'll be late for school, get on with it. Betty, those boys haven't even brushed their hair.'

'I've had a letter, Iestyn' Mrs Lloyd jumped up, guiltily, 'from Evan. You remember, Evan Llŷr.'

'I remember,' said Iestyn, none too warmly.

'He's coming here!'

'Is he now?'

All at once, hairbrushing conveniently forgotten, the kitchen was full of boys' excited questions. 'Would Iolo's room be large enough for a soldier? Where would his boots go? Would there be weapons under the bed?'

'Not if I've got anything to say about it!' Mr Lloyd might be a butcher but his lust for blood did not extend beyond his trade. He regarded soldiery with suspicion. 'Now, up those stairs and make yourselves tidy!'

So the children had to wait until tea time before they could squeeze further information from their mother.

'Who is Evan, really?' Nia asked for the second time.

17

'I've told you, my brother's son,' her mother sighed, patiently.

That was no answer. 'Yes, but who…?' Nia persisted.

'I'll tell you.' Mrs Lloyd, easier now that all ten plates were filled, sat down and embarked on a history of Llŷrs, past and present. 'As you know, there were three of us girls: Auntie Megan, Auntie Cath and me. Well, I was the youngest and your Uncle Dai was fifteen years older. He was a half-brother, my mother's child but not my father's!'

'So he's not a Llŷr!' Nerys put in.

'Well…no…'

'Nor is Evan then!' Nerys went on. She was always one for grabbing at little details. She liked backgrounds to be neat.

Her mother didn't want to linger on complications but she knew Nerys would give her no peace until she had every bit of the puzzle. 'Dai was only a baby when my parents married,' she explained, 'so my father adopted him, legally; gave him his name.'

'Who was Dai's father then?' Nia asked.

'I don't know!' Mrs Lloyd seemed surprised by her own answer. 'I never knew. I never asked.'

This piece of information fascinated Nia.

So there's a part of Evan that we'll never know about, she thought. Aloud she said, 'Go on about Uncle Dai.'

Relieved to have got off lightly this time, Mrs Lloyd continued, 'Well, Dai never did like farming, so he was off to work in the bank, in Wrexham. Did very well, too. Must have been quite a catch in those days. He was handsome, too, your Uncle Dai.'

'What's a catch?' asked Iolo, grasping at the only point of interest in his mother's story.

'Like a fish,' Alun said quickly.

'Is he dead, then?' Iolo inquired.

'Dead? Why should he be dead?' Mrs Lloyd was in danger of losing her thread.

'He means like a fish being caught,' Nia cheerfully came to the rescue.

'I do not!' Iolo said indignantly. 'You said *was,* Mam. You said he *was* handsome!'

'Oh, in those days. He's quite old now.'

'Where is he?' Nia asked.

'Where? In Australia. Where was I?' Mrs Lloyd looked at her eldest daughter. Nerys could usually be relied upon at such times, but she was polishing her spectacles. Catrin was gazing into a space that was probably occupied, Nia thought, by a boy on a black horse. Catrin was in love with Michael McGoohan, the doctor's son.

Nia had not lost the thread. 'Uncle Dai, who was handsome and rich because of being a bank manager, went to Australia,' she said. 'But what about Evan??'

'There were two of them,' Mrs Lloyd said absently, then all at once she seemed to regret having launched herself thus far.

'Two what?' Nia prompted eagerly.

'Evan had an older brother, Emrys, but he died when he was only eight' Mrs Lloyd disclosed this sad and dreadful fact as though she intended to end her story there, and for most of her family it had the desired effect. The awfulness of dying when you were eight had to be respected in silence.

The twins managed a mumbled 'Aw!' and glanced at Iolo, but Nia needed to know more about the survivor. 'And then what?' she asked.

'Then what? Then what?' Mr Lloyd mimicked irritably. 'It's like a pound of flesh you're wanting, Nia Lloyd. Haven't you had enough Llŷr history?' It was clear that he had had a surfeit; his own family was not so numerous, nor as interesting as his wife's.

'But I want to know about Evan,' Nia stubbornly persisted.

'Go on, then! Go on, Betty! I'll get my own cup of tea!' Mr

19

Lloyd made a great to-do about squeezing himself out of his chair at the end of the table.

'Sit down, Da,' said Nerys, reaching for his cup.

'And go on, Mam,' said Nia. 'Emrys died and then what?'

'Then, sometime after, your aunt and uncle went to Australia, but Evan wouldn't go. He wanted to be a soldier.'

'A soldier, and he's coming here,' the twins yelled at each other.

'A soldier, yes, but one that's been to college.' Mrs Lloyd was proud of her nephew. 'Duw, he was bright, that Evan. He's a major now, it seems, and still only in his thirties.'

'He's getting on, then,' Nia began to be disappointed.

'He's younger than I am,' her mother laughed. She wasn't old, Nia thought, her curls were still golden-brown and her eyes as blue as Catrin's.

'But for a cousin he's old,' Iolo said. 'I mean, he's past playing, isn't he?'

'He's a soldier,' scoffed Gareth.

'A fighter,' added Siôn.

'Yes,' Iolo sadly agreed. He lived in the hope of finding someone who could share his games. His older brothers were into violent activities where he was always the victim.

'There was another side to Evan, as I remember,' Mrs Lloyd told Iolo, but she refused to be drawn further.

When tea was over and Catrin had carried Bethan away for her bath, Nia surprised her family by demanding to take Alun's turn with the drying up. She wanted to be alone with her mother.

'What was on the other side, Mam?' Nia probed while she gently dried her father's favourite mug.

'Other side of what, cariad?' Mrs Lloyd was thinking of beds now.

'You said there was another side to Evan Llŷr.'

'Yes.' Mrs Lloyd became suddenly wary. 'Well – I meant he wasn't all soldier.' She caught sight of the kitchen clock. 'Is that the time? I want to watch the news!' She peeled off

20

her rubber gloves and left the kitchen for the front room.

Nia dogged her. She wasn't going to let it go at that.

The news hadn't started. They remembered the kitchen clock was ten minutes fast. Mrs Lloyd switched off. She sank on to the sofa and drummed her fingers on one arm. Nia wriggled in beside her.

'Go on about Evan, Mam!'

'What do you...' Mrs Lloyd began and then something caught her eye in the street beyond the lace curtain.

A horse and rider came into view. The horse was huge and glossy black, the young man on his back had attractive youthfully rounded features, thick brown hair that curled over his collar, and skin that seemed permanently flushed, giving him the appearance of someone always on the edge of a violent emotion.

The sight of the boy and the horse seemed to irritate Mrs Lloyd. 'That Michael McGoohan,' she muttered. 'Thinks he's grand, doesn't he, loafing about on a big black horse.'

'You can't loaf on a horse, Mam,' Nia said. 'Anyway, they ride horses a lot in Ireland.' She felt she had to defend Catrin's interest. 'They think nothing of it.'

'Why doesn't he get a job? He's left school.'

'He's waiting for the right one. Catrin likes him.'

'I know. She could do better!'

Michael McGoohan glanced towards their window, hoping perhaps for a glimpse of Catrin. Nia and her mother, safely concealed behind the lace, stared out at him. The young man looked up and scanned the second floor windows. Disappointed, he moved his horse on.

Nia waited until the rhythm of hoofbeats had receded then prodded her mother. 'Mam, about Emrys. How did he die?'

'Oh, Nia,' Betty Lloyd gave a long, sad sigh, 'I've kept it to myself for so long. It's something I'd like to forget.'

'No one else knows, then.'

'Of course they do. When a boy dies, people have to know.

21

You can't keep it a secret.' She took a breath. 'He fell out of a tree. There!'

Nia had annoyed her mother and it was the last thing she'd intended. But she felt compelled to pursue the subject. If she let go of it now, she would never know the story as it should be known.

'Oh Mam, please tell,' she begged. 'I know that isn't all of it. It can't be. There's more. The bit that hurts you.'

Mrs Lloyd gripped the arm of the sofa. Nia thought she'd pushed too far and that her mother was going to fling away the subject of Evan and Emrys, in favour of the television news. Then Mrs Lloyd relaxed, she put her arm round Nia and said, 'Emrys was the one we watched. The one everyone loved for his brave ways. Evan was quiet; a kind little boy, always behind Emrys, always following, and a bit of a coward. Emrys loved to climb trees; Evan would watch, too frightened to climb, and Emrys would taunt him.

'They were gone a long time that day. It was autumn, the conkers were ripe. Emrys had climbed the chestnut tree to reach the best...

'I was sent out to find them. I was twelve. When I saw them I thought it was a bit of play-acting, but they were too quiet for that, and so still, and all at once I knew why. I'll never forget that day, not as long as I live. He never cried, see, Evan, not once, just walked away and left me calling to his mam. And the next day, when we were all wandering about, still shocked, I suppose, and hardly knowing what we were doing, he slipped out, that strange child, and climbed the very tree that had killed his brother, almost to the top. I followed him and waited till he came down, all serious-looking but somehow satisfied and when I asked him, 'Why did you do that, Evan? How could you?' he just said, 'I climbed higher, Betty, higher than Emrys.'

'I thought he'd lost his wits and must have shown what I thought because he put his arms so carefully round me and said, 'Don't cry, Betty, Evan is here!' He was so gentle.'

22

Betty Lloyd had never spoken about the past at such length. Perhaps it was because she had been able to sweep her daughter into the hours that still startled her when she remembered them. And now Nia, too, saw the fierce dead boy, and the gentle one beside, unable to cry.

'He came again, often,' Mrs Lloyd went on. 'I don't think his parents understood him any more. He came every summer. Long summers they were, and always hot, as I remember, and, this will sound heartless to you, but we didn't miss Emrys any more.'

So Nia thought she knew all about Evan Llŷr. She'd heard his voice, seen his letter, knew his childhood. She believed she was armed against whatever it was that Gwyn Griffiths wished to save her from.

The weather broke at last. A wind swept down from the mountains and blasted arctic wet into the valley. Chimneys toppled and the trees flung ripe fruit and fading leaves over the sodden fields. The river rose and spilled into basements and back gardens. It had happened before and would do so again.

For two days, inky black clouds threatened with thunder. Roads became muddy torrents of debris. The wind screamed through pylons, snapped at hedges, gleefully toyed with loose bricks and litterbins. Traffic was diverted and Pendewi would have been a quiet place if it hadn't been for the wind.

The prince still came, though later than expected, so the boys were into their noisy after-tea time, and Mrs Lloyd was busy with Nerys in the kitchen. It was Nia who answered the door. She opened it very slowly and carefully; even so, she was unprepared.

Evan Llŷr was tall, but not in uniform as Nia had expected. He wore a dark sweater and jeans and something flung round his shoulders in the manner of a cloak. His appearance caused a jolt in Nia's mind and the reception

23

she'd intended became disorganised. 'Aw,' she mumbled. 'Is it… are you?'

'Hullo!' said Evan Llŷr.

And Nia could not reply to this because, in all her eleven years, she had never been alone with anyone so startlingly handsome. Black-wing eyebrows accentuated a brilliant blue gaze; abundant black hair sprang away from fine aquiline features and the faintest of blue shadows echoed the long curves of his upper lip. Evan Llŷr was the prince from every fairy tale; he was fierce and kind – and immensely troubled.

'I'm Evan Llŷr,' he said.

'I know,' Nia opened the door wider.

Her prince smiled and Nia felt so small she wondered if he could really see her.

They stood a moment, regarding each other, a moment in which Nia came to know her cousin more intimately than in all the imminent hours of close conversation.

And she was still standing there, wondering at the intense and unfamiliar sensation when her mother came up behind her exclaiming, 'Nia … Nia, what are you doing, girl? Let the man in … is it? It is, it's Evan!'

And then the prince was walking past Nia, and there were boys whooping down the stairs, and her mother was bouncing like a girl and planting sugary kisses on the noble cheekbone.

Nia turned from these intimacies to close the front door and as she did so, noticed something black and bronze in the misty road, steaming like a tired beast. Such a car did not seem appropriate for a prince, but more the sort of vehicle a demon would choose.

She followed the company into the kitchen where her father gave Evan Llŷr his own seat at the head of the table. But it didn't seem right that a prince should be sitting there, with clutter and crumbs still on the cloth, with sticky jars on the dresser and stained tea-cloths hanging on the door.

24

He seemed happy with his lot, however; a plate of stew piping hot and a glass of plum wine, the last bottle, kept specially for such an occasion.

Between mouthfuls the new cousin made up for lost years; counted heads, repeated names and asked all the questions expected of a long-absent relative. And although someone was missing he never mentioned it, but turned his head very slightly, now and again, to listen to the sonata that Catrin was playing in the room beyond.

No one could stem the twins' eager curiosity. What weapons did a major use? How many men did he lead? When was he wounded and how? The soldier parried these questions gently, some he answered, some he left and then Gareth asked, 'How many men have you killed, cousin Evan?'

And Nia noticed a sudden stillness fall about Evan. He seemed to depart from them. His fingers tightened round the cut-glass tumbler, then abandoned it. And he withdrew a shaking hand into safe shadows beneath the table.

'How many?' Sîon pressed.

'Leave Evan in peace, boys,' Mrs Lloyd said in what seemed to Nia a meaningless way, for her mother was beside herself with a sort of silly excitement.

'You're no different, Betty,' Evan remarked, almost himself again. 'Last time I saw you on the lane from Tŷ Llŷr you had a baby in your arms; its the same now, and you're the same.'

'Don't tease, Evan!' Betty Lloyd blushed, although she was a few years older than the soldier, and pressed her face into Bethan's dark curls. 'It's ten years; Nia was the baby then.'

For a moment Nia had her cousin's undivided attention and then someone came into the room behind her and took her moment away. Nia, watching closely, saw a hint of dismay and then confusion in Evan's dark blue eyes.

25

'And this is Catrin,' Mrs Lloyd said.

Catrin walked into a space where the light was brightest. Her hair shone as though she had brushed it a thousand times, just for the occasion. But she looked nervous and unsure.

Evan smiled. 'The musician,' he said quietly.

'Catrin took your message,' Mrs Lloyd told him, 'but she kept it to herself,' and she immediately tried to make light of her remark by giving a diffident laugh.

She is aware of something, Nia thought, and so am I, and so is Catrin. We have changed, each one of us, but we won't speak about it, not yet. All this happened before, long, long ago, it's like a story being retold. But how are we going to find the way to a happy ending?

Chapter
3

'He's come then, Alun's soldier cousin?' said Gwyn's mother. She'd been toiling away at the new stove, a French contraption that did radiators and hot water as well as the cooking. Gradually, Glenys Griffiths was dragging her reluctant husband into the twentieth century.

There was a glass oven door in the smart new stove; you could see the bread, and it wasn't rising. You couldn't have bread, it seemed, as well as radiators.

'He's come,' Gwyn said. 'Alun says he's not like a soldier. Won't talk about the army, nor nothing like that.'

'Just as well!' Mrs Griffiths flung herself back into an easy chair. 'I thought that storm would blow the heat away but it seems to be back, just as close, and it's nearly October.'

'He wants to come and see Tŷ Llŷr, this Evan,' Gwyn said. 'They're bringing him up this afternoon. Think I'll go and have a look at him.'

'Have a look?' his mother smiled. 'Sounds like he's a toy soldier.'

'You know what I mean. Can I bring him back for some tea?'

'How many? There'll be no bread.' Mrs Griffiths glanced ruefully at the oven.

'Cake then. I don't know how many. Maybe the soldier will want to stay at Tŷ Llŷr. He loves that place, Alun says.'

'I remember him,' Gwyn's mother disclosed with a coy and unfamiliar expression. 'A tall young man, quiet, with eyes like – the summer sea.' Memories of Evan released the poet in her, it seemed.

'He used to come and help the Lloyds at lambing time,' Glenys continued. 'He was good, too, up all hours, out in all weather, never complained. He didn't get on with Alun's dad, though, I don't know why. He'd have been good on a farm, shame there was no place for him.'

'Sounds drastic to be a soldier instead,' Gwyn remarked. 'Like going in the wrong direction.'

'Well, he was strange, too!'

Gwyn knew that. He'd heard the voice reaching into Nia's home. 'I'll try and bring him back, then,' he told his mother. 'So you can look into his sea-blue eyes!'

'Gwyn!' Was it the heat, or did she blush?

'It'd better be a grand cake,' he teased and leapt away from his confused mother, closing the door against her muttered protestations.

He decided against walking down the lane. His grandmother might be in her front garden and he was still not ready for a discussion. So, feeling a little foolish, he walked through the farmyard and climbed the gate. The binder twine that secured the broken bolt took too long to unravel.

Wishing he did not feel so furtive and ill at ease on his own territory he walked round the back of the outbuildings and then downhill, through two fields of sheep. There was a shaggy little horned ram in the second field. He stared at Gwyn with his sharp hazel eyes and moved protectively along the ranks of ewes until the boy had left his field.

Gwyn scrambled over a drystone wall and dropped into Nain's ground. The wild acre behind his grandmother's cottage was choked with weeds; burdock and thistles scrawled round giant artichokes, cumfrey and green alkanet. None of this was accidental, nor was it a 'crime' as Iestyn

Lloyd would have it. 'It's a prime bit of pasture and she's let it go,' he would complain. But Gwyn knew that every centimetre was planned, every plant known. Birds flocked to Rhiannon Griffiths' fruitful meadow, bees found untainted pollen there, ladybirds thrived, rodents happily multiplied.

'Everything has its use,' Rhiannon would say, 'and there's a cure for all ills in the things that spring from the earth!'

And Gwyn knew that his grandmother was not mad. He also knew that none of her herbs would solve his problem. They would not help him to grow, nor stop the burning in his hands. He needed something else, something or someone?

He passed the copse of ash trees that separated the weeds from his grandmother's more formal herb garden. The feathery leaves were already yellowing in the dry weather. Nain loved the ash above all trees. Gwyn dared not look towards the cottage, but couldn't resist a guilty glance at the garden where he suddenly became aware that he was looking straight at his grandmother, who was staring at him. She'd been so still, wrapped in a green shawl and kneeling on the path, he hadn't noticed her at first.

Gwyn started, then smiled. It was too late to run away. She didn't speak, didn't move.

'Hullo, Nain!' he said at last, and his voice sounded withered and unwilling.

His grandmother looked away from him. She was holding a trowel which she began to poke into the dry soil. When she spoke she seemed to be addressing the earth. 'Snooping are we, Gwydion Gwyn?' she said.

'No, not snooping, Nain,' he said.

'Why didn't you come to the door, then, instead of lurking in my ground like a thief?'

'I wasn't lurking, Nain. I was just passing,' he said huffily. He felt silly peering through the sprays of coloured leaves.

'I see. Not coming to see *me*, then!'

'Well...' he shifted from one foot to the other.

29

'So run along, then,' she said coldly. 'Don't let me detain you from your urgent business.'

All at once Gwyn felt that he should speak to his grandmother.

It wasn't pity that led him to her at last. He went to seek her advice, to arm himself with a little of her ancient wisdom before facing the owner of that dark and worrying voice.

He sidled past the trees and walked up the path. When he was standing beside her he said, 'I'm going to see that soldier.'

'Soldier?' She was too obviously casual to be uninterested.

'You must have heard,' he said. 'The Lloyds' cousin. He was wounded, in Belfast.'

'That one!'

He could tell, in spite of her digging away at the earth, that she was profoundly interested. 'D'you know him?' he asked. 'He came to Tŷ Llŷr, when he was a boy, Alun says. Says he's not much of a soldier neither, though he's a major and won medals.'

'Poor creature,' Nain said.

'Poor creature?' he repeated, surprised.

'That one, that soldier. Poor injured soul.' She shook her head.

'Why poor, Nain? He's better.' Gwyn was intrigued. What was she on about now?

'Is he better? Is he?' She turned for the first time and darted a fierce black look up at her grandson. 'Why has he come here, then?'

'To recover. There's no mystery!' He wished he could believe that himself.

'But why here, eh? After all this time?'

He wasn't sure whether she expected him to know the answer or was trying to kindle an interest. Couldn't she tell that he was already on his guard? 'His relations are here,' Gwyn explained.

'It's not so simple, Gwydion Gwyn. It's not just his

30

relatives. I know that man. And I knew he'd come back, to finish a story. Perhaps you can help him.'

'Me?' He was genuinely astonished.

'Of course, you. Who else? You're the magician.'

'Oh, Nain, don't...' he groaned and kicked at the pebbles on the path.

'You can't just shake it off, boy. You're a magician. I'll shout it. Nothing you can do will unsay it.' Nain stood up and clutched at his shoulder. She was such a tall woman. He felt buried in her shadow. 'Listen, it isn't my fault. I didn't make you what you are. I just woke you up. And weren't you pleased, Gwydion Gwyn, when you discovered your power, and didn't it bring you joy to see your lost sister, and to save your cousin Emlyn with a spell?'

'Yes, yes!' He shrugged her off and turned away. 'But I don't want it any more, see! I'm sick of it. It's making me tired!'

He began to run towards the trees but when he'd passed through the copse and couldn't see the tall figure on the path, the words he'd meant to keep to himself burst from him. 'I want to grow,' he cried and he tore through the wild acre as though every second he spent there would diminish him further.

But as he broke free of the giant weeds and tumbled on to smooth-cropped grass he heard a voice sing-songing after him. 'You *will* grow, Gwydion Gwyn. You will, I promise you!'

He believed his grandmother, as he always had and always would, and rushed down towards the Tŷ Llŷr fields, feeling lighter and more hopeful than he'd done for many months.

Ivor Griffiths now farmed the land that had once belonged to the Lloyds, but the ancient farmhouse was owned by Idris Llewelyn, the painter. The chapel where Idris worked was too small for his growing family and ever since the fire there,

31

four years earlier, his wife Elinor had refused to live in the place. Elinor and Gwyn's mother were sisters and Gwyn now considered Tŷ Llŷr a second home. Nia, too, used it as a refuge; the only house where she felt truly at peace. In fact there was an embracing atmosphere about Tŷ Llŷr that suggested it had been the site of a well-loved home even before the present farmhouse had been built. And so it had become a meeting place, where children from three families would come to find each other and discuss their problems.

A stream ran past Tŷ Llŷr; a wild, rocky stream of clear water that sprang from the mountain summit and spilled in a silvery torrent beside the lane until it found the Lloyds' old farmhouse, perched on its granite rock, and there the water, seeking an easier passage, found soft shale that allowed it to meander gently round the back of the farmyard. The bank, here, was formed from the roots of willow and alder, it was an untidy network that twisted and curled into the riverbed.

Gwyn found Evan Llŷr sitting on a wide rock, his feet supported by the trellis of blanched roots, with Nia and Iolo either side of him. The man and the boy each held a string with a polished conker tied to the end. The conkers flew on their strings, they spun and cracked while the soldier issued instructions. 'Keep the string short, Iolo! Hit it on the top, now. Harder! Ah, you've got me!'

Iolo laughed and Nia smiled; she watched the soldier, not the battling conkers, Gwyn noted. And then she saw him and exclaimed, 'It's Gwyn!'

Gwyn faced the group across the stream. The soldier looked up, lifting his hand to shade his eyes from the sun. 'So you're Gwyn Griffiths,' he said and there was nothing in his voice except a gentle curiosity.

Gwyn stepped into the stream, and the current pushed against him, little billows of shining spume lapping round the top of his boots.

'It's deep there,' Nia shouted. 'You'll get your socks wet.'

But Gwyn took his time, feeling for the smooth higher

pebbles with his feet. He paced slowly through the stream, watching his step, aware of a sea-blue glance marking him out, until he came within a metre of the bank and then he stopped and looked up at the trio.

Evan Llŷr regarded him eagerly, intrigued and puzzled and, for a moment, Gwyn was thrown off his guard because the soldier's smile was so truly welcoming. And then he remembered the voice that had snaked through the air, repelling the same three people who now found its owner so irresistible. And Gwyn sensed a terrible contradiction. He was in the presence of something utterly unfamiliar. There was an emptiness about Evan Llŷr, a fearlessness that had nothing to do with courage, and it betrayed the kind and gentle smile.

Does he know who I am? Gwyn wondered.

'Here!' The soldier held out his hand and Gwyn accepted it. There was no warmth in the soldier's flesh, it was smooth and dry and his touch sent a tiny circuit of pain trickling through Gwyn, like a ghost; it was so fleeting Gwyn did not even gasp, but the soldier's hand tightened round his own and he was sure Evan knew what had happened between them.

'Don't fall,' the soldier said.

And Gwyn replied, 'It's my boots, they're slippery!' And as he clambered up beside Nia's cousin, he was baffled by a sense of being quite alone with Evan, in a place where giant trees replaced the hedges and a midnight cloud obscured the sun.

'I won,' Iolo shouted into the quietness. 'D'you want a game, Gwyn?'

'No, not now,' Gwyn said, trying to shake off unreality. 'Got to get my hands in the right mood.'

'Look!' Nia held out a handful of conkers. 'Aren't they beautiful when they're new? There are hundreds this year, all over the lane, big and shiny.'

Gwyn took the largest from her. It gleamed brown and

velvet smooth; the underside white and soft as down, just plucked from its shell. 'I'd like to grow this up at home,' he said, 'but it would die; it's too cold and high for chestnut trees. Nain says it's strange that a chestnut tree should grow on a mountain at all.'

'It's in a sheltered spot,' said Evan, 'away from the north wind. The topsoil has collected there just so such a tree could thrive.' And then he added, 'I climbed that tree once, long ago.'

Iolo began to attack the roots at his feet, but his victorious conker broke free of its string and bounced into the water. 'Aw!' he cried. 'My conqueror, he's gone,' and he leapt up to follow the prizewinner downstream.

'Let it go, Iolo,' Evan said, 'and I'll get you another, an even greater winner.'

'We're going for a walk,' Nia reminded him. 'You wanted to see the mountain again, you said.'

'So I did, and so we shall.' Evan got to his feet. 'But I have forgotten the best way, so you'll have to keep close to me.'

'We'll all go,' Gwyn said. He felt protective towards the mountain; it was his place, his and his father's; Griffiths land right to the summit. 'And we'll take Emlyn,' he added when he saw his cousin, a tall boy with wild corn-brown hair coming through the yard.

'Take Emlyn where?' his cousin asked. 'I'm busy.'

'No, you're not,' Gwyn winked slyly.

Emlyn showed no surprise. 'Oh, I'm not,' he said.

Gwyn knew he would help. They were as close and comfortable as brothers, even if Emlyn did not always understand how his cousin could sometimes ache with apprehension on a sunny day. Emlyn had no space to waste on the inexplicable, his mind was reserved for the animals he made. He already showed a considerable talent for woodcarving and it was clear that he would follow in his father's footsteps. His four year old brother Geraint, on the other hand, longed only to be a farmer like his Uncle Ivor.

34

In the end it was the four children who walked up the mountain leaving Evan Llŷr to follow, because Emlyn's mother came to her door and begged the soldier to stay for just one cup of tea. Mrs Llewelyn was usually shy of strangers but the major had charmed her with his quiet diffidence. His request to wander through her garden had been so courteous, his smile so irresistible, she was eager to share more of her home with him, and to show him round the places he had loved.

'I'll catch you up,' Evan told the children. 'Wait for me at Tŷ Bryn.'

So the children walked up to Gwyn's home where they visited the cat and her three white kittens lying in a barn. Then Gwyn mentioned the kite he had observed hovering over the lower mountains, and Nia couldn't wait to see it.

'We'll need field glasses,' Gwyn said, 'just to make sure. It might have been a buzzard, but I think it was too big, and the wings had touches of red.'

'I'll get the glasses,' Iolo offered. Gwyn's attic, crammed with books and maps of the planets, was always worth a visit.

'They're hanging on my bed,' Gwyn called after him. But Iolo knew exactly where to look.

He was away for some time. Gwyn would have gone after him, to see what he was up to, but Nia and Emlyn had already started up the mountain track. It was the sort of breezy day that seemed to forbid the indoors. It spun Gwyn through the farmyard, infecting him with a reckless forgetfulness, and leading him up the mountain away from the thing he should have remembered.

Inside Gwyn's room Iolo was reaching for the field glasses when a dark shape fluttered through the open window. It flipped over Iolo's head, knocked into a cupboard, and swung away. Iolo ducked, the little creature dipped past him then flew up to a shelf above the bed, where it came to rest.

Iolo straightened up. He saw a tiny bat clinging to something that lay on the very edge of the shelf. He cautiously extended his hand toward the bat, but the creature sensed movement; it wheeled away and this time headed straight for the open window. As it went, something toppled off the shelf and fell on to the pillow. It was a small wooden animal: a horse, maybe, Iolo thought, but without ears or tail, its mouth a jagged row of teeth, its eyes bulging and fierce.

He picked it up to replace it but found that it was looking at him and he couldn't do what he'd intended because the horse didn't want to be abandoned. It clung to his hand with an almost human insistence. So he put it in his pocket, took the field glasses and left Gwyn's room.

The others were already in the high field where Gwyn had first caught sight of the kite. And, as if to reward them, the great bird reappeared. They had no need of field glasses, it soared above them, an autumn bird, red-gold in the soft light, its tail spread in a wide triangle, the distinctive blaze of white on the underwings clearly visible. It swept down to the woods and they jumped on a stone wall to prolong the event.

'It lives here,' Nia cried. 'Right here, with us. Let's not tell anyone, ever. Let's keep it a secret, our bird!'

'Better warn Iolo it's a secret then,' said Emlyn nodding at a small figure bobbing up the track.

And Gwyn saw Iolo sprinting towards them, the field glasses clutched in his hand. He waited until Iolo reached them before telling him the news. 'Don't broadcast it, Iolo, we don't want strangers on our mountain.'

'Looking for our kite,' Nia added.

Iolo climbed up beside them, held the field glasses to his eyes and trained them on to the wood. But the kite didn't emerge. It had important business down there, behind the screen of coloured leaves.

They sat on the wall and ate the apples that Emlyn's mother had provided and then they remembered Evan.

'He can't be lost,' Gwyn said.

And Emlyn remarked, 'My mam's taken a fancy to him, I reckon.'

It was intended as a joke but, for some reason, no one laughed because Evan Llŷr was the sort of person who might pose a threat to the most stable relationship. Gwyn knew this because Elinor Llewelyn's glance had excluded everyone but Evan; even Gwyn's own mother had recalled the soldier with a hint of something deeper than affection, and now cheeky childish Nia had begun to watch this older man like a real, wide-eyed girl at last.

'Let's go,' Gwyn said suddenly, 'and find out where the major's got to.'

They followed the stream down to Tŷ Bryn. It was a favourite route. They could leap over the water from side to side, on to dry islands of rock that rose clear of the sparkle and the spray.

Emlyn lead the way with Nia close behind him, singing delightedly as she slipped and splashed through the water. Her voice was high and fluttery but she didn't care, the mountain always drew songs from her. Gwyn couldn't help laughing, and then he turned to see what had become of Iolo. The sky smouldered gold and scarlet where the sun had left it and he was about to remark on this when he noticed Iolo, unmoving, on his tiny island, staring at something in his hand.

'What've you got, Iolo?' Gwyn called. 'Not a fish?' No, it was not a fish. He knew very well what it was. He could see the tiny label. He stepped into the stream, but he was shaking now and couldn't trust himself to move further.

Iolo, looking up, said, 'It's a horse, I think. I found it in your room and put it in my pocket. I didn't mean to keep it, honest!'

'Give it to me!' He couldn't convey urgency, his words carried across the water in a dismal mutter.

'O.K.' Iolo raised his arm.

'No! Don't throw...' This time Gwyn found a scream, but

it was too late. Distracted by Gwyn's cry, Iolo's aim went wild. The horse was free! It sailed over Gwyn's head and landed, with a soft splash, beyond him. The stream carried it away.

'Stop it!' Gwyn shrieked.

Nia looked back, still singing, and Emlyn shouted, 'What's the matter?'

Gwyn couldn't explain, even if he had had the time, they wouldn't understand, and who could blame them. 'Destroyer...' he mumbled. 'Guard the prince...me...only me...dark...' Shaking, he tottered to the bank and crawled along the side of the stream crying, 'Stop it! Stop it! *Please!*'

'Stop what?' Confused, Nia slithered into a deep pool and water gushed into her wellingtons.

'Horse,' Gwyn moaned. 'Black, very small.' Willing strength into his knees he got to his feet and ran past Nia, his eyes fixed on the water. 'You wouldn't know,' he gabbled feebly. 'It's got no ears, no tail. Must stop it, see! Stop it! Stop it!'

'What's so special about it?' Emlyn peered into the stream.

'There isn't time,' Gwyn mumbled breathlessly. 'Help me, Emlyn. If you see it, keep it safe. It's a terrible thing.' And he ran on helplessly, seeing nothing in the stream but weeds and pebbles.

'You'll never find it now,' Emlyn called. 'The current's too fast, and once it reaches the river...'

'I must!' Gwyn screeched and pelted on, now hopping sideways to scrutinise the water where it rippled over shallow pools, now trying to race the current. But he couldn't stop shaking; fear shattered his concentration. He knew the others were staring at him, bewildered and concerned. It was such a small thing. They must think him mad.

All at once the shaking stopped and Gwyn stood very still, reluctantly remembering who he was. Then, leaving the others without any explanation, he ran home.

He kicked his boots off in the porch and crashed through the kitchen door, provoking an angry, 'Mind that door,' from his mother scrubbing potatoes in the kitchen.

'Don't let anyone come upstairs, Mam,' Gwyn cried.

'Whatever...' she began.

'I'm dead serious, Mam,' he said.

The urgency in his voice must have impressed her because she said gently, 'All right, cariad!'

He leapt up two flights of stairs, burst into his room and, taking a deep breath, sank on to his bed. He mustn't panic now. He could see a boy, himself, fearful and wide-eyed, staring out of a small oval mirror on the wall opposite. 'Nothing ever comes quietly into your life, Gwyn Griffiths,' he sadly told himself. 'A soldier arrives and you know he's not what he seems. Then a mad prince decides on some devilment, and you're the one to stop him, the only one. If it wasn't so tragic I'd laugh,' and he smiled ruefully at his troubled and too youthful reflection.

Something glistened in a dark recess. His spider was at work already. She had known what he needed even before he himself had become fully aware of it. He sat very still, watching a glossy cobweb begin to form. Like a tiny spark, Arianwen darted back and forth in a series of breathtaking acrobatics while her gossamer grew into a vast and glittering screen.

Gwyn got up and closed the curtains so that the luminous threads would reveal more clearly the landscape where he must work. There was no turning back. He couldn't dismiss the magic. He must trap the demon before it was too late.

The web was spattered with green and gold, like swathes of paint, changing hue in places, to form shadows and sunlit trees and hedges. Now autumn leaves fluttered below the green and Gwyn could discern the lane where it twisted beyond Nain's cottage and descended to Tŷ Llŷr. And there, on the bend where the ground levelled out beside the stream, the chestnut tree surged up beside its neighbours, towering, like a huge pavilion hung with rosy-golden banners, and Gwyn saw what he had been hoping for: a dark figure stepping out of the stream; a crouching demon, hardly yet formed into a man, stealthy, believing himself free again. Gwyn held his breath, and gathered his strength. He had to order his thoughts, chance his power, even if it stunted him for another year, there was no other way.

The shadowy figure moved beneath the low branches of the chestnut tree and then emerged on to the lane. It was tall and straight now, more prince than demon. 'You don't fool me,' Gwyn muttered as his victim took three paces, one! two! three! into the centre, the very heart of Arianwen's web.

'Daliwch ef!' Gwyn cried. 'Take him!'

And the tiny streak of silver flared toward the web's heart, covering in a shining blanket the image that trembled there. It took less than a minute.

'We have him!' Gwyn whispered triumphantly, and then from the shelf above Gwyn's bed the silver pipe rocked and a cry issued from it, filling the room. The sadness of the sound overwhelmed Gwyn. His confidence ebbed and his clever victory all at once seemed meaningless. He had heard the captured demon howl before, but this voice was different. It was full of despair, and a kind of submission.

Arianwen crept along a rafter and dropped on to his arm, as if in consolation.

The green and gold landscape began to dissolve. The shining threads slackened and drifted apart; coloured strands floated to the ceiling and disintegrated. And the silver core dropped to the floor, a pile of glittering fragments. Gwyn knelt and touched them. Hard to believe that a moment ago they had formed the image of a man. He blew and the tiny particles melted into the dust of his room.

'What have we done, Arianwen?' Gwyn asked softly.

Chapter
4

The other children had reached Tŷ Bryn. They stood by the gate not knowing whether to seek out their friend or leave him in peace. Emlyn and Nia understood Gwyn well enough to respect his sudden impulses, his request for solitude. But they had never seen him in such a violent state of agitation. It frightened Nia.

'Let's go and see the kittens again,' Emlyn suggested. 'We can wait in the barn till Gwyn is ready.'

'I didn't mean nothing,' Iolo said for the tenth time. 'It was only an old bit of wood. How can it be precious?'

'It'll turn up,' Emlyn reassured him. 'Come on, we'll go and find out what it's all about.' He turned in through the gate and walked up the path, with Iolo hopping nervously after him.

Nia held back; she noticed that Gwyn's curtains were drawn. Something was happening in his attic room. It must be dark in there. It reminded her of sickness and unnatural sleep. She walked away from the house calling, 'I'll see you later.'

She had just turned the last bend before the lane made its steep descent to Emlyn's home when she saw someone climbing out of the stream behind the chestnut tree; Evan must have been wandering there, she thought; perhaps he had found Gwyn's horse.

Yes, it was Evan; he was tall and had to stoop beneath the branches. He stepped into the lane, took three paces towards her and lifted his hand to wave; then he fell – and went on falling!

Nia found herself running. The prince had made no sound when he slipped to the ground but Nia sensed a cry so terrible it seemed as though her own breath was caught in it. She saw a man lying motionless, but she could still feel him falling, falling, falling, and could hear his descending sigh, while all about him was utterly silent, utterly still.

When she reached Evan he had turned on his back. He was lying among the broken conker shells, his arms spread wide, his fingers buried in dead leaves. He smiled at Nia and said, 'Don't be frightened. No bones broken!'

Then he sat up and brushed himself free of dust and dead leaves, while Nia watched, speechless. But when he eventually got to his feet, she flung her arms round his waist and buried her face in the rough wool of his sweater. 'I thought you had died,' she murmured.

Evan laughed and said, 'I am very much alive!'

She felt the laugh deep inside his body and a pulse racing through him, angry and irregular, as though it had just been awakened. His arms round her shoulders were hot and heavy, but he was shivering.

They walked up the lane to fetch Iolo for the journey home, Evan keeping Nia's hand in his own, and gradually his shivering subsided.

I shall protect him, Nia thought. He is my prince and in danger, but I shall save him, somehow. From whom or what she should save him she didn't know. Nor did she know that she was too late!

Gwyn's curtains were still drawn when they reached Tŷ Bryn and Nia was reluctant to go in, so she called to Iolo from the gate, and heard a muffled pleading for 'Just one minute longer with the kittens, *please!*' and then Gwyn's mother saw Evan from the window, and ran to open the kitchen door.

'Come and have a cup of tea while you wait,' she suggested. 'It's Evan Llŷr, isn't it?'

'It is, and your sister Elinor has already entertained me,' the soldier told her.

'I see,' Glenys Griffiths looked disappointed. 'Did she give you cake, too? Elinor doesn't like baking. I've got fresh *bara brith* here!'

'I can't resist,' said Evan Llŷr.

Glenys' smile seemed to indicate more than ordinary pleasure, in fact Nia had rarely seen Gwyn's mother so animated, but Mr Griffiths came through the yard just then, and his wife's expression stiffened into awkward uncertainty. 'You remember Evan Llŷr, Ivor, don't you? He used to help the Lloyds with the lambing.'

'I don't remember,' Mr Griffiths muttered.

'Of course you do,' Glenys pulled at her apron, nervously.

'I said I don't,' said Ivor Griffiths. He did not welcome visitors but on this occasion his hostility seemed personal.

The soldier, however, seemed unperturbed. 'It's been ten years,' he said, 'and people can't be expected to remember.'

'Evan's stopping for a bit,' Glenys said boldy. 'Are you coming in then, Ivor?'

Ivor stood rooted to his earth. 'What is this, a party? It's milking time. Where's Gwyn?'

He could be so savage, Gwyn's father. 'I'll fetch him, if you like,' Nia said.

'Well, he's ... busy, Nia,' Mrs Griffiths began.

'Tell him, it's five minutes or it's no pocket money,' her husband growled.

'Yes, and I'll knock,' she told Gwyn's mother.

As she left them she heard Evan say, 'I'll help with the cows, Ivor, I haven't forgotten how.' But Nia did not hear the reply.

She knocked on Gwyn's door, as she had promised, but

43

receiving no answer, went in. Gwyn's room was dim and airless. It seemed to be full of a kind of dust; particles of gossamer drifted just beneath the rafters; tiny, broken threads sparkled in the gloomy recesses under the beams. So Gwyn was back at work. She knew how reluctant he was. What had forced his hand at last?

Gwyn was sitting on the bed with his strange silver spider nestling in his hand. 'I know, it's milking time,' he said.

'Are you all right, then?' she asked. 'Did you find it, that horse?'

'In a way,' he replied, and then he looked sideways at her and mumbled, 'I had to use the power though.'

He hadn't mentioned his power for a long time. He used to call it magic, but considered himself too old for that word now.

'What did you do?' she sat beside him.

'It was Arianwen,' he said. 'She showed me where he was and we caught him, she and I, we wrapped him up. Trapped him!'

'How?' she asked gently.

'In the web. I saw him under the chestnut tree. He'd escaped you see, from the horse.'

'Who escaped? What was it in the horse?' Nia asked, alarmed by the unnatural glitter in his dark eyes.

'A demon,' Gwyn said.

She thought of the cry that had taken her breath away and her prince lying among the broken conker shells. 'Evan fell under the chestnut tree,' she said. 'I thought he had died!'

They regarded each other, trying to relate what she had said to a captured demon. And it seemed to Nia that Gwyn suddenly reached a conclusion he might be afraid to share with her. Then he shook his head and said, 'Perhaps I'd better remind you of a story.'

Nia might have warned him of his father's threat then, but Evan would help with the cows, and Emlyn, probably. She had to know this story. 'Remind me, then,' she urged.

44

'Remember the presents Nain gave me for my ninth birthday,' Gwyn said, 'The seaweed that brought a ship from outer space, and the scarf that called my lost sister back for a while.'

Nia nodded. She had been the only one to share Gwyn's secret and it was not so long ago that the extraordinary ship had returned and nearly taken Emlyn away forever. It was only Gwyn's power that had saved his cousin. A little sadness always seemed to linger about Gwyn, however, because he had been unable to keep his sister with him. But Nia felt that, in many ways, the lost girl was still there, on the mountain. Mrs Griffiths kept her daughter's room just as she had left it; with rose-petals in the drawers, dresses hanging in the wardrobe and dolls displayed on the dressing-table, as though any day Bethan might walk through the door with a bouquet of flowers she had wandered off to find. It was Nia who had chosen Bethan's name for her new baby sister, two years ago.

'And there was the brooch,' Gwyn went on, 'that became Arianwen when I gave it to the wind.'

'The broken horse was another gift,' Gwyn said, and then he grunted, 'Some gift! I wouldn't be telling you this if I didn't think you'd understand, Nia. But I believe you're the only one who can believe in the impossible. Am I right?'

Honoured by this description of herself she eagerly agreed, 'You are!'

'The horse was given to my grandmother by her great-great-grandmother, who was a witch,' he glanced at her, 'if you can believe that.'

'I can,' she said.

'I must keep it safe, she told me, never let it go. For I was the guardian, the magician who had inherited the power of Gwydion. But even Nain didn't know what that horse contained.'

'And did you find out?' Nia asked.

He avoided a direct answer. 'I had to search the legends,'

45

he said, and from beneath his pillow took a book already open at a page that had evidently been more than just slept on, for it was stained with thumb marks and wrinkled with damp breath.

'They say this story is more than two thousand years old,' Gwyn went on. 'For hundreds of years bards and storytellers kept it alive until it was written down, maybe hundreds of years later. Shall I read it?'

'Yes please,' Nia said fervently. Gwyn was the best story-teller she knew, describing events with such passionate meaning that heroes and heroines seemed to leap before her, drawing armies and castles behind them, in a dazzling atmosphere that quite excluded all her immediate surroundings.

Gwyn cleared his throat in a rather theatrical way and began, 'Long, long ago, when Britain was a land of wild forests, Bendigeidfran, the Blessed Bran, son of Llŷr, was King. He was a mighty man, a giant. Men thought him a god. He had a brother, Manawydan, and a sister, Branwen...'

'The fairest maiden in all Britain,' Nia said, happy to demonstrate her knowledge.

'D'you know it all, then?' Gwyn asked tersely.

'No, no! That's all I can remember. Please go on.' Nia begged.

'The next part is what matters,' Gwyn told her. 'Will you promise to keep quiet?'

She nodded, obediently mute.

'Bendigeidfran had two half-brothers, sons of his mother, Penarddun. Nisien was a kind and peaceful man, Efnisien, his brother, the very opposite. Wherever there was peace, Efnisien would cause strife!'

'On a sparkling summer day, Bendigeidfran was sitting with his nobles on a rock at Harlech, when he saw a most wonderful fleet sail into the bay. One ship outstripped the others; bright banners waved, its prow was painted gold and

46

it flew an ensign of brocaded silk. Even from afar it glittered like a wonderful toy, but for all its joyful colour, its promise of good tidings, it brought nothing but future sadness. It carried Matholwch, King of Ireland, who had come to ask for Princess Branwen to be his wife.

'And it was agreed that Branwen should marry Matholwch. But when Efnisien discovered this he was consumed with rage. 'My sister shall not marry Matholwch,' he ranted, 'a maiden so excellent as she belongs in Britain and married to a British Prince.'

'D'you think he loved her then?' Nia asked, forgetting her promise.

Gwyn frowned severely and continued, 'And he maimed the Irish King's horses; he cut off their lips, their ears, their tails and even their eyelids until they screamed and no one could lay a hand on them. And because of this and the shame Bendigeidfran felt on Efnisien's behalf, he gave to Matholwch Britain's most precious possession – the great cauldron of rebirth wherein a dead man could be born again. Matholwch took the gift but he was still not appeased, and once in his own country he treated his new wife, Branwen, in a terrible fashion. He banished her to the kitchens where she was beaten every day and although she bore Matholwch a son, still he would not honour her. In her lonely cell Branwen found a starling and trained it to seek out her brothers telling them of her misery. As soon as he received word of her plight King Bendigeidfran and his brothers crossed the Irish sea with their army. The Irish were mortally afraid, for Bendigeidfran strode waist-high across the sea. They did not want to do battle with such a man and they hastily built a mighty house to honour him, for he was of too great a stature for any of their buildings.

'But the wily Irish did not intend to let the British live. Inside the great house they hung two hundred bags of hide and in every bag hid an Irish soldier, and that night every Briton would have died were it not for Efnisien, who was their greatest warrior in strategy and courage. It was he who first entered the house to ensure King Bendigeidfran's safety.

'What is in those bags?' Efnisien asked the Irish.

'Flour,' they answered.

'Efnisien approached the first bag; he touched it, suspiciously, and knew it to be a soldier. With his great hands he ruthlessly crushed the skull he felt inside the bag. And this he did with every one until he had killed all the soldiers hidden there and the Irish, being too ashamed to admit their treachery, could do nothing to stop him.

'And that night a feast was held in the house and it was agreed that Gwern, the son of Branwen and Matholwch, should be heir to both the kings thus uniting their countries. But, of a sudden, Efnisien rose up, wrathfully, and cast the boy into the fire, and it was done so fast that no one could stop the deed.'

Nia knew now why she had tried to forget the story. She wanted to ask if it was madness or hate or terrible love that had caused Efnisien's dreadful act, but she realized that in the passing of time and the route from bard to bard, the meaning and the cause had become blurred and then forgotten. 'Go on,' she whispered.

Gwyn looked at her over the rim of the book and continued without looking at it. It was obvious that he knew the next part by heart.

'And then there was a tumult in the house as the Irish and the British took up arms against each other. And when the Irish saw that they might be defeated they began to kindle the cauldron of rebirth, so that their army would be reborn again. Efnisien, seeing that his soldiers had no hope against a ghostly army, cried, 'Woe is me that I should cause the death of the men of Britain, and shame on me if I do not seek their deliverance!' And he lay down among the Irish dead, and, believing him to be an Irish corpse, they threw him into the boiling cauldron, a living man. And he stretched himself out in the cauldron and burst it into four pieces, and his heart burst also!'

Gwyn looked into the book again but did not continue the story. He had told Nia all she needed to know. The sadness increased on every further page, for in the end she remembered, Branwen and the king died too.

'We are Llŷrs, of course,' Nia said thoughtfully, 'through our mother, though I can't believe we're related to a legend in any way.'

'I seem to be,' Gwyn said wryly.

Should one be consoled for being a magician, Nia wondered, but asked instead, 'You think it is the spirit of Efnisien then, trapped in that horse?'

'Yes! I do believe it is!'

'And when Iolo lost him in the stream, he was free for a while.'

'For a while, but I caught him, didn't I?' he attempted a reassuring grin. 'Before he could do any harm.'

'Then where is he now?'

Gwyn shrugged. 'I don't know, Nia! I made a spell and it went astray somehow. I don't know why. Don't worry, I'll find the horse. Right now I'd better get downstairs or I'll be late for milking!'

But the cows were already in the barn and Mr Griffiths, in a better mood now, was chatting to Evan in the yard. Evan seemed reluctant to leave the mountain. 'You keep the sun so long up here,' he told the farmer.

When they went home, at last, the sky was a riot of violent colours and a lonely bird, hidden in the chestnut tree, cried out, like an augury.

They soon became used to having a soldier at Number Six. His was an easy presence; quiet, unobtrusive. He took his breakfast early and was out of the house before the morning scramble; the banging on the bathroom door, shouts for more milk, more toast; the noisy hunt for combs, clean socks, sandwiches and school books. There was seldom a time when all seven children had everything they needed; never a time when one hadn't had to run to catch up with the rest.

He caused quite a stir in Pendewi, though, did Evan Llŷr.

'Related, is he?' Mrs Bowen, the wool, asked Betty Lloyd, who had taken Nia to choose colours for a new cardigan.

'My cousin,' Betty smiled possessively.

'Dashing, isn't he?'

'Well, I wouldn't...' She was proud of Evan but had never been one to boast. 'Yes, he is good-looking, isn't he?' she coyly conceded.

'And a major too, I hear!'

'That's right. Nia, come closer, cariad. Nia's good with colours. I never choose without her now.'

'Been in the army long, has he?' Mrs Bowen resumed her ferreting.

'Fifteen years or more.'

'On leave then, is he?'

'That's it. Sick leave!'

'Wounded, was he?'

'That's it! In Belfast!'

'Whereabouts?' Mrs Bowen leaned closer, eager for details that might have to be confided in a whisper, because of Nia.

'Whereabouts? Oh, well...I don't ask.' Mrs Lloyd stepped away from Mrs Bowen's prying black eyes.

Nia shuffled inside the door. She hated the way Mrs Bowen probed for every detail. Dissecting her prince like a specimen, caught under glass, going on about his wounds. Why wouldn't they leave him alone? The twins were as bad. As soon as Evan returned from wherever he fled in his dark car they would start, 'What happened, Evan? Was it a bomb, Evan?'

'A bomb was it?' Mrs Bowen nosed for the scent. 'Belfast, you said. Bound to have been a bomb!'

'Well, it's difficult, Joan.' Betty was flustered. She didn't

50

know, that was the truth. No one knew, for sure, what Evan's trouble had been. Questions often flickered on her tongue but were always left unspoken. She feared they might drive her Evan away. He had never volunteered information.

'Lucky his face wasn't scarred or we wouldn't be so interested, would we?' Mrs Bowen giggled. 'Are you with me?'

'Yes.' Mrs Lloyd shuffled the bundles of wool. 'Nia, come here and look at this pink.'

Nia, gazing through the window, had seen a black car gliding smooth and quiet down the High Street. Evan was home early today. Where did he go, she wondered, every day? Out all day and at night restless; moving about in the room beneath hers. She would lie awake holding her breath, taut with curiosity, listening for every small sound: a step, a creak, a cough, a sigh. Her prince was so near and yet so completely mysterious.

'Nia,' Mrs Lloyd called impatiently.

The black car pulled up outside Number Six. Nia rushed to the counter. 'That one's too pale, and those are too bright,' she said, pushing the balls of wool back across the counter. 'And that one's really horrible, like plastic flowers.'

'It's a very popular colour, is flamingo!' Mrs Bowen bristled.

'I'd go for green, Mam,' Nia said.

'But, Nia, we agreed on pink, I thought, to go with Bethan's dress.' Betty Lloyd rubbed her forehead.

'I give up then.' Nia made a dash for the door.

'Green now, is it?' Mrs Bowen sighed dramatically and bent under the counter.

Mrs Lloyd, confused, muttered. 'I'm not sure, Nia...?' she turned to her daughter.

'I've got piles of homework, Mam,' Nia said. 'And green will do,' and she slipped through the door leaving it open so that the shop bell rang continuously at the back of the

51

building, where Mrs Bowen's mother made baby clothes and never answered the door anyway.

She heard her mother shout as she sped away, but she didn't try to decipher the message. She was afraid Catrin would be playing hostess. She was right. When she leapt into the house Evan was stepping through the kitchen door and Catrin was already pouring tea for him.

'You're early today,' Nia said boldly. 'Where've you been?'

'Nowhere and everywhere,' Evan replied.

'Is that a riddle?'

'It could be but it's not. I've been in the mountains. I climbed, sat and watched clouds, went to sleep!'

'Were you tired, then?' Nia thought of the nightly creaks and sighs.

'Shut up, Nia,' Catrin snapped. 'Leave Evan alone.'

It wasn't like Catrin to be harsh. Stung, Nia decided to tease her sister. 'Had a bad day, then? Didn't Michael say "hullo!"?'

'Don't be ridiculous!' The tea that Catrin was pouring would have overflowed the cup, if Evan had not put out a hand to steady her. He gently removed the teapot and set it on the table. Then he held Catrin's hand in both of his and looking from one sister to the other, said quietly, 'Let's not have quarrelling in the kitchen.'

Nia burned with unspoken sentences. The sight of those clasped hands troubled her. Perhaps something of her worry conveyed itself to Evan for he released Catrin and said, 'You've asked me questions, Nia, now tell me about your day.'

She sat beside him on the bench, not too close, but near enough to notice a tiny fleck of red in his black hair, just behind the ear. 'I've been to school,' she said. 'There's nothing interesting about that, is there?'

Evan laughed and it was such a carefree sound the girls laughed with him, and gradually the tension that had filled

52

the cramped little kitchen was diffused and they even noticed that the evening sun, slanting into the room, was bouncing reflections from silver on the dresser, up to the low ceiling. Evan took a spoon and twisting it through the air made light dance over Catrin's golden hair, and then on Nia's dark plaits. So both the girls had to take silver, Nia a teaspoon and Catrin a knife, and turn the lights on Evan, over his face and round his head, like a glittering crown. And Nia noticed yet another streak of red in the black hair, and then another.

'We're going swimming!' The twins were in the doorway, watching the show.

'D'you want to come?' Sîon addressed himself to Evan.

'No, it's too cold,' Evan said.

'It's not, it's great, warmer than summer!' Enthusiasm always made Gareth yell.

'All the same, I'd rather not.' The soldier drummed his fingers on the table.

'We go down by the bridge, it's not deep, but you can swim a bit,' Sîon persisted.

'Evan's busy,' Catrin interceded. 'Go on, twins, we'll come later.'

Sîon would have gone then, but Gareth was always one to push even when the cause seemed hopeless. 'Is it your scars, then?' he asked hopefully. 'We don't care. Are there scars where you were wounded? I'd be proud if I had scars!' He edged closer to the table trying to fathom his unsoldierly cousin, completely unprepared for the onslaught he provoked.

Violence sliced through the air as Evan leapt to his feet and thundered, 'There are no wounds! No scars! Nothing, understand? Nothing…nothing…nothing!' He towered above them, his fine face distorted with fury and Nia felt the room shudder at the outrage that poured into it. A monstrous stranger glowered there, not Evan, and to her horror she saw tears on his face, as though he despaired of the wrath that had shaken through him.

Instinctively she covered her eyes and heard the boys shuffle away, frightened into silence. The emptiness that followed their retreat was all the more alarming after such a tempest.

When she dared to risk a furtive glance into the room she found the prince sitting beside her, looking pale and all used-up, as though he was bewildered by the anger, and wondering who he was.

Catrin's voice broke into the stillness, saying shakily, 'We'll go and watch the boys, shall we, Nia?'

Nia nodded, still too nervous to speak, and to their surprise Evan said, very slowly, 'I'll come with you.'

And then they heard Bethan crying from the room above.

'Bethan!' Catrin cried. 'I forgot her. I told Mam I'd look after her.'

She ran out of the kitchen and was about to mount the stairs when Mrs Lloyd came through the front door, flustered from her interview in the wool shop and calling, 'Nia, why did you run off? Mrs Bowen persuaded me to get flamingo pink and now ...I don't know...Are you going out again?'

Nia and Evan had come to meet her in the hall and Evan said quietly, 'We're going to watch the twins in the river.'

'But Bethan's crying, Mam,' Catrin told her.

'I'll see to her. You go on!' Mrs Lloyd ushered them out, awkwardly. She wanted a bit of peace before her husband came in from the shop. She wanted to think about flamingo pink wool and what to cook for supper. 'No hurry,' she called after them and added, 'You'll be stopping in tonight then, Evan?'

He turned back, confused again it seemed, and said, 'Yes, I'll be with you.'

The weather was still extraordinary. There had hardly been a breeze since the storm that had preceded Evan's arrival.

Every day, after school, boys would migrate to the river, trying to prolong the sensation of a never-ending summer. And the evening mist would close about them, settling softly into the brittle bronze fields; a warm mist, scented with ripening fruit.

The girls wandered up the High Street with Evan between them, and Nia was aware of fluttering lace curtains and glances across the street. Middle-aged mothers smiled at Evan over their bundles of late shopping and Catrin's friends stared, openly envious, while the boys suspicious and ill-at-ease pretended disinterest, but watched their progress all the way to the bridge.

'Anyone would think you were an alien,' Nia whispered to Evan. And he bent down and said, very seriously, 'Perhaps I am!'

No, Nia thought, you are not from Out There, and neither are you from Here. She began to think of the gods and princes who inhabited the Celtic Otherworld, sometimes leaping out to breathe real mountain air before slipping back into their misty legends. 'Perhaps you're from the Otherworld,' she murmured.

Evan heard her and asked, 'Do you believe in pagan gods then, Nia?'

'I don't know,' she truthfully replied.

Catrin, puzzled, inquired, 'Are you two having a game?'

'It could be a game,' Evan mused.

They had reached the bridge and looked down on the four boys in the river. Alun and Iolo waved when they saw Evan, but the twins ignored their audience, they splashed and shouted at each other still unable to bring themselves to look at their cousin after his stormy outburst.

'Let's see, now, do you know your legends, Catrin?' Evan pursued the matter of gods.

Catrin struggled. 'Nia's the expert,' she said.

'Don't tell me you've forsaken words for music!' Evan's tone was light and teasing, but Catrin would not answer. She

55

had seen a horse and rider approaching down the hill.

So Evan stroked her hair over and over, while he gently reminded her of the stories she seemed to have forgotten. And, as the horseman drew nearer, he put his arm about her shoulder and his mouth close to her hair and whispered something that made her turn from Michael McGoohan and look at Evan with astonishment and, it seemed to Nia, recognition.

And, all at once, Nia felt isolated. She ran to the end of the bridge and began to shout encouragement at the boys, trying to stifle the bewildering ache she felt at the sight of those two heads, black and gold, so close. But she never took her eyes off the horseman. She saw him reach the figures on the bridge, saw Evan turn, slowly, still keeping Catrin close, and look up at the rider.

And then there was a scream. It was the horse. Something must have startled him. The sound he made was awful and full of pain. He reared up, his front hooves cleaving the air, while Michael clung to his back, terrified, shouting angry oaths at the man and the girl.

It was usually such a quiet horse, big and gentle, Nia knew it well, they all knew it; its name was Glory.

Michael almost had the horse under control when it began to cavort about the bridge. Catrin called out helplessly, 'What did I do?' but Evan stood watching, very calm, and did nothing. Then Michael began to use his whip, a thing he rarely did; he pulled at the bit and Glory screamed again, then he charged, straight at Nia.

She crouched against the wall and the great animal thundered past, close enough for her to smell his terrible fear and to feel the thud of Michael's helpless body on the saddle, and then Glory had left the bridge and was hurtling down the bank.

Nia leapt up and followed. Perhaps believing that by doing this she could help in some way. But the horse plunged into the water and began stumbling and rearing across

56

the river, while sheets of spray burst over him. The terrified bathers floundered out of his way and Michael cried, 'Glory! Glory, boy!' as his boots skimmed the water.

Black Glory careered towards the far side of the river; as he trampled the rushes a bird soared out, shrieking; the horse screamed in panic, vaulted on to the bank and sped over the yellow fields, slipping through the close air as though he was haunted.

When Nia turned back, the mist was settling and she could hardly make out the figures on the bridge. Even as she watched Evan and Catrin they began to leave her; became as insubstantial as ghosts, receding into a world of their own where she couldn't follow.

She ran home, superstitiously urging herself out of the misty ring of enchantment where there was no special place for her. The sound of Bethan's crying was almost reassuring until she remembered that her little sister rarely cried, and had never been inconsolable.

When Nia tumbled into the kitchen Bethan glared sullenly from her mother's lap. Her tear-stained face was crumpled with exhaustion.

'What is it, Nia?' Mrs Lloyd asked, alarmed at Nia's sudden arrival, afraid that a boy was drowned or damaged at the very least.

'I didn't – like it there, Mam,' Nia said, fumbling for a description of events. 'Michael's horse – he's ill or something!'

'No one's hurt?' Mrs Lloyd stroked the distressed child's head.

'No, Mam!' Only me, she could have said; because they've shut me out, those two on the bridge, and something is happening that I don't care to understand.

Bethan began to sob again and Nia asked, 'What's the matter with Bethie? She's been crying for ages. It's not like her!'

'Oh, Nia, I don't know!' She gave a familiar hard-pressed

57

mother's sigh. 'I found Iolo's toys all broken on the landing. He shouldn't have left them there, but all the same, they could have brushed them aside, whoever it was, not stamped on them in such a way.'

'Was Bethan there?' Nia inquired. The little girl had broken precious things before, in an accidental baby way.

'She was in Catrin's room,' said Mrs Lloyd indignantly. 'Besides her tiny fingers couldn't have done – that!'

The damage was worse than usual it seemed. Nia went to inspect.

Iolo's farm animals lay scattered on the dark uncarpeted floorboards. At first glance they seemed to have been kicked about or trampled underfoot by someone carelessly hastening towards the stairs. But when Nia knelt to gather them up she found herself touching severed limbs and tails, twisted heads and tiny slithers of metal. The boys had never destroyed each other's toys with such deadly purpose, and only the horses, Iolo's favourites, had been broken: shire horses, hunters, tiny Shetland ponies, even a mare and her foal had been damaged almost beyond recognition, while the other animals, and even a farmer and his milkmaid still stood, unharmed, beside the wall.

She dropped the small sad pieces into her pocket, wondering how she could break the news to Iolo. What had possessed the person who had done such a cruel thing? She couldn't believe that it was someone she knew, one of the family.

Outside the mist intensified and a purple dusk invaded the house, ironing shadows out of corners and spreading them thickly through the rooms. Bethan began to wail again and the thin hunted sound made Nia shiver. Bethan had been a witness. She knew who had destroyed the toy horses, but could not speak his name.

Chapter

5

Gwyn's French book fluttered out of reach. The school bus waited halfway up a high and windy hill in Pendewi where anything light and unguarded was at risk. Gwyn had no liking for French but he hadn't thought the wind would take him literally when he had prayed aloud that he'd never have to see or hear a foreign verb again. But he'd packed his bag carelessly after the last lesson; a crisp packet had flown out and as he'd bent to catch it the bag had flapped open leaving his homework at the mercy of the wind.

As he crawled along the path, grabbing at his drifting paper, he saw Nia running up towards him. She should have been going in the opposite direction. The Lloyds had no need of a bus, they lived ten minutes away from the school.

Nia caught the escaping French book, stifled its flapping and thrust it under her arm crying, 'Gwyn, can you come home with me?'

'I've got homework,' Gwyn said half-heartedly. Not that he was keen on the stuff but it was embarrassing to have a girl waylay you under the eyes of a busful of children; they were already laughing at him. He knelt on the path, stuffing pens and papers back into his bag.

The bus drew level with him, its door invitingly open, giving him a chance at least. 'Are you getting on or not, boy?' Mr Roberts, the driver, looked down at him. 'Or is it the

59

girlfriend, tonight?' He was keen on jokes at other people's expense, was Mr Roberts.

'Please, Gwyn?' Nia stood panting beside him. She held out the French book.

'Look, I've got to…' Gwyn glanced helplessly at the bus.

'Well, boy!' Mr Roberts said.

'Please!' Nia begged.

Mr Roberts, star of Pendewi Amateur Dramatic Society, sighed theatrically. 'I can see we're not wanted,' he shouted back into the bus and was rewarded with giggles and donkey brays.

It was now impossible for Gwyn to get on the bus. The door slammed shut, but as the vehicle drew away Gwyn saw Emlyn peering from the back window. One sympathetic face made up for all the rest.

'Tell Mam I'll be late!' Gwyn mouthed at his cousin.

Emlyn nodded and the bus vanished over the lip of the hill.

'Heck, Nia!' Gwyn said angrily. 'Couldn't it have waited?'

'No,' she said and he became aware that she was anxious and lost, like someone clinging to a hope, and he was it.

'O.K.' he grinned amiably. 'Thanks for saving the book.'

'I don't want to go straight home,' she said.

'I'm not staying up here, at least let's go down the hill a bit. He pulled the hood of his anorak over his eyes, squeezing a smile out of her at last. Things were easier then.

They sat on the stone wall that curved round the base of the school hill. It was an ancient wall, patched and rebuilt over the years, reinforced with concrete and thickened with sand-coloured rocks so that, where the stark grey stones remained, it seemed as though the wall had been blasted by thunderbolts. No one knew its beginnings. Perhaps if it were not there, hill and school would have tumbled into the river.

'I've told Alun to tell Mam I'm at Gwyneth's,' Nia began, 'so there's no hurry.'

'Nia, why do you lie?' Gwyn groaned. 'There was no need.'

'It's a habit,' she replied, kicking the wall, 'and it's easier.'

'It's a bad habit,' he remarked, 'and in the end it makes things worse, you know that. You're so daft sometimes.'

He realized he was going to have to pay for that remark. She would keep him up here for another half-hour before coming to the point if he didn't watch out. 'Come on, then,' he nudged her encouragingly.

'It's difficult.' She looked at her dangling feet. 'A horrible thing happened yesterday. We were all there but we can't talk about it; everyone's pretending they didn't see it, even the boys. So I have to tell you, because you're outside it all and can tell me if it matters, or if I'm silly about a...a maddened horse.'

'Horse?' It was the word made him shiver, not the cold.

'Glory!' Nia said.

'Glory?' Gwyn had no liking for the McGoohans, show-offs the lot of them, but Glory was not a McGoohan, he was a beautiful creature, you couldn't help admiring him. 'What about Glory?' he asked.

'We were on the bridge,' Nia went on. 'Catrin, Evan and me, watching the boys in the river. And Michael rode up on Glory. He always does a bit of an act, you know. He takes off his hat and sweeps it through the air, and then he bows to Catrin as if she's a princess.'

'I know, I know,' Gwyn said hastily. He'd seen Michael's little show and thought him a fool stuck up on his great horse, acting like a lord. If only he knew how Pendewi boys laughed. And Catrin was so taken with it; Gwyn hated that.

'Sometimes he lifts Catrin on to Glory's back,' Nia continued. 'They don't go anywhere. Just sit there whispering, and she should be practising you know, for her Grade Eight music.'

Gwyn began to wonder how many details he would have to suffer before Nia got to the point and then she said, 'But yesterday it all went wrong,' and he realized that she was still so frightened by what she had seen that she didn't know how to describe it.

'Go on.' He hoped he sounded sympathetic. He was eager for more, and sorry for the way he had begun the discussion.

'Like I said, we were on the bridge, when Michael rode up but when Glory saw us he screamed, and then he ran as if...he had seen a ghost. There was nothing else, you see, no frightening sounds, nothing to startle him, and he's such a quiet horse, even in traffic. He never, never panics.'

'Who was he looking at, Nia?' Gwyn peered into her troubled face.

'It wasn't me,' she replied, 'because I was further away, and I don't think it was Catrin.'

She was so distressed she couldn't bring herself to name the man. Images moved in Gwyn's mind: sensations, just out of reach: the telephone, the soldier by the water and the bleak touch of his hand, the howl dredged out of the past when the spider had caught her prey. And Nia knew what was on his mind, she had been with him at every step because she said in a surprised tone, 'He was hurt when he fell, more than we know; part of him called out so sadly but,' she screwed up her face so that every feature frowned at Gwyn, 'he didn't make a sound.'

'And you don't make sense,' Gwyn said, trying to cheer her up. They had been tossing the soldier between them, now it was time to name him. 'So Evan Llŷr frightened a horse; Evan Llŷr fell and did some silent crying!' He tried to sound matter of fact because he was going to need her help and she must remain calm. 'Evan Llŷr is a strange man,' he said. 'What's his past? Who is he? Do we know he is your cousin for sure?'

Her reply to these questions was not what he expected. A rosy tint began to liven up her pale face and she looked away from him as she murmured, 'I've been thinking he was a prince or something, you know, like in the stories, Sleeping Beauty and Cinderella.'

'Aw, come off it!' He jumped down from the wall.

'The frog prince,' she said desperately, 'or Rapunzel's poor blind prince... or...'

'Let's get on a bit,' he said.

But she remained where she was, high on her ancient wall, demanding his attention and what had begun as a silly list that he had been eager to dismiss, gradually evolved into a sort of index that could, if he chose the right name, lead him to the core of his search, for she began to name the heroes of Wales.

'Prince Pwyll,' she cried, leaping to her feet and running along the wall, 'or brave Culwch and the giant's daughter, or', she gazed over the town to where the mountains unfolded in waves of fading blue, as though the hero she sought still slept there, waiting for her cry of recognition, 'or maybe a king,' she said. 'Arthur or Bran.'

Why didn't she mention that other prince? Was she too frightened even to think of him? After all, Gwyn admitted to himself, there was still no proof. 'Not Bran,' he muttered, but he kept the rest of his information locked inside his head where it could hurt no one but himself. It hissed and made him feel sick and dizzy, and he longed to shout, 'Efnisien, prince of madness and the dark,' but instead he began to run into the wind hoping his fears would be blown away.

'Don't go,' Nia leapt down and ran after him. 'I haven't told you all of it.'

'Well, what then?' He stopped and waited, almost dreading the rest of her story.

'When I got home,' she said, 'I found Iolo's toy horses on the landing. They'd all been broken in terrible ways, twisted, flat, stamped on, and,' she hesitated, 'their tails and heads had been torn off, and Bethan was crying and crying, but it can't have been her, she's too small.'

No, not Bethan, Gwyn thought, but perhaps she had been there, watching, while someone stormed past her, overcome by a two-thousand-year-old rage.

63

'No one knows who did it,' Nia went on, 'but we're all watching each other, wondering, and there's a horrible feeling in the house. And I thought of you and your horse. You said if you didn't find it something terrible would happen. Well, where is it?'

'I've been wondering myself,' he said miserably. 'I was so sure I had trapped that mad spirit, even though I couldn't find the horse. But something's wrong. I've been careless.'

She tapped his arm and asked, 'What have you done?'

'It's what I haven't done,' he sighed. 'I have a foreboding, but I can't tell you yet what it's about.'

'Can I help?'

'Yes! Keep an eye out for that horse I lost. I believe you might find it. I didn't describe it, but I will now. It has no ears, no tail; its lips are gone, its eyelids are cut away, so the eyes are always afraid, and the mouth is always screaming.'

She stood away from him, screwing her face up again; it was a habit she had but anyone would have done the same.

'And there's a label round its neck,' he went on. 'It says "Dim hon! Not this!" Because it must never be used, never left unguarded where its spirit can escape.'

'But it has escaped, hasn't it?' she accused him. 'Because all that stuff about your spider catching it just wasn't true, was it? Was it?' And she jabbed nervously at him.

'Look,' he tried to sound confident. 'I may not like what I am but Arianwen and I, well, it's no use denying it, we can make things happen, and yes, we did stop that spirit. If we hadn't there'd have been a storm, don't you see? There would have been hail and thunder, things would have died. As far as I know he's a little pile of dust, it's just...'

'Just...?' she echoed.

'Just that I don't like losing things.' His half-hearted laugh suddenly became real because she looked so funny, her small scowling face twisting round like a puzzled bird. 'Let's get on now, and perhaps your mam will give me some tea before all that business about who's fetching me or who's taking me home.'

'Evan might take you,' she smiled, 'and give me a ride too.'

He did not like to consider her suggestion. 'I could always fly,' he said and then, in an attempt to keep the conversation light-hearted, added, 'I don't see why ski-lifts are reserved for Switzerland.'

Nia giggled aloud and they ran, still laughing, round the curve of the hill and on down into Pendewi, only to discover that they were about to take part in a curious drama.

There were three people outside Number Six, obstructing the passage of the butcher's customers. Michael McGoohan, a pedestrian today, was hopping on and off the kerb like an angry wasp in his tweed jacket and yellow corduroys. He was shouting at Catrin so that people turned to stare at her, while she stood with her back to the wall, her arms folded, head down and golden hair hiding her face. Michael seemed small without his horse, a wispy man with faded curls, but perhaps he looked that way because Evan Llŷr was there beside Catrin, his dark presence holding the focus like a magnet, so that all about him seemed incidental: unnecessary paraphernalia that hovered beneath him like so many insects.

'Poor Michael,' Gwyn murmured without compassion.

They gathered speed and then came to a halt, simultaneously, as though each knew what the other felt, for they had come within the circle of the extraordinary scene and were not part of it.

'You'll have to!' Michael cried in his sweet Irish tenor. 'Come with me now and see for yourself.'

'I don't want to, Michael,' Catrin tossed her flowing mane.

'Don't want to? But, Cat darling, you must. He's so troubled, he may die. He's been ridden half to death, and surely to God, whoever it was had a mind to kill him!'

'I'm sorry, Michael,' Catrin spoke softly, 'but not now. Please understand.'

'I do not! I do not! You'll come with me! I need you!' His attempt to excite the affection she had so recently felt for him was disastrous, for his voice rose to an hysterical shriek.

'Leave her alone, boy,' Evan said. It was a challenge. Gwyn knew that this was not Nain's poor wounded creature. He was triumphant, his few words filled with quiet menace.

Michael stood very still. A king toppled from his throne; angry and undignified. 'So your uncle's the boss now, is he?' He glared at Catrin vainly trying ridicule to move her.

'He's not my uncle,' Catrin declared.

The significance of her remark was too much for Michael McGoohan. He walked away from Catrin, muttering oaths about older men.

The soldier ignored his insults, instead he singled out Gwyn for a special greeting. 'How are you, Gwyn Griffiths?' he said with a thoughtful smile.

'I'm well,' Gwyn replied.

'And did you find your toy?'

'It was not a toy,' Gwyn said meaningfully. But he could not fathom the bright glance that followed this so he turned from Evan and called to Michael, 'I'll come and see your Glory!'

'Let me come,' Nia leapt after him.

'Clear off, both of you!' Michael made a futile gesture with his arm and began to run.

The children were not put off. They dogged the Irishman. 'I know about horses,' Gwyn called after him. This was a lie but Gwyn felt that if he saw Glory it might, in some way, help him understand what sort of ghosts had frightened the horse.

Michael ignored them for a while but as they insisted on pursuing him, he slowed his pace and allowed them to fall into step beside him. He needed them, after all. He needed someone to share his trouble for he would be a lonely man without his Catrin. He was still a stranger in Pendewi, even after two years and, being well-off and slightly arrogant, was not welcome everywhere. But now Gwyn was afraid for him.

Just outside the town they turned through a white gate and, descending a gravelled slope, soon found themselves in an avenue of giant beech trees where rhododendrons spread like a dark curtain excluding the outside world. They had entered another kingdom: an usurped kingdom, Gwyn thought wryly, and wondered if he had inherited the thought from Nia's prince.

A breeze loosened the dying leaves and they fluttered like tiny fragments of topaz across their path, heralding the approach to the McGoohans' grand house; too grand for an ordinary G.P., but Doctor McGoohan's wife had money and was descended, so Michael boasted, from the ancient kings of Munster.

The house was built of grey stone; it was beautifully symmetric with long Georgian windows, sixteen on each of the two floors. Two huge oak columns supported the slim porch roof, and the heavy black door was decorated with a worn pattern of scrolls and flowers. It was a Welsh home, four centuries old; a refuge for Welshmen, Gwyn found himself thinking. The McGoohans did not belong there, and again he realized he had caught the drift of ancient enmity that had very briefly flared in Evan Llŷr's remarkable blue eyes.

Michael led them across the front of the house, over a gritty drive that crunched and rolled under their plimsolled feet. Somewhere inside, his sister Mary played Bach on the grand piano, not half so well as Catrin. And then they were walking down a moss-grown path to the stables.

The top of Glory's stable-door was open, the lower half remained closed. Michael would not let them in. They stood in the warm cobbled yard, looking into the darkness and the sunshine, all about them, made a chilling contrast with the deathly gloom of Glory's stable.

The big horse was covered in a blanket. His eyes were open; they could see a glint of white, but the rest of him was just an endless sound in the dark, a reproachful groan that rose and fell on his every breath.

'What happened?' Nia asked fearfully.

'Someone rode him,' Michael murmured into the oppressive air. 'Rode him all night, God knows where. There were thorns in his hair and mountain flowers. They rode him on to his knees, kicked him until he was more dead than alive.'

'But who…' she began.

'I'll not be the one to accuse,' Michael groaned. 'It has to be a madman!'

Gwyn stepped away, into the light where the sun might help him to sort out a nightmare. 'It's terrible,' he said, 'I'm sorry!' He felt an inexplicable guilt.

'Will he die?' Nia breathed.

Michael shrugged helplessly, and his voice broke as he said, 'I don't know,' then tears came into his eyes and he folded his arms along the stable door and laid his head upon them.

'Come away, Nia!' Gwyn grasped her sleeve. They must leave Glory in the safe quiet where he might recover.

Nia seemed reluctant to leave the young man who had once been everything to her sister, but whose power had been so publicly damaged. Clearly embarrassed by his emotion she had to move closer to Michael so that, perhaps, he might know that he was not entirely alone.

'Nia!' Gwyn said quietly.

And this time she came with him, across the drive and into the shadowy lane again, and only then could Gwyn bring himself to question her.

'You never answered when I asked about your cousin,' he said. 'You put me off with guesses about fairy-tale princes but I want to know more, Nia!'

'Why?' She stopped and faced him, hands on hips. 'Why

68

all the questions?' She stamped her foot. 'You're hounds, all of you!'

'I'm only concerned,' he said gently. 'He seems so ... strange!'

She sighed and contemplated the bright leafy arches above her.

'No one has seen him for ten years,' Gwyn prodded.

Nia considered the branches for a while in her irritating airy-fairy way then, almost by chance, hit upon an answer that was more than adequate. 'Evan's father is not really a Llŷr,' she said. 'He's my mother's half-brother. So there'd be no in-breeding if we married him.'

'Marry? Evan and who?' Gwyn asked, incredulous.

'I don't know, any of us, Nerys, Catrin – me!'

'You?' he glared at her. 'That man's old enough to be your father, and Catrin's!'

She ignored these observations. She had more to offer. 'He had a brother called Emrys. He was fierce and brave and when he was eight he fell out of a tree and died and Evan, who was gentle before, suddenly became just like Emrys.'

Gwyn quickened his pace. He needed this history yet dreaded it.

She hopped beside him and said, close to his ear, 'He was in Belfast and dreadfully wounded but – he hasn't any scars!'

They emerged on to the main road and Gwyn closed the white gate behind them. Now it was Nia who ran eagerly forward and Gwyn who hung back, frightened of betraying his suspicion if he met the soldier.

But the black and bronze car had gone and Evan Llŷr was not in the house; he had left, with Catrin, on one of his mysterious 'trips of remembrance', as Betty Lloyd called them. Instead, they found Gwyn's uncle Idris and his cousin Emlyn in the kitchen. There was a stifled atmosphere in the room, the sort that follows accident or death. Uncle Idris looked as if he hadn't been able to wake himself out of a very bad dream.

'Dad's been visiting the police,' Emlyn explained, 'and we stayed to give you a lift home.'

'Thanks,' Gwyn said, 'but police? Why?'

Emlyn looked at his father, but Idris seemed unable to mention his problem.

'Someone broke into your uncle's studio, Gwyn,' Mrs Lloyd told him. 'The unicorn was broken.'

'Mutilated!' Idris roared, suddenly awake. His furious lion's eyes narrowed. 'It was deliberate, careful mutilation!'

'How?' Nia asked, not understanding.

'With an axe,' Idris said slowly. 'Quite small, I'd say, and precise. They defiled my creature. Hacked at its ears, its eyes and its tail; cracked my unicorn's lovely gold eyes.'

The unicorn was the artist's favourite work. Marked 'Not for sale' it stood in his studio window, its magical presence brightening the gloomiest of damp Welsh days. That it should be so dreadfully disfigured was too much for Nia. She leapt protectively towards Idris. He had always been her friend. 'Why?' she cried.

'Why?' Idris repeated patting her hand, as helpless and confused as she.

His studio, high on the hill road that led out of Pendewi, had once been a chapel. But Idris had decorated it with silver and gold, pink and blue, in a flamboyant gesture that had once caused suspicion and resentment in the town. Now, however, his beautiful work, his paintings and brightly-carved creatures had earned him respect and admiration. No one who passed the chapel on their way into Pendewi, did so without a tingle of excitement, a feeling that, somehow, they were stepping into another world, for the unicorn held their gaze. Setting his hooves upon an invisible mountain, he seemed to be declaring that fairy tales could, after all, be true.

'It was drunks, most probably,' Iestyn muttered. 'Who else would do a thing like that?'

'Vandals!' Betty put in. 'What will they do next?'

70

'No,' Idris told them calmly. 'Not vandals, not drunks either. It was like,' he sighed, 'a ritual. Don't ask me how I know, but I felt the deed still in there; I could smell it.'

A chorus of subdued and anxious murmurs broke out. They were all, in their way, trying to dissuade Idris from his terrible conviction.

But Gwyn, clinging to the door like someone drowning, knew it to be true. The voices throbbed in his head, tunelessly, like a warning drummed through time. Careless magician that he was, he had failed. The demon was free again! Visions of faces that he loved peeped in at him, through the dark. Who would the madman choose next? He had destroyed so many that first time, more than a thousand years ago. Would he repeat himself? And then Gwyn thought of Nia's prince, his pale face, his perplexing summer-sea eyes and empty fingers, and he gave a remorseful little sob that caused his friends to shiver and turn in his direction.

Chapter
6

When Gwyn and the Llewelyns left Number Six they exchanged glances with no one, but it seemed to Nia that they were silently supporting each other in a manner that united them. She tried to catch Gwyn's eye but he would not look at her. News of the unicorn seemed to have alarmed him as much as the Llewelyns. She wanted to know why. Why had he hurried away as though an apparition had reared up in their cosy front room?

Mrs Lloyd held back the evening meal and they waited for Catrin and Evan. No one knew where they had gone. At last the family began to eat, uneasily, expecting interruption at any moment. Mr Lloyd was irritable, his stomach had lost its rhythm, he said.

Nerys blinked and peered; she'd left her spectacles somewhere and she was wearing lipstick, the first time she'd done either of these things as far as Nia could remember. She wondered what had tempted her eldest sister into such an unlikely adventure.

It was dark when they heard the familiar roar of the black and bronze car. Catrin came into the kitchen with Evan close behind. They were hungry; they had not eaten; the sea had delayed them, Catrin said. The tide had been out and they had wandered across the empty sand until they had reached the water. They had removed their shoes and socks and splashed their feet in the waves and when they had turned back, the lights were just coming on in Aberdovey.

'It was like magic,' Catrin said. Her eyes looked electric. She stared at the plate of food her mother put before her, toyed with a fork and replaced it. She could not eat. She wasn't hungry after all.

Evan ate slowly. Nia, making a pretence of tidying kitchen drawers, watched him. She found it reassuring to see him eat. It made him accessible.

'I wish you hadn't stayed out quite so long,' said Betty Lloyd. 'There's your music exam soon, Catrin.' Then, almost as an apology, 'I suppose the sea air does you good, though!'

'Course it does, Mam,' Catrin said too brightly. 'And the water was so warm; I've never seen Aberdovey so ... beautiful.'

Nia pictured two figures, standing very close on a shining stretch of sand; dark silhouettes touching, then folding together, the taller bending over the other just like they did in movies. An uncomfortable knot formed in her stomach.

'Shouldn't you be in bed?' Catrin asked suddenly. And Nia, startled, dropped the drawer, scattering its contents, paper doilies, plastic bags and clothes pegs, all over the floor.

'Oh, Nia, she's right,' Mrs Lloyd sighed irritably. 'Look at the time. You'll be in trouble if your dad catches you.'

No chance of that, Nia thought, scrabbling on the floor. She could hear the television in the next room. The snooker had just started. There would be another half-hour to engross him.

Evan bent down to help her. He smelled of the sea and there was sand on his jeans. He put a peg into her hand, gently closing her fingers over it and made her look at him. 'Next time I'll take you,' he said quietly. 'I promise!' His smile was secretive and she noticed that the chestnut streaks in his hair had multiplied; they burned through the black like tiny living flames.

Evan withdrew his hand and Nia, reluctantly, stood up. She replaced the drawer, saying quickly, 'I'll go to bed now, then. *Nos da,* everyone.' She kissed her mother, looked at Evan and left the room.

'*Nos da,*' they called after her. 'Good night, Nia.' She ran up the stairs thinking of tomorrow and the sea.

She couldn't concentrate on anything the following day. She was planning her evening trip in the black and bronze car. They would take slices of *bara brith,* she thought, and apple juice and marmite sandwiches. She knew these to be Evan's favourites. They would spread a rug on the dunes and later wander down to the sea and she would capture the magic that Catrin had found. As for standing close, she would leave that for a while, she thought, until she was tall enough to do justice to such an event. She never doubted that Evan would stay forever, or at least return to them for every holiday.

After school she ran almost all the way home, passing the waiting bus where Gwyn watched her progress with interest, from his high window seat. Nia had always been one to linger, dreaming on the hill road.

The car was there, outside the house. Evan would be waiting for her. She sprang, breathless, into the kitchen and began to gather her picnic. She was adding half a loaf to the pile when her mother came in and exclaimed, 'What are you doing, cariad? Can't you wait for tea?'

'I'm out for tea, Mam,' Nia said happily. 'Evan's taking me today.'

'Taking you where?'

'To the sea, Mam, like he did Catrin.'

'I don't think so, Nia. He's not here!'

'But the car, Mam. The car is there,' Nia said, a little pang of misgiving beginning to gnaw at her.

'The car maybe but Evan is out.' Betty Lloyd looked hard

at her daughter. 'What did Evan say, Nia, to make you think he'd take you?'

'He said that it was my turn,' she said quietly. 'He meant it, Mam, I know he did.'

'Well...' Betty's mouth closed in a thin line. It was difficult to determine what she felt. 'We'll wait and see,' she said.

So Nia left her incomplete bundle on the table and went to change. She refused to believe that she was not going to have her journey so she chose her clothes carefully; her thickest sweater, creamy Aran wool handed down from Catrin but still her favourite; black jeans and new pale trainers. Then she took up a position on the landing where she would be the first to claim Evan when he came through the front door.

The boys were already in the kitchen scrabbling for crisps and lemonade.

Nerys, coming in late from the library, saw Nia on her perch and asked, 'How is Catrin?'

'I don't know,' Nia replied. 'Is she ill?'

'Came home in the dinner hour,' Nerys said. 'She looked awful.'

Nia gave a strangled little 'Oh!' Her eyes pricked and she chewed her lip to distract her tears of suspicion. 'She's not at home now.' Her sisters' bedroom door was open and she could see that the room was empty.

Nerys looked up, then went briskly into the kitchen. There was a commotion. Raised voices. Mrs Lloyd ran through the hall followed by Nerys. They both went into the shop. Nia watched the door and listened. Loud conversation in the shop. Mr Lloyd emerged in bloody apron. 'Are you sure, girl?' he said over his shoulder, then seeing Nia, commanded. 'Look in Catrin's room, see if she's there, Nia. Look in all the rooms!'

Nia obeyed. She looked swiftly and calmly into every upstairs room, certain that Catrin was not alone, wherever she was, and quite safe from kidnappers.

'No,' she called. 'Catrin's not here.'

Mr Lloyd was reaching for the telephone, his wife pulling off her apron when the front door opened and Catrin sailed in. She was breathless but hardly unwell. Her hair was tumbled, her eyes wide, her face all smiles.

Very clever, Nia thought, to make an entrance just in time, before a fuss is made and police sent searching in the hills.

Her sister was swept into the kitchen with questions and complaints. 'Where've you been, girl?' 'Why didn't you say?' 'Why leave school so early?' 'Are you sick?'

The boys scuttled out before they could be included in the trouble that was brewing. Treats might be withheld. The television banned. But Nia, plunging through their retreat, heard Catrin object in a shrill voice. 'I'm sixteen now. I'm not a child who has to tell everything. I went for a walk. I went for a walk, a walk, a walk, right?'

To Nia this disdainful repetition was proof of her sister's guilt. She wanted to know more. Trying to provoke her parents into further questioning she asked innocently, 'Were you alone?'

Her mother cast her an agitated look. 'It's none of your business, Nia!'

Temporarily rebuffed Nia left the argument and went to take up her post on the stairs. She met Evan in the hall. She was angry now. Angry with everyone, especially Evan. 'I'm ready,' she said defiantly.

He looked exceptionally handsome: windswept and buoyant. 'Very nice,' he murmured abstractedly.

'You said you would take me to the sea,' she furiously reminded him. 'Remember?'

'Ah,' he said. 'Ah, yes.' And then, shaking his head in a suddenly thought-out explanation, 'The car's not right, Nia. It needs fixing.'

'You've had all day,' she said, unable to stem the deliberate rudeness.

He hardly noticed her tone. 'I've been … preoccupied,' he told her. 'Problems to solve.'

'I suppose you've been walking off your 'problems' with a friend!' She glowered at him, hating herself.

The wonderfully carefree expression vanished. 'Ridiculous child,' he said roughly.

She dropped down on to the top stair. Chastened. He strode past her into his room, not giving her the satisfaction of a slammed door, as a friend would have done, but closing it firmly behind him.

Nia brooded on the darkened stair. She was hungry for descriptions, information, anything that would give her a picture of Catrin's mysterious afternoon. She would waylay her sister. Get at the truth. When Catrin came out of the kitchen and began to mount the stairs, Nia deliberately set herself in the centre.

'Nia,' Catrin sighed. 'Let me pass.'

Nia stood aside but followed Catrin into the room she shared with Nerys. Her sister did not object, but Nia ventured no further than the door. She stood with her back against it, ready to attack. She envied her sisters. They had made their room so pretty; painting the walls creamy yellow to match all the old pine furniture they had gleaned from Tŷ Llŷr. They had stripped and polished chests and cupboards, burning themselves with acid sometimes, chafing their fingers on sandpaper, reeling from the smell of spirit but determined to recreate the bygone age that beckoned from the pages of glossy magazines. Nerys had even forbidden posters, instead she had begged samplers and flower paintings from ancient aunts, and hung them round the room.

'You're so lucky,' Nia said, but her sister would not respond to this. She stood beside the window, looking out. Michael hadn't been seen for a week but Catrin still seemed

77

unable to break her habit of watching for him. Perhaps, after all, Nia thought, Catrin had been ill at school. She knew that her parents would have asked the usual questions about time and place. These did not interest her. She wanted to get at events. Ruthless and daring she challenged, 'Has he kissed you?'

Catrin turned into the room. 'Kissed?' she repeated.

'Evan? Has he? Has he?'

'Ssh! What if he has?'

'No,' Nia cried. 'Not *that* way!'

Catrin approached her. 'He's not a goblin,' she said coldly. 'I'm not bewitched, see!' She stretched her long pale fingers towards Nia then flipped her hands over, palms upward, like a baby who has cleverly hidden a forbidden sweet.

'Has he, then?' Nia whispered.

'I'll never tell,' Catrin taunted, launching herself into a series of sad and frantic giggles.

Nia fled.

October broadened into a month of extremes. Frosty nights and warm, bright days lit by the violent colours of dying leaves. But the mountain chestnut was more colourful that year than any other tree. So startlingly splendid were its leaves that, from a distance, it appeared to blaze like an enchanted fire above the wreaths of evening mist.

And Evan Llŷr's luxuriant hair was growing longer. He seemed unable to comb it into any conventional shape. A mass of red and black framed his narrow face so that he took on an unreal, fairy-tale appearance. The superstitious were alarmed. Nia, forgiving everything, was entranced, for it seemed to confirm her belief that Even was, indeed, a hero from the Celtic past. She felt as though by recognizing him she had breathed life into the troubled prince she had welcomed on that stormy day.

It was Nain Griffiths who gave Evan the name of Chestnut

Soldier. On one of her rare visits to town she had met him striding down the High Street and boldly re-introduced herself, remarking on his hair and its resemblance to the flaming chestnut tree. And he had laughed his deep abandoned laugh and swept her into Number Six for tea. Nia was amazed to see how girlish Gwyn's grandmother became in Evan's company. She would not leave until she had extracted a promise from him, to visit her.

Others did not feel so comfortable about Evan Llŷr. He was seen too much with Catrin Lloyd, a girl young enough to be his daughter. His hair was too long for a soldier. When would he return to the army? What was his past?

At school girls pestered Nia for information about him. But Gwyn Griffiths and Emlyn Llewelyn were the worst. They wanted to know everything. Where the soldier went, and how he behaved when he returned. Why his hair was turning red? How Catrin felt and why she was so pale now and so very slender. And was the soldier ever angry or violent?

Because she needed these two to be her friends, she told them she would watch her cousin and report. She would have watched without being asked. And every time she saw Evan and her sister walking together or laughing secretly, she would try and ignore the painful twist inside her and forgive him, always trusting in his promise, that one day it would be her turn to be his companion by the sea.

By now the twins had given up trying to draw Evan into their games. They had hoped for a swaggering soldier, a violent man whose stories they could boastfully repeat. They felt cheated. Evan was a romantic who spent time only with their sister and who excited the female population of Pendewi for reasons they did not approve. Sometimes Nia would hear them arguing with Iolo who would always champion Evan. Alun felt himself to be above the quarrel but tended to side with the twins. No one seemed to notice Iolo's increasing distress; the way he would hide his face behind his hands as though by obstructing his view of the family he could prevent them from recognizing him. Sometimes they would discover his toys in strange places; in his mother's drawers, behind the old dresser, inside the piano. Even when Mr Lloyd found a toy garage in the deep freeze he merely thought it another of Iolo's little idiosyncrasies.

Rehearsals for the Christmas Concert began. This year it was to be excerpts from Fauré's Requiem. The Male Voice Choir, the High School Orchestra and half their relatives were roped in for the most ambitious project yet attempted. Every evening music filled the valley from the Church, the School and the Community Centre. Siwan Davis had been chosen to sing solo soprano and in order to achieve perfection she spent all her spare time listening to a tape of Victoria de los Angeles. Long after dusk *'Pie Jesu'* issued from the open windows of the Davis's hill farm. It might have been this wistful accompaniment to the autumn that made it so unforgettable.

One afternoon Mr and Mrs Davis called into the butcher's shop. Bryn was a friend of Iestyn's and a good customer. He liked his meat. Besides his daughter, Siwan, he had a son, Dewi, whom nobody liked. Dilys, Bryn's wife, vied with Mrs Bowen, the wool, for the position of most informed busybody; she was never one to withhold advice or practical help. The Davises came into the shop just before closing time and were taken through the house to see Betty. There began a low and earnest conversation in the kitchen.

Nia, overcome with curiosity, burst in on them, saying through the sudden taut silence, 'I forgot my homework.' She sidled behind Mr Davis to a pile of newspapers on the dresser where she had planted her books, and then left the room.

'Shut the door, Nia!' her mother called after her and Nia meekly replied, 'Yes Mam!' However she had perfected a method of clicking the door shut and then immediately opening it a fraction. The adults, reassured by the first 'click', began to resume their conversation, never noticing the narrow crack through which Nia, hidden by the door, was listening.

'You're not worried then, Betty?' Dilys Davis continued where she'd been interrupted.

'Well, as I said...' Mrs Lloyd began.

'You should be, Betty!' Mr Davis broke in. 'If it was my daughter...!'

'It's innocent, I'm sure,' said Dilys. 'But people talk, and it's not nice, Betty. Not right, I mean, for Catrin's sake.'

'Can't you do anything, Iestyn?' Mr Davis asked. 'It's a man's duty.'

Mr Lloyd's chair squeaked on the tiled floor. He stood up, paced toward the window. 'It's difficult, Bryn. He's a relative, see, and recuperating – had a terrible time just lately. His family's in Australia and he's nowhere else to go. The other cousins are all gone from Wales; in England now, they are...'

'And he had to come back to Wales,' Betty added softly.

'What happened out there, then, in Northern Ireland?' Dilys Davis inquired, her quiet tone hardly disguising an unpleasant eagerness.

'Well, from what we can gather,' Betty Lloyd reluctantly began, 'it was a routine search for arms, no danger expected. Evan sent his platoon into a warehouse, I think it was, then suddenly there's this explosion and Evan rushes in. The radio operator tried to stop him, madness he said it was and not the right thing to do at all, but Major Llŷr must reach his men. He brought two out, horribly burned they were, and then went in again when the whole place went up like a... like a...'

'Wired like a cage, they said,' Iestyn explained dramatically. 'Four bombs in all. They didn't stand a chance. Then, after, when the fire was out, they found our major under a pile of girders, not a mark on him!'

'A miracle!' Dilys breathed.

'A hero!' Betty added.

'Duw, I remember now,' Mr Davis declared, banging the table. 'It was in the papers, like a cauldron they said it was, and only one man left alive. He was in a coma for days. They never released his name. Duw, I never realized it was him!'

'Nor did we,' Betty said. 'He wouldn't speak of it. But Iestyn wrote to his regiment, just to make sure, you know, of what his accident had been. They'd kept his name out of the papers because it was all too extraordinary, a mystery!'

Outside the door, Nia was getting cramp, yet she dared not move. She wondered when her father had written that letter. When had he become suspicious?

'The army don't like mysteries,' Bryn said gravely, and his wife excited by the talk added, 'His hair, all streaked red like that, it'll be the shock!'

'It would be!' her husband echoed.

'The shock,' Iestyn agreed. 'So we must have sympathy. And Catrin, well, perhaps she helps. She's a kind girl, and sensitive!'

Nia began to tiptoe away. Filled with this new knowledge of her cousin, her mind raced back to that first day, when her prince had come to them out of his long sleep. She did not watch her step and tripped on the stairs. Books tumbled out of her arms and slipped into the hall. She turned to retrieve them just as the front door opened and a gust of wind sent the pages into a frantic flutter, while Evan stepped in amongst them and stood looking down at her.

Without exchanging a word, they gathered the books together and put them in a pile on the stairs. Nia found herself sitting beside Evan on the second stair, and couldn't stop herself from asking, 'Will you take me, this time, Evan, to the sea?'

He stared at her for a moment, smiled and said, almost savagely, 'Yes, I damn well will!'

'Now?'

'Right now. Get your coat.'

She hurried upstairs, hardly able to believe her luck. When she came down again they were all crowding into the hall. Dilys Davis, seeing Evan in a new light, was gazing almost shyly at him while he said, 'I'm taking Nia for a ride, Betty. Is that all right, with you?'

'Nia?' Betty asked, surprised.

'Yes, me this time' Nia said, childishly triumphant.

'We'll see you at rehearsal then, Iestyn,' Mr Davis reminded his friend of his duty to the Male Voice Choir. Then he steered his wife towards the door, nodding respectfully at Evan, before stepping into the street.

Mrs Lloyd buttoned Nia's jacket fussily. 'You won't be too long now!' She addressed herself to Evan. 'You'll be back for supper?'

He answered indirectly. 'I'll take good care of her, Betty.' He took Nia's hand and, stepping into the street, they approached the bright car together, like conspirators.

'D'you like to travel in the air?' he asked her and when Nia nodded, he jumped into the driver's seat and pressed a switch, conjuring his strange car into a gleaming roofless chariot.

Nia stood on the kerb, almost afraid. If she entered the prince's chariot would she turn into something her family would not recognize?

'Hurry! Before the sun sets,' he commanded. And to reassure her, he climbed out and opened a door. 'Into the back,' he said. 'Where children are safe!'

She grimaced and got in. Evan laughed and said, 'Time will fly, Nia. You'll soon be old enough to sit beside me!'

Like Catrin does, she thought, and said, 'Let's make time fly now!'

The engine growled into action and they sailed up the High Street, passing Gwyn Griffiths on the bridge. He was talking to Alun and Emlyn. Two boys returned her vigorous waving but Gwyn looked glum and seemed to shake his head.

'We'll go to Harlech,' Evan declared. 'Where it all began.'

She did not ask what he meant but pressed herself into the seat and half-closed her eyes, enraptured with the smell of leather, the freshness of the wind and the whirl of mountains, sheep and sky.

They travelled in silence for nearly an hour and then came within sight of the sea. A huge sun balanced on the edge of the horizon and, against the mountains, the great castle was defined by shadows.

The road that led to the castle on its giant rock was deliciously steep and narrow. There were no visitors in the car park, they had the place to themselves. But the castle was closed so they stood by the south-eastern tower where a statue of the dying King Bendigeidfran, turned away from the sea. Behind the King on his weary horse, lay a dead boy: Gwern, the King's nephew, a victim of the mad Efnisien.

Nia had forgotten the statue and remembered only the view: Mount Eryri, the rugged towers that swept towards the sky and the delicate blue line of the Llyn peninsula curving into the sea. When she had been younger, she purposely put sad things out of her mind; she had been prone to nightmares.

'It's so old, this castle,' she murmured.

'No,' Evan retorted. 'Not so old!'

'But...' she began.

'It wasn't here,' he said abruptly, 'when they were. He half-turned his head toward the statue but wouldn't look at it. Then he paced away from the dying King and added, 'There was only the rock.'

'Oh!'. Hugging herself against the wind, Nia twirled about trying to turn the landscape into a wild kaleidoscope. At last she came to rest beside him. He would not even glance at the scenery that so delighted her but remained very still, glaring across the sea. In spite of the wind beads of sweat glittered on his face and she wondered what mirage could be there, beyond the horizon, that had suddenly called up so much wrath. Her prince had slipped away again and left a demon in his place, his wild hair ruffled like some mythic beast, his windblown jacket surging darkly all about him.

Adrift between the elements and this grim stranger she felt afraid. She wanted to bring him within her reach but could not think how to do it. At last she ventured, 'What is it like – to be a soldier?'

He turned to her, very slow, and replied, 'It depends on who you are!'

'But being who *you* are?'

He seemed to be sizing her up, deciding if she was worthy of a true answer. Then all at once he leant towards her and softly confided, 'Glorious!'

Astonished she mumbled, 'But…'

'Glorious,' he repeated. For a moment his smile was wicked and his eyes mirrored colours that were not apparent in their surroundings, brimstone and flame-green. She moved away from him and watched him looking across the sea again. He was far away now, somewhere where it troubled and excited him. Then he thrust his fingers through his wild hair as though he were trying to rub away the rage. 'A soldier is a hero to half the world,' he murmured uneasily, 'the others,' he shrugged, 'would rather be without us!' This time his smile was sorrowful. He was almost her quiet prince again. 'Let's go down to the beach' he said.

They climbed into the car and sped down the narrow cliff road, then over the railway track and down to the sea. The sun had almost set but the clouds were bright and reflected gold glittered over the sand. They left the car on a verge then, abandoning their socks and shoes, plunged through the dunes to the beach.

Nia immediately run to the water. She splashed a path along the tidal line of shells and seaweed, aware that Evan was watching, his hands in his pockets and almost happy again. He began to march across the sand and Nia ran before him and around him, laughing and leaping backwards sometimes, in a little dance that had a pattern to it, and because his strides were measured and unhesitant their movements took on the shape of a strange ritual that they might always have known.

When they climbed back across the dunes the wind, singing in the marram grass, flung handfuls of sand at them and Nia had to keep her mouth closed tight against her giggles.

She insisted that she wasn't cold and so, with the roof open to the dark sky and darker mountains, they sped away from the sea and the coloured clouds and, as all light faded, she watched the headlights beaming them forward through a bright tunnel. Swathes of mist drifted across the road and when she looked back, the mountains had vanished. Nothing was familiar. Huddled against Evan's shoulder, Nia fancied that she was plunging into the Otherworld in a war chariot driven by some fantastic legendary god or chieftain. She did not mind that her time with the prince had not lasted as long as her sister's, that certain events might have been omitted from her adventure. Evan had given her enough to puzzle over and to cherish.

At Number Six the meal was waiting for them. Nia entered the kitchen with a challenging stare, meant especially for Catrin. Her sister deliberately avoided her glance but Nia, watching closely, saw a listening expression cross her face when Evan came in. Catrin would not look at him.

Nia had intended to boast of the warm beach and the sunset. She had thought that she would tell about Mount Eryri and her dance beside the water but she found that she could not. It had become something special that could not be shared. And when her father asked how their journey had been and had they seen the sea, she could only answer, 'It was great!'

The atmosphere was strained. The younger children had

86

eaten earlier and where the twins' noisy chatter would have been there was an uncomfortable emptiness. Alun tried a few jokes. Evan smiled and Mr Lloyd laughed seconds too late. Nerys had nervously applied make-up to her long thin face. It was a disastrous experiment; the colour was wrong and she looked like an unsuccessful clown. Everyone wondered what had possessed her but she seemed so sadly ill at ease that no one could bring themself to ridicule her efforts.

After supper when the household had dispersed, Nia heard a monotonous and desultory tune coming from the piano in the front room. Catrin seemed unable to perform. Nia opened the door and peering round it asked, 'Can I listen?'

Hunched over the piano, Catrin said nothing.

Nia slipped quietly into a chair. Catrin toyed with the keys and then thrust her hands across the piano, pounding out discordant ugly chords. She was too musical to bear the sound for long, however, and gradually brought her fingers under control until the notes softened into a tune again. It was then that Nia became aware of the high treble accompaniment of sobbing. 'I can't play any more,' Catrin wept quietly. 'It's beyond me!'

Nia stood up, ready to leave the room. Her sister's distress seemed too private. But as she touched the door Catrin said, 'Glory is dead!'

'No!' Nia cried. 'Oh no,' and she ran to Catrin who flung her arms about her sobbing, 'Michael blames me, I don't know why. He's so cruel now. Won't speak to me. And he's seeing Lluned Price every day.'

Astonished that Catrin should be sharing this news with her, Nia marvelled, nevertheless, at her sister's self-deception. Surely Catrin must know what the town and, therefore, Michael thought. She had been seen so often with Evan Llŷr. She had refused Michael when he needed her. Surely he was a boy of the past. But perhaps it hurt that he had chosen someone else. It was all such a puzzle. As Catrin sobbed against her shoulder Nia resolved that she would never find herself in such a quandary. She would love always and forever, to the very end.

'Don't tell them,' Catrin brushed her wet cheeks with the back of her hand.

'Course not,' Nia said. She stood at Catrin's side a moment longer, studying the tortuous black patterns of her sister's music. Catrin began to fumble with the keys again and Nia wondered how she could avoid the age of sixteen when it was possible to be hurt by so many things at once: a dead horse, a boy's rejection, music that you couldn't play.

When she let herself out of the room Catrin had begun to draw something almost tuneful from the piano.

All that stuff she gave me was only part of the truth, Nia thought. It was Evan taking me to the sea, that was the real hurt, but it came out as all sorts of other things.

She climbed the stairs wondering if Evan had left the house. What would he be doing if he was in his room? Did he read? Write? She had never seen him with a book. She glanced towards his door. It gave nothing away. The house was exceptionally quiet; even the boys' voices were low. She began to mount the narrow flight of stairs that led to the top bedrooms: her parents' and the room she shared with Iolo and Bethan.

Bethan was asleep in her cot but in the corner, where a soft light glowed on the sloping roof, Iolo lay in a tense huddle. Nia knew he was awake. She crept over to him and touched his shoulder. 'Go away,' said a muffled voice from the mounded bedclothes.

'What's the matter, Iolo?'

He turned on his back and glared at her, his eyes red-rimmed with drying tears.

'What is it? Shall I call Mam?' Nia asked. She had little confidence in her nursing abilities.

Iolo shook his head.

'Shall I turn the light out?'

Another shake of the head, then screwing up his face he blurted out, 'He promised me. He promised to take me!'

'Who?' She knew, of course, but had to play for time while she thought of a way to settle him.

'Evan. He said he'd take me in the car, one day. But he never does. It's always Catrin, and now it's you. He said I could walk with him, but he never waits. And he never talks to me now.'

Nia didn't know how to comfort her brother. 'Perhaps you're too shy,' she suggested. 'Ask him about the car tomorrow. I'll help you!'

Iolo stared at her searchingly. 'O.K.' He yawned, burrowed into a comfortable position and closed his eyes.

Nia undressed, turned out the light and got into bed. She lay very still listening intently for sounds from the room beneath. But there were none. She fell asleep and dreamed that she was riding in a chariot through a cloud of larks that whirled about her head like the butterflies in Idris Llewelyn's studio. Distant hoofbeats drifted into her dream and fixed themselves in her head, edging out the smoother singing sounds. In her confused and drowsy state she wondered if it could be the poor broken unicorn, or the spirit of black Glory come to take her to the Otherworld.

All at once she was wide awake and the hoofbeats had rolled out of her dream and into the night of the street. She must see this phantom for herself.

Kneeling on the dressing table she reached up to the high dormer window, opened it carefully and peered down into the street. The horse, or whatever it was, was coming closer. Suddenly its speed increased and it galloped across her narrow line of vision. A wild white horse, a stallion perhaps who had left the mountain herd or been stolen from it by the dark rider on his back; a man who wore something bright that billowed round him like a cloud.

Nia closed the window and went back to bed. 'A ghost,' she told herself. 'Farmers do not wear cloaks and gallop about at night.' She thought of telling this story at breakfast, knowing very well that she would not tell anyone.

On Saturday mornings Number Six was always more than half empty. Alun went to football, the twins to cheer him on. Catrin visited Miss Olwen Oliver for extra music lessons. Nerys was always in the library. Mr Lloyd would be in his shop, his wife in the kitchen singing to Bethan while she cooked cottage pie and Iolo drew pictures of animals and tall coloured houses. This Saturday, Evan had left the house before anyone was up. His note on the kitchen table told them that he would be away for a day and a night.

Alone in her high bedroom Nia reflected on the events that had crowded too fast into the recent hours: her visit to the sea, her sister's tears, the phantom horse. She must share some of these secrets soon, she thought, with someone she could trust, or they would tumble out where they should not.

She left the room and descended in a drifting way to the landing. She glanced down the passage. At the end Evan's door invited her from its deep shadows. She walked slowly towards it, put her hand on the doorknob and found herself looking through the open doorway into Evan's room. It told her nothing. Its tidiness was depressing. Only the jacket left on the back of a chair gave a clue to the room's occupant. Nia wandered into the room. It was a cool, featureless place, but in the mornings a slither of sunlight would creep through the window. She patted the pillow, straightened the coverlet. She ran her finger along the top of the dressing table, not daring to open a drawer. He had left nothing for her to do, except perhaps tidy the jacket into smoother folds. She picked it up and must have turned it upside down, for something fell out of an inner pocket.

It lay on the pale carpet; a small dark object, wooden, an animal without ears or tail. She knew it to be Gwyn's lost horse. Holding her breath she knelt down and touched it, ready to sustain the fear that Gwyn had prepared her for. But it was not a dreadful thing at all. It was light. Harmless. She threw it up, caught it and, almost laughing, passed it from one hand to another.

'Oh, Gwyn,' she said to the sunshine in the air. 'There's no demon here. It's empty!'

And then the fear came.

Chapter
7

Gwyn was on the mountain when he saw Nia and Iolo arriving. He was gathering bracken for the cattle's winter bedding, in a field that was too steep to mow. He dumped the last bundle into the trailer and began to run down the track. Nia had something to tell him at last. He had been waiting, anxiously, for something to jolt her out of her ridiculous loyalty to her cousin. As he ran he speculated on what could have led Nia to seek his help. His downhill race became a wild plummeting.

His visitors were already in the house when he reached the porch. He dutifully flung off his muddy wellingtons and ran into the kitchen. The Lloyds were sitting, waif-like, at the table, waiting for hot chocolate.

'I've brought Nia and Iolo for the weekend,' his mother explained as she heated milk on the stove.

'The weekend?' Gwyn noticed two bulging plastic bags beside the door. A pyjama sleeve dangled, pathetically, from one. Their departure must have been hasty.

'What's happened?' he asked nervously.

Nia frowned, trying to decide on an answer. 'Iolo was in a state,' she said at last.

Iolo obviously did not object to this remark. He nodded vehemently.

Gwyn was disappointed. He had hoped for something more impressive. 'Why?' he asked.

'He keeps losing things and – people are being unkind.' She looked furtively over her shoulder and whispered, 'I'll tell you the rest later.'

Here was better news. If it could not be spoken aloud it must be interesting, Gwyn reasoned. He joined them at the table and begged a cup of chocolate for himself. Mrs Griffiths had automatically added more milk to the saucepan. She looked as though she could not quite grasp the situation and was comforting herself with a quiet and familiar routine.

Gwyn and the Lloyds sipped their hot drinks, slowly postponing further conversation while they avoided scalding their tongues on the hot liquid.

'Perhaps you two would like to take your things to Bethan's room,' Mrs Griffiths suggested when the mugs were empty. She never said, 'the room where Bethan used to sleep,' because she had never relinquished the hope that, one day, her daughter would return to claim her place, although it was eight years now since Bethan had vanished.

Nia loved the room. She had once confided to Gwyn that she felt peaceful, surrounded by Bethan's dolls and clothes. It was a state that always seemed to elude Nia in her own home.

'Come on, then,' Nia nudged her brother and made for the door.

'I'll bring a mattress for Iolo later,' Mrs Griffiths called after them.

'Iolo can share my room if he likes,' Gwyn proposed. He could not think why he had said this. Later he assumed that it was intuition.

The Lloyds stopped in their tracks. Nia astonished. Iolo round-eyed with enthusiasm. 'Yes, please,' he said.

'Take your stuff and put it on my bed then,' Gwyn told him. 'I'll sleep on the mattress.'

'That was kind, Gwyn,' Mrs Griffiths said when the Lloyds had gone.

'Iolo's all right,' Gwyn murmured. 'He's different from the twins; quieter. We'll be O.K. What happened, Mam? Why are they here? Why not Alun? It's all a bit sudden.'

'Alun had a big match on, and I don't know why those two are here, that's the truth. I was in the shop for the weekend joint when Nia bursts in from the house.' Mrs Griffiths lowered her voice. 'She looked, quite frankly, terrified. I don't know what's been going on. Poor Betty, I don't know how she manages it; eight children and I've only one to worry about.'

They eyed each other but did not mention Bethan.

'Go on about Nia,' Gwyn encouraged. 'Why did you bring her here?'

'Well, she stared at me, I don't know, as if I were her salvation and almost yelled, "*Please,* Mrs Griffiths, can I come and stay with you, *please, please!*" Her father looked quite put out. Well, I went into the house and, of course, Betty was very happy for Nia to come. She said Catrin needed a bit of attention, she wasn't herself, and then all at once Iolo cries out, "Can I come too?" And Nia put in her bit, "Let him come," and added all those "pleases" again, so I couldn't refuse, could I?'

'I'm glad you didn't. Was Catrin ill, then?' He asked the question in an off-hand way, not wishing to appear too interested in her.

'No. But she hasn't looked well lately, and always about with Evan...'

'Yes.' Gwyn curtailed any discussion that might revolve around Evan Llŷr. He knew where his mother's sympathies lay.

'That poor man, his hair...I heard from the Davises...'

'Yes, yes!' Gwyn said, not waiting for a story he would have found enlightening. 'I'm going to see what those two are doing.'

Nia was sitting on the patchwork quilt that covered his sister's bed. She had Bethan's rag dolls in her lap and was tidying their hair. Gwyn sat beside her.

'Will she come back again?' Nia asked.

'Bethan?' Gwyn shrugged. 'Perhaps. If I call her!'

'Will you?'

'No,' Gwyn said and then added, regretfully. 'She's happy in another place. She'll always be a child and I'm afraid if I've outgrown her, we'll have nothing left to say to each other. When she came back, that other time, we were almost the same age.'

Nia hugged all three dolls, sighing hugely. Gwyn laughed and said, 'Come on, it's not that sad. Now tell me what's happened.'

'I don't know what came over me,' she said. 'I was so scared, I didn't know what to do. I didn't know who to tell, and then there was your mother, just like an answer to a prayer I hadn't thought of. I feel a bit silly now.'

'So tell me!' Gwyn demanded.

Nia felt inside her jacket pocket and brought out the broken horse. Gwyn stared at it, almost disbelieving. 'Thank God,' he said. 'Where was it?'

Nia hung her head and murmured reluctantly, 'It fell out of Evan's coat.'

Gwyn grabbed the horse from her. 'Duw,' he said. 'I knew it. All the time I've known it. But I didn't want it to be true.'

'You knew he had it?'

'Not just that. I know why he had it!'

'Perhaps he meant to give it back but had forgotten?'

Gwyn shook his head. He yawned, longing to lay his head down. It was like having flu without the pain. Just knowing he was going to have to embark on an impossibly ambitious spell exhausted him. And it would have to be soon, before the demon grew confident and completely overcame the soldier. But how could he stop him, and with what? 'You realise,

Nia, what has happened, don't you?' Gwyn said.

'No!'

He knew she lied.

'That day Iolo lost the horse, and I believed I had trapped his spirit, even though we never found it. And Evan fell under the chestnut tree, and you thought he cried out, silently...'

'He's a poor wounded soldier,' she said reproachfully.

'Listen,' Gwyn cried. 'That mad, black spirit was free for a while, but I caught it, Nia, in Arianwen's web. Only Evan got in the way, somehow, and now he is possessed.' He peered into her averted face and made her look at him. 'The dark soul of Efnisien is there, Nia, in your great prince.' He almost enjoyed the way her rebellious expression began to crumple. At last she must believe him.

Defiant to the end, she muttered, 'No! He's a hero. And I'll tell you why. When he was in Northern Ireland he ran into a burning warehouse to save his men; he shouldn't have done it, they said. He broke the rules. It was hopeless, you see. And they all burned to death except for him. And he had no wounds at all. It was a mystery. They never gave Evan's name to the papers because it was, unnatural, I suppose. Impossible. I was outside the door when Mam told the Davises, Tŷ Coch. I don't think we're supposed to know. But you see, he's a hero, not a demon.'

She didn't realise that instead of contradicting Gwyn she'd given him all the proof he needed. Reasons and events whirled in his head, sorting themselves into a dreadful pattern. It was terrifying and yet exhilarating, discovering the ability to fit the pieces of a story together.

'I can see now that Efnisien has been calling to Evan for a long time,' he said, 'so that he could enjoy life again in the form of someone like himself. Evan's life is almost an echo of his own – a soldier, a Llŷr who is not a Llŷr; a man who is the opposite of his own brother; Nia, he even tried to sacrifice himself in a fire, but at the moment when Evan's hate matched his own, Efnisien was able to reach the soldier and save him for himself. The rest was inevitable. Hatred is a dreadful force; it makes things happen.'

'But what about me?' Nia's voice called plaintively into his excited speculations. 'Was I meant to find the horse again?'

Gwyn stopped pacing and thought about that. 'No,' he said. 'It was an accident. You went into that room because you are ... silly about Evan.'

She bristled. 'Not *so* silly. I knew he was a prince!'

'Prince!' Gwyn exclaimed, exasperated. 'This isn't a fairy tale, Nia. We're sliding into a real tragedy, a parallel story if you like, that might not have a happy ending. And I have to stop it, somehow. I'm the only one.'

'All the same,' she quietly persisted, 'Efnisien was a prince.'

'Huh!' was all Gwyn said. But he couldn't deny it. 'Evan found the horse in the stream and would have given it to me, but I prevented that, idiot that I am. Always an idiot with my spells. Once the demon was there, safe within his soul, he hid the horse so that I could never again use it to trap him. Don't you see, Nia? It's so clear. Glory was afraid of Evan the moment he saw him. His memory inherited from the horses Efnisien maimed. Fear of that prince had become an instinct. And the unicorn, Iolo's toy horses, they were a repetition Evan couldn't help.'

'Evan didn't do those things,' Nia broke in.

'Of course he did,' Gwyn said roughly. 'Efnisien is beginning to relive his story.'

'And Catrin is Branwen.' Nia said flatly.

Did Nia wish it could have been her role, Gwyn wondered?

'I believe so,' he said.

'What shall we do?' she asked helplessly.

Gwyn was forming an answer when the door handle rattled and Iolo's face appeared. 'I'm going to help your dad with the ewes in the top field,' he told Gwyn proudly.

'We're going to see my nain, sure you don't want to come?' Gwyn asked, sure that Iolo would not.

'Heck no!' Iolo disappeared.

'Your nain!' Nia had brightened immediately Gwyn mentioned his grandmother, as though their problems were half solved already.

Nain Griffiths welcomed them as a glorious excuse for a party. She wanted them to try her new seed cake, her fresh apple juice and hazelnut cookies. Spreading all this tempting food over a lace cloth on her lawn, she bundled cushions out of the house and pushed the children on to them while she hummed and twirled to show off her new three-tiered skirt. Gwyn couldn't break through her persistent cheerfulness. At last he almost shouted, 'Look, Nain, we've got a problem!' and her bird-bright glance told him that she had known it all along but needed her tea party to celebrate this longed-for visit.

'Well?' she said, perching, in a temporary way, on the remains of a cane chair that had obviously housed many generations of mice.

But they didn't know where to begin and Nain was about to fly off for another plate when Gwyn brought the broken horse from his pocket and put it on the white cloth where it couldn't fail to catch her eye.

Arrested in mid-flight, she glared at the animal and said hoarsely, 'Why have you brought *that* here, Gwydion Gwyn?'

So Gwyn told his story from the beginning, when they had walked up the mountain to admire the red kite, and Iolo had found the horse and let it fall into the stream. He left nothing out but neither he nor his grandmother had the whole picture until Nia added her part.

When she described her visit to Harlech there were moments of terror for him, but his grandmother remained calm. He could not understand this when she must have

98

known why Evan had glared across the Irish sea, must have remembered that Efnisien had sailed across, perhaps from that very spot, to fight and die for his sister Branwen. And Nia was pitching herself back into those hours with Evan as though they were the only true and wonderful moments of her life. Women, Gwyn thought, were unfathomable.

'You're not afraid,' Gwyn accused his grandmother. 'Once, you could hardly bear to look at that horse. You wouldn't forgive me for setting it free four years ago. What's so different now?'

'For one thing, it isn't free!' Nain grinned in an irritating way. 'This time, I know I'm not at risk!'

'You're very smug, I must say,' Gwyn exploded. He leapt up, jerking the cloth, and the broken horse gave a little jump against a cup that tinkled like a tiny warning, or so it seemed to him. The others, however, appeared to be enchanted with the incident and laughed delightedly.

'Heck, you two,' Gwyn stormed. 'Grow up! We're all at risk. There's a madman on the loose, lusting for glory, and murder too, most probably.'

'You're wrong, Gwyn!' Nain said, suddenly grave. 'Our chestnut soldier will fight the violence he's been saddled with.'

'And if he loses?'

'Then he will need your help, won't he?' she retorted. 'It's your fault, boy. You've bewitched that poor soldier as surely as your ancestors ensnared each other into the lives of animals. And you said that you were tired of magic!'

Gwyn ignored her last remark.

'You admit then,' he said, 'that we could be in for trouble. That there's danger about.'

'Duw, duw!' His grandmother set out on a little dancing journey through her orchard, flinging tuneful messages over the fields. 'You think you've pinned him down, don't you?' she sang. 'Foisted that poor soldier with some convenient mythical personality to suit a coincidence of horses. But do you really know, Gwydion Gwyn? Stories take a tortuous route through time. Perhaps this one isn't quite true? Yes, I began it all. I gave you the horse. I knew it was a dreadful thing. But it was you who decided it held the tortured soul of that poor prince. Did he really commit the murders ascribed to him? If he did, then he atoned for them. He was flung into the boiling cauldron, a living man, stretched himself until it broke into four parts, and his heart broke also.'

Gwyn was determined not to be impressed. 'Something of him was left,' he muttered darkly. 'The diabolical part. I had it safe and now it's on the rampage.'

'Oh, la, la, la, la, la!' his grandmother trilled mockingly.

'You've been led astray,' Gwyn furiously accused her. 'Why have you allowed it?'

'Because I am a woman,' she replied.

'A mad one,' he said grimly. She's lost, he thought, hoodwinked by a blue-eyed Llŷr. She can't help herself. And then he told her of the recent Irish fire and Evan's part in it, how he had tried to throw his life away to save his men, and failed.

And Gwyn knew his grandmother believed at last, but although she looked anxious, it was not in the way he had hoped for. 'Poor man,' she murmured.

Overhead white mare's tails were racing through the blue sky and a little wind burrowed beneath the cloth. Nia caught the broken horse as it rolled on to the grass. 'What shall I do with this?' she asked. 'He'll know I've found it.'

'Let him know,' Nain said. 'Gwyn, you must soon show him who you are, that you'll help him.'

'Perhaps he is enjoying his new soul. He seemed lonely without one,' Gwyn muttered. He was thinking that after all, he had not been entirely responsible for the change in Evan. It had begun far away, in an Irish fire.

They gathered up the cloth and the empty cups and plates and took them into the kitchen. But before Nia and Gwyn left

Nain took them into her forest of a room, where plants held sway over everything, even the furniture. Nia was commanded to relax while Gwyn cleared the table of books. Then his grandmother produced a large deck of cards wrapped in black silk. She laid the cards on the table, face down, in a fan shape.

'What are we going to do?' Intrigued, Nia began to count the cards.

Nain tapped her hand. 'Let them be,' she said. 'There are seventy-eight. You must choose one. This is not the normal route to the truth, but it will serve my purpose. I may not be a wizard,' she glanced at Gwyn, 'but I have my ways. Have you heard of Tarot cards, Nia?'

Nia shook her head. 'Is it like fortune-telling?'

'No! It is a way of seeking the truth, and thereby a solution.'

Gwyn sighed. He knew the cards. They told stories, relayed lives, caused thought when action was needed.

'No need for that,' Nain chided him. 'If I am not wrong, Nia is close to the heart of this matter. If she chooses the right card then it is she who will take our story to its happy conclusion. Now, Nia, take your time. Empty your mind and choose a card.'

Gratified, but anxious not to jeopardise the proceedings Nia made a show of closing her eyes, flexing her fingers and biting her lip.

'That will do,' Nain said sharply. 'It is in your heart, Nia, not your fingers.'

Nia relaxed and Gwyn found himself regarding the cards with reluctant fascination. The smooth sweep of black and gold hid pictures he'd once longed to play with. Nain would never let him. The Tarot cards must be respected, she had told him; left in peace so that they could tell their stories, do their work unhindered. Whatever work should that be? He had been too impatient, then, to find out. He watched Nia stretch her hand towards the left of the fan. She was

101

thoughtful now. Carefully she withdrew a card and handed it to his grandmother.

'I knew it,' Nain lay the card face upwards on the table and clasped her hands. 'The chariot!'

Gwyn beheld a blue-eyed man with copper-coloured curls beneath a bronze helmet. He wore a bronze breastplate over a blood-red tunic and stood in a bronze war chariot. In his left hand he held the reins of a white horse, in his right hand, the reins of a black horse. The animals appeared to differ in their preferred route. The black horse veered to the right, the white horse to the left. Behind the chariot a red desert stretched beneath a dark and stormy sky.

Gwyn observed Nia's face as it registered puzzlement and then pleasure. 'Who is he?' she asked.

'You have chosen Ares the war god,' Nain told her. 'He embodies conflict and bloodshed. His driving force is aggression.'

'That's not very pleasant for a hero,' Nia remarked. 'I bet he came to grief!'

'He didn't,' Nain said. 'The goddess Aphrodite fell in love with Ares. She loved him for his strength and vitality. A strange match, you might argue. The war god and the goddess of love. And yet what came of it?' She waited, her head on one side.

'What?' Nia asked, suddenly realizing an answer was expected.

'Harmony!' Nain told her joyfully. 'They had a daughter, and her name was Harmony. Don't you see?' She lifted her hands and her silver bracelets caught the sunlight and shimmered wonderfully. She opened her fingers and sparks flew from her jewelled rings. 'Harmony!' she chanted. 'Now do you understand?'

'Harmony,' Nia repeated, beginning to enjoy the word. At last it dawned on her that she might have an equal share with Gwyn in determining the outcome of the story. If he must defeat demons, she could happily supply love.

There was a fizz of excitement in the air. Gwyn was uneasy. He had learnt nothing from the strange experiment. His grandmother folded her cards into a neat pack and laid them gently in their black cloth. 'That was very satisfactory,' she said.

'We'd better go,' Gwyn told her. 'Iolo's back at home. I ought to keep an eye on him.'

'You'll come again, won't you?' His grandmother looked suddenly anxious.

'Of course,' he said.

They left the house by way of the fallow field, where Nia remarked on the number of birds that flew complaining out of the thistles.

'Can I come tomorrow?' she called to the tall woman, all in green, who looked like a sapling in her golden copse.

'Someone will be here,' came the enigmatic reply.

'You know,' said Gwyn as they strolled through the fields, 'I don't think you're taking this seriously enough, Nia.'

'I am,' she replied earnestly. 'I was really frightened when I found that horse. But Evan is wonderfully strong, your Nain has helped me to see that. I can't believe he'd do anything really wicked.'

'I hope not,' Gwyn said grimly. 'Once I was almost persuaded that legends are not true. But I know better now. The names and places may be different, but there were princes and battles, there was jealousy and murder and terrible love, and there were magicians.' He looked at his hands and added, 'And they're all still here. Perhaps it's because our land is so ancient. Ghosts feel at home; they find it easy to slip into our lives like long lost relations.'

'I don't seem to fit any story,' Nia said. 'I've just wandered in by accident!'

And now you're part of it, Gwyn thought. 'Nain seems to believe you're as close to finding a solution as any of us!' he said.

103

They found Iolo sitting on the yard gate. He was bursting with pride. 'I helped your da sort out the ewes,' he told Gwyn. 'We've brought a hundred down from the mountain for dipping. Fly was brilliant. She kept them all together with a bit of help from me and Cymro.'

Fly had been the Lloyds' dog once, when they had lived at Tŷ Llŷr. But they had parted with her when they went to live in Pendewi. She had lasted one miserable, whining day in the town and then come to join Cymro, the Griffiths' sheepdog.

Gwyn, Nia and Iolo spent the rest of the day on the mountain together, searching for the red kite. The weather was hardly cooler than on that burning September day when Iolo had lost the broken horse. Now it was found. Too late. The kite did not appear for them and Gwyn couldn't enjoy the walk. Nia, however, seemed happy, knowing that his grandmother felt so confident about her chestnut soldier.

That night Iolo refused Gwyn's offer of a bed. It was more fun, he said, to sleep on the floor. He was happy with his mattress and sleeping bag. When Gwyn came to bed, however, the younger boy was still wide awake.

As Gwyn climbed into bed he was beginning to frame a question which, he knew, had risks attached to it. He turned off the bedside light and, in the darkness, asked, 'Iolo, how d'you like your cousin, Evan?'

What answer did he expect? Perhaps the one he received.

'I don't!' Iolo said.

'Why?'

'He was nice to me once; now he never has time. It's like I don't exist.'

Gwyn was surprised by the anger. He sought to turn it to his advantage. 'Will you do something for me?'

'What?' Iolo asked cautiously.

Gwyn judged that he was keen. 'Will you follow your cousin for me? Watch him, but always secretly. Find out what he does and where he goes. Never let him know what you are doing, though. It could be dangerous.'

'Dangerous?'

'I believe Evan broke your horses, Iolo, and my uncle's unicorn.' He plunged on, aware of the effect his words had already had, 'I think he was responsible for Glory's death.' He had no need to fuel Iolo's dislike, but couldn't help himself.

The little boy was sitting bolt upright, staring at the pale moonlit curtains. 'How could he?' he exclaimed. 'He was my friend. What's happened to him?'

'I can't tell you yet,' Gwyn said. 'If you watch him, we'll find out. Will you do it? I'm not sure if I can trust anyone else.'

Iolo was flattered. 'Yes,' he said, and Gwyn knew he had an ally.

'Are you allowed to use the phone?'

'If I ask,' Iolo replied.

'When you've something to tell, ring me after six. Say you want to see me, nothing more. I'll make the arrangements.' Gwyn said this, aware of the perils of such an operation, but never dreaming how much he would regret it.

On Sunday morning Emlyn and Geraint came up to the farm. They loved to lend a hand. The ewes and the weaned lambs had to be sorted, ready for dipping on Monday. The older animals were already suspicious. They remembered the smell, the stinging in their eyes and ears, the terrible taste. Idris Llewelyn would have to come and help. It needed strong hands to subdue the big mule rams and at six foot three and fifteen stone, Idris was one of the strongest men in the district.

After their work the children began to walk down to Tŷ Llŷr. They rounded the bend from where Nain's cottage could be seen, just as a dark figure emerged from her garden. For some reason they all stood quite still as the man stepped into the road. He was tall and wore a black jacket round his shoulders. He did not see them and began to walk in the opposite direction, then suddenly he turned and looked back. He didn't wave. The sun was in Gwyn's eyes and he couldn't see the man's features. Nia cried, 'It's Evan.'

Gwyn laid a hand on her arm but she pulled away from him and ran down to her cousin. The four boys stood watching as the two figures disappeared into the trees that bordered the river.

Emlyn, always sensitive to Gwyn's moods, asked, 'What's up?'

Iolo's eyes widened. He nudged Gwyn, enjoying their new relationship.

'It's all right, Iolo,' Gwyn reassured him. 'Emlyn's with us. It'll need some explaining,' he told Emlyn. 'Can you wait?'

Emlyn nodded. 'Is Nia in trouble?' he asked.

'Not exactly,' Gwyn sighed. And added, 'I think I may need your help.'

'My sister's crazy,' Iolo said unnecessarily.

Mr Griffiths returned Nia and Iolo to their own home on Sunday afternoon. Before Iolo parted company with Gwyn he winked and gave a rather obvious thumbs-up sign.

Gwyn worried that he'd piled the drama on too thickly. Was an eight-year-old capable of such a dangerous mission?

Three days later, at six o'clock in the evening, Iolo rang him.

'Hullo, it's me!' a perilously creaky voice informed him. 'Nothing's happened yet, but *he's* just gone out – alone. I'm going to follow him!'

'Iolo …' Gwyn began, but there was a click and the line went dead.

Gwyn stood in the dark passage wishing that, somehow, through the maze of wires that had momentarily connected them, he could drag Iolo back to hear his warning. A tiny tremor rippled through the floor and a sudden wind burst

106

through the gate, seeking out loose straw and driving it in a ghostly dance across the yard. Gwyn went into the kitchen and watched, fascinated, through the window. It was one of those unnatural winds that was up to no good.

At nine o'clock that night, his mother called up to his attic room. 'Gwyn, have you seen Iolo? Betty Lloyd's on the phone. She's frantic. He left the house some time after tea and hasn't been seen since!'

Chapter
8

Gwyn didn't know how to tell her and so he called back, 'No, I haven't seen Iolo.' And then, suddenly, in wild indecision, 'Well...'

'What was that?' his mother shouted.

'Nothing,' he said miserably. He'd lost his chance.

Emlyn Llewelyn had been the last person to see Iolo. He had passed the chapel, Emlyn said, at half past six. He was alone and appeared to be making for the mountain.

Mrs Lloyd rang the police. A search party was organized: Idris and Emlyn, Gwyn and his father, Mr Lloyd and a few neighbouring farmers and their sons. Twenty men set off, on foot, to comb the mountain fields. A bitter wind thrashed against their faces but the rain held off and the moon was full. Clusters of stars could be seen, glittering through the driven threadbare clouds.

It was Fly who found Iolo. Memory and her sixth sense must have told her where to look. He had fallen into a stone quarry that bordered the river.

Gwyn and Mr Griffiths, attuned to Fly's whining signals, ran to the cliff top immediately above her. Mr Griffiths trained his flashlight down into the quarry. Fly was standing beside a small figure lying in the mud that had been churned into thick liquid by the frequent passage of animals.

'*Duw!*' Ivor swore. 'Go and tell them, Gwyn. And get Mam to ring the ambulance.'

But the pathetic sight had launched Gwyn into a violent trembling that almost immobilized him.

'For God's sake, boy. Get hold of yourself.' His father grasped his shoulder. 'We need help. Tell them to walk down by the road. We can reach him from the lower fields.'

Gwyn rallied his limbs into a disorderly run that several times sent him crashing to the ground. 'It's my fault,' an inner voice muttered to him while his own cried into the forest of swinging lights, 'He's found. Iolo's here!'

'What's that?' called Mr Lloyd.

'He's found.'

Someone took up the call. Voices sang out and vanished on the wind. 'He's found.' '*Rydym ni wedi ffeindio fo.*' 'This way!' '*Ffordd hyn!*'

'Go by the road,' Gwyn yelled. 'He's in the quarry by the river.'

Lights and voices began to converge towards the road while Gwyn raced on to the farmhouse.

Betty Lloyd was in the kitchen with his mother. Her face was an angry tearful red. She practically fell upon him when she heard the news. 'Where?' she cried.

'In the quarry,' Gwyn panted. 'They're going down by the road.'

'Is he all right?'

'I don't know, Mrs Lloyd,' he said. 'We were on the cliff. We couldn't reach him that way. Dad says to call the ambulance, quick.'

'Oh, my God,' Betty sobbed. 'It's always one of mine. I've too many, that's the truth!'

Mrs Griffiths leapt to the phone and gave directions to the ambulance while Betty Lloyd rushed out into the night, letting the wind blast through the open door, rattling windows and sending loose papers flying round the kitchen.

109

Gwyn had turned to follow her when his mother shouted, 'Stay here, Gwyn,' as she replaced the receiver.

'I must go, Mam,' he told her.

'But there's no need, cariad, now he's found. You look dreadful. You should be in bed. Look at the time. Eleven o'clock!'

'I've got to go back,' he cried savagely and leapt out. The wind slammed the door for him.

He followed Mrs Lloyd's frantic footsteps down the lane.

Every time he turned a bend, he lost her on another. At his grandmother's gate he stopped, longing to take shelter with her. Her softly illumined window sent out welcoming messages, but he tore himself away and trudged on, past Tŷ Llŷr, and another inviting light. Mrs Lloyd's retreating footsteps were drowned now by the hissing of the turbulent stream.

Just before the lane joined the main road Gwyn turned on to a narrow footbridge that crossed the stream where it tumbled into the river. He went no further. Beyond the turn two landrovers were parked, their nearside wheels deep in the verge. Behind them the blue light of a police car shed a melancholy glow over the dark hedgerows.

Gwyn could see a circle of lights on the bank beside the quarry. Emlyn came stumping away from it and along the muddy path towards him. 'He's O.K.,' he yelled when he saw Gwyn.

The relief that flooded through Gwyn was almost like a pain. It drained him. 'Really O.K.?' he asked weakly when Emlyn stood beside him.

'He's alive,' Emlyn gasped for air and continued breathlessly, 'but he's been concussed, they think, and may have broken some bones.'

'Aw, heck!' Gwyn said.

'I'm going home now,' Emlyn told him. 'D'you want to walk up with me?'

'No,' Gwyn said. 'I'll wait for Dad.'

Emlyn moved off just as an ambulance screeched round the corner and began to ascend the rocky lane, its accompanying siren shrieking above the wind. Gwyn left the bridge and stood against a drystone wall, whose topmost stones had begun to spill into the river, so that it offered a rather precarious protection from the torrent beyond. Mr Davis, Tŷ Coch, and two neighbours approached. They began to run and Mr Davis shouted, 'He's down there!' Then, recognizing the ambulance driver as he stepped out of the vehicle, 'You'll need the stretcher, Tom. We dursn't move the lad. He's injured bad!'

Gwyn watched the uniformed men move swiftly into the dark with their torch and stretcher. Dappled moonlight glimmered on the water beside them. Perhaps someone had intended Iolo to drown, Gwyn thought. He could not help imagining how Iolo's body might have bobbed among the waves. For some reason the picture called to mind the small wooden figures that ancient Celts had thrown into their sacred springs, in the hope of a cure. It gave him the beginning of an idea.

'That you, Gwyn Griffiths?' Mr Davis had seen him. 'Better go home now, lad. There's nothing you can do!'

Gwyn did not move and couldn't trust himself to speak.

Mr Davis peered at him. 'Are you all right, Gwyn?'

'Yes,' Gwyn mumbled.

Mr Davis turned away. He had never been a friend and was always suspicious of Gwyn, who had once wounded his son with a spell.

It began to rain. A slow procession of lights pressed through the gale towards the bridge. Gwyn tensed himself against an inward shaking that threatened to overwhelm him. My fault, he thought. Always, my fault! It always turns against me, my nature. Always getting people lost! He stood back as they passed him. Iolo's face looked deathly white against the dark blankets on the stretcher; he was making faint sounds like a small wounded animal. Mr

Griffiths brought up the rear. He saw Gwyn and put an arm round his shoulder. 'All right, Gwyn. I'll be with you in a minute.'

They lifted Iolo into the ambulance and Mrs Lloyd climbed in beside him. The doors closed and they tore away into the night.

Police and farmers murmured in groups beside the parked vehicles. They couldn't fathom why Iolo had come to be in that lonely field, or how he had fallen into the quarry. There were three strands of barbed wire flanking the cliff edge, the lowest strand only a few centimetres from the ground. The wire was fixed, at intervals, to stout fencing posts, and Mr Griffiths checked and renewed the fence every season. Why had Iolo crawled beneath the wire? He wasn't that sort of boy, Mr Lloyd exclaimed. Iolo had never ventured alone beyond the town.

Gwyn, shivering outside the uneasy gathering, couldn't bear the grave and doubtful voices any longer. He backed away then ran up the lane. When he reached his grandmother's gate he flung it open, tore towards the beacon of her window and tapped on a pane. She was reading by her lamp, looked up when she heard him, saw his face and ran to open the door.

'What is it, Gwyn?' she asked. 'Emlyn was here. He said they'd found Iolo.'

He nodded.

'He's all right, then?'

Gwyn began to toss his head about. 'Oh, Nain,' he cried. 'Oh, Nain, I don't know. I don't know!'

'Stop it, boy. What is it?' She removed his anorak and drew him towards the log fire.

'Nain,' he whispered. 'It's my fault. I couldn't tell them. What shall I do?'

She took his hands. 'What have you done, Gwydion Gwyn? Tell me?'

'I asked him to follow Evan Llŷr. I knew it was dangerous

112

but I did it all the same. The soldier must have pushed him; he meant to kill Iolo, Nain. I know it!'

'What rubbish is this!' She flung his hands away and sat in her chair, glaring up at him. 'Wicked, silly boy!'

'Listen,' he begged. 'Iolo phoned me at six o'clock. He told me Evan had just gone out and he was going to follow him. But the soldier knew. He tricked him, led him along that cliff and ... and...'

'Stop it!' Nain commanded. 'You're not rational, Gwydion Gwyn. You've no proof at all. And why didn't you tell the Lloyds about this phone call?'

'I don't know,' he said mournfully. He could feel her cold disdain and shuffled away from it to stare into the flames. 'What shall I do?' he asked.

'You're coming with me,' she said, slipping into a black mackintosh that lay ready on a chair. 'And you're going to tell them everything.'

They left her house and walked up to Tŷ Bryn without speaking a word to each other but in the farmhouse porch Nain peered closely into Gwyn's face and asked. 'Why did you tell that poor child to follow Evan?'

Gwyn seemed to find courage in that question. He remembered his anger with Evan, or whatever Evan was, and declared, 'He's a devil! I'll prove it to you somehow!'

His grandmother opened the door and prodded him inside. As he removed his wellingtons he could hear the solemn rumble of voices coming from the kitchen. A late-night inquest was taking place. Gwyn's heart sank.

Nain led him down the passage, opened the kitchen door and announced into the crowd of wet and weathered faces, 'Gwyn can shed some light on this mystery!'

Gwyn stepped inside, was about to deliver his message when, to his horror, he noticed a tall figure in the shadowy corner beyond the stove.

'What is it, lad?' Mr Lloyd had swung round in his chair.

'I...' Gwyn began. The room was a sea of shapes and

113

faces. He could see nothing distinctly except the dark, utterly motionless soldier; the searching glint of his blue eyes swept through him, seeming to know everything. Instinctively, Gwyn thrust his hand into his pocket and felt for the broken horse. As his fingers closed over it, Evan Llŷr smiled at him.

'Have you got something to say, Gwyn?' his father asked. 'What is all this?'

Outside the storm seethed. Every door and window rattled.

Gwyn cleared his throat. 'I forgot to tell you,' he said lamely. 'I'm sorry. Iolo rang me, see, said he was going out. It was six o'clock exactly.'

'Why didn't you say, Gwyn?' Mr Lloyd sprang out of his chair.

'Rang you?' his father bellowed. 'What the hell for?'

'Gwyn, how could you forget?' his mother asked.

'I don't know,' Gwyn said. 'I didn't think it was important – then!'

There were angry protests at this remark but Mr Lloyd hushed them saying, 'What did my boy say? Why was he going out? And why ring you, Gwyn?'

The soldier moved at last. He took one pace forward. The slight smile never left his face. He is mocking me, Gwyn thought. Daring me to accuse him.

Gwyn accepted the challenge and said loud and very clear, 'He said he was going to follow Major Llŷr. I asked him to, see.'

'It was a silly game,' his grandmother said quickly.

Was it Gwyn's imagination or was there a slight shifting of blame? Now they were looking at Evan. The soldier stepped boldly into the light and told them, 'It was someone else the boy followed, not me!' But his extraordinary storybook appearance seemed to deny this statement. How could anyone in the world be mistaken for such a strange and colourful figure?

114

Iestyn looked at the soldier, his doubtful black eyes narrowed and he asked, 'Who then?'

'Ask the boy,' Evan replied and although his mouth curved into a smile the look he shot at Iestyn had ice in it.

'I will,' the butcher mumbled, and almost ducked away from Evan's deadly stare. The whole room seemed to sway uneasily around the arrogant unnatural man.

'Better get going, man! It's midnight!' someone said.

The kitchen began to empty. Shoulder to shoulder, friends shuffled to the front door, retrieved their boots from the pile and dragged on their wet jackets. Outside they called sympathetic messages to Iestyn through the wind. Iolo's father, hunched against the weather, made for his van without a backward glance at Evan.

Evan Llŷr was the last to leave. '*Nos da, teulu Griffiths,*' he said. 'Good night, Griffiths family.'

Gwyn remained in the porch while his family retreated to the kitchen. There was something odd about Evan's departure.

'He hasn't forgotten his Welsh,' said Nain, who had claimed the armchair by the stove.

'Thought he didn't know the language,' Ivor said suspiciously.

'Oh, I'm sure he did,' his wife put in. 'Little things, you know!'

'His car wasn't there!' Gwyn said abruptly. 'How did he get here without a car? How will he get home?'

'He's probably left it at the bottom of the lane,' his grandmother retorted. 'And you ought to be in bed!' she added tersely.

'I'm going,' Gwyn said. I've turned the tide a bit tonight, he thought. I've put them on their guard.

In his room, he flung himself back on the bed, and immediately thought of Iolo wrapped in pale hospital sheets. But he was so exhausted that the fears that had held him awake for so many hours during the past few nights began to

115

fall away from him. To a tiny glow, circling the bed post, he murmured drowsily, 'There's work to come, Arianwen. I have to stop the mad prince soon, or else...' He fell asleep trying to dream of a solution.

The following day they heard that Iolo would recover. He had suffered two fractured ribs, a broken arm and leg, and a nasty head wound. But his limbs would mend and his concussion had not lasted long enough to cause permanent damage. There was one disappointment. He could remember nothing of the incidents that led to his accident. He's afraid to remember, Gwyn thought.

That evening he went to see Emlyn. He found his cousin where he expected to, in the barn that Idris Llewelyn had converted especially for his son. It was where Emlyn could happily indulge his passion for woodcarving without damaging the neat and polished interior of Tŷ Llŷr.

Once inside the barn Gwyn slid the bolt across the big oak door.

Emlyn grinned. 'What's all that for?' he asked, without taking his eyes off the block of wood before him. He already knew of Gwyn's suspicions. If he found them hard to take he never showed it.

'I don't want anyone to know about this!' Gwyn said.

'Know about what?' Emlyn slid a chisel carefully along the side of the wood. As he approached Gwyn could see that something was taking shape there under Emlyn's hands. He walked round his cousin and the tall three-legged table that supported his work, and, to his surprise, saw a head that he recognized. The lines were still rough, and the eyes not yet defined but there was no mistaking the long coiled horn.

'You're making another unicorn!' Gwyn exclaimed.

'He'll rise again, like the phoenix, as brave and bold as before. He's Caradog, the unbowed Celt. And if they defile

116

him, I'll create another and another and another. There'll always be a magical welcome in Pendewi!' Emlyn's speech had always been flamboyant. It came of being born in France, Gwyn had decided.

'I came to beg a favour,' he began.

'Fire away,' Emlyn said.

Gwyn hesitated. 'Hope you won't laugh but I want you to carve a soldier for me. You know, as they are today, in battledress. A beret, a camouflage jacket and boots. Not too big,' he held his hands twenty centimetres apart. 'It's for, well, a trick.' That wouldn't do, he thought. Emlyn deserved better. 'No, a bit of witchcraft,' he confessed. 'Of the healing sort.'

Emlyn appeared to accept this as a perfectly normal request. 'D'you want me to paint it?' he asked.

This hadn't occurred to Gwyn. 'Yes,' he said. 'Thanks!'

'I'll enjoy it,' Emlyn told him. 'Copper streaks an' all.'

'Heck, Emlyn. I'm glad you're around.' Gwyn drew up a stool beside the unformed unicorn and sat down. 'When can you finish it?'

'I've got some seasoned chestnut wood.' Emlyn said. 'It's used for making toys. D'you remember, Dad had to lop a branch off that old tree up the lane a couple of years ago. It'll take me two or three evenings.'

'It'll be another chestnut soldier.' Gwyn found himself laughing with a desperate kind of relief.

The door shook and Emlyn's brother Geraint called plaintively through it, 'Emlyn, Dad wants you!'

'I'll be there in a minute,' Emlyn shouted. He lowered his voice. 'Gwyn, I know what you're into. But this sort of thing has to be done gently. You can't cast him into the depths in anger. You want him cured, not dead.'

Gwyn realized, with a shock, that this was perhaps what he had intended, and even now, if this unlikely remedy did not work, it might come to that. 'You're right,' he said. 'Emlyn, you will be careful, don't...'

'It'll be safe enough in here,' Emlyn told him. 'No one else will know!'

'Thanks!' He unbolted the door and ran past Geraint, who was pressed suspiciously close to the wall of the barn. 'Ta ra, Geraint!' Gwyn yelled to him.

Confidence surged through him, propelling him into a jaunty downhill sprint to nowhere in particular. He was whistling merrily when he turned on to the bridge where, the previous night, events had reduced him to a wreck. He recalled that snivelling incoherent self with something like contempt. He was returning to the quarry to prove, somehow, to himself that Iolo's fall had been no accident. He didn't know what he expected to find.

The water had dropped considerably. It ran fast but clear. The rocks were visible and the spray that lapped around them was frosty white.

He was walking purposefully towards the quarry when he saw a fisherman stepping through the water, stealthily, a furled rod in his hand, a basket hung, slantwise, across his back.

It wasn't too late to run away, the man hadn't seen him, but Gwyn lingered, fascinated by the man's sure movements against the current, and the elegant swing of his arm as he cast his line over a deep pool. A silver flash indicated the belly of a salmon as it leapt to catch the fly. Evan began to wind in his line, slowly. A battle ensued as the fish thrashed through the spray, desperately unwilling to lose its life. It was a war of wills as well as strength lasting several minutes. But the fisherman held steady, playing the line with incredible skill as he edged his way towards the bank. At last he had the writhing fish in his hands. He held it on the stones, dashed a rock against its head and when the fish lay still, deftly removed the hook. He showed no surprise when he saw Gwyn. *'Noswaith dda,'* he greeted him. 'Good evening, Gwydion Gwyn!'

'He's using the language like a true Welshman,' Gwyn thought wryly. And how does he know my other name? *'Noswaith dda,'* he returned. 'You're catching salmon out of season, Major Llŷr. It's against the law!'

'Are you going to betray me, then?' Evan asked. He curled the fish into his basket and walked towards Gwyn. 'How will they punish me?'

'I won't tell them,' Gwyn said, standing his ground. If they were to have a conversation, he might discover what sort of man would be left, should the healing spell prove effective.

'Sut mae'r teulu?' Evan asked. 'How is the family after that long night?'

'Da iawn, diolch,' Gwyn replied. 'Very well, thank you!'

They began to stroll upriver until they found themselves on a beach of wet stones where the brittle reeds had parted round a huge slab of shale. They shared this seat and began to talk about the moods of the river, the mountains and clouds, mentioning, on their way, the myths that seemed to have been born out of such a landscape. They spoke in Welsh, the only language that was appropriate for such a discussion. And all the time Gwyn kept thinking, We're so calm! Is it always like this before a battle?

It was dusk when they walked together towards Nain Griffiths' house. Evan had promised her a fish for tea.

When they passed by the still splendid chestnut tree, Evan gazed up at the topmost branches and murmured, 'My brother died of that tree.'

Gwyn asked, 'Were you there?'

'I was standing where you are now,' Evan told him, 'watching every move my brother made, so that I should remember and repeat his route. He looked down, so triumphant, lost his footing and fell. I thought he was diving into my soul.'

They silently regarded the tree and Gwyn sensed that, for Evan, the moment was critical. He was absorbed in the shape and colour of leaves and branches as though he were committing them to memory, for a journey he would make, after which time all things would have changed beyond his recognition.

In all the world, Gwyn thought, there can't be a man as lonely as he is!

They continued their walk without exchanging another word, but when Evan reached Rhiannon Griffiths' white gate he held out his hand and said, *'Nos da,* Gwydion Gwyn. Thank you for your company!'

Gwyn took the soldier's hand. *'Nos da,'* he said. It seemed like saying 'goodbye'.

Chapter
9

The Lloyds lived uneasily after Iolo's accident. They seemed unable to talk to each other in the comfortable way they had been used to. Mr Lloyd held opinions he was too afraid to voice, as though, once uttered, they would divide him even further from his wife and daughters.

Every day Mrs Lloyd would visit the hospital and stay an hour with Iolo. Sometimes her husband would accompany her, sometimes she would take one or two of the other children after school.

On the fourth day Nia begged to go with her parents. She had always disliked hospitals and prepared herself the way she did for a horror movie, expecting a mummy-like figure strung up with wires and surrounded with bottles of plasma. She arrived outside the ward clinging to her mother's hand, handkerchief at the ready, tense and jumpy.

'Calm down, Nia,' her father said, his nerves already jangling. 'We don't want Iolo upset now!'

'Perhaps you'd better stay outside,' Mrs Lloyd suggested. 'I don't think this was a good idea!'

'I'll be calm. I'll be calm, I promise!' Nia assured them breathlessly.

'Well, just nip out if you feel bad,' her mother said.

They went in.

In many ways it was not nearly as horrific as Nia had expected. There were no bottles of blood in sight and Iolo was not swaddled in white. A narrow bandage encircled his head like a tiny crown. But his fractured ribs were safely concealed beneath pyjamas and a hump in the bed was the only indication of injured legs. He was even smiling. But as soon as Nia had taken all these reassuring signs of recovery into her mind she was immediately alerted by the expression behind that cautious smile. Iolo was frightened. Terrible memories were chasing through his head and his eyes betrayed him. Like Nia and Bethan, Iolo had inherited his father's dark colouring. His anxious umber-coloured eyes lurched out of the small sallow face, dense with unrecounted nightmares.

'He's still a bit – distressed,' a genial nurse explained. 'Perhaps his sister will cheer him up!'

But Nia could do no such thing. She was too shocked by her brother's helpless fear.

Mrs Lloyd took Iolo's hand. 'Have you been eating, cariad? D'you like the food better now?'

'You'll be home soon,' Mr Lloyd said with forced heartiness and, unmindful of the alarm that flickered across Iolo's face, added, 'We'll have a slap up meal, all your favourites, won't we, Mam? Roast lamb and mashed potatoes, and apple crumble, you'll like that, won't you?'

Iolo nodded weakly and Nia suddenly realized her brother was being primed for other, more important questions.

'Have you remembered yet, why you were on that cliff? No?' Iolo shrank against the sheets but his determined father lumbered on. 'Gwyn Griffiths has told us it was a game, and that you phoned him!'

'Leave it, Iestyn,' Mrs Lloyd warned softly. 'It's not the time!'

Her husband was unable to do this. Someone was responsible for his son's sorry condition. He had waited long enough. The mystery was tormenting him. 'Gwyn says you were following Evan...'

'No!' Iolo cried, jerking himself away from the pillows. 'I wasn't following no one. It was a game, see, but the spirits played a trick on me!'

'Spirits? What spirits, cariad?' Mrs Lloyd attempted to touch him but he ducked away from her.

'Evil spirits, Mam,' Iolo said gravely. 'I know because I could feel them!'

'Feel them?' his parents repeated in alarmed unison.

'Yes,' he lowered his voice to share the next secret, 'and I saw one, shining!'

'Shining?' said Nia, her mind racing. What had Gwyn been up to? Why had he chosen Iolo for this mission and not her?

'Here,' Iolo told her, touching his wrist, 'something shining, and here,' he pointed to his shoulder.

Iestyn, still bent on a different answer quietly pressed, 'Are you sure, Iolo, that it wasn't your cousin Evan?'

'No! No! No!' Iolo cried, drawing the white sheet up to his face. 'It wasn't anyone real, it wasn't!'

A nurse materialized through a distant door as Mrs Lloyd exclaimed, 'How could you, Iestyn? He's not ready.' Again she tried to touch her son and again he resisted her.

'We've got to get to the bottom of this,' Iestyn argued.

Nia couldn't bear her favourite brother's confused and troubled stare. Unable to comfort him, she turned away from the scene and began to run, passing the nurse whose stride had quickened into an anxious jog.

Nia slipped through the swinging door and raced down a long cool passage of numbered and mysterious doors. She didn't stop until she was out in the air. She crossed the car park and flopped down on a low brick wall beside the butcher's van. Why was her father, all at once, intent on proving Evan a villain? Gwyn doesn't trust me, she thought resentfully, because I've defended Evan.

123

When her parents emerged they were still arguing and they didn't stop on the journey home. Nia had never heard them so angry with each other. Their quarrel alienated her from both of them, making her feel helpless and unhappy.

The atmosphere that waited in Number Six was no better; Bethan in a storm of tears in Catrin's arms; Nerys complaining of the noise. Gareth and Sîon had been fighting; Sîon sported a black eye and Gareth, in an attempt to comfort himself, had reached for the special biscuits and knocked a precious glass duck on to the tiled floor, where it still lay in glittering fragments. Alun had locked himself in the bedroom and was shouting, to anyone who cared to listen, that he wasn't 'bloody well going to open the door until people grew up!'

Betty Lloyd, unable to console her tearful baby, declared that the whole family had gone mad. 'Can't you stop fighting?' she appealed to them. 'What's happening to us?'

'It would never have happened but for that Gwyn Griffiths,' grumbled Iestyn. 'Trouble always follows him. Clings to him like a shadow, it does!'

'It's not his fault,' said Nerys. 'It's his grandmother, giving him strange ideas. You know what she's like, all those silly stories.'

'They're both mad, then,' her father muttered.

'How could you?' Betty cried at her husband's retreating back.

He stumped into his shop just as the front door slammed and Catrin said, almost to herself, 'That's Evan!'

They listened to soft footfalls on the stairs. He never marched or thumped as Nia imagined a soldier used to wearing boots would do. Evan's strides were light and almost musical, like an animal or forest Indian.

'Evan doesn't like crying babies,' Nia remarked, in an attempt to explain his avoidance of the kitchen.

'He doesn't like babies at all,' Nerys said, as though she sympathized with his point of view. She had tied a pink scarf in a bow on top of her head and was wearing a very un-Nerys blouse with frills all down the front.

'You're just too much at times, Nerys Lloyd!' Catrin cried, 'and who said you could borrow my scarf?'

Bethan began to howl again. Catrin left the room and Nia followed, leaving their mother and Nerys to continue a noisy argument.

What *has* happened to us, Nia wondered. Something has sneaked into the very heart of our family and it's gnawing away like a treacherous rat. She wished she was out of it all, up at Tŷ Llŷr with the Llewelyns, where everything was safe and calm and beautiful. Where Idris would laugh her out of her fears and Elinor would be singing in the garden. But she knew she was needed here. Any little crack in the family might cause it to break apart altogether.

She went to the top of the house but remained on the small landing between her room and her parents'. She was aware that she was spying but past caring now. In fact she realised that she was quite likely to develop this unpleasant trait of hers further; recent events did partly justify a lurking, furtive Nia.

A few seconds after Catrin's door had closed it opened again, just as Nia had expected. She heard her sister cross the passage and knock on Evan's door.

Tap! Tap! Tap! Very gentle. No answer.

'Evan, are you there?'

A door opened. Two sets of footfalls on the passage, down the stairs, across the hall. The front door opened and closed.

For a brief moment Nia hesitated. Perhaps she thought of Iolo's near-fatal journey, but curiosity eventually sent her bounding down the stairs and out in the street.

They were strolling towards the bridge, Evan's exotic hair unmistakable beyond the few late shoppers.

She tried to keep up without being seen, but it was impossible. Catrin kept stopping and turning into shop windows. It soon became apparent why she was doing this.

125

On the other side of the street Michael McGoohan was walking arm in arm with Lluned Price. So what does everyone think about *that*? Nia wondered. Michael smiled at her. She smiled back, feeling guilty somehow, at having a foot in both camps. None of it was Michael's fault anyway. When she looked back up the street Catrin and Evan had vanished.

'Damn!' Nia muttered, and a voice behind her asked, 'What's the problem?'

She turned to see Gwyn grinning at her. 'What're you doing here?' she asked ungraciously.

'Nothing! I'm innocent!' He held up his hands in mock surrender. 'I came down with Dad to get some chicken feed. It's not like you to swear!'

'We've just been to see Iolo!' she told him.

A shadow fell across his face, drawing his confident grin into an anxious line. 'How is he?' he asked.

'He's mending, physically!' She repeated a nurse's description, 'But he's not too good up here!' She touched her head. 'And I don't mean mad; he's frightened, so frightened he can't even bear our Mam to touch him!'

'I'm sorry,' Gwyn said and then, too casually, 'He's forgotten, I suppose, what happened?'

'Not exactly.' She watched Gwyn's face for signs that might give him away. 'He says a spirit pushed him. Its arm was shining.' Gwyn seemed to find this description very promising. 'Dad says you told Iolo to follow Evan. Why did you do that? Why didn't you tell me? It's horrible at home. Everyone's angry and hating each other, and none of us really knows why!'

'Look!' Gwyn broke into her angry flow. 'It's going to be all right, Nia!'

'What is? What've you done now?' Out of the corner of her eye she saw Mr Griffiths emerging from Alwyn Farmers, where they sold everything from chicken feed to gumboots. 'I wish you would leave people alone,' she added.

'Gwyn!' Mr Griffiths bellowed across the street.

'It's too late for that,' Gwyn said grimly. He turned his back on her and crossed the road, waving his hand. She couldn't tell if he was feeling the air for rain or had flung a spell into it, for tiny drops of water began to tickle her face.

She ran towards the bridge, regretting her effort at spying. She was too old. Gwyn could enjoy his childish games; they always seemed to bring bad luck. She decided to take a pondering sort of walk beside the river; the rain would soothe her nerves and, in this way perhaps, she would find a solution to the trouble at home.

After crossing the bridge, Nia took a narrow path that wound between bushes and brambles until it reached the river. The water was very low. She hopped along the beach from rock to stone, while the rain beat a companionable rhythm on the water beside her. There was no one in sight. Beyond the reach of all the worry and grimness she began to sing chirpily, 'Who cares, anyway? Who cares?' She found herself wading through a forest of reeds and, crouching down among the thick stems, it occurred to her that she was in an excellent position for a spy. The thought was hardly formed when she realized that it was exactly what she was.

On the other side of the river where the bank rose, house-high, beyond the beach, two figures were clambering down. They stood a moment on the narrow strip of pebbles, enjoying the shower. Evan's hair was all black now, it drooped about his head like a slippery helmet. Catrin's sweater clung, tight as skin, and her hair hung in long coils almost to her waist.

Unseen, Nia froze. She watched, as she might have watched an illustration to a fairy tale, waiting for the picture to spring to life, yet dreading it. And when it did she observed every detail, preserving it somewhere in her mind as something that happened outside her life, to creatures in a story, that she didn't know at all. For Evan's kiss was not

127

gentle. Like dreadful sorcery it turned Catrin to stone and, for a moment, all the fairy tales turned backwards as in an ugly mirror. The prince didn't waken this sleeping beauty, he sent her scrambling away from him, up the narrow path, all mud and tears.

Nia, wishing she was a hundred miles away, could only focus on the prince as he paced the rainy beach, roaring with terrible laughter. And then, as he slipped down on to the stones, until he was almost lying in the water, his laughter gave way to the howl she'd heard before, a dreadful sound that sank deep into her and made her sob against her hand, 'It isn't him. It isn't him at all!' Catrin had seen the terrible brimstone eyes, she'd seen the monster and been kissed by him. At that moment Nia hated Evan, not for hurting Catrin but for kissing her.

Soon the only sound about them was the rain. Nia grew stiff with waiting. Her eyes ached with watching the solitary form beside the water. She couldn't move for his gaze seemed to bore straight through the reeds that concealed her. She became convinced that he could see her, but at last he stood up, wearily, and began to walk upriver. She watched him slowly recede into the curtain of rain, stumbling through the pools but still tall and straight, welcoming the weather as a sort of sanctuary. When she lost all sight of him she ran home, slipped upstairs and managed to change out of her wet clothes before anyone saw her.

Evan didn't appear for supper. Catrin's eyes were red and she had dried her hair carelessly into a great mound of yellow candyfloss. Her wild appearance caused Nerys to remark, 'Good grief, Cat, you look as though you've been ravaged by the hounds of hell!'

Catrin leapt up with a screech, and made for the door, shouting, 'Shut up! Shut up! Shut up!' to all the walls and furniture, before she ran out.

Mrs Lloyd frowned reprovingly at Nerys. 'Why can't you be more sensitive?' she sighed.

'I am sensitive,' Nerys returned, 'only none of you realise it. You all think *she's* the only sensitive one because she fits the picture of a talented and temperamental person. Well, I've got feelings too. But no one tells *me* 'How pretty you are!' 'How lovely your hair looks today!' You don't even notice what I'm wearing.'

This uncharacteristic outburst stunned Betty Lloyd, who began to look at her eldest daughter with dawning sympathy, but Iestyn, refusing to believe his daughter's moods had anything to do with growing up, said 'You're all working too hard. Exams for this, exams for that, music as well!'

No one argued with him.

At eight o'clock the big oak dresser gave a little shudder while Nia and Nerys were washing up. A drawer fell out and cutlery jangled on to the tiles like an eerie percussion. At half-past eight a glass rolled off the bathroom shelf. Ten minutes later the bookcase in the hall emptied itself. It did this in a helpless desultory way, dripping books on to the floor one by one, as though it was trying to disguise its tipsiness. 'This house is crooked,' Alun complained as he attempted to stem the flow of ancient weighty tomes.

At nine o'clock the television trembled into silence, the news presenter glowed brilliant pink then vanished and a blank screen seemed to advise that bed was the only answer. Then the lights went out. A power cut, they thought, to wind up their unhappy day. They all took candles and went upstairs in a defeated weary way, longing for sleep but, somehow, not expecting it. The rain became a steady downpour, beating through their dreams.

It was past midnight when the knocking began. Except for Bethan the household was awake but they seemed to think that if they didn't acknowledge the noise, it would disappear.

It grew louder. Nia switched her light on and sat up. The room was shaking now. The temperature had risen by twenty degrees at least. Sweat trickled down her back.

Downstairs a deafening crash sent the family tottering to their doors, calling to each other, 'What's that? Mam, Dad, what is it?'

Mr Lloyd, candle in hand, went down to the kitchen. 'By heck, it's the dresser,' he exclaimed. 'Smashed the table, right through. Duw! We can't do anything about it now.' Something roared above him, the ceiling cracked and flung hot plaster through the air. He leapt out of the kitchen crying, 'It's a 'quake!'

The Lloyds clattered downstairs and huddled together in the front room, blessing the day they had decided to bring the oil lamps from Tŷ Llŷr. They sat very close to each other, Bethan clinging to her mother, too afraid to cry; the girls holding hands, tense against the sudden jerks that followed the thunder.

'It's so hot,' Alun remarked in a whisper. 'Like there's a fire in the cellar.'

'Is it the end of the world?' Sîon asked.

'No, No! It's a disturbance, that's what it is,' their father reassured them. But he sounded too confident. 'Weather patterns all gone wrong. It'll sort itself out,' he added emphatically.

Nia bravely joined Gareth by the window. The street lights were out, and there wasn't a flame or a glow to be seen in any of the neighbours' windows. Perhaps they were sleeping through the storm. Hail began to tap against the panes; for a few seconds each tiny stone glowed red as though it was an ember from some monstrous bonfire in the sky.

Nia and Gareth stepped back while, behind them, their family gasped, 'It's impossible. It can't be! What's happening now?' And then a groan descended through the storm, hardly distinguishable as human. They all knew where it came from but no one mentioned it.

He's alone, Nia thought, but they're pretending he doesn't exist. They don't want him in here with them.

She took her candle from the sideboard and went to the door.

'Where are you going, cariad?' her mother whispered.

'I'm tired,' Nia replied. 'I'm going to bed.'

'Careful on the stairs,' her father advised.

Before anyone could decide to follow her, Nia slipped out and closed the door. She slowly mounted the stairs, while the candle flared in sudden draughts that disarranged the neat shadow creeping behind her. There were sounds in the house that she could not identify; rustling, hissing noises that might have been raindrops but when she tried to picture them, she could only imagine little buds of flame sprouting through the walls. Try as she might she couldn't calm the shaking hand that held her candle on its saucer. On the landing the sounds intensified, they rippled towards her down the narrow corridor like amplified waves in a tunnel. She longed to let the tide drive her away but, instead, clung to the balustrade for a moment and then set off to the room that held that secret fire.

It seemed such a long journey. So many times she might have turned back, but each time she felt a quiet and desperate call tugging at her, and pressed on. At the end of the corridor she put a hand on Evan's door. It almost burned her. Nia, who believed in ghosts and magic, did not believe that disturbing weather patterns had caused this terrible heat. Nightmares had overflowed into their home.

She opened the door and stepped into a room that sweltered like a melting pot. Colours flared across the walls: scarlet, orange, green, too bright to watch. They sang and crackled in a shining circle; tormenting little flames that threatened to break into the room, greedy for life. Nia stood on the threshold, petrified, telling herself that nothing was real except the man surrounded by his dreams.

Evan was lying on the floor. Whether he had fallen there or had chosen this position she couldn't tell. His head was turned towards the curtained window and his eyes were closed. His face glistened with sweat.

Nia tiptoed carefully round the tall prone figure, drew the curtains and flung open the window. A wonderfully cold breeze rushed past her, breathing reality into the room. For a moment the flames brightened, angrily fighting back, and then they died. Evan stirred and gave a low moan but he didn't wake. Nia set the candle on the floor and, kneeling beside him, gently touched his damp head.

'Please help this poor soldier,' she implored the cool night air. 'His dreams are burning him up!'

Chapter
10

Nia told no one that she'd seen the epicentre of their fiery storm. She left Evan, still sleeping, but more peaceful. She liked to think that she had coaxed a calm spirit into the room. The thunder gradually receded and a cool nocturnal breeze roamed through the house, comforting the Lloyds into a few hours of sleep.

When Nia went downstairs next morning she found that Evan had left the house. He had gone even before Mrs Lloyd made her way to the kitchen to discover how she could make breakfast in a room full of broken china. Confronting her, the huge oak dresser lay at a treacherous angle across the broken table, blocking the light, daring the family to touch it.

'I'll ring Morgan-the-Smithy and we'll have it right in no time,' Iestyn said with forced cheerfulness.

Morgan, proud of his strength, was always ready to oblige. 'By heck,' he said when he saw the chaos. 'Have your lads done this?'

'It was an earthquake,' Iestyn told him gravely.

'Never,' said Morgan winking at the boys. 'There was a bad storm, but no 'quake, Iestyn. What were you drinking last night?'

The onlooking family didn't laugh.

They soon learnt that, although their neighbours had

suffered a power failure, none of them had noticed a rise in temperature or seen glittering hailstones in the sky, they hadn't even had their houses rocked.

'I don't think they believe us,' Mrs Lloyd complained. 'They still think we're superstitious mountain people!' She rang the Griffiths' farmhouse where she knew she'd always find sympathy.

Gwyn heard the news just before he left for school and wondered if he was responsible. The previous evening he had collected a small carved soldier from Emlyn. He had taken it high on to the mountain, where shining clear water sprang from the rocks, filling a dark ice-cold pool. Gwyn had thrown his wooden soldier into the centre of the pool, watched it vanish and chanted a tranquil poem across the water. Widening concentric ripples spilled towards him and he had begged the spirit of the pool to forgive and heal Evan Llŷr. He had waited in vain for the light wood to surface but the water had swallowed it up. He had thought it a good sign at first, the spring water had taken the soldier to its heart and would cure him. But as he had walked home the clouds had felt leaden and wrathful about him, threatening to disgorge something far worse than rain on to his bare head.

So he was not entirely surprised to hear Alun's unsure voice recount the night's disturbance. Gradually Gwyn learned of the shaking walls, the display of hailstones and the inexplicable smell of burning that had crept through Number Six.

'I only made him angry, then,' Gwyn muttered.

'What've you done?' Alun asked, not really believing his friend could have been responsible for such amazing incidents. He knew Gwyn had a power he didn't understand, but he disliked the supernatural.

Gwyn hesitated to burden Alun further. 'I can't explain now,' he said. 'I'll pop in after school.' He was eager to discover, for himself, any trace of the extraordinary fire that Evan had, without a doubt, drawn about him.

It was far worse than he imagined. The house was possessed by a quiet chaos. Alun's mother sat beside the broken table while her husband wearily hammered and plastered the ruined room about her. Mrs Lloyd mumbled about hallucinations. It was like a giant had thumbed through her house, she said, tipping up furniture, breathing filthy smoke into the rooms.

Embarrassed by their mother's temporary madness, the children foraged for bread and biscuits. Nerys made the tea and tried to cheer her mother, while Catrin withdrew to share her troubles with the piano. Tragic and unfamiliar music began to penetrate the house, even following Alun, Gwyn and Nia to the very top, where they had retreated to discuss the night's events.

They sat side by side on Nia's bed, staring at Iolo's reproachful empty one, while Gwyn described his attempt to rid Evan of the dreadful prince he harboured.

Alun's face was a mixture of distaste and alarm. He might have dismissed his sister's stories, but he couldn't argue with his friend. 'You really believe in this demon, don't you?' he said glumly.

'I know it almost as well as I'd know a friend, now,' Gwyn told him. 'And I honestly thought I'd help Evan to fight it. But it's stronger than I dreamt!'

'And the fire in our house was his nightmare, wasn't it?' Nia said, peering at him.

'It was real,' Alun insisted.

They both turned to Gwyn for confirmation. 'Nia's right,' he said. 'But – which nightmare? How can we know if he was dreaming of the fire that burned his friends, or that other one nearly two thousand years ago.'

'Aw heck,' Alun groaned. 'How can you have someone else's dream?'

'When you're possessed,' Gwyn told him fiercely.

Still Nia kept the secret flames to herself. They belonged only to him, she thought. She had trespassed and shared his nightmare. Nain Griffiths had told her she would be the one to find a happy ending.

Alun kicked the bedpost, hating the inexplicable. 'O.K.,' he said at last. 'Supposing it's true what you say and Evan is – possessed by an old Celtic prince, supposing he's reliving terrible memories, trying to murder Iolo, stealing Catrin, burning our house, what are we going to do about it?'

A crash from below diverted Gwyn from an answer. They leapt to the door and ran down the first flight of stairs, expecting more of the same sounds to follow. But on the landing Gwyn held up his hand, warning them not to approach the second flight. The melancholy piano had stopped but the ensuing silence was, somehow, even more menacing.

Peering cautiously over the balustrade they saw Evan standing in the hall. He wore a huge scarf round his shoulders, deep crimson striped with gold, and a brooch glittered on his chest. There were rings on his hands and a gold band peeped from the edge of his sleeve. He had flung the front door open so violently that it had crashed back too far, fracturing the wooden frame. The fanlight, too, had cracked and slithers of glass suddenly fell on to the floor with a muted little tinkle.

Iestyn emerged from the kitchen. He sidled past Evan who neither moved nor greeted him. The butcher felt the splintered wood and closed the door, nervously murmuring, 'It can't be helped. I'll see to it later!'

Mrs Lloyd came into the hall; she stared at Evan and the broken fanlight, rubbed her mouth with her knuckle and asked, 'Evan are you – all right?'

A fearful sound came from him; an even deeper voice than the one they knew. Betty Lloyd cringed away from it, moved round him, bent almost double, and knelt to pick up the

136

broken glass. Evan strode further into the hall and turned to watch her as Catrin appeared in the doorway of the front room.

Mother and daughter looked at each other and then at Evan. He kicked a fragment of glass he'd spied towards the kneeling woman and crunched his heel upon another.

'It's not him,' Nia croaked in a desperate whisper. 'It's not Evan.'

He looked up at that, and hurled an oath at them.

'Who is snooping on the stairs?' he roared.

Alun, Nia and Gwyn pelted back to the top of the house. They stood in the narrow landing, searching each other's faces in the gloom and Alun, all at once believing everything, said, 'What shall we do now?'

'Something impossible,' Gwyn told him.

Nia stared hard at Gwyn, trying to guess what he might have to do, but she realized that Gwyn himself was not entirely clear about what it was.

After a moment of silence she went down to help her mother with the broken glass. Music came from the room beside them and when she asked where Evan had gone Mrs Lloyd directed a quick frown at the closed sitting-room door.

They're together then, Nia thought. Has Catrin recovered from the monster's kiss, or has he captured her at last?

The front door creaked open again and Gwyn's father thrust his head inside. 'Was this the storm then?' he nodded at the cracks that threatened to set the door free.

'Indeed it was,' Mrs Lloyd said, carefully avoiding her daughter's gaping stare. But Nia had no intention of telling the truth.

'He's here, then?' Mr Griffiths looked up the stairs to where Gwyn and Alun had appeared. 'Thought he would be!'

'Will you have a cup of tea now, Ivor?' Betty Lloyd asked a little unwillingly.

'D'you need some help, Betty? You look real shaken up.'
She shook her head. 'Morgan came round this morning.'

'We'd best be off, then. There's a heck of a lot to do.'

She knew, of course. She'd been a farmer's wife and was beginning to wish she was back there, safe on the mountain, where there were no ghosts to trouble her children and shake her house.

Gwyn winked at Nia as he passed her. He hoped he wore a confident look but doubted it. She smiled bleakly at him and said, 'See you at school.'

Mr Griffiths closed the door on harassed Number Six and climbed into the landrover after Gwyn.

'Done quite a bit of damage then, that storm,' he remarked as they drove past a broken gutter.

'A heck of a lot,' Gwyn agreed.

Mrs Griffiths was visiting her mother-in-law when they got home. Father and son helped themselves to tea and slabs of bread and honey before each went to his own work. Mr Griffiths to his cattle, Gwyn upstairs, ostensibly to do his homework. His room reeked of chemicals. Five hundred sheep had been dipped that week and the pungent smell would hang about the farm for days. Gwyn closed his window but made no attempt to get out his books.

He had to do something very soon, and he needed help. It wasn't enough, this time, to rely on a trickle of energy through his fingers. He had two monsters to face, one reinforcing the other, not fighting it. And he'd been the cause. He'd bound that poor soldier into another story, sent him tumbling into a state of madness where he couldn't forgive or forget the fire that had taken his friends. Gwyn knew what he had to do, of course. He had known for some time but had refused to recognize the directions his own small voice was giving him. It was such a very big step. He needed to think about it.

For a long time he sat watching Arianwen spinning in a

138

corner. She was exceptionally busy today, providing an entrance to the country he would have to visit. Once Nia had slipped into the mysterious time beyond that web, but he'd been nearby to help her back. How should he return, with no one to guide him? He'd have to trust his familiar: a tiny spider that looked quite ordinary in daylight.

Should he have more to eat before he set off? No. Poets and magicians fasted before attempting feats of great magnitude. He brushed his hair for the occasion and emptied his pockets. In case he was delayed, he tore a page from his exercise book and wrote on it: *Gone to see Emlyn about homework. Might stay late!* He took the note to the kitchen and left it on the table propped against the honey jar. Then, noticing the half-moons of grime under his fingernails, he gave his hands a good scrub in the kitchen sink.

When he got back to the attic the web was ready. It hung across an entire corner from ceiling to floor: a huge screen that capriciously mirrored his room in false shapes and colours; his bed had become a frothy green bank, the cupboard had multiplied into a wood of twisted grey trees; the carpet was tufted with wild flowers where a reed-like shadow stood, who must have been Gwyn's own reflection.

He searched the beams for his spider and identified her at last; a tiny glimmer beside the silver pipe. She seemed to indicate that he should take it, so leaping on the bed, he seized the pipe and immediately felt his legs lighten. In a strange, almost airborne fashion he stepped down and walked towards the web. The pipe began to tell him things he did not understand but when he touched the gossamer it began to make sense. 'Come, forward, and bow your head, now your feet!'

Gwyn held his breath. He shut his eyes against the sticky threads, lowered his head and moved through the web, remembering to call a brief farewell to the spider watching from her perch. When he opened his eyes again he was met with such a blackness he panicked himself into believing he was blind. But the pipe in his hand hummed in such a comforting way that he took a courageous step forward and, finding nothing to resist him, took another and another, until he was moving confidently forward to where a faint light illumined the landscape.

He was in a forest, a vast never-ending sea of trees. He knew it was vast as though he had lived there always. He could feel the endless repetition of branches stretching to the fringes of the land. It was an ancient forest, the slowly brightening dawn light showed him huge moss-grown trunks, plants that festooned the branches like Christmas decorations and a deep carpet of undisturbed leaves that smelt indescribably old and earthy. Gwyn became aware that he was following a thin track where the undergrowth had been brushed with a silvery dew, like the wake of a snail, and he knew that he was not alone.

Creatures crept behind him, accompanying his footfalls with soft breathing and busy scurrying that was not at all alarming. Once Gwyn glimpsed a great stag moving in the shadows, but he was not afraid. He felt every animal to be his friend.

The light became sunshine beaming into a glade where someone sat motionless on a huge seat, roughly hewn from a single rock that glittered with threads of quartz. The man had his back to Gwyn. He wore a cloak made of strips of fur intertwined with dark feathers whose colour shifted through a hundred variations with every breath of air. His hair was singing white and lay in a stiff mane down to his shoulder blades.

The stranger heard Gwyn's approach and turned in his direction. He showed no surprise on seeing a twentieth-century boy, in fact he seemed to expect him. Gwyn, however, stopped dead in his tracks; he might have been looking at a matured and weathered version of himself. The white-haired man was not old; he had every one of Gwyn's features: the dark eyes, and heavy eyebrows, even the

Griffith dent in his chin. He smiled, showing excellent white teeth and said, in perfectly understandable Welsh, 'Croeso, Gwydion Gwyn! Welcome!' He motioned the boy to sit at his feet and when Gwyn was comfortable began to talk as naturally as a parent embarking on a bedtime story.

Gwyn slowly came to realize that he was hearing a story told, not as a legend but as an episode in someone's life, where spells were just as commonplace as cups of tea. Gwydion, the magician, the greatest storyteller in all the world was relating a chapter that had been missed in the writing of the legends. He spoke for a long time and while Gwyn listened the sun died and a brilliant moon filled the open sky above them. It was the story of two princes, brothers, one kind and gentle, the other wilful and strong. They were so close they might have been two sides of one man. But somewhere in their lives the stronger man had swept his gentle brother into his own fierce life, swamped him so that he had no place in the story. And the strong prince loved so passionately, hated so savagely, committed crimes of such enormity that, even when he died, his spirit was stranded outside the Otherworld where all great warriors live, until Gwydion, almost by accident, trapped the violent spirit into an exquisite carving, a small ebony horse that had been a gift from his brother Gilfaethwy. But when his spell was accomplished, the horse had twisted and screamed itself into such a monstrosity that Gwydion had locked it out of his sight. 'And that mad prince was Efnisien, my own nephew,' the magician said a little sadly. 'He was my sister Penarddun's son.'

The storyteller's voice had almost sent Gwyn into a state of dreaming. 'I had forgotten he was related,' he said, shaking himself into action. He stood and told his ancestor, 'Efnisien is free again.'

Gwydion said, 'Well, boy, I know. Why else would I have told you all this?'

141

'Forgive me,' Gwyn persevered, 'but it isn't an answer to my problem.'

'A story is an answer,' Gwydion replied. 'Perhaps you haven't asked the right questions.'

'Very well, then. What must I do?'

'Whatever you do, don't do it in anger,' Gwydion said gravely. Then all at once he took a long stick of ash wood that lay beside him, spun it three times in the air and let it fall. And where it touched the earth sparks flew out in a brilliant display of forms and colours : dragons, flowers and butterflies, beasts and birds blazed about Gwyn's head and then slid away in a bright procession through the trees.

Gwyn regarded the wand for a moment, wondering if it was a gift. He could not bring himself to touch it. 'Gwydion,' he said. 'I'm afraid of magic. Everything I do – it always turns on me. My decisions are hopeless. I've made too many mistakes.' He looked up at his ancestor, hoping for a word to set him once and for all on the right road for a magician.

But Gwydion said, 'I too!'

'You?'

'We all do!' Gwydion laughed. 'My uncle Math turned me into a stag once, for misbehaving, and on another occasion a wild sow.' He threw back his head and gave a delighted guffaw. 'Imagine,' he roared, 'a sow. I can't tell you what it was like. I found myself relishing, well, you wouldn't believe it!'

'I would,' Gwyn said, joining in the laughter. 'We've kept pigs.'

At this Gwydion's laughter redoubled and Gwyn fell back on the ground, giggling hysterically. In all his life he had never felt so carefree. If only he'd known that magic did not have to be a burden. 'You mean a magician can misjudge?' he asked breathlessly. 'Can blunder?'

'Nothing is straightforward,' Gwydion replied. 'It's like life. But isn't it fun to leap in the dark?'

They smiled at each other in perfect understanding.

142

Friends forever and Gwyn, at last, felt able to murmur, 'Gwydion, I haven't grown for nearly four years.'

For a moment he thought his ancestor was going to find another excuse for laughter, but instead he nodded in a thoughtful way. 'I'm sure you will,' he said. 'But is it so important?' And when Gwyn grimaced he added, 'You're not blaming your genes, are you? I'm no dwarf! Bear up, boy! Laugh a bit more. Let a chuckle grow inside you until you have to stretch to keep up with it. Now take my ash wand and see what you can make of it.'

It was a slim uncomplicated-looking stick, and yet it had released a cloud of magic. When Gwyn picked it up he felt the echo of his touch ringing through the wand like music. He knew he must give something in return for this precious gift and tentatively offered the pipe that Gwydion had sent him four years before.

'I'll keep it safe!' his ancestor said.

A quietness hung between them and Gwyn was aware that there was still something unfinished about their exchange. There was a meaning to the story that he had missed and, running through it quickly in his mind, he found what surfaced every time he thought of the broken horse, causing him a restless sort of anxiety. 'Will that tormented prince ever be happy?' he asked. 'Can I help him into the Otherworld?'

He was rewarded with a golden smile. 'You've already taken the first step,' Gwydion said, sliding gracefully from his seat, and without another word he vanished into the black shadows of the forest. Gwyn could not even hear a footfall. And yet when he had curled himself into a sleeping pattern on the ground, he thought he heard a voice, very close to his ear, whisper, *Pob hwyl*, Gwydion Gwyn! Good luck!'

When he woke up he was lying on his bed with his mother leaning over him, an expression of irritated concern on her face. 'Gwyn, what's the matter with you?' a rather distant voice came grumbling through to him, and then more loudly, 'Emlyn's downstairs; he says he hasn't seen you. Why leave that note?'

'Sorry, Mam.' He tried to wring a reasonable response out of himself. He felt utterly exhausted. 'I meant to go. Must have fallen asleep!'

'Supper's ready!'

He thought he'd spent twenty-four hours in a forest, had it been only one? He swung his legs over the side of the bed, knocking something on to the floor.

'What's that?' Mrs Griffiths frowned at the stick beside his bed.

He was about to inform her that it was a wand, of course, when his twentieth-century self caught up with him and he replied, 'It's for measuring, Mam.'

'Gwyn, love.' She gave him a sympathetic glance at last. 'You're not still worried about growing, are you?'

'Heck no,' he assured her. 'I'm measuring furniture and that, for school. It's a project.'

She gave a sigh of relief and left him to tidy himself up.

His legs felt like lead. I suppose I've walked a fair bit, he told himself, and then he looked in his mirror. It was not Gwyn the boy who returned his puzzled stare, but a full-grown man with white hair and deep lines etched into his parchment-brown skin. It was Gwydion the magician. Yet Gwyn's mother had noticed nothing.

Had he exchanged more than a gift with Gwydion, then? Had unseen age come with the wand, while all his youthful undisturbed features had been left in the forest, for a middle-aged wizard to enjoy? What a trickster!

'How old am I?' Gwyn asked the mischievous reflection. 'Two thousand years, or forty?' The wizard wasn't telling. 'Will I be thirteen on Sunday? You surely can't take my birthday away from me! Tricks are all very well,' he went on, facing the mirror squarely, 'but will I be strong enough now,

144

to fight the prince, or will I crumble to dust the moment he touches me?'

Chapter
11

When Mr Lloyd had repaired the table well enough to withstand a meal, the family settled down to a cold supper. Only the twins had an appetite but the others forced themselves through the motions of eating as a way of comforting their mother who seemed more distraught than ever.

Nia couldn't rid her mind of the wild presence that had burned into every corner of their narrow hall. He had shone like the spirit who had tricked Iolo; he had gleamed gold with his glittering bracelet, his rings and jewelled brooch. Had he stepped back through time to retrieve the effects of a warrior prince? Or had madness driven him to buy an exotic costume for the final seduction, the moment when he would carry her sister thousands of years away?

Evan went out after his brief visit and did not return. Catrin left her music looking as though goblin's kisses were burning both her cheeks. No one alluded to the soldier's outlandish appearance. They tried to wish the memory away.

The rain fell steadily through the night. By morning the river had risen more than a metre. The mountains were scribbled with tiny white torrents that gushed down through the rocks and the scree. The ditches swelled and spilled across the narrow roads, making them almost impassable.

Nia caught a glimpse of Gwyn in school; he was dragging himself along the corridor and coughing like a geriatric.

'He's a real wally, that Gwyn,' said Gwyneth Bowen. 'Did you see what happened in the playground?'

Nia had not seen. She'd spent her break trying to catch up with homework.

'Fell flat on his face, he did,' Gwyneth informed her gleefully, knowing Gwyn was a friend of Nia's. 'Just because one of those old jets flew over. Shaking like a leaf, he was. What a laugh!'

'Perhaps he knows something we don't,' Nia retorted. 'They crash sometimes, those jets do.' She had heard the jet, rumbling overhead. It was a familiar sound but she could never help reacting, hunching her shoulders and blocking her ears. She wasn't the only one either. No one, however, had gone as far as flinging themselves to the ground. What had become of Gwyn, just when she most needed him?

Nia caught Gwyn's eye in the dinner queue and he gave her a sly half-smile. After school he accompanied the Lloyds to Number Six, but instead of following Alun into the kitchen he hung back and touched Nia's arm. She waited in the hall while he gasped for breath.

'What is it?' she whispered. 'You're like an old man.'

'Not old, just out of touch,' he replied. 'It's household air, I'm not used to it.'

'What do you live in then, a forest?'

'You don't realize how funny that is,' he said wryly.

'I heard you were diving for cover when the jets flew in today!'

'Took me by surprise. Look, can you come outside, there's a dreadful smell in here!'

'It's only Mam's cooking,' Nia said indignantly, and then admitted, 'It could be disinfectant, it does pong a bit.'

He opened the front door and pulled her out on to the pavement. 'That's better,' he said, breathing in a more normal fashion. 'I suppose I look quite ordinary to you.'

147

'I wouldn't say that,' she replied. 'You've never looked absolutely average and today you're really weird.'

'But you'd recognize me?'

'No, I think I'm talking to a buzzard.'

He gave a high plaintive 'Hee-haw' in response and then laughed. He was not someone else and yet he was not quite Gwyn. It was very unnerving to think that this heavy-breathing, rather jokey person was all that she had to rely on.

'Gwyn,' she said gravely. 'Are you going to help us?'

He looked up the road, frowned at a passing car and said tantalizingly, 'I suppose you're shouting because of all this.'

'I'm not shouting!' She had the impression that he was trying to adjust to the atmosphere, as though the world of traffic and conversation was too overwhelming for him to give her the attention she needed.

'Yes,' he said at last. 'I know what to do, but it'll be up to you, too.'

'What do I have to do?' she asked, reluctant to commit herself to any frontline activity.

Having adapted himself to the situation, he became quietly efficient. 'Tomorrow's Saturday,' he said. 'Catrin will be rehearsing in the Community Centre. Tell Evan Llŷr she wants to see him by the bridge. Say it's urgent!'

'But...' she said wildly.

'There's no room for dithering, Nia. He'll be there, in your house and you'll all be glad to get rid of him. I'll put things right!'

'When?' she cried, beginning to panic at the deceit she'd have to use.

'At dusk,' he told her. 'You'll know. Now I've got arrangements to make.'

She watched him swaying up the road, wanting to ask him so many questions, yet knowing he'd moved on, somewhere far beyond her little problems. What did he intend to do? Would he harm her cousin? Was there a place on the clock for dusk? Suppose she didn't time her mission properly?

148

Gwyn walked all the way home; surveying his territory, marking footsteps in his mind; judging the swell of the river and feeling the approaching weather. After a while his feet became accustomed to the hard tarmac. He would have to drag himself a little further into the present, he realized, to grapple with a soldier whose anger burned in two worlds. He needed a storm – drowning weather.

When he reached his grandmother's cottage he found her in the garden, piling leaves ready for a bonfire. 'Are you coming down tomorrow, then, Gwydion Gwyn?' she asked. 'To share my Hallowe'en fire?'

Hallowe'en? He'd forgotten. How appropriate, he thought wryly. But there would be no fire. 'It'll rain, Nain,' he told her, 'and I'm sorry, but I'll be busy.'

'Rain? Rubbish!' she snorted, and then she looked intently at him, as though something in his attitude had filtered through to her at last. She came to the gate and asked, 'How do you know?'

He felt himself give the same smile that his ancestor had passed on to him, 'I know,' he said lightly.

She peered at him, searched his face with her bird-bright eyes and whispered, 'Gwydion Gwyn, have you been back?'

He nodded, still smiling.

'And did you meet…?'

'I did,' he told her.

She gave a long happy sigh. 'I'm so glad for you, Gwydion Gwyn.'

'I'll tell you one thing,' he said with the air of someone who was passing on information about a mutual friend. 'Gwydion is a rascal. He blunders like I do, and I know that sometimes I shall have to leap into the dark, but Nain,' he was amused by the crooked little expression of gladness that had gradually crept into her face, 'I'll never turn from it again. It's not a burden, you see.'

'You speak of him in the present,' Nain said.

'Do I? Well, he's here, isn't he?' Gwyn spun, arms akimbo,

149

in the lane, his hands eventually coming to rest on top of his black hair.

They laughed together in a way they hadn't done for a long time and Gwyn, at last, confided, 'He's in my reflection, Nain. He's taken me over, he breathes through me, laughs inside my head, and he's not above a bit of wickedness. I'll have to watch that!'

'And has Gwydion shown you how to solve your – problem?' she asked carefully.

'He's given me the means,' Gwyn said, 'and I know what to do.'

'You won't harm the soldier, Gwyn?'

'I told you, I'm leaping in the dark. I'll save the Lloyds, I'll trap the demon, but as for Evan Llŷr, I can't tell!' He was sorry to disappoint her. 'Not everyone can win,' he said regretfully. 'You know that, Nain.'

'I know.' She gave a disconsolate little shrug and then asked hopefully, 'But you'll try, Gwydion Gwyn, won't you, not to cause him any more pain?'

Gwyn couldn't promise that.

Just before she disappeared into her house, Nain called, 'It's your birthday, the day after tomorrow. Thirteen is a special age. How shall we celebrate?'

There may be nothing to celebrate, he thought. 'Let's wait and see,' he said.

He continued up to Tŷ Bryn, wondering if this older man, this alter ego, would always be with him. He needed Gwydion's strength but what if he never broke free of the quizzical middle-aged reflection, the long weatherworn fingers and the forest-dweller's cough. I'll put my worries aside, he thought, as Gwydion would have done – is doing. Because I'm him, or he's me. He found himself laughing a lot louder than Gwyn Griffiths usually did.

When he reached home he resolved to sleep in the air that night. He would take a blanket out to the open barn where the weather could sing him to sleep. He needed to dream.

A distant rumble heralded the storm he'd predicted.

Saturday was a dark day. The sunlight was obscured by a thick blanket that drizzled steadily into the valley. The river swelled to a dangerous torrent and children were forbidden to play on the banks. Nia wondered how she would know dusk from daytime.

The prince returned at noon and joined them for a meal. His tartan scarf had been discarded in favour of a scarlet shirt, pinned at the neck with the same shining brooch. He was a stranger to them now. The stare he levelled at Catrin across the table was quite outrageous, and when she shied away from it embarrassed and afraid, he gave another of his desperate laughs.

Nerys tried to diffuse the atmosphere by talking of the weather. She'd curled her hair and looked almost pretty. She chattered on, rather wildly for her, until Evan suddenly laid a hand on hers and said, with quiet venom, 'You talk too much, my dear. Plain girls should always keep quiet!'

Stunned, Nerys's mouth snapped shut. She stared ahead at a cup on the dresser. A single tear rolled down her cheek. It was, somehow, even more dreadful than Catrin's awkward fear.

And then another laugh descended on them, striking every member of the family a blow from which they couldn't recover. Even the twins were silent. This was the soldier they had wanted, but he terrified them.

At either end of the table, Iestyn and Betty gazed helplessly at each other, wondering how to end the madman's occupation of their home.

My prince has gone, Nia thought, vanished; swallowed up by someone else's life. The window showed a sky of endless grey and she began to worry that her part of the magical proceedings would go wrong. Suppose she called Evan too soon and he returned from an empty bridge, outraged and even more violent.

He spent the rest of the day in their front room, leaving the door open to flaunt his possession of the sofa; his feet over one arm, his head resting on the other; eyes closed, hands clasped across his chest. Now and again he emitted a faint snore. The beast at rest. No one thought of closing the door.

'What's happened to Evan?' Gareth asked his mother, whispering even behind the closed kitchen door. 'He's like another person.'

'He's ill, cariad,' Mrs Lloyd told him.

'Is it – the wound?' Sîon asked.

His mother nodded. 'Doctors have pills for that sort of thing now,' Sîon said helpfully, and then, worried by his mother's closed uncomfortable expression, 'He'll get better won't he, Mam?'

'Oh, Sîon, I don't know,' she confessed. 'I hope so!'

At three o'clock the twins thankfully departed for a friend's Hallowe'en party. Mrs Lloyd took Bethan to visit Iolo. 'He'd like to see you, too,' she told Nia, offering her a way of escape. 'He's much better now, not so gloomy.'

'I'll stay,' Nia said firmly.

Catrin gave the remaining family their tea before she left for the Community Centre with her father. 'It's only up the road, so if you need us ...' she said meaningfully to Nia. 'Or would you rather come with us?'

Nia shook her head. 'Nerys will be here. We'll keep each other company,' she said. They didn't mention the sleeping soldier. She followed Catrin and her father into the hall, where Mr Lloyd switched on the light. None of them looked into the room where he lay, though Nia could have described his attitude exactly. One arm hung loose, its gold and bronze ornaments caught in a bright beam that slid through the open door.

Mr Lloyd moved uneasily from one foot to the other. 'Perhaps you'd better come with us, girl,' he said.

'Then poor Nerys will be alone,' Nia said, hoping to

152

remind her father of the tear that had been wrung from his eldest child.

'Ah yes.' As he and Catrin stepped out of the house, the street lights came on. It was dusk. Nia closed the door. She went back to the kitchen and sat at the table. Above her Nerys creaked across a room. The light seemed to be fading in seconds.

It has to be now, Nia told herself, another day might be too late. She forced herself into the hall again and stood on the brink of the dark room where he slept. Would he detect the lie in her voice? She took a deep breath and walked in.

'Evan,' she called faintly into his sleep, then gaining courage, loud and steadily, 'Evan! Evan!'

His eyes opened and, for a brief moment, her own dear prince looked out. The sorrowful blue gaze shook all her resolve. He knew. She couldn't trust herself to speak. But the dark soul betrayed him. Something stirred behind his eyes, leaking tiny yellow flames into the blue. Nia was tipped into action and the lies came pouring out. 'Catrin wants you. She's on the bridge. She sent me to fetch you. It's urgent, she says.' Shame confined her voice to a tight little croak and she was sure he could see deep inside her where the truth lay all mixed up with love and dread.

But he swung his legs on to the floor, stood up, rubbed his eyes and walked past her. In the hall he touched her shoulder with his ringed fingers and said quietly, 'Thank you, Nia!' She longed to keep his hand and hold him back, but he whisked himself away and was gone.

She waited behind the closed door then suddenly flung it open and leapt out. The town was deserted except for the tall figure striding towards the bridge. Rehearsals were in full swing and the *'Sanctus'* came pouring into the street like water; it washed around the soldier, causing him to stop and lift his head in a listening attitude as though he was willing the music to keep him there, safe against the future. Slowly he released himself and continued on his way. The rain had stopped but the wet pavement glimmered gold under the street lights.

Close to the houses, Nia followed, watching every movement of the man ahead. When he walked on to the bridge she slid behind a wide buttress at the end, and peeped out. Evan was alone, staring over the wall at the wild flood.

Where was Gwyn? Suppose he let her down? Would Evan, sensing the trick, rush furiously back to her? And then something that had been there all the time began to move. It was an indistinct form, topped with a cloud of white, startling in the twilight.

The soldier turned and faced the magician.

All through the day Gwyn had been torn by indecision. Perhaps, after all, he wouldn't have to exert himself. He thought of using the telephone to postpone the meeting. The persistent rain and the distant forlorn murmur of thunder made him restless. But towards dusk he became very calm. He went to fetch his ash wand and was amazed by the energy it sent through him.

When the rain had stopped and the melancholy sky waited for night, Gwyn began his journey to Pendewi. He had to wield the wand carefully, for when it struck the ground a hollow sound came from it, as though its echo reached to the world's beginning. Every chime filled him with a wonderful optimism, but he didn't want to alert the countryside. He discovered that Arianwen was travelling with him, couched in a little hollow at the top of the stick. She had decided to play a part, it seemed, though Gwyn couldn't guess what it would be.

He passed Idris Llewelyn's chapel, and the unicorn, remade and even more beautiful, beckoned him on, into the land where he would make the last spell of his childhood. Tomorrow he would be thirteen. He felt invincible.

Yet when he saw the soldier, peering into the deadly water, a little qualm kept him at the end of the bridge where a damp mist wrapped him safely out of sight, tempting him to retreat. But he could feel the wand aching like one of his own limbs, and he moved on to the bridge. They were quite alone now, he and the soldier, together on an island, from which only one of them would return.

All at once the soldier, feeling his presence, turned to face him, and Gwyn almost lost his courage for another creature swooped out of Evan Llŷr, adding extra height to his already tall frame. A great warrior stood there, shining with royal jewels, and a scowl of such hatred coursed out of the familiar features, it took all Gwyn's strength to look at it. But he held steady and, without averting his eyes, brought the broken horse from his pocket and held it out.

His action was greeted by a dreadful sound, deeper than any natural voice. It rolled around his head, confusing all his senses and threatened, 'You'll die this time, old man, if you attempt to keep me in that!'

His hatred towers above anything I can feel, Gwyn thought, and began to weaken. But, once more, the ash wand jerked against his fingers and an icy glow, perched on the tip, floated across and settled in the crest of bright hair. The warrior hardly noticed it. He took a step towards Gwyn. The wand bowed in the magician's hand, alive with energy. It twisted toward the wall and a shaft of light travelled from it deep into the stones; they burst into fragments and tumbled into the river, leaving a jagged hole that gave on to the still rising tide of water.

Again the warrior bellowed but this time Gwyn detected a note of anxiety, a loss of confidence. The spider had begun to work. Tiny threads criss-crossed the monster's face. He tried to brush them away but the spider floated out of reach, and spun on, faster and faster, over the plume of chestnut hair, across the eyes, forming a ghostly mask. The soldier took another step towards Gwyn; again he swept his hands over his face, this time clutching the air as though he would crush it with his huge fists. He leaned forward; powerful, shining

155

arms reached toward Gwyn who knew that if this warrior fell he meant to take the magician with him. Helplessly, Gwyn closed his eyes so that what followed became a secret ceremony, known only to the men from the past, leaving the two who remained forever doubtful of what had happened.

Gwyn only knew that his right hand became a weapon wielded by someone else. It raised the wand and struck something with such furious energy that he was rocked off his feet. He opened his eyes, wondering how he should protect himself from the assault that must follow. But the bridge was empty and beyond the breached wall, there was a man in the water, struggling for his life.

'I don't hate you,' Gwyn called across the water. 'Forgive me, Evan Llŷr.'

An answer came from Evan Llŷr: a drowning howl that carried on the waves like receding music, an age-old lament composed of many voices. And then a girl tore past Gwyn crying, 'Gwyn Griffiths, you have murdered my cousin!' And Nia bounded down the bank, following the current that bore Evan Llŷr away.

Nia, racing beside the river, couldn't understand why the town was still singing. Her prince was drowning. All the Hosannas in the world couldn't save him now. She tore helplessly along the bank, trying to keep pace with the current, calling 'Evan' endlessly, as though the name could keep him safe. Three times she saw his arm strike through the grey tide, the last time was hardly a stroke at all, but more a lonely gesture of farewell.

She sank on to the wet grass and turned her face away from the river where all her happy dreams had died. But a surprising gust of wind urged her to look again. On the far side of the river where slim alders clustered on the bank, the wind, in a sudden frenzy, tore at the red leaves, dispatching them in a cloud across the torrent. Startled birds flew out, calling to each other in alarm. It seemed to Nia that every bird she had ever known had a place in the great flock that

156

soared above her, their wingbeats clattering into the air like a mighty orchestra.

Then into the band of golden sky that rimmed the distant hill, a line of horsemen drew up and began to descend toward the wooded bank. Nia's vision was blurred by tears and they seemed to seep through the naked trees like drifting streams of smoke, but she could still make out the dull bronze of spears and helmets and the occasional glitter of gold.

Struggling against unreality, Nia watched the silent, shadowy army follow their prince beneath the water, safe into the Otherworld. She watched until every tiny gleam had drowned, until the bank was deserted and the river, the same unassailable sweep of water as before. Then she made her way back to the bridge.

She found a crowd of men surrounding Gwyn Griffiths, who lay perilously close to the place where Evan had slipped into the river. He looked bewildered and years younger than the last time she had seen him. There was an old stick beside him that looked as if it had been used by lightning and his hands, clasped round something small and black, were bleeding. Making her way across his sleeve was a tiny silver spider.

'Doesn't seem to know where he is,' someone remarked. Nia recognized Morgan-the-Smithy.

'Come on, lad,' another said. 'You'd better shift from there. It's dangerous!'

'A man fell in,' Gwyn said dreamily. 'I couldn't save him.'

'In that?' asked Morgan in disbelief, nodding at the angry current.

'It was my cousin, Evan Llŷr,' Nia murmured through unspent tears.

'Then he's gone, girl, that's for sure,' said Morgan. 'That flood would take the strongest man alive!'

Chapter
12

He had no right to be outside her room, tapping away like an intrusive woodpecker. The door was open anyway and Gwyn could see that she didn't want company. Why didn't he go away?

'Nia, you've got to talk to me!' He came in, cautiously, hands in pockets while she quickly hid her treasure on the bed beside her. 'What's that you've got?' He looked so jaunty.

'Nothing,' she replied sullenly.

He came and sat beside her.

The whole world ached. A grim mist had lain in the valley for days, a ghostly shroud left to shame them. A heavy, featureless climate hung about the town, only the mountain rose above it. Impossible events had set Pendewi adrift from the universe, untouched and unloved. No one wanted to know about a soldier who had carried a family into his dark past. Some things were better left unsaid, it seemed. For weeks Nia hadn't even heard his name.

'Nia, he's not dead!'

When she had taken in the full meaning of what he said, she stared at him stupidly, her life upside down again.

'He swam ashore downriver,' Gwyn told her gently. 'Didn't know his name for a while. He's been in hospital.'

'Why didn't Mam tell me?'

'They've only just heard. And you two girls have been so – frantic, we thought it would be better to break it gradually.'

'Is he coming back?'

'How could he, Nia?' His dark eyes, truthful and very kind, held hers.

She turned away.

'I cured him, Nia,' he said firmly.

'You tried to murder him!'

'No, not Evan. It was that other one. I was trying to save Evan. I had a head full of spells, and Arianwen, ready to convert him but my ancestor had a mind of his own. Perhaps he doubted my will, so he reached through me to quieten Efnisien forever, not caring how he did it. He didn't know our soldier, you see!'

She felt behind her and brought the little carving on to her lap. 'I found this in the reeds beside the river,' she said. 'It's yours, isn't it?'

The paint had washed off and the soldier looked little more than a piece of wood, the face and clothing vaguely sketched in lines of fine silt.

'It was a mistake,' he confessed. 'I thought of those little sacrificial figures they found in Celtic springs, thrown there to heal the owners of some dreadful illness. I don't know what I expected. I certainly didn't realize that he'd fight it and bring a storm to your home.'

'Well, you'll never save him now,' Nia said dramatically.

'He *is* saved,' Gwyn told her cheerfully.

She looked up. 'What do you mean?'

'Gwydion may have done his worst, but his descendant won a battle too!' He brought from his pocket a wooden horse that resembled the animal she'd found in Evan's room. If it was the same horse, it was transformed. Polished and handsome, its severed features all restored, it glowed.

'Is it …?' she began.

'The same,' Gwyn confirmed.

'What's happened? It's so beautiful.'

'This is how it was in the beginning, when Gwydion's brother gave it as a gift, before it was used for magic. Gwydion told me.' She darted him a suspicious look which he refused to acknowledge, ploughing on in spite of her impatient fidgeting. 'After he'd – gone into the water the horse began to kick at my hands and when I wouldn't give it up it punished me. I don't know how I held on, but it was something I had to do, to cling on and soak up all the anger. It seemed to reach every part of me with hooves and teeth and bony head. I hung on until the pain knocked me out, and when I came to my hands were bleeding, but the horse was – like this!'

'What does it mean?' she asked, wanting only to hear about her prince.

'Efnisien's anger is all spent. He's a hopeful prince now, riding through the Otherworld.'

'But Evan?'

Gwyn shrugged. 'It's hard to say. Perhaps we'll know one day if he's forgiven us.'

He's saved his prince, Nia thought, but left mine wandering without a soul, alone and unforgiving. 'Can I keep this?' she held up the wooden effigy.

'As a substitute? If you like.' He got up and walked away from her. He seemed such a sunny person now, she hardly knew him. But when he reached the door he turned back and said, almost bashfully, 'By the way, there's something else.'

'More good news!' she said, more resentfully than she'd intended.

'In a way,' he said, still cheerful. 'Look!'

She looked at him and saw nothing but Gwyn Griffiths, black hair rather too long and bushy, not even halfway to being well-built, a lean face with eyes so dark they could conceal a thousand mysteries, and an annoyingly smiley mouth.

'My ankles!' he said, directing her gaze to a pair of wrinkled grey socks.

'I can see your ankles. They're fantastic!'

'Don't be like that, Nia!'

'Your trousers have shrunk!'

He beamed at her. She seemed to have found the right answer. 'Not at all. My trousers have not shrunk. I've grown. Two inches to be precise.'

'He looked, all at once, so shy and so joyful she couldn't deny him his congratulations. 'Well done,' she said, and before she could bite it back, 'You'll be a giant!'

'Hardly,' he returned. 'Average will do for me!'

Average he would never be, she thought, and with one of her queer little spins into the future saw an unusually fine young man, glowing with secret knowledge and as mysteriously handsome as a mature magician should be.

Nia took her wooden soldier to school every day after that. She wrapped him in a piece of velvet and kept him at the bottom of her bag. At night she would tuck him under her pillow. Once he fell out of the bag and Dewi Davis pounced on the little figure, threw him in the air and launched him into a game of catch. Nia, helpless with inexplicable rage, wept for its return, but this only drove Dewi's gang to heap further indignities on the soldier. They kicked it across the playground, purposely tripping and treading on it. It wasn't restored to her until Gwyn came out and thumped Dewi on the chin. The game stopped abruptly. Dewi was afraid of Gwyn.

'Why don't you keep it at home?' Gwyn said, putting the soldier safe into her hands.

'I can't,' she replied. 'He'd be alone.'

Gwyn shook his head. 'You've got to snap out of it, Nia!'

She couldn't. Someone had to keep faith.

Catrin was almost her old self again. The enchanted kiss was fading and she began to blossom with extraordinary

161

talent. The piano rocked under a passionate torrent of sonatas, preludes and fugues. She'd passed Grade Eight with distinction. A few days after her exam results had arrived, Michael McGoohan came round with a congratulatory bouquet. Catrin received her visitor warily. They spent half an hour in the front room, then Michael went home. The following week he took her to a concert. Michael had embarked on a second diffident courtship. Catrin had emerged from her association with Evan mysteriously glamourized. She was definitely not to be an easy conquest, but obviously well worth the effort.

'What if Evan comes back?' Nia asked her sister one day.

'What if?' Catrin airily replied. She was cured of the kiss. That part of the book would remain closed, never to be reopened. It was just an episode on Catrin's route to being seventeen. If she was aware that she'd been a heroine in someone else's story, the knowledge belonged only to her.

When Iolo returned home his bones soon mended but it took him a long time to become a cheerful little boy again. Gradually, with Nia's help, he spent less and less of his time remembering the shining spirit who had tricked him. One day he even ventured, 'Nia, will we see Evan again?'

To which she replied, 'Perhaps, if we all want him enough.'

'I do!' Iolo said.

If he hadn't been too old for sisterly embraces, she'd have hugged him.

At Christmas they had a short letter from Evan Llŷr, tucked inside a card. It was like a letter from a stranger. He thanked them for their hospitality and was sorry for any trouble he had caused. There was no address.

Nia begged to keep the card, not string it up with all the others on a silver ribbon. No one objected. She took it to her room and tried to read some special message in the picture. But there was nothing there. Only a decorative golden

'Greetings' on an emerald background. At least it isn't red, she thought. And took comfort from that.

She decided to colour her soldier for the festivities. She went to Idris Llewelyn's studio for advice and found Emlyn working there. 'D'you want me to paint him the way he was before?' he asked. 'Or give him a different character? I could carve the beret away and give him a good head of hair.'

Nia thought about it, and remembering the way Evan had looked on that very first, long ago day, described him to Emlyn.

'I'll bring it round tomorrow,' he said.

That wouldn't do. She couldn't be without her soldier, she explained. Intrigued but obliging, Emlyn let her wait in the chapel until he had finished the work and then walked home with her. The paint was still wet and she held it before her on outstretched palms, like a precious offering.

Outside her front door Emlyn suddenly asked, 'What are you up to, Nia? There's nothing very special about that carving. It's only chestnut wood and paint!'

'I have to keep him safe,' she told Emlyn. 'No one else will.'

'You ought to get out more,' he said. 'I'm going to the cinema next week. 'Ape-man's Revenge' is on. D'you want to come?'

It wasn't her sort of film but surprising herself, she said, 'Yes.'

As it was they went in a foursome; she and Emlyn, Alun and Gwyn. But she was aware of a subtle difference in their relationships. She'd achieved a new position in the group and hadn't tagged along just as one of the boys.

She kept her carving wrapped up in wool all through the long winter and the chilly spring. She even made a scarf for him and a smart felt hat with a golden band. Now he was a little prince.

Nerys came upon the bundle, tucked in a towel beside Nia's place on the kitchen bench. 'You're too old for this, Nia,' Nerys complained. 'Why don't you give it to Bethan?'

'He's mine,' Nia cried vehemently, snatching her toy from Nerys. 'Leave him alone.'

'Willingly,' said Nerys. 'Just keep him out of my way!' She knew who it was meant to be. Emlyn had done his work well. Nerys still hadn't forgiven Evan Llŷr for that tear.

One May weekend, Mr and Mrs Lloyd were told to have a holiday. They were to go to the sea and leave their children to their friends. Catrin and Nerys stayed at home, the boys went to the Griffiths' farm, Nia and Bethan to Tŷ Llŷr.

Nia was blissful in her old home. The Llewelyns had made it so alive and beautiful. On her first evening she took her toy prince up the lane to visit Nain Griffiths.

'He's very fine,' Nain said, regarding the little figure that stood on the summit of her tallest pile of books. Nia had supplied him with a new fur cape and a gold belt made of Christmas string.

'He's out there, somewhere, all alone,' Nia said, knowing she would be understood. 'He went away believing that we'd rather he didn't exist. But we were his family, the only people in the whole world he could trust. I wish I could tell him that I'm sorry.'

'Perhaps he knows,' Nain took the little figure from its perch and stroked the soft fur cape.

'Then why doesn't he tell us where he is or if he's well?' Nia burst out. 'It's not fair. Gwyn has saved his old prince. He's got all that magic piled inside him and ancestors to back him up but he can't seem to help my cousin.'

'You're doing that,' Nain said gently. 'If you care as much for him as you do this little carving, then he'll know.'

'How?' Nia asked, frowning.

'One has ways.' She smiled enigmatically. 'Remember what I said about Ares and Aphrodite?'

'I'm not a love goddess,' Nia said sheepishly.

164

Nain laughed and put the toy prince into her hands. 'You don't have to be a goddess!'

It was getting dark when Nia began to walk back to Tŷ Llŷr. The candle blossom on the chestnut tree glowed white against the evening sky. Nia stopped and gazed at the tree, imagining the blossom to be real white flames. When she half closed her eyes she thought she could make out a familiar face smiling down at her; it was so lightly etched into the shadow it could have been a wisp of lichen clinging to a branch, yet gradually she became sure of what she was seeing and at last knew, with joyful certainty, that it was the true forgiving prince and that every candle was a lost soldier, peacefully remembered.

She laid her wooden prince beneath the tree, covered him with last year's leaves, and went back to Tŷ Llŷr.

It was Nain Griffiths' birthday in June. She wanted a special celebration, she said, for herself and Gwyn whose thirteenth birthday had been overshadowed by Evan's disappearance. The whole family must be there, Llewelyns, Griffiths and even Lloyds, who were part of her family even if not directly related. They would have a party in the field behind her house. The weather would be glorious.

Gwyn sensed buried excitement in his grandmother. She was keeping the lid on a delicious secret, something that she would save until the very last moment, to flabbergast them all when they least expected it.

'I'll pay you back if you spring something nasty on us,' he warned.

'Wizard!' she snapped. 'Whatever gave you that idea?' She had made a primrose yellow dress for herself (the colour of madness, Gwyn had told her) and was flaunting it a week too soon, for his approval. 'You never had your party because of all that – trouble. So we'll have a double celebration and I'll make a towering cake. By the way,' she lowered her voice, 'will the ancestor be with us?'

Gwyn laughed. 'He's been gone for ages, Nain. The mirror

165

tells me I'm thirteen and just the right size. It seems a long, long time since you brought me those five gifts. They've taken me on a strange journey but now I feel I've finished with them. I'm grateful for the adventure but I don't believe I'll need magic for a while. Arianwen shall keep me company, but as a peaceful friend. I won't use seaweed and a scarf to bring my sister back to me; I'll let her stay in the place where she's happiest. And the horse, as I've shown you, is a precious ornament. I'll never need to hide him now.'

'That was your greatest achievement, Gwyn,' Nain said thoughtfully, 'to bring the dark prince peace at last. No one else could do it!' And then, all at once remembering the strange toy her great-great-grandmother, the witch, had left in her keeping, she asked, 'But what has become of the pipe?'

'Ah, I've exchanged the pipe,' Gwyn said, 'for an ash stick, a wand to keep me in touch with all my ghostly relatives.'

'Perhaps it comes from a tree that fathered my own wood,' Nain suggested happily, more to herself than Gwyn.

'It feeds me, Nain,' Gwyn told. 'It gives me so much energy I feel I'll reach the clouds some day.'

'I wish you could spare some for your little friend,' Nain said.

'Nia? Yes, she does look a bit weary.'

'I never knew a child could store up so much loyalty,' his grandmother said thoughtfully. 'She'll be rewarded though.'

'Nain, what have you planned?' He had an inkling of what it might be, but still couldn't really guess it.

'Nothing! Nothing! Now go home and leave me to plot!'

It was a glorious day. Three families in a field of flowers, mown just enough to spread a huge white cloth, covered in treats. In the centre a gaudy five-layered birthday cake listed crazily into the breeze, the leaning tower of Pisa surrounded by Nain's wholefood biscuits, bara brith and endless plates of sandwiches. And not to be outdone, Gwyn's mother had contributed two versions of her prizewinning sponge, one chocolate and one vanilla.

'How old are you, Nain Griffiths?' Nia asked. 'There are only thirteen candles on the cake!'

'The candles are for Gwyn,' she said. '*I* am ageless, and anyway I've forgotten.'

When all the plates were empty she still wouldn't cut the cake. 'Have a game,' she commanded. 'You're still not ready for my treat!'

Nia had a feeling she wasn't referring to the cake. She joined in an unruly game of rounders. Out of danger, on the far side of the field, Catrin and Michael lay in a pool of buttercups, feeding each other with whispers. Neither of them was aware that, from a distance, Idris Llewelyn was capturing their mood with coloured pencils.

Nia watched Nain Griffiths tiptoe lightly over to the artist, all brimming with excitement, as though she longed to share some wonderful secret. Perhaps she has made magic somewhere, Nia thought. Perhaps there's a genie in the wood, waiting to grant us all three wishes. I could make do with just one.

Something sailed over her head and bounced into the lane beyond the hedge. 'Neeeeaaa!' came seven shouts. She ran and flung herself over the gate. Gwyn, not trusting her speed, was hard on her heels. But Nain came to open the gate and called him back.

The ball trickled down the lane, teasing her with unpredictable little twists and turns. At last it came to rest, wedged safely into the stony verge. But she didn't pick it up. A stranger was approaching; a tall figure with raven hair and something thrown round his shoulders in the manner of a cloak. Not strange at all when she came to study him.

The mountain lurched, the trees spun and the earth rolled away from her feet. She could feel the welcome that Nain and Gwyn were restraining, so that it should belong only to her; it was as though they had jumped off a seesaw and left her tumbling in a dangerously fast descent. It might have ended in disaster if he hadn't caught her.

'Evan Llŷr has come to trouble you again,' he said, holding her very tight.

She knew it wasn't true. He was her prince but, in a way, quite new, his gaze untroubled and his smile completely hopeful.